Welcome back to Sullivan's Island.

You won't believe what all's been going on...

Trouble's Turn to Lose

Seaside Southern Mysteries
BY SUSAN M. BOYER

Carolina Tales Series

Big Trouble on Sullivan's Island

Beginnings: The Sullivan's Island Supper Club (*prequel*)

The Sullivan's Island Supper Club

Trouble's Turn to Lose

The Liz Talbot Series

Lowcountry Boil (A Liz Talbot Mystery # 1)

Lowcountry Bombshell (A Liz Talbot Mystery # 2)

Lowcountry Boneyard (A Liz Talbot Mystery # 3)

Postcards From Stella Maris (Five Liz Talbot Short Stories)

Lowcountry Bordello (A Liz Talbot Mystery # 4)

Lowcountry Book Club (A Liz Talbot Mystery # 5)

Lowcountry Bonfire (A Liz Talbot Mystery # 6)

Lowcountry Bookshop (A Liz Talbot Mystery # 7)

Lowcountry Boomerang (A Liz Talbot Mystery # 8)

Lowcountry Boondoggle (A Liz Talbot Mystery # 9)

Lowcountry Boughs of Holly (A Liz Talbot Mystery # 10)

Lowcountry Getaway (A Liz Talbot Mystery # 11)

The Talbot & Andrews Investigation Series

Hard Candy Christmas (*coming October 27, 2026*)

Trouble's Turn to Lose

A CAROLINA TALE

SUSAN M. BOYER

Trouble's Turn to Lose

A Carolina Tale

First Edition | April 2026

Stella Maris Books, LLC

5000 Old Buncombe Road

Unit 27, Unit #273

Greenville SC 29617

https://stellamarisbooksllc.com

This is a work of fiction. All of the characters, places, organizations, and events portrayed in this novel are either products of the author's imagination or are used fictitiously.

All rights reserved. Thank you for buying an authorized edition of this book and for complying with copyright laws by not reproducing, scanning, or distributing any part of it in any form without permission. Brief quotations embodied in critical articles and reviews are the sole exception.

Copyright © 2025 by Susan M. Boyer

Cover Artwork © 2024 by Marina Kaya, Qamber Designs, used by exclusive license

Cover design by Elizabeth Mackey

Author photograph by Mic Smith

ISBN 978-1-959023-36-4 (E-book)

ISBN 978-1-959023-37-1 (Trade Paperback)

ISBN 978-1-959023-39-5 (Hardcover)

ISBN 978-1-959023-38-8 (Large Print Paperback)

ISBN 978-1-959023-40-1 (Audio Download)

Printed in the United States of America

 Formatted with Vellum

For Ciera...
I became a cat person for her.

Chapter One

Saturday, April 1, 2023

The day that would change my life forever, that would divide it precisely and irrevocably into two eras, before and after, started out like any other. I woke at 5:00 a.m. and was on my bike by 5:10, just like always. I rode down the beach from my house near Station 28 1/2 on Sullivan's Island, then took the path at Station 18 1/2 Street and zigzagged my way down the island, past the lighthouse, past Fort Moultrie, and all the way to the end of Middle Street, near where the trolleys once came over from Mount Pleasant on Pitt Street Bridge.

There's something magical about having the island mostly to yourself, which you can only do very early or very late. The feel of the salt air blowing through me as

I whiz along quiet streets while most of the island is still asleep somehow makes me feel like I'm the keeper of all the island's secrets, and there are sacred things only the island and I know.

I weaved my way to the other end of the island and settled in at Thomson Park just before first light. I spread my towel on the sand and sat back to enjoy the show.

The horizon glowed ember-orange, a thin line of fire separating the dark waters from the awakening sky. I hugged my knees to my chest as the first sliver of sun peeked above the water. The sun climbed higher, transforming from orange to yellow-gold, its reflection creating a shimmering pathway across the water. A pair of dolphins broke the surface about fifty yards out, their sleek bodies arcing gracefully before disappearing beneath the waves.

My mother is never far from my mind, but I always feel her close at sunrise. She brought me here to watch my first sunrise before I was old enough to remember, and countless times after. What would she think of the way things had turned out, me living here, on Sullivan's Island, the way we'd always dreamed? It hurt my heart that she wasn't here to live it with me.

There are people in my life who hold the opinion that my relationship with my mother was unhealthy for us both. Gavin, who I guess you'd call my grandfather figure, is the only one who's ever voiced that opinion, but some people imply a lot with their eyes. My mother was my best friend. She had me young, and it was just the two of us. It was only natural for us to be close. It would soon be twenty-five years since she'd passed away. I missed her every day, and yet I still felt her close to me.

The colors intensified as the sun fully emerged—lavender, peach, and gold streaking the sky. The breeze picked up, carrying the familiar scent of salt, pluff mud, and possibility. Watching day break over Breach Inlet soothed my soul. I took a long, salty breath of air and was just about to stand to leave when she appeared—right there beside me on the towel, as if I'd conjured her.

She just sort of…faded in, from thin air.

My mother—Vivienne Joanna Cooper.

The one who died nearly twenty-five years ago.

She looked exactly the same. No—she positively *glowed* with health, not at all like the last time I'd seen her, when the cancer had ravaged her body. She'd been thirty-five years old when she passed away on my seventeenth birthday. We were closing in on my forty-second birthday, which meant I was older than her now, which was hard to wrap my head around.

Surely I was hallucinating. Was this a symptom of a sudden-onset nervous breakdown? I hadn't eaten anything odd…

"*Momma?*" I whispered.

She smiled at me, all the love shining in her eyes, grinned a little grin, and shrugged. She looked gorgeous in her favorite blue sundress.

My hands went to my mouth in wonder.

Then Momma held up three fingers—I'll never forget this as long as I live.

"Three things," she said. "One—I'm so sorry. Please forgive me." Her eyes glistened and her lip quivered. She seemed to gather herself, square her shoulders. "Two—help her...*help her*, Hadley. And three—yes, this is real, but I'm not supposed to be here. In fact, I have to go. I love you, Twinkle. So very much. Never forget that. Promise me."

And then her edges started shimmering and she just faded away.

I focused on breathing in and out.

Innnnn and *ooouutt*.

I hadn't started any new medications—I didn't take any medications at all.

Of course I'd heard ghost stories all my life—I lived in Charleston County, for goodness' sake. They have tours for the ghosts. They're part of the fabric of our world. Some of them probably vote. But I'd never actually *seen* one before, and certainly not one that I knew.

I needed to talk to someone. Who, I did not know just yet—maybe a therapist would be a good start. I gathered myself and pushed my bike back towards the house. It was only a few blocks, but I was a little shaky, didn't trust myself to ride it. Across the street from Thomson Park, Sunrise Presbyterian Church beckoned. Maybe that was the thing—Christian counseling. I should talk to Pastor Ben. Maybe I'd call the office over at First United Methodist and make an appointment.

Halfway home, I'd convinced myself I'd fabricated my mother simply because I'd been thinking of her. She wasn't really there—of course not. I simply missed my mother and wished her into being there with me. It was perfectly normal.

Maybe I'd still talk to someone, just to be on the safe side...

I punched in the gate code at the entrance to my driveway and waited for the gate to swing open, then I pushed my bike through. Thankfully, the sprinklers had finished their morning rounds. I keyed in the code to the garage and pushed my bike through the stained wooden door on the far left. I had just stowed my bike in the bike rack and was headed towards the stairs when I heard the pitiful caterwauling.

I froze, straining to hear over the rush of the incoming tide. What *was* that? Something was definitely calling for help from somewhere beneath my house. Following the wails, I made my way towards the back wall, near the utility closet. There, stuck in the lattice ventilation panel, was the head of a grey cat with dazzling green eyes.

"Oh, no...poor kitty." I hurried over and dropped to my knees peering closer to see how I could help. Leaning in, I craned and twisted my neck, trying to find an angle that gave me a better view of the problem. "My goodness, what have you gotten yourself into?"

Kitty howled pitifully.

"How did you get your head in there to begin

with?" Her head seemed too large to have ever fit between the slats.

Kitty howled in answer, but I didn't understand her language. From the other side of the lattice screen, I heard a second cat chime in, pleading for my help.

I sat on the coated concrete floor and probed the lattice around the stuck kitty's head. That's when she went to licking me.

"Oh no...please don't do that." I winced. I'm highly allergic to all pet saliva.

Kitty paid me no mind whatsoever. She was so happy to have me there in the situation with her, trying to help, that she felt compelled to show her appreciation.

I've never been a cat person, for the simple reason that I'm so allergic to pets—both their dander and their saliva. But I knew enough about their temperament that I was very much afraid of being bitten the second that, in my efforts to free her, I did something Kitty didn't care for.

Gloves. I needed gloves.

I climbed up and dug through the various totes and boxes on a shelving unit next to the closet. Kitty objected loudly to what she no doubt feared was my abandonment. Finally, I found a pair of gardening gloves. I pulled them on and settled back in front of the traumatized cat.

"It's okay, Sweetheart. We're gonna get you loose. You just hold still now," I told her. "How about we sing a little song? Do you know 'I Love Beach Music,' by The Embers? My momma used to sing that song to me, and now my doorbell plays it." I sang soft and slow, like a lullaby.

Ten minutes later, I had somehow negotiated Kitty's head free of the lattice. I stepped out the pass-through door to the garden to make sure she was okay. Two large cats rushed to greet me and express their thanks by rubbing up against my legs. The one who'd been stuck was the larger of the two—a huge grey cat with stripes so faint she appeared solid until you looked closer. Her friend was a rich brown tabby with tiger eyes and a bit of white around her mouth and under her chin. Neither cat had a collar. Both appeared quite well fed and cared for.

"Where do you guys live?" Did they have chips, perhaps?

The previously stuck kitty attempted to answer. She was quite chatty, but we still had the language barrier.

I called my friend, Sarabeth Boone.

"Hey, do you have carriers to take pets to the vet?" I asked.

"Yeah, the girls have those for Hutch and Daisy. Why? What's up?"

Hutch and Daisy were the two medium-sized dogs Sarabeth's granddaughters had brought with them when they, their dad, and an exotic blue iguana moved in last year. Sarabeth led an unconventional life.

"Do you think I could borrow them? There are two cats in my yard. I don't dare leave them outside because of the coyotes, but they don't have collars. I thought I'd take them to the vet and see if maybe they have chips. They seem to be well cared for, aside from the fact they're wandering alone through my yard."

I reached down to scratch their heads.

"Sure. I'll run them by. Do you have calamine lotion?"

I pulled off my gloves. "It's the strangest thing. I don't have a single hive, and the big cat licked me good."

"I'll bring some just in case."

"Thanks—and hey, would you post in the neighborhood Facebook group? Let folks know I've found someone's kitties?"

"Of course. See you in a few."

I crouched to easier pet the cats, who were the friendliest felines I'd ever run across. Maybe it was just dog saliva I was allergic to. I'd broken out in heinous hives after being licked by friends' dogs numerous times. My mother always said I was allergic to *all* pets. I never even asked for one because she convinced me it was a health risk. Maybe Momma simply didn't like cats. I'd have to ask her if she turned back up.

Hush it. I admonished myself.

Not happening.

My dead momma did *not* appear to me that morning. I simply wanted her to be there so badly I—

Wait—was this kitty the "she" Mom had referred to when she told me to "Help her?"

Nope—not losing my mind today. I did *not* see my mother at sunrise.

But...

She'd seemed so *real*.

And if I'd imagined her, surely I wouldn't've dreamt up that business about three things. What was that all about?

What on earth would she be sorry about anyway? See—that made no sense at all. There was absolutely nothing in this world my mother had to be sorry about, at least not as far as I was concerned. Nothing she'd say "I'm sorry" to *me* for.

There I went again, trying to decipher the thing that absolutely did not happen.

Both kitties lay down and rolled onto their backs, purring as they invited me to rub their tummies. I surprised myself by obliging. There was something so appealing about these two characters, and they seemed accustomed to being petted. They were also a welcome distraction just then from the business with Momma.

Four hours later, after Sarabeth arrived and helped me load up the kitties, after I took them to the vet over at PetSmart on Long Point Road in Mount Pleasant, I knew that both kitties were mixed breed, with some percentage of Maine Coon. The larger cat—the one who'd been stuck—was actually a male, who weighed in at a whopping twenty-two pounds. His lady friend weighed slightly less at nineteen pounds. Neither cat had a chip. Both had been fixed. I bought cat food and other essentials to last until their people could be reached.

Back at home, the kitties sat transfixed, staring at the floor-to-ceiling aquarium that formed the wall between my kitchen and dining room. Meanwhile, I set up the litter box on one end of the laundry room and food and water at the other. I half expected to break out in delayed onset hives at any given moment, but so far I'd suffered nary a sneeze nor itch. When I called them to come check out their quarters, I was disappointed by their complete lack of enthusiasm. They did not budge from their spots.

I padded into the dining room to explain their setup, feeling a bit like a hotel desk clerk with no available upgrades.

"I know it's not ideal, having your buffet and your powder room so close together," I told them. "But it's temporary. Your people will come for you soon. You're such nice kitties. Someone is looking for you. I bet they're worried sick."

"*Raowwww*," opined the big grey kitty in a mournful tone, without taking his eyes off the fish.

If only we understood each other.

So I eased down onto the floor beside them and together we watched the flamboyantly colored fish parade by. "Looking at the fish relaxes me too," I murmured, reaching out to rub the spot between Big Kitty's ears as Tiger Kitty crawled into my lap without taking her eyes off the aquarium.

Usually it does.

But just then my mind slipped straight back to Momma.

Chapter Two

The third life-changing event visited upon me that day came in the form of Carolyn Talbot. I was doing paperwork in my office—not the one in my house, the new one on Coleman Boulevard in Mount Pleasant. Business had been good lately, and meeting clients at Brown Fox Coffee had its share of challenges, so I'd finally splurged on bona fide office space for Cooper & Associates Investigations. I was still dreaming about hiring an actual associate. I didn't have anyone to answer the phones and greet people when they came in either. It was just me, Hadley Cooper, in the three-room suite between The Village Bookseller and FitLife Charleston.

I hesitated to leave the kitties alone, but work called. Cats were fairly independent, I'd heard. Hopefully, they wouldn't make a mess.

I wasn't expecting anyone. It was a gorgeous Saturday afternoon, but I was stuck indoors finishing up the report for the Wheeler case, and I was eager to be done with it so I could go home, check on my feline houseguests, and take my time getting ready for dinner. Cash—Walker Cassius Reynolds, my guy, my significant other—was taking me to Maison, a French restaurant on King Street we hadn't tried yet, and I was looking forward to the evening.

I was in my office, at the end of a hall behind reception and a conference room. By the time the knocking registered, it was urgent. *What in this world?*

The front door was locked. I only ever unlocked it if I was expecting someone. Mildly cranky at the interruption, I walked out of my office and started towards the front door. Probably someone selling something, and I definitely was not buying.

The knocking stopped.

I pulled up short. An auburn-haired lady peered through the glass door overlooking Coleman Boulevard, her hands cupped around her face. When she caught sight of me she straightened, smiled, and waved. Maybe she needed directions.

Her eyes narrowed and her face creased. She looked at me like I was a puzzle she was trying to solve.

I studied her as I unlocked the door. She was petite, maybe 5' 4", with a high-volume bob, bright blue eyes, and perfect posture. Her creamy complexion made her age impossible to guess. She wore cream-colored slacks, a pink tweed jacket over a silky cream shell, and low-heeled shoes. She might've been on her way to a Women's Club meeting or a charity luncheon.

I pulled the door open. "Hey, can I help you?"

"Are you Hadley?" Her drawl was laced with urgency, but there was a note of confusion as well.

"Yes, ma'am."

She reached out and placed a manicured hand on my arm. "Darlin', I'm so glad I caught you. I'm Carolyn Talbot. Please forgive me for not making an appointment. It's a disgraceful breach of manners, I know. Sarabeth Boone gave me your name. I need to speak with you regarding a pressing matter. May I come in?"

"Of course." I stepped back further to let her through. It never occurred to me to deny her—to ask her to come back another time. There was just something about her that made her impossible to refuse. "Sarabeth gave you my name?"

"She tells me that you are the best private investigator in the state."

"Well, Sarabeth loves me. You should probably take what she says with a grain of salt." I tilted my head at her sympathetically.

Her squint deepened. "Do you by chance have family in the area?"

"I do, actually." Was she asking who my people were? I didn't get that a lot professionally, but it was a common question in our part of the world. "Legares on my father's side. My mother was a Cooper."

"I see...well." She smiled warmly, patted my arm,

and shook her head, as if to clear it. "Forgive me, darlin'. You remind me of someone, is all."

"Are you in need of a private investigator?"

"Yes, I'm afraid that I am."

"You'd better come back to my office then and have a seat."

"Oh—thank you so much. You just don't know how much I appreciate this."

"My pleasure," I said. "Right this way." I took a step towards the short hallway.

"Your offices are just gorgeous. Who was your designer?"

"Ha—that would've been Sarabeth and a few of our friends. I haven't been here but a month. They threw me an office-warming party and surprised me with decorating the reception area. Tallulah—you'd have to know Tallulah—insisted that my 'public-facing space' must 'set the right tone.'"

"It looks like an art gallery in here." Carolyn stopped and ran a hand along the live-edge desk.

"Another friend makes those. He has a shop here in Mount Pleasant. He made the bookcases too. Anyway..."I smiled, antsy to get down to business.

Her gaze slid along the wall of bookcases behind the desk. They were expertly styled with sweetgrass baskets, blown glass vases, and all manner of beautiful things. It made me happy just to look at it, but it was all Sarabeth's doing. Carolyn shook her head in admiration as her eyes slid around the room and landed on the oil painting over the blue leather sofa. "Is that a Betty Anglin Smith?"

"It is."

"I love having local artists on the walls. It's stunning."

I nodded. "It is indeed. That was a gift from my father." Even now, two years after my father became a part of my life, saying those words made my heart feel all soft and warm and safe.

"Your family and friends have exquisite taste."

"Thank you." I moved down the hall. "Can I get you something to drink? Water? Iced tea to sip on?"

"Iced tea sounds lovely, thank you."

"Please have a seat in my office. It's in the back here, just past the conference room. I'll just get us a couple of glasses." I gestured towards the doorway and slid over to the beverage bar at the end of the short hall. Carolyn was the first new client I'd had in the new offices. As much as I loved Brown Fox Coffee, for initial client meetings, this was a vast improvement—much more private.

I added ice to our glasses and filled them from the big glass jug I kept in the fridge. It was only a few minutes past two. I could meet with Carolyn, finish my report, and still be home by 4:15. Cash was picking me up at 5:30. It would be tight—no time for soaking in the tub with a face mask—but doable.

Why had Sarabeth not mentioned Carolyn to me?

I slid a lemon slice onto the rim of each glass, spun

around, and walked back into my office. Carolyn sat in one of the two leather armchairs in front of my desk. I set her iced tea on a coaster atop the table beside her. "It's slightly sweetened with a stevia blend and just a touch of agave."

"Sounds perfect." She picked up her tea glass and took a sip. "Delicious." Carolyn exuded warmth and the air of confidence that came with being completely secure in your place in the world. If a Hollywood director ordered a Southern matron from central casting, he'd be quite pleased with Carolyn Talbot.

I settled into my chair, set my tea glass down, and lifted my chin to gaze across the desk. "So…what brings you by?"

Carolyn took a deep breath and squared her shoulders. "I'm not unfamiliar with your profession. My understanding is that whatever I tell you is confidential."

"That's generally true," I said. "I can't, of course, conceal a crime. But I seriously doubt that's an issue here." I smiled warmly, indicating what a silly notion that was—that she might be involved in anything criminal.

Carolyn's face creased again. She gave me an odd look, then blinked and gave her head a little shake. "Naturally. Do you know all the other local private investigators? Do y'all go to meetings and what have you?"

"I know most of them, I suppose." Where was *this* headed?

Carolyn nodded. "Are you familiar with Talbot & Andrews Investigations?"

"I've heard of them. I understand they're no longer in business. Wait...you said your name was Carolyn Talbot. Are you related to Liz Talbot?"

"She's my daughter. Do you know her?" She raised a perfect eyebrow.

"No, we've never met. I know the name, that's all."

Carolyn nodded. "She *cannot* hear about any of this...that I've hired a private investigator."

"I give you my word I won't tell her." It's not like our paths had ever crossed before. I couldn't see this coming up.

"Liz lived and breathed her job. She loved being an investigator, solving things. She misses it. I know she does. But it's a dangerous job. I'm sure I don't need to tell you that. She and her husband Nate had *several* close calls. I used to lie awake at night worrying about their safety. But I don't anymore, and I'm grateful for that." Carolyn studied me, a worried look on her face. "Now that I think about it, I wouldn't want to be the cause of you being in harm's way either. Perhaps this isn't a good idea after all."

"Mrs. Talbot—"

"It's Carolyn, please."

"Carolyn, this is my job. If I don't work for you, I'll work for someone else. I'd like to help if I can."

She nodded, sipped her tea, and glanced around the room. "Liz and Nate have a new business now. They run a foundation that does all sorts of positive things for the community. They're mostly involved in measures to protect Stella Maris from hurricanes and so forth, but they have their fingers in other pies as well. This is where things get sticky. With these other pies..."

"Oh?"

"It's all quite complicated. I suppose I should start with what needs investigating."

"That sounds right." I nodded and reached for my glass.

"Have you read in the papers about Patricia Gaillard? She was murdered in her home on Logan Street a little more than a week ago."

I choked as I nearly inhaled my iced tea. Red warning lights flashed on and off in my brain. I sat back in my chair, and when I could speak again I said, "I'm afraid I can't take any case that's related to the Gaillard murder. The lead SLED agent, Agent Reynolds, is my...significant other." Cash's job with the South Carolina Law Enforcement Division had collided with mine before. It wasn't conducive to a harmonious relationship.

"Oh dear." Carolyn's hand went to her pearls. "I can't tell you how devastated I am to hear that. I don't know what I'll do. I don't know of anyone else to call." Her blue eyes clouded with worry.

I was torn between my natural desire to help this sweet lady find a good investigator and my determination not to so much as glance in the direction of Cash's case. We were in a good place. I couldn't jeopardize that. My mother always told me that when I found the right guy, I had to put him first no matter what. The choices you make advertise your priorities, she said, regardless of the words you have to say on the matter.

And it was right then, as I was hearing my mother's words in my head, that I remembered what she'd said that very morning: *Help her, Hadley.*

But that was a direct contradiction to the thing she'd always taught me. This couldn't be what she was referring to. If she'd actually been there, I mean, which was of course ridiculous.

"I'm so sorry. I wish I could help."

"I understand," said Carolyn. "I just *have* to find someone who can help poor Bridget. She could lose her children. She could go to jail—or worse."

"You know Bridget Donovan?" What was wrong with me? I should not have encouraged this conversation one single second further. Bridget was Patricia Gaillard's former maid. Cash had arrested her late yesterday.

Carolyn nodded. "Quite well. I volunteer at Southern Grace Initiative. It's a nonprofit that supports single mothers here in the Lowcountry. As does Sarabeth. That's how we met. Bridget is a client. She has the two most adorable children. Hutton is seven and Delaney is six. Hadley, Bridget would never in a million years commit murder. She doesn't have that in her, I know it. But even if she did—which she most certainly does not—she would *never* jeopardize her children."

My stomach twisted into knots, the instinct to help a young mother in trouble wrestling with the instinct to honor my commitment to Cash.

"I really wish I could help," I said. And I meant that more than Carolyn could possibly know. Fighting for the underdog was the reason I got into private investigating to begin with.

"Do you know *anyone* else I could call?" She clutched her pearls and stared at me with those big, watery blue eyes.

"Who is her attorney?" I asked. "They'll likely have investigators of their own."

Carolyn shook her head in sorrow. "Bridget doesn't have the money for an attorney. They'll assign a public defender. I seriously doubt they'll have those kinds of resources."

"Why not just hire her an attorney?" I asked.

"I don't have a lot of experience at this. None is more accurate. But I imagine high powered defense attorneys will want a huge retainer in a case like this."

"I'm certain you're right about that."

"We're talking probably a hundred thousand dollars or more. That's beyond my disposable resources unless I involve my son-in-law, which I *cannot* do, because that would mean dragging my daughter into it. And this is exactly the kind of case that would have her diving headlong back into the world of exploding ferry boats, blue-blooded psychopathic crime lords, and gunfights in dark alleys. It would happen so fast all our heads would spin clear off."

I felt my eyes grow. Liz Talbot had led a far more exciting life as a private investigator than I had, at least up until that point.

"I understand. She'd want to help, no doubt about it. *I'd* love to help—truly, I would." This was exactly the kind of case that was nearly impossible for me to turn down. A dear friend of mine had been wrongly convicted of DUI homicide years ago. It ruined his life. I couldn't allow a miscarriage of justice if there was any chance it was in my power to stop it. How could I possibly live with that?

It was simple. I couldn't.

But...Cash and I had an agreement, one that served our relationship very well. I never took cases he was assigned to. Well...I didn't anymore, anyway. And Cash was good at his job. If he arrested Bridget, and he had, then he had very good reasons for doing that.

And yet...he had arrested innocent people before. Virtually every officer had at some point. It came with the territory. Sometimes law enforcement had to go with the evidence they had and let the court system sort it out.

"What makes you so certain Bridget is innocent?" I asked.

"Aside from the fact I know she isn't capable of murder, she depended on her job to support her children. Patricia's death put Bridget out of work. She lived from paycheck to paycheck as it was. It doesn't make any sense that she would kill the woman who paid her above average wages."

"Sometimes people do things in the heat of the moment—"

"No." Carolyn closed her eyes and shook her head. "I'm telling you, Bridget is innocent."

"But...didn't the SLED agents find Patricia Gaillard's diamond necklace hidden in Bridget's car? Along with the gun that killed Patricia?"

"Someone planted that, I can assure you. Whoever killed Patricia no doubt saw Bridget as an easy target to cast suspicion upon. And now she's being held and those poor precious children..."

I shook my head in sympathy. "That's just awful. I wish there was something I could do to help. But honestly, I don't know of another investigator to recommend. Everyone I know either specializes in a different area or works exclusively for one of the local defense attorneys."

"It just simply can*not* be the case that there is no help for Bridget. I refuse to believe that's the world we live in. Surely someone will stand up for this wrongly accused single mother." Carolyn's eyes challenged me, her tone appealing to my sense of justice. It was as if this woman I'd only just met knew exactly what made me tick.

I felt my hand grasping at my hair. I shook my head. "I just can't—"

"Won't you just talk to her, Hadley?" She leaned in, her big, blue, tear-filled eyes imploring me.

"I'm so sorry. I'd like to help, truly—"

Help her, Hadley, my momma's voice whispered in my ear.

"Just talk to her. See what you think," coaxed Carolyn. "If, after you meet with her, you're not absolutely convinced she's being framed...if your sense of fair play and justice for all doesn't demand that you help her...well then, I won't trouble you further."

"Carolyn, I—"

"Just *imagine* what that poor girl is going *through*..." Empathy glistened in her blue eyes, and a flush crept high into her cheeks.

"I can't even—"

"Innocent...locked up like an animal with creatures who prey on innocence for sport..." She pressed a hand to her chest, and shook her head in sorrow.

"It's just—"

"Charged with a crime she did *not* commit..." Carolyn was afire with indignation, her whole posture alive with righteous anger.

"Please—"

"Knowing she doesn't have the resources to defend herself...worried sick day and night about her poor, innocent, precious children..."

"*All right.*" I raised my voice and held up both palms in the universal sign for *stop*. "I give up. I'll talk to her."

"You will?" She smiled, her face all aglow, like I'd just solved World Peace.

"I'll talk to her," I said. "But I can't promise anything beyond that." I must be out of my mind. This was *so* not a good idea.

"Oh, thank you so much, sweet Hadley. I just can't thank you enough. Do you have a contract for me to sign? Liz and Nate always got a signed contract. I have your retainer..." She reached for her purse.

"No contract. No retainer. This—I'm just going to talk to her. That's it." With any luck at all, she would do something to convince me she was guilty. Maybe she would confess. Then I could walk away with a clear conscience.

As soon as I locked the door behind Carolyn, I called Cash.

"Hey, listen, I'm so sorry, but could we postpone Maison until another night?"

"Ah...sure, if we need to. I'll make a call. What's up?" We were both accustomed to last minute schedule changes. It came with the territory for both of our jobs. But I could hear the echo of my own disappointment in his voice.

"I had a walk-in this afternoon...it's a heartbreaking situation. You know me," I said, like *you knew what you were getting into*. I would never lie to Cash. But I was choosing my words very carefully, still hoping hard Bridget Donovan would give me a reason to wash my hands of this case. Maybe I'd never have to tell Cash I even considered it.

"Hmm...well, your soft heart is one of the things I love about you. I'll change the reservation. But you still have to eat. Want me to pick up some takeout?"

"I'm not sure how long I'll be."

"Just call me an hour before you want dinner delivered," he said.

"I don't deserve you."

"You deserve much better than me. But I'm hoping to convince you to settle. Thai sound good?"

"Always. I'll see you later." I prayed for a way out that wouldn't involve blowing up our relationship.

Chapter Three

Bridget Donovan was being held at the Sheriff Al Cannon Detention Center in North Charleston. Like many jails, nowadays they restrict most visits to video, which dramatically reduces the amount of contraband being smuggled in. There are exceptions to this video visitation policy, the biggest being attorneys. I needed to see Bridget in person to get the sense of her.

I *might* have implied I was visiting on behalf of Charlie Vanderhorst, senior partner at Middleton, Bull, & Vanderhorst, whom I'd worked with on occasion, but I never actually said that. Middleton, Bull, & Vanderhorst was one of the top-tier law firms in Charleston. If someone inferred Charlie was going to be taking Bridget's case, well, I couldn't be held responsible for that. It was a testament to how much pull Charlie had that I was able to get in to see Bridget on such short notice late on a Saturday afternoon.

A female guard escorted Bridget into the visitation room. "You have thirty minutes," she said before stepping back into the hallway and closing the door behind her.

Bridget shivered as she sat in the grey molded plastic chair across the table from my identical chair. Everything in the utilitarian room was white, or grey, or both, including Bridget's grey-and-white-striped uniform. She hunched over like she was trying to curl up as much as possible, crossed her arms, and rubbed them like she was freezing.

"Are you my attorney?" asked Bridget in a near whisper.

"No," I said. "My name is Hadley Cooper. I'm a private investigator. Carolyn Talbot came to see me on your behalf. Are you cold?" It didn't feel particularly cold to me in the room, but Bridget's teeth rattled. Was she in shock?

"Please," she said. "Have you seen my children?"

"I'm sorry, I haven't. Can you tell me what happened?" I asked. "With Patricia Gaillard?"

"She was my employer." Bridget seemed to gather herself. She sat up straight and looked me straight in the eye, her words firm and clear. "I cleaned, did laundry, cooked occasionally...basically whatever she needed me to do on any given day. Someone must've broken into her house, a week ago last Thursday night, and killed her. I showed up for work Friday morning at 9:00 like always. I didn't know..." Her voice broke. The shivering got worse. After a minute she continued. "...I knew something was off because normally she was downstairs by the time I got there. There'd be coffee in the pot, a dish in the sink...I had no idea. I thought maybe she wasn't feeling well...I went to take a basket of laundry upstairs around 9:15 and I found her in her bedroom. I called 911. That's all I know. That's all that happened." Her eyes implored me to help. "I just need to know that my kids are okay. They were at daycare —at Southern Grace Initiative—when I was arrested. Did my ex's mother pick them up?"

My heart broke for her. "All I know about Southern Grace Initiative is that Carolyn Talbot and my friend Sarabeth Boone volunteer there. I just met Carolyn this afternoon, but I can tell you for sure there's no way on God's green earth those ladies let anything bad happen to your kids. I'm sure they got them safely to their grandma."

"*No.*" Her eyes went wild. "No, please. They cannot be left with them—with Mary Ellis and George Donovan. They need to be with my friend Imani. Imani Wright. She lives next door to me. Please. If Mary Ellis Donovan gets her hands on my kids, I may not get them back."

"Where is their father?" I asked.

"Arlo—my ex-husband, their father—is in Nashville, trying to become a country music star. Please. I am begging you. Make sure my kids are safe with Imani."

"I will." I nodded. "I will." What was wrong with me? I had no business making this poor woman promises I had no idea if I could keep. "Have you had a recent falling out with Patricia? Is there any conceivable motive you could've had to want to see her dead?"

"*Noooo*." She recoiled, shaking her head. "She was good to me. She paid me well, treated me with respect. We've never so much as had an argument."

Cash must've concluded Bridget was desperate for money and the necklace was the motive. But anyone could've planted that necklace and the gun in Bridget's car.

"You told me about Friday morning—discovering Patricia's body. Back up now and tell me about Thursday. Did you work that day?"

"Yes. My regular schedule. I was there from 9:00 a.m. until 5:00 p.m."

"Anything out of the ordinary happen?"

"It was a typical Thursday. I cleaned out the refrigerator."

"Can you think of anyone who might've had a motive to kill her?"

"No. She was good to everyone who knew her as far as I've ever seen. I've never known her to have a cross word with anyone. This is just an unbelievable nightmare." Her eyes held a plea.

The pressure in my chest was building. "I can't even imagine." It was possible I'd been taken in by a convincing liar, but I really didn't think so. I read her as innocent. And if she was, this was the exact same kind of nightmare my friend North had survived.

She unwrapped her arms and commenced rubbing

the tops of her legs and her knees. Her forearms both had nasty looking bruises.

"How'd you get those?" I looked at the purple blotches.

She glanced at her arms and shook her head. "A creep who didn't want to take no for an answer. It was nothing...not important. Can you help me?" Desperation rolled off her. "If I can't somehow prove I didn't do this, my kids will end up with Arlo's parents. I may never see them again."

I closed my eyes and inhaled slowly. There was simply no way I could walk away and not help Bridget. Momma's apparent pleas on Bridget's behalf aside, I didn't have it in me to do anything less than my absolute best for her. Somehow, I would have to make Cash understand.

Resolved, I squared my shoulders and met her gaze. "I'll do everything I can."

"I don't know how I'll ever pay you, but I will. It may take me a while."

"Carolyn Talbot hired me on your behalf. My bill is the last thing you need to worry about. Patricia Gaillard was killed sometime between 11:00 p.m. on March 23 and 3:00 a.m. the next morning. Where were you?"

"At home with my kids. Ten o'clock is my bedtime."

"Can anyone corroborate that aside from your kids?"

She shook her head. "No."

"Did they photograph those bruises on your arm when you were processed in?"

"Yeah." She glanced at her arms and shrugged. "They've actually faded quite a bit. I figured they wanted to be able to prove I didn't get them here or something."

"Maybe," I said. "But they may have a theory of the crime that includes a struggle. This could be used against you. I know you said it wasn't important, but tell me anyway...how'd you get those?"

She rolled her eyes and shook her head. "It was stupid. I met this guy at the grocery store. He was asking me which breakfast cereal was a healthy choice. He seemed nice. It was a Wednesday, and the kids were with Mary Ellis. Sometimes I let her take them to church on Wednesday evenings. Anyway, I agreed to have coffee with him nearby, at Mercantile & Mash over on East Bay. I thought he was a nice guy, but he wasn't. He was kind of a jerk. I decided to cut my losses after ten minutes and a few sips of a chai latte. I made my excuses and walked out. He considered that rude. He followed me, grabbed me by the forearms. I stomped on his instep and he let go. End of story."

"Does this dreamboat have a name?"

"Corey something." She dismissed him with a wave. "I should know better than to date guys I meet on the cereal aisle."

"Fair enough...tell me about Patricia Gaillard... clearly someone had a problem with her. Who might it have been? Tell me about her family." I would do a deep dive into whatever could be found online about Patricia and her family. But some things weren't stored in databases.

"She's a widow, no children. Her husband, Chalmers, passed away around Christmas in 2021. Covid complications."

"How sad."

"It was." Bridget nodded. "They were both nice people."

"So you worked for them when he was alive?"

"Yeah. I went to work for them about a month after my divorce was final. May of 2018."

"Anyone else in her household currently?" I asked.

"No, just the staff. Myself and Scarlett Hathaway. She's—she was—Mrs. Gaillard's personal secretary. I did everything Scarlett didn't."

"Any trouble between Patricia and Scarlett?"

"No." She shook her head. "Not as far as I know."

"What about family…brothers, sisters, parents?"

"Her parents are deceased. She had one sister, Corinne. They had a complicated relationship, but not so bad Corinne would kill her. Corinne has a husband and two daughters around my age—mid-twenties."

"What about Patricia's husband's family?" I asked.

She jerked with a little chuckle and raised her eyebrows. "I've only ever met Senior—Chalmers's father. He's a character, but harmless, I think. He must be pushing ninety. As far as I know he and Patricia got along fine."

"So who stands to inherit Patricia's estate? Any ideas?"

"I would assume Corinne and her daughters, a couple of charities Patricia supported. But I don't really know. That's not the kind of thing she'd discuss with me."

"Okay, tell me about you...is there anyone who you can think of who would frame you for murder? Anyone who wanted you out of the way?"

"That's easy," she said. "Arlo's family. His parents—especially his mother. They want my kids. They don't think I'm fit to raise them by myself with Arlo out of the picture. But as awful as Mary Ellis Donovan is to me, I can't see her killing Patricia just to frame me. Mary Ellis is a church lady."

"Is Arlo an only child?"

"No. He has three brothers. But Arlo is the youngest, and Mary Ellis and George spoiled him rotten—ruined him."

"Anything else you can think of I should know?"

She shook her head. "I wish I knew something helpful."

"You haven't met with an attorney yet?"

"No. They told me an attorney would be assigned, but no one's been here yet. It feels like years, but I've only been here about twenty-four hours."

"I'll make a call and see who's been assigned. I know one of the public defenders, Dana Smalls. She's excellent. You'd be in good hands with her."

"I thought public defenders always wanted you to make a deal. I'm not pleading guilty. I did not do this."

"Dana would never pressure you to enter a guilty plea when you're innocent. One of the biggest advantages in having a private attorney is that they have their own investigators to explore theories of the crime the police have either set aside or not discovered. You have me to take care of that piece. Dana and I have worked together before."

"I can't thank you enough…just please make sure my kids are with Imani. I left her a message, when they let me make a call." She rattled off the phone number.

"I'll call her."

"They know her at Southern Grace Initiative. She's listed as someone authorized to pick them up. Imani is the *only* person authorized to pick them up. She works —she's a driver for Amazon. She'll need to continue taking them there. Please let Carolyn know."

"Of course."

"I don't have any money. I rent an apartment in North Charleston. I have no assets except an eight-year-old Honda Odyssey minivan. And since Patricia was killed, I no longer have a job. I was on my way out for a job interview when I was arrested—I can't afford to be out of work even a day if I can help it. I don't have any hope of getting out of here on bail. My only hope is for you to find who did this and clear my name."

I nodded slowly. My every instinct told me she was telling me the truth, that she was an innocent person caught up in an imperfect system without the means to extricate herself. She was the personification of my very reason for being a private investigator. I was both eager to get started and terrified at the awesome responsibility.

In addition to the house on Sullivan's Island, my dad had made me the beneficiary of a generous trust on my fortieth birthday. I'd never touched it for anything other than upkeep expenses for the house, which were automatically paid. I had resources—I honestly didn't even know the extent of them. Maybe I should hire Charlie Vanderhorst to represent Bridget myself. That would be a switch. Normally Charlie hired *me*.

As I crossed the parking lot, I tried to reach Charlie, only to learn from her executive assistant that she was out of the country on an extended vacation. Well, that was that.

When I was back in my car I called Dana Smalls.

"To what do I owe the pleasure?" Her words were coated with sarcasm. We had a complex relationship. Dana was my friend, and we'd worked several cases together successfully at that point. But she liked to pretend I was a thorn in her side. I knew she loved me. Well, I was pretty sure she did, anyway.

"Bridget Donovan," I said. "Is that your case?"

"Nah, that's Boyd Taft."

"He hasn't met with her yet. Can you request the case?"

"Why would I want to do that?" she asked. "I have

a full case load, and that promises to be a pain-in-the-ass case."

"Oh yeah, why's that?"

"*Why's that*? What do you mean *why's that*? You know exactly—are you really going to call me after seven p.m. on a Saturday night and play that? That's a dead rich lady from South of Broad. That's the *ultimate* pain in the ass."

"Well, if you don't think you can handle it..."

She muttered something that might've been laced with curse words. "Let me tell you something—"

"Smalls, she's innocent."

The line went silent. Dana huffed out a long breath and mumbled another string of colorful commentary.

"...and she's got two little kids...pain in the rear in-laws—ex-in-laws—trying to take her kids. This girl's got trouble flying at her from every direction. And if you and I don't help her, she's probably going to prison for the rest of her life, and that's if she doesn't end up on death row."

"And she's *your* client? How? Where'd she get the money for that?"

"Someone hired me on her behalf."

"Who?"

"A woman from Southern Grace Initiative."

She was quiet for so long I thought the call had dropped.

"Dana?"

"Your boyfriend know what you're up to?" Dana

knew this was Cash's case. Anyone connected with the criminal justice system in Charleston County knew that.

I sighed. "Not yet."

"Mmm-hmmm. That's fixin' to bite you hard in the—all right. Fine. I'll make a call. Taft'll be happy to be rid of that mess."

"Thanks, Dana."

"Oh, don't thank me. You gonna *owe* me."

"Yeah, yeah. Whatever. I gotta go. Cash is bringing dinner over.

"Mmm-hmm. Girl, I hope you know what you're doin'."

"Yeah...I'm afraid I do." I was very likely about to destroy my relationship with a good man who I cared deeply about. I sent up a prayer that by some miracle that wouldn't be the case.

I left messages for Bridget's friend Imani and Carolyn Talbot. I needed to verify where Bridget's kids were and ease her mind on that score.

Then I called Cash to let him know I was on my way, shuffled my favorites playlist, and pointed Jolene—the teal blue 1966 Ford Fairlane XL500 convertible I'd inherited from my mother—towards home. Appropriately, the opening strains of "Flirtin' With Disaster," by Molly Hatchet sounded through the speakers.

I turned it up.

Chapter Four

Cash's grey Jeep Grand Cherokee was in the driveway when I pulled in. He must've been sitting in the parking lot of Basil Thai waiting for me to call him. Why was he being so sweet right now? *Not helpful.* It made it harder still to deliver the bad news that I needed his agreement on my breaking our agreement, and I was really hoping he could please not be angry at me. It was a big ask.

I dropped my backpack on the bench in the foyer, called out to Cash, and looked around for the cats. They'd certainly made themselves at home. The bigger of the two was perched on the back of the sofa in the living room, with his friend curled up in the corner of the loveseat.

"Hey, there, big boy." I scratched the previously stuck kitty's head. He moved his head around, rubbing me back. "You sure are affectionate."

I gave the other kitty a quick rub, then headed for the kitchen.

When Cash wasn't there, and there was no sign of food, I knew where I'd find him. Our favorite spot to have dinner this time of year was by the fire pit on the pool deck. I grabbed a sweatshirt—early April evenings got cool right on the beach—and headed through the sliding glass door in the living room.

The sound of their laughter greeted me, drifting on the breeze as I descended the wide stairs to the pool deck. Of course Cash had called out to North and invited him to join us for dinner. I knew as I approached the semi-circle of Adirondack chairs with the spread of food on the sidebar that North's favorite—Thai noodles with beef—would be a part of the buffet Cash had put together. His kindness towards North never failed to touch me.

Tonight, it complicated things.

North Pickens and I had been friends since childhood. The product of broken parents, North was raised by his grandmother. A prodigy when it came to computer technology, he'd gone to Georgia Tech on a full scholarship and would've had a bright future had he not agreed to drop his junior-year roommate off at a party. The evening ended with the roommate driving North's car into a telephone pole killing the young man in the passenger's seat. The only one in the car who had been neither drinking nor driving, North was framed, convicted of felony DUI homicide, and went to prison. When he was released ten years later, he was a broken person with a PTSD-related phobia of enclosed spaces. North was basically homeless by choice. He just couldn't bear to be inside.

The architect who designed my house—and this is a whole nother story—created several outdoor "rooms" with landscaping providing privacy, including an outdoor kitchen on the pool deck and an adjacent open air bathroom. Everything was designed for North's comfort, and yet he still wandered Sullivan's Island and even parts of Mount Pleasant sometimes. Being anchored to one place troubled him. But, as long as he was free to come and go as he liked, he chose to stay more often than not lately, and could often be found in the magical space he called my "hidden garden" on the other side of a row of magnolias from the pool deck.

Cash understood the situation, and went out of his way to be kind to North, which I was so, so grateful for. But tonight, I'd really needed to talk to Cash alone. On the other hand, part of me was grateful for the reprieve.

"It's fabulous out here," I said as I approached the fire pit. The breeze off the ocean was gentle, the evening air soft and cool. Overhead a few eager stars sparkled in the darkening sky.

"There she is," Cash said as they both stood.

I gave him a hug and maybe held on a little longer than I should've given that North was there. Cash was solid and warm and smelled really nice—a little woodsy, a little spicy—like he always did.

He pulled his head back to look at me. "Everything all right?" His soft, warm brown eyes queried mine. At six-foot-three, Cash was fit as can be, and wore his toffee-colored hair cut short and neat, just like I liked it. In his Levi's and light blue button-down shirt, he was far too handsome for my own good.

I smiled and looked away. "Sure. Just hungry." There was no way I could tell him what I needed to with North there.

"Well, you're in luck," said Cash.

I pulled out of his arms and gave North a quick hug. "How you doing, buddy?"

"I'm great. Sorry to intrude on your evening." North squinted at me like he was clocking something wasn't quite right with me too.

Both of these men read me well.

I took in the assortment of Thai food on the teak sideboard near the edge of the pool deck, just beyond the fire pit. "This looks delicious. Thank you so much for getting dinner and setting everything up. Shall we?"

Cash handed me a plate. "Ladies first."

We all piled our plates high with Vegetable Delight, Red Curry Tofu, fried rice, and egg rolls. The guys also had Thai noodles with beef and steamed dumplings. It was a feast, and there would surely be leftovers for lunch tomorrow.

After we settled into our chairs around the fire pit, Cash poured me a glass of a Tuscan red blend. As he handed it to me, he said, "Hadley, is there anything you want to tell me?"

My heart seized.

I nearly dropped my plate.

"Wh—what do you mean?" I asked. *Dangit. Dangit, Dangit.* News traveled fast in the law enforcement community, but this was ridiculous. Not now, please. Let me figure out what words to use. I need more time—

"I couldn't help but notice the two extraordinarily large cats in the house. Neither of them attacked me, well, I nearly tripped over them while they were rubbing up against me, but—I thought you were allergic to cats?" Cash gave me a look that was a mix of confusion and amusement.

Oh, sweet relief. I laughed. "I have had a crazy day..." I told them all about the cats. "...hopefully, Sarabeth will locate their family on Facebook."

"And you haven't had a reaction to them?" asked North.

"Nary a single hive nor sneeze," I said. "It's the strangest thing. Of course, I have only my mother's word about the cat allergy thing. My friends all had dogs growing up. I don't guess I've ever touched a cat until today."

"Yeah, Vivienne probably took advantage of your dog allergy to nip every other pet in the bud," said North.

"Momma wouldn't've done that to me." My tone was perhaps a touch defensive. "Our relationship was... well, we were very close."

"She was a single mom...pets are expensive. I don't blame her," said North.

"Did you ever want a cat?" asked Cash.

"I asked for one a time or two, I guess."

"Well, now you get to test-drive having two. See how you like it," said Cash.

"Hmmm..." I was thinking I could get used to them pretty easily.

"I had an interesting day," said Cash.

"Oh yeah?" I popped a bite of spring roll in my mouth.

"I had a call from the mother-in-law of that cleaning lady I arrested in the Patricia Gaillard case."

I somehow inhaled part of the spring roll and choked.

Cash gave me a concerned look. "You okay?"

I nodded and sipped some wine. One of the nice things about agreeing never to work the same cases is that we could both feel free to talk about our day without fear of a conflict of interest. Cash didn't yet know we had one.

"I've been following that case," said North. "What did the mother-in-law want? Is she trying to help her or feed her to the wolves?"

"I'd say there's no love lost there, anyway," said Cash. "But what she really wants are her grandkids. She insisted I come by and talk to her, led me to believe she had information about the case."

"I thought she was divorced, the woman you arrested," I said. Imani must have the kids, thank goodness.

"Yeah, she is," said Cash. "I guess she's her ex-mother-in-law. But she's not an ex-grandmother."

"But surely it's up to the children's mother to make arrangements for their care," I said. "What does this woman want from you?" I needed to hush up and change the subject.

"She's a piece of work, for sure," said Cash. "Has it in her head that I can somehow force my murder defendant to relinquish her kids. I thought I'd never disentangle myself from that conversation and get loose of her."

"Aren't the kids with their father?" asked North.

"Apparently not," said Cash. "He's in Nashville pursuing a career in country music. His mother seems very proud of that. Gave me a little promotional flash drive with his debut album. The woman gave off vibes like those stage moms with little girls in the beauty pageants."

"Poor kids," said North. "Sounds like a mess. Looks like that's something the grandmother should take up with family court."

"Seems she thought she could save the attorney's fees by getting me to take care of the matter for her," said Cash. "She's got a long list of complaints against the children's mother. I told her to call social services."

"Why would you do that?" The last thing Bridget needed was to have to deal with social services. Apparently, she trusted her friend Imani with the kids. That should be good enough.

Cash shrugged. "The daughter-in-law—who's in jail and headed to prison for murder, so it's reasonable to call her judgment into question, I'd say—apparently left the kids with a friend the grandmother says is unfit. Even if that's not true, the kids can't stay with a friend forever. They need a permanent home. Who better than the grandparents?"

"I think the cart is before the horse is all," I said. "The mother is the custodial parent, and she's innocent until proven guilty, is she not?"

"Well, technically, of course—"

"Due process is not a technicality." I bristled like a porcupine.

Cash squinted at me.

"...I mean, naturally, you think she's guilty, or you wouldn't've arrested her. But I'm just saying you can't go taking a woman's parental rights until guilt is established beyond a reasonable doubt, right?"

"Hadley, I am not trying to take the woman's children. That's not my place. But I do believe permanent arrangements are going to have to be made in the best interests of the children, and of the options I'm aware of, the grandparents seem like the best one."

There was no getting around it. I was going to have to tell him now, or later, when he found out, he would remember this conversation and it would make things so much worse.

I looked at North and was about to ask him to

maybe take his plate to his hidden garden when Cash's phone rang.

He glanced at it. "I've got to take this. Cash Reynolds," he said as he put the phone to his ear.

He listened a minute, then said, "It'll take me about thirty-five to forty minutes. I'm on my way." He ended the call and said, "They found the baker from West Ashley who went missing overnight. It's Charleston PD's case, but he was mugged, and there's a potential tie-in to a string of muggings in Columbia and Greenville."

"Oh my gosh. Is he all right?" I asked. Stanley Mahaffey's picture had been all over the news, his wide, open smile capturing everyone's heart. Reporters couldn't get enough of the story about how he handed out free cupcakes to kids who couldn't afford them, saying no one should ever leave his bakery empty-handed.

"Sadly not. They found his body in the woods behind his bank branch. He was dropping off a deposit from the bakery."

"That poor man," I said. "That's just awful." I sent up a prayer for him and his family.

Cash left, and North and I finished our dinner. I commenced stress-eating in earnest, staring at the fire, shoveling Thai food in my mouth, and trying to figure out the best way to explain myself to Cash.

"You're working for the cleaning lady, aren't you?" asked North.

"Yep." North knew me well, and his powers of perception were uncanny.

"Wanna talk about it?"

"No thanks. I need to think."

"Well…if you change your mind…"

"You think I'm terrible?"

"Never. But I think this is not in your best interests."

"You got that right."

"Hadley, you don't have to save everyone, you know. Let someone else have a turn."

"That's the trouble. No one else is in line for a turn. And I can't live with leaving this woman at the mercy of the system."

He nodded. "Let me know how I can help."

North went about clearing up dinner and packing the food away. I sat by the fire brooding for another hour or so, then turned off the gas logs and headed inside. I didn't notice what had happened until I climbed the steps to the wide walkway that bordered the back side of the house. I'd situated a table there as sort of a reverse drop zone. North usually left things there for me that he'd carried up the steps.

But the Thai food wasn't there.

I wandered into the kitchen and pulled open the refrigerator. All the leftovers were stacked neatly in their takeout containers.

That evening, for the first time since he'd been home—the first time in more than eleven years—

North Pickens had voluntarily gone indoors. I was certain he'd left the sliding glass doors wide open, and I'd bet he'd come and gone quickly, but it was progress.

I smiled as I made my way upstairs for a shower.

An hour later, in my pajamas, pink fluffy robe, and cow slippers, I was checking to make sure the cats were settled—they weren't, and they wanted to play with my slippers—when Cash texted.

> You still up?

> Sure.

It was only a few minutes past ten.

> Mind if I stop back by?

> Of course not.

This was it then. I had to tell him.

He knocked on the door. Of course. He must've texted from the front porch.

I pulled the door open, and he stepped into the foyer.

His eyes, those beautiful, soulful brown eyes, wore an expression that was a mix of question and hurt. He stepped close but didn't reach out to touch me. "I figured it out on the way to West Ashley...the heartbreaking situation that walked into your office this afternoon…it was Bridget Donovan, wasn't it? You've taken her case. The Patricia Gaillard case."

I closed my eyes, pressed my lips together, and nodded.

"Why, Hadley? We agreed…we both said this wasn't good for us…"

"Because there's no one else, and she needs help, and I believe her."

"You believe she's innocent you mean?"

"I do."

"Of all the PIs in Charleston, how did she get your name? How did this happen?"

"Sarabeth volunteers at Southern Grace Initiative. It's an organization that helps single mothers. Bridget Donovan is a client. Her kids go to their daycare. Sarabeth gave my name to another one of the volunteers who wanted to hire a PI. She came to see me this afternoon. And I tried so hard to say no, I did Cash. I told her no many, many times…emphatically. But this woman is hard to say no to. She somehow convinced me to just talk to Bridget…and if I didn't believe her, I could just walk away."

He just kept looking at me, with that hurt look, waiting for me to go on.

"But I do believe her, Cash. I can't help it. I think she's being framed, just like North was, and there's no one else to help her. Most of the other PIs work with attorneys, and she can't afford an attorney. Dana Smalls is going to take the case. Cash…I am so sorry, believe me. You can't even imagine how sorry I am…

but I just can't walk away from this. I have to help her if I can. And I'm not saying you don't have a good case, or that you're not good at your job...you are. You are such a good detective..." Tears streamed down my face. I was a blubbery mess. "Please don't be mad at me. No—you should be mad at me. I'm a horrible person."

He closed his eyes and shook his head. "That's absurd. The last thing you are is a horrible person. I just think sometimes you see the world through your heart and not your eyes. We're going to have to have a Chinese wall. We cannot discuss this case at all. That's it. Agreed?"

"Agreed." I nodded.

He winced. "I just hope this agreement holds better than the last one we made. You go do your thing, whatever you need to do. Just don't ask me any questions."

"Chinese wall." I nodded.

He gave me a perfunctory kiss on the forehead. "Good night. I'll talk to you tomorrow."

As I closed the door behind him, the cats rubbed up against my legs, as if trying to pet me.

"Y'all want to sleep upstairs?"

"*Rawooooow*," Big Kitty replied.

I picked up their beds, carried them up to my room, and situated them near the windows where they could see out. They promptly hopped into my bed and looked at me as if to ask what I was waiting for.

"Oh, what the heck." I climbed into bed and

propped against my pile of pillows. Big Kitty settled into my lap, and Tiger Kitty sat beside me and pressed against me. Soon they were both purring. There was something so soothing about their presence.

I was going to miss them when their family picked them up.

Chapter Five

Monday, April 3, 2023

Southern Grace Initiative was housed in an utterly charming renovated Victorian house on Rutledge Avenue, a couple of blocks up from Colonial Lake. Surrounded by mature live oaks, the wrought-iron-fenced yard appeared larger than typical for the neighborhood. I parked on the street that Monday morning and waited for Imani Wright to arrive to drop off Bridget's kids. Imani had never returned my call, and while Cash's comments had certainly led me to believe the kids were with Imani, and Carolyn Talbot had assured me this was the case, I wanted to lay eyes on these kids and get the measure of the woman Bridget's former mother-in-law considered unfit. At that point, I'd had only a thirty-minute conversation with Bridget and didn't know any of the rest of these folks at all. I needed to make sure the kids were okay. Once I'd set my mind at ease, I could reassure Bridget, check this box, and focus on proving her innocence.

At 7:05, a light-skinned black woman in an Amazon delivery uniform unloaded two towheaded kids with backpacks from the backseat of a blue Honda Civic. This had to be them. I snapped a picture as they hurried down the sidewalk holding hands and swinging arms, chattering happily, through the wrought-iron gate. Cute kids. The little girl looked up at the woman and laughed out loud at something. From what I could tell, Hutton and Delaney looked clean, typically dressed, and happy.

I was waiting for the woman when she came back down the front walk a few minutes later.

"Imani Wright?" I asked.

She gave me a steely-eyed glare and kept walking.

"Imani, I work for Bridget. Carolyn Talbot hired me. I left you several messages..."

She spun around on the sidewalk.

"Carolyn hired you?" Her tone dripped with skepticism.

"Yes, I said that in my messages—"

"Yeah, well, people can *say* anything, can't they? Look, I don't know you. For all I know, you're one of Mary Ellis Donovan's henchpeople."

"Why not call Carolyn and ask her?"

She shrugged and gave me a look that inquired who the heck I thought I was to question her. "I've been busy...dinner, baths, bedtime stories...do *you* have kids?"

"Fair enough. Look, I'm not trying to take the kids. I just wanted to reassure Bridget they were with you. Now that I've seen it for myself, I can do that. So we're good."

"Of course they're with me. Where else would they be?"

"Bridget was worried somehow her ex-mother-in-law had picked them up at daycare after she was arrested."

"But Bridget knows Mary Ellis can't do that. She's not on the list."

"I guess Bridget freaked out a little bit. Being arrested will do that. She just needs to be reassured the kids are okay."

"The kids are just fine."

"Great."

"All right then." She gave me a look like, *why are you still in my face?*

"Fabulous. Do they need anything?"

"I just told you they were fine."

"Okay, okay." I raised my palms, then reached for my business card. "If that changes, or you need to reach me, here's my card. You know, in case you forgot to write down my number from the four messages I left."

She muttered something under her breath. "Look, I'm sorry, all right? There's only one thing I can do for my friend right now, and that's take care of her kids, and make sure they don't end up with that witch Mary Ellis." Her words were a tad more colorful.

"Hadley?" I turned to see Carolyn Talbot coming down the sidewalk, with a large bag from Harken Cafe. She did not appear overjoyed to see me.

I wondered why. "Hey, Carolyn. I was just checking on the kids for Bridget."

"I see that. Good morning, Imani."

"Hey, Carolyn. You vouch for this woman?" Imani raised an eyebrow at me with a half grin.

"Yes, of course." Carolyn smiled and glanced around nervously.

What was up with her?

"I'm late," said Imani. "You ladies have a good one."

"I didn't realize you'd be here this morning," I said to Carolyn. "As long as you are, we can get that contract signed if you like."

Carolyn's eyes grew wide. "Oh—how about if I drop by your office later this morning? I know you must have a million things to investigate. Don't let me keep you."

I squinted at her. "Is everything all right?"

"Why, of course. Why wouldn't it be? I just don't want to hold you up this morning. And actually...I have an appointment myself. Please excuse me—" She started through the wrought-iron gate.

"Mamma?"

Oh.

I'd lay good money on the blonde strolling easily down the sidewalk being Liz Talbot.

Carolyn hurried down the path, as if she hadn't heard the woman call to her.

"*Mamma?*" The woman called louder, staring after Carolyn, who was up the steps and crossing the porch at a fast clip.

The woman glanced from Carolyn to me and said, "Good morning," before turning back to stare towards the house with a quizzical look.

Then her head snapped towards me, her face registering surprise. "What are..." She tilted her head and squinted.

"Good morning," I said.

She gave her head a little shake. "You look so much like—I'm sorry. Where are my manners? I'm Liz Talbot." She held out a hand.

"Rhonda Swicegood." I pulled a name out of thin air and shook her hand. "I was just admiring the restoration work they did on this house. My husband and I are working on a similar Victorian, and I wanted to ask who the contractor was. But the lady I was speaking to was in a rush. I'll drop back by another day. Nice to—"

"Oh—I can help you with that. Come inside, please. That's my mamma you were speaking to. She volunteers here. The house is the headquarters for an organization that supports single mothers here in the Lowcountry. Southern Grace Initiative. My husband and I actually bought the house and had it restored.

I've got tons of information in several three-ring binders. You're welcome to—"

"You're so kind to offer." A piece of the puzzle clicked into place. This was why Carolyn had said the situation was "sticky." Liz was already too close to this case for comfort. She and her husband were the benefactors of the organization where Carolyn met Bridget. "But I—"

"*E-liz-a-beth*. Hadley."

Liz and I both turned to the front porch. Carolyn stood there staring at us imperiously.

"Both of you come inside," she said. "Breakfast is in the kitchen."

Dagnabbit, Carolyn, I had this covered.

Liz was looking at me with that confused expression again.

I covered my face with a hand, then grinned. "Actually, I'm Hadley Cooper. And your mother will explain."

"Well, I simply cannot wait to hear that. Do come inside."

I followed her through the wrought-iron gate, past the Palmetto palm in the front yard, down the sidewalk, and up the front porch steps to where Carolyn waited for us.

"Let's get some coffee and food inside us and then we'll talk." She turned and led us through the door, across the gleaming heart-of-pine floor of the foyer, and back to a large, modern kitchen. Sandwiches, pastries, and yogurt parfaits, formed a bountiful buffet across a wide butcher-block island.

"Coffee's on the bar," said Carolyn. "I don't know how you like it, Hadley. Please help yourself."

I poured myself a cup and watched as Liz selected one of the parfaits and settled in at the built-in banquette in front of a large window.

"The breakfast sandwiches are quite good," said Carolyn. "There's plenty. Try a couple of them."

"Mamma always has at least three times as much food for everything as she thinks she'll need," said Liz. "It's her policy. Trust me. There's only half a dozen employees and volunteers scheduled to be here all morning. The kids will have breakfast more geared to their tastes."

"This all looks amazing," I said. "But I've already eaten." No need to get into my dietary issues this morning.

"Nonsense," said Carolyn. "You'll need something to snack on while we chat."

"Resistance is futile." Liz raised an eyebrow in my direction. "Mamma feeds everything that breathes. It's her love language."

Carolyn gave Liz a look that might've meant *that's quite enough out of you young lady*.

I grabbed the closest sandwich, which didn't appear to have meat on it, and really did look delicious, and slid into the chair across from Liz.

At the end of the table, Carolyn sipped her coffee, the expression on her face serene.

Liz took a bite of her parfait, caught my eye, and grinned. "Mamma is gathering her thoughts."

Carolyn sighed and set down her coffee cup. "Now, Elizabeth, I know what you're thinking…"

"Do you, Mamma?" Liz squinted and canted her head sideways. "Because I'm honestly just trying to figure out why our friend here gave me one name—Rhonda Swicegood, was it?"

I nodded and sipped my coffee.

"…until you called us into the house, at which point she admitted to being Hadley Cooper—a name, I confess I am somewhat familiar with. Professional awareness, let's call it." Liz smiled warmly at her mother. "It would seem she was trying to hide her true identity. Any idea why that would be, Mamma?"

"I imagine that's because she's a professional. And because I specifically asked her not to reveal to you that I'd hired her," said Carolyn, in a tone that clearly established who was in charge.

"You what?" Liz stared at her mother.

"You heard me," said Carolyn. "I hired her."

"*Why?*" Liz wore a stunned expression.

"Do you know Bridget Donovan?" asked Carolyn. "She's one of the Southern Grace Initiative clients."

"I don't," said Liz. "But the name rings a bell."

"That's because she was arrested for murder," said Carolyn. "It's ludicrous, of course."

"Right." Liz nodded. "I saw that on the news. So you wanted to help her, but make sure I wasn't tempted to investigate myself. Is that it?"

"Precisely," said Carolyn. "I'm aware that you miss your former vocation. But the last thing any of us need is you being drawn back into all of that. You and Nate have a great many important projects to manage. You don't need this distraction."

Liz and Carolyn met and held each other's gaze for a long moment. There was clearly a lot being communicated between mother and daughter nonverbally. I'd had the same sort of channel with my own mother. A wave of longing for her swept through me.

"I trust Hadley will get to the bottom of this for us," said Carolyn. "Can we leave it at that, please, Elizabeth?"

Liz sighed, closed her eyes for a few seconds, then looked at her mother. "Hell's bells, Mamma, do you really think in all this time...in the last seven years—since Poppy was kidnapped in St. John, and Nate talked me into retirement—that I haven't investigated *anything*?"

"Watch your language. And of course that's what I think. You work for the foundation...you're involved in all sorts of environmental and charitable projects. When would you have time to sneak around after adulterers and other miscreants?"

Liz shrugged. "I've occasionally dipped a toe in. My PI license is still current. So is Nate's."

"What?" Carolyn blanched.

"Mamma...it was my career for a very long time. It's part of who I am. It's impossible to completely walk away from it. Now, I haven't taken on the kinds of cases I used to...I've just...dabbled a bit here and there. Things I could do from the office."

"Does Nate know about this dabbling?" Carolyn asked.

"Of course. Nate and I don't have secrets. He dabbles too."

Without realizing it, I'd eaten half my breakfast sandwich, a delicious egg and cheese biscuit concoction which I had no business eating, watching this drama unfold. It was almost like they'd forgotten I was even there.

"This is a slippery, slippery slope, I fear," said Carolyn. "But I know you well enough to know that my opinion in the matter—my stress level, lying awake at night and worrying about you—that won't enter into your calculations."

"Of course it does, Mamma," said Liz. "Relax. I'm not out following criminals around, or anything remotely like that. I'm just...looking into things online, occasionally...when situations capture my attention. And it's likely I would've been poking around in Bridget's case once I figured out she was one of your clients."

Carolyn closed her eyes and gave her head a little shake. "There is no need for you to do that. As I said... I'm certain Hadley will get to the bottom of things. She comes very highly recommended."

"I have no doubt." Liz smiled brightly. "Hadley, are you originally from Charleston?"

"Yes. Well, Mount Pleasant, actually."

"Mount Pleasant is lovely," said Liz. "Do you have a big family?" She exchanged a glance with Carolyn.

"Not really. My dad, stepmom, and my half brother. My mother passed away when I was seventeen."

"I'm so sorry," said Liz. "I didn't mean to bring up sad memories."

"It's been quite a long time." Although not so long since I'd last seen her. *Did not, did no*t*, did not*. "So... you don't actually work here at Southern Grace Initiative?"

"No," said Liz. "I just dropped by this morning on my way to the office because I love the breakfast parfaits at Harken, and I knew Mamma was going by there. She brings breakfast in for the staff once a week. Our foundation, mine and my husband's—the Talbot & Andrews Foundation—contributed to getting Southern Grace Initiative started, but we're not hands on here. There are other organizations involved as well, and a full staff, some paid, some volunteers. I have an office at our foundation headquarters over on Broad Street. You should pop by and see me sometime. We can talk shop."

Carolyn gave me this look that discouraged comment, so I just smiled.

"Carolyn, shall we get that contract signed while I'm here?" I asked. "I mean...now that we're all on the same page..."

"Yes, of course." Carolyn reached for her purse. "Let me write you a check. Is a check all right?"

"Perfectly fine," I said. "My usual retainer is twenty-five hundred. Is that okay?"

"Oh, no indeedy, it most certainly is not," said Liz. "Seven years ago, my retainer was five thousand dollars. Mamma, make that check for seventy-five hundred. How much are you billing an hour, Hadley?"

"One twenty-five."

"Again, that's what I was charging seven years ago. With inflation, you're losing money. You should charge at least two hundred."

"Thank you, Elizabeth." Carolyn flashed her daughter a quelling smile and handed me a check with a flourish.

Liz shrugged. "She should be compensated fairly. As you so often point out, Mamma, it's a dangerous job."

"I do have a question for you, Carolyn." I passed her the contract. "What can you tell me about Bridget's family dynamics? The ex, and especially the ex-mother-in-law, Mary Ellis Donovan?"

"That woman is a bona fide piece of work," said Carolyn. "She's specifically not allowed to pick up the kids, which tells you all you need to know about her relationship with Bridget."

"She's apparently going to appeal to social services to deliver the kids to her," I said. "She tried getting SLED to get involved, but they referred her to social services. I wouldn't be surprised if she retained an attorney and filed a petition with family court. With Bridget not likely to make bail, this could be an issue. I know she doesn't want the kids with Mary Ellis. I'd like to be able to reassure her, but...who knows how a family court judge might rule?"

"Let me look into that aspect of things," said Liz.

Carolyn looked alarmed.

"Just the bail and custody issues, Mamma," said Liz. "We have funds set aside for that sort of thing in our legal relief program."

"I've never heard you mention that," said Carolyn.

"It's never come up. I'll talk to Nate. He may have some ideas. Bridget is a client at Southern Grace Initiative. We'll do what we can to help her."

"I'm grateful for that." Carolyn's tone was careful, like she was torn between two impulses—keeping Liz out of Bridget's case and helping Bridget.

"Who's her attorney?" asked Liz.

"Dana Smalls is a public defender I've worked with in the past. She's an excellent attorney. At my request, she took the case from one of the other attorneys."

"I could ask a friend to look at the case," said Liz. "Fraser Rutledge III...he's one of the best in the area, particularly for this kind of high-profile murder case..."

"I thought about Charlie Vanderhorst," I said, "but she's out of the country. I'm sure your friend is excellent...the thing with Dana is that she has a heart for this kind of underdog case. I know she'll make it her mission in life to get Bridget acquitted."

"Let me know if there's anything she needs aside

from you." Liz passed me her business card. "I'm not surprised SLED is involved. This is a high-profile case. But Patricia Gaillard was murdered inside the city limits. Do you know whose case this is? From the Charleston PD?"

"Sonny Ravenel, I understand." I handed her my business card. "And Cash Reynolds is the SLED agent. Which complicates things for me tremendously. Cash is my...significant other."

"I imagine that is messy." Liz winced. "The good news is that Sonny Ravenel is a friend from way back. Let me know if you run into a roadblock."

I nodded, all the ways this could blow up in my face with Cash sambaing around my brain.

"Well look who's here! Good morning everybody." Sarabeth Boone breezed into the kitchen.

We all chimed in with our hellos and good mornings. Sarabeth went about the business of getting her coffee and selecting breakfast.

"Carolyn, I'm just tickled you were able to get Hadley to look into things for Bridget. Heaven knows that poor girl needs a break," said Sarabeth.

"I hope I can help," I said. "We were just talking about her family situation. Do you know the ex-mother-in-law?"

Sarabeth slid into the chair beside me. "Oh yes, I have had the misfortune to cross swords with her. She knows she's not on the pickup list, but she keeps trying, thinking she'll get someone new she can talk into letting her have the kids."

"Does Bridget not let them see their grandparents at all?" What happened to church on Wednesday evenings? "Is it that bad?"

"Oh, they spend plenty of time with Mary Ellis and George," said Sarabeth. "Bridget would never keep them from them entirely. But she has a schedule, and she keeps to it. I think they get them twice a month—one full weekend and a Saturday."

"That sounds reasonable to me," I said. "But what do I know about this sort of thing?"

"It's more than reasonable," said Carolyn. "But Mary Ellis isn't interested in being reasonable. She would like full custody."

"Oh, I know it," said Sarabeth. "And she's smart enough to realize that would never have happened. Bridget is an excellent mother. But these murder charges change everything and give her leverage she would never have had otherwise. Trust me, she will use it for all it's worth."

"So what's the deal with the kids' dad?" I asked. "I'll do research on all these people, of course, but in this case, the most important stuff isn't on a computer somewhere."

"Arlo Donovan is the best country singer you've never heard of," said Sarabeth. "Just ask his mamma. She makes excuses for the fact that he's basically abandoned his family to chase a pipe dream in Nashville because, in her mind, he's one song in front of the right person away from being the next Blake Shelton."

"Oh yes," said Carolyn. "And when he makes it

big, he'll sue Bridget for custody and give the kids to his mother to raise while he's on the road. This is Mary Ellis's master plan, as I understand it."

"Why on earth would she want to take the kids away from a loving mother?" Liz asked.

"She thinks it's the Christian thing," said Sarabeth. "Women like Mary Ellis reflect poorly on Christian women everywhere."

"I'm sorry, what?" I squinted at Sarabeth.

"Mary Ellis and George are in church every time the doors are open, and want the grandkids there with them," said Sarabeth. "Eternal Hope First Baptist Church of Ladson. Don't let that name fool you. These are off-brand Baptists, and they have no hope at all to share. This church is more hellfire focused than most, if you know what I mean. Less about Christian love and more about beating religion into folks. If Bridget would go to church with them and bring the kids, Mary Ellis and George might, possibly leave her more or less alone. Maybe. But Bridget has different ideas about their religious instruction. She takes them to a United Methodist Church, which Mary Ellis seems to think is a danger to their souls."

"And this woman is okay with her son chasing a career in country music?" asked Liz.

"Anything Arlo wanted to do would be fine with his mamma," said Carolyn. "She's his number-one fan, and I'm here to tell you, he does no wrong. Of course, she probably has an idealized vision of the type of music he's singing."

"Is he an only child?" I asked. "Wait—Bridget said he's got brothers if I remember right."

"Youngest of four boys." Sarabeth nodded. "And there was something else weird...for a while, Mary Ellis was acting all nice...almost sucking up to Bridget."

"Right," said Carolyn. "I remember that. Bridget mentioned that her employer's—Patricia Gaillard's—college roommate is married to some big Nashville music executive. Mary Ellis wanted Bridget to somehow get her to send Arlo's demo CD or some such thing to this man."

"*Yeeees*," said Sarabeth. "She worried the fool out of Bridget about that. Bridget wanted no part of it. She didn't want to bother Patricia with it. I think the whole idea embarrassed her. But her refusal to help Arlo—those were Mary Ellis's words—made things infinitely worse between them."

"Which one would've been hard pressed to imagine," said Carolyn.

I sat back in my chair. "Anything else I should know about this family?"

"One could write a long, colorful novel about this family," said Carolyn. "But aside from protecting Bridget's rights to her kids, I don't think there's any need to bother much about them."

I stood to leave. "I guess I'd better get going. Thanks so much for all the info."

From the corner of my eye, I noticed Liz Talbot studying me. She and Carolyn both had given me odd looks, and they'd exchanged odd glances a few times.

As I left Southern Grace Initiative that morning, I couldn't help but wonder what they were thinking. Were they sizing me up? Did I somehow fall short? I was a solid investigator. But somehow, I left there feeling like I had something to prove.

"I'll walk you out." Sarabeth followed me out onto the front porch.

"I have a favor to ask," she said at the top of the steps.

"Of course. Name it," I said.

"I'd like to shadow you on this case."

"I'm sorry—what?"

"I want to ride along. It's research for the book I'm working on." Sarabeth was a cozy mystery author. She'd always asked me a lot of questions, but this was the first time she'd ever asked to watch me while I worked.

"Ride along...like every day? I mean some days are office days. I'm on my way there now..." This was something I needed to give serious thought to. Sometimes my job was dangerous. Okay, not really very often, but still...

"No, not every day. Just, you know, when you're doing something interesting. If you'd rather I didn't—"

"No...no...let me give some thought to when would be a good day."

She squealed a little and hugged my neck. "This will be so much *fun*."

"It will," I said, perhaps not quite as enthusiastically. I'd worked by myself a very long time. "Hey... have you heard anything on the cats yet?"

"Not a single thing," said Sarabeth. "I guess the owners aren't on Facebook."

Chapter Six

By ten o'clock that Monday morning, I was in my office. The first thing I needed to do was set up a case file and board. I spent the next couple of hours profiling the victim, Patricia Gaillard, and figuring out the various players in her orbit. I also added people in Bridget's circle, because it was possible one of them killed Patricia for motives more related to framing Bridget.

Several online subscription databases gave me all the data I needed. An app North designed for me pulled it all together, combined it with publicly available information, displayed it on my screen, and gave me the option to print. North was amazingly gifted with all things technical. Perhaps I wasn't *completely* comfortable that all his data sources were strictly legal, but I managed not to let that trouble me too much. I was on the side of the angels.

Patricia Anne Pinkney Gaillard grew up in

Charleston, South of Broad. She attended Vanderbilt University and graduated with a bachelor's degree in music. Interesting...she'd studied voice, but married Chalmers Gaillard, Jr., another Charleston native ten years her senior, three weeks after graduating.

I found no evidence Patricia ever pursued a singing career. She became the socialite and charity volunteer she was apparently destined to be. She had no criminal record and no civil actions filed against her. Nothing in her background hinted at any sort of scandal. But I did find numerous photos of her online with Uma and Trevor Jennings, a Nashville power couple, apparently. Trevor was the head of Riversong Records. Uma, his wife, was Patricia's friend from college. I could see why Mary Ellis had been so eager for Bridget to slip her a demo album. Patricia Gaillard had legit connections in the Nashville music scene.

Sadly, in most murder situations, the most likely culprit is someone close to the victim. I always start my digging with those closest and work my way out. Typically, you look at the spouse or significant other first, but as Patricia was a widow with no known partner and no children, I focused on her next closest relative, the sister. While I was an only child, and had never experienced it myself, I understood sisters could be tricky.

Corinne Pinkney Barnwell and her husband Porter had two daughters in their mid-twenties, Emerson and Everly. Interesting...according to the marriage database, the Barnwells married in Vegas in March of 1995. Not the big society wedding you might expect. When I dug a bit deeper, I saw the likely reason: their oldest daughter, Emerson, was born in October later that same year. I filed this tidbit under irrelevant family drama.

Porter was an executive at a local shipping company, and the family seemed well-off—no financial red flags that might make them eager to collect an inheritance. I needed to get a look at Patricia's will to verify who her beneficiaries were. That was one thing I could not access through North's handy app. My best bet was to get inside Patricia's house and do a bit of snooping.

The biggest surprise from my morning's research came in the form of an apparent love child. When he was twenty years old—twelve years before he married Patricia—Chalmer's Gaillard Jr. had a child with a woman named Nadine Phillips. There was no evidence they'd ever married, but the child—who was now thirty-nine years old—was named Chalmers James Gaillard III. Interesting. I wondered if he had axes to grind with his stepmother?

By lunchtime, I'd constructed a preliminary list of possible suspects and motives, some of them far-fetched, but I liked to start with every possibility I could think of and then eliminate suspects from my list systematically, preferably because they had a rock-solid alibi. Murders happened for a finite list of reasons. At the start of any case, I looked at everyone who might've had one of them. And I always included the client because until I could prove otherwise, it was possible my client was guilty. Here's where things stood on my dry-erase case board at noon that Monday:

MOTIVE	SUSPECT
Money / Greed	Corinne and / or Porter Barnwell
Money / Greed	Emerson and / or Everly Barnwell
Money / Greed	Chalmers Gaillard III
Money / Greed	Unknown beneficiary
Anger / Hate	Chalmers Gaillard III
Anger / Hate	Mary Ellis and / or George Donovan
Love / Benefit someone else	Unknown subject
Jealousy / Sex	Unknown lover
Revenge / Vendetta	Unknown subject
To Keep a Secret	Unknown subject
Urge to protect	Unknown subject
Violence / Thrill	Random psychopath
Unknown Motive	Nadine Phillips
Unknown Motive	Scarlett Hathaway (Patricia's secretary)
Unknown Motive	Arlo Donovan (Nashville connection?)
Unknown Motive	Adam, Aaron, or Andrew Donovan
Unknown Motive	Bridget Donovan

There were a couple of other possible motives for murder—like freedom from your spouse—that didn't apply in Patricia's situation. I was staring at the case board musing over my list when I heard a knock at the front door.

When I stepped out of my office and looked down the hall through the glass front door, Gavin stood there grinning and waving his hand like a magician over a picnic basket covered with a blue-checkered napkin. I hadn't realized it was lunchtime. Suddenly, I was starved.

I unlocked the door and pulled it open.

"Grub's up, Twinkle."

"Gavin, you are Heaven-sent." Since I'd opened my office a scant few blocks from Gavin's house, he'd taken to dropping by with food on occasion. He'd called earlier, on an obvious pretext, to ask if Cash and I were planning to go with him and Joe Vincent—his best friend and the former PI I interned with years ago—to the Blessing of the Fleet in a few weeks. I'd recognized this for the ruse it was, designed to determine if I was in the office.

I always go with Gavin and Joe to the Blessing of the Fleet, which is pretty much what it sounds like: a boat parade, with a ceremonial blessing of the shrimp and fishing fleet. There's also a line up of some of Mount Pleasant's best chefs offering samples of their signature dishes, a craft fair, an art exhibit, a shrimp eating contest, music, and dancing. It's really a fun day.

When I was a child, Momma and I would go with Gavin and his wife, Maribel, to the Blessing of the Fleet at Alhambra Hall, just a short walk from the house I grew up in. It was tradition. The festival had gotten so big they'd moved it years ago to Memorial Waterfront Park, near the base of the Mount Pleasant end of the Arthur Ravenel Jr. Bridge, or as any bridge over the Cooper River would always be called inside my head, the Cooper River Bridge.

I lifted the napkin over the basket and peered beneath it.

"Nothing fancy," said Gavin. "Just chickpea salad on homemade sourdough with some fresh sliced strawberries. But it'll hold you till dinner. Stand back now, I'll put it in the conference room."

He walked with purpose past me towards the hall, a clear sign he had something on his mind aside from dropping off lunch.

"I brought mine along so we can eat together," he called over his shoulder. "People shouldn't eat alone so much."

I nodded. Yep. The lovable old codger was up to something.

By the time I'd poured us both a glass of iced tea, he had a tablecloth on my conference table, matching napkins at our places, and food set out.

"This looks amazing. Thank you," I said.

"You're welcome." He took a bite and chewed thoughtfully.

"Anything on your mind?" I asked.

"What do you mean?" He flashed me an innocent look.

I shrugged. "You know, anything you wanted to talk to me about?"

"What, I need an excuse to bring you lunch now?"

"No, of course not. Just wondering…"

"Whatcha working on? Got a big case going?"

I nodded. "Did you talk to Cash?" Gavin and Joe were definitely what you might call fans of Team Cash. It was hard to say sometimes which of the three of us was happier when Cash and I patched things up after a breakup a couple of years back.

"I did not," said Gavin. "Joe mighta mentioned something about you were working on the Patricia Gaillard case, but I know that can't be right, because that was Cash's arrest, and you two have an agreement about that sort of thing."

I sighed. "It's complicated, Gavin. Bridget Donovan needs someone in her corner—"

"Well, sure. But why does it have to be you?"

"Because there's no one else."

"You're the lone avenging angel of mercy, now, are you?" He sat back and gave me a look that might've suggested I was too big for my britches.

"There's not another PI available who works this kind of case who isn't busy with a case load from the attorney they work for. You know how this goes." I didn't add how this case pulled my heartstrings right out of my chest because Gavin already knew that.

"What I know is, you will never put your needs before anyone else's. And while that's an admirable quality, sometimes you need to take a longer view of things."

"What do you mean?"

He screwed up his face into a pained expression. "The timing here is just bad, Twinkle."

"I'm sorry?"

"I mean...how long have you and Cash been...you know...on an even keel, so to speak?"

"Nearly two years." I took a bite of my sandwich.

Gavin could do amazing things with chickpeas. This tasted remarkably like chicken salad.

"Exactly what I'm telling you." He nodded meaningfully.

"What...is what you're telling me? Gavin, you're not telling me anything at all."

"Well, I'm trying to just give you a little perspective, is all."

"You're going to need to be more direct."

Frustration washed over his face. He looked towards the ceiling, then back at me. "I'm only saying that after a couple a years a smooth sailing, you and Cash might be thinking about the future."

"And you think I might jeopardize our future by taking a case that's also his case?"

"Well, *yeah*." He gestured with both hands wide, as if to say, *isn't that obvious*?

"Well, I hope that's not what happens. You know how I feel about Cash—"

"But does *he* know? That's the point Twinkle. Maybe he sees this as a sign you're not really committed to him."

"I really don't think—"

"Actions, Hadley...it's your actions that count. Not your words. Maribel, God rest her soul, and I, we always put each other first, no matter what."

"And you had a wonderful marriage. The best. And I understand you want the same thing for me. But...Cash and I are different people from you and

Maribel...and he understands this is something I just have to do."

"The timing—"

"It's all going to work out, Gavin. Or...it won't. I hope it does. I love Cash. But I could not live with myself if I walked away from Bridget Donovan. I have to help her if I can."

Gavin closed his eyes and raised a sun-spotted hand to his forehead. He shook his head. "Maybe Joe knows someone—"

"He doesn't. I already spoke to him, as you know. And anyway, if he did, I'd know them too."

"I just don't want to see you get hurt."

"Me either." I smiled and patted his hand. "It'll be okay. Hey, I have a question for you."

"Yeah, what's that?"

"Do you ever remember me having an allergic reaction to a cat?" Gavin had known me my entire life. He and Maribel lived in the house next door to where I grew up and my mother too. They'd witnessed both of our entire histories—well, Gavin had, anyway. Maribel was killed in a hit and run accident, by a suspected drunk driver, when I was fourteen. Her unsolved case was one of the reasons I'd gravitated towards a career in investigation.

Gavin shrugged and consulted the ceiling. "Not as far as I recall. I don't remember there ever being a cat around. Dogs, now...you had some pretty dramatic reactions to dogs in the neighborhood. More than once your momma took you to the doctor with hives all over you."

"Yeah, I remember. But she always said I was allergic to cats too. I'm not so sure that's true."

"Guess it was a chance she didn't want to take. You figuring on getting a cat?" The look of distaste on his face asked, *why on earth would you do such a thing as that?*

"Nah, just curious." I told him about Big Kitty and Tiger Kitty as we finished our lunch, then he packed everything up and headed out.

He'd been gone maybe five minutes, and I'd just barely glanced back at my case board, when someone tapped out a rhythmic knock on the door. I sighed, thinking maybe Gavin had thought of something else to allow on the subject of my current case.

But when I stepped out of my office and headed down the hall, Liz Talbot stood on the other side of the glass door. I smiled as I opened the door and let her in.

"Hello again," I said.

"Hey...sorry to drop by unannounced. I just...well, to be honest, I'm having a hard time keeping my mind off your case. I was hoping you wouldn't mind letting me just kind of...look over your shoulder. Ordinarily, I'd just dive right in finding what I could online, but it seems...not in Bridget's best interests to simply duplicate what you're doing, and I—"

"Sure." I opened the door and stepped back. "Come on in."

"Thanks. Great office. We always just worked from home. Well, in Stella Maris, anyway. At one point we had an office in Greenville, but that's been ages ago."

"I haven't had this space very long." I led her back to my office. "I used to just meet clients at a coffee shop—usually Brown Fox. That's not ideal."

"I love Brown Fox Coffee," said Liz. "The Mexican Fox is my favorite."

"Mine too. I just finished the case board this morning," I said. "Maybe you can spot something I missed." I led her back to my office, where she settled into the swivel chair her mother had occupied on Saturday and spun around to have a look.

"Oh, my stars." Liz stared at the dry-erase board that hung on the wall opposite my desk. "This looks a lot like the way I used to do it."

"You miss the job a lot, don't you?"

"Every single solitary day. Have you seen the electronic video walls? They're like having a big tablet with multiple touch screen windows. You can add stuff with your computer, or your iPad, or your phone…you can drag things around with your fingers."

"I haven't," I said.

"Ssshhh…I might've put one in my office—the one at the foundation, but don't tell Mamma. You really need one—you'd love it. So…do you have any early favorites for who killed Patricia Gaillard?"

"You know, I try not to have a favorite, but if I had to place a bet, it would be on someone who stood to inherit a chunk of her considerable fortune. I just don't know who those people are yet."

"How are you going to get a copy of the will?" she asked.

"The old fashioned way. Breaking, entering, and snooping."

"I *sooo* miss the snooping. Do you wear disguises?"

"Yes, of course. Everyone and their cousin Eddie have cameras that record all their neighbors' business."

"Indeed." Liz studied the board for a few moments. "Corinne Barnwell is the sister, right?"

"That's right."

"I'm thinking there are several possible motives there aside from the money. As Mamma is fond of allowing, 'I think the Lord our God made few things as intricate and complex as the relationship between sisters.'"

"Sounds like you speak from experience."

"Oh, I do indeedy." Her eyes grew large. "But no matter how much we squabble, Merry and I are much more likely to kill defending one another. Still...could be some sibling rivalry with Patricia and her sister... some old wound that festered..."

"I'll see what I can find out about their relationship. Can I ask you a question?"

"Sure."

"If you miss it so much, what keeps you from just jumping back into the fray, so to speak?"

Liz sighed. "Two things, I guess. Those last few years, things were pretty hairy. Nate and I were both hospitalized a time or two. He's been shot. I've been shot at too many times to mention. I guess I figured it was time to stop pressing our luck. I worried about him. He worried about me. After a point, it wasn't worth the price."

"And the second thing?"

An odd look spread over Liz's face. She seemed to be staring at something over my shoulder. I turned to see what it might be, but there was nothing back there but my credenza.

After a minute, she said, "Now I need to ask you a question."

"All right."

"Believe me, I know full well precisely how insane this is going to sound...but have you ever run into anyone close to you who had passed away, maybe years before? Have you ever seen a ghost?"

Ice ran through my veins. I stared at her for a long moment, then nodded slowly. "I saw my momma Saturday morning at sunrise."

Liz nodded. "Is that the first time that's ever happened?"

"I...I thought I'd imagined it. Sort of wished her into being there."

"My best friend died the summer we were seventeen," said Liz. "She popped back into my life about ten—twelve years ago. No one knows except Nate. No one else can see her. And in all that time, she's never asked me to pass along a message to anyone else. Until today."

"She has a message for *me*?" I felt my face stretch into what was no doubt an unattractive expression. "That's not...I don't—"

"She said your mother is like her... a guardian spirit. But one of the rules is, these guardian spirits, they're not supposed to contact family. Apparently, your mother bent the rules a bit by contacting you. You probably won't see her again. But she's fine. And whatever message she had for you, well, it was important enough for her to take a pretty big risk."

"That's..."

"Crazy as sunbathing raccoons, I know." Liz nodded slowly, then shook her head, her eyes large and full of import.

"I had no idea Monday was going to be this complicated when I got up this morning."

"I was telling you, the second reason I gave up being a PI is that Colleen—that's her name, my best friend, the guardian spirit—she convinced me that my mission in life was to run this foundation with my husband. The dead can be very convincing."

Chapter Seven

To put it mildly, Liz Talbot had given me a lot to think about on the drive to James Island, which was where Scarlett Hathaway lived. I decided to start with her because, aside from Bridget, Scarlett was the only person who saw Patricia Gaillard most days. Scarlett could give me perspective on Patricia's life—Scarlett had a front row seat, which made her both a suspect and a witness.

She agreed to see me at three. With the top down on Jolene, I headed towards Charleston at two to allow plenty of time to scope out the neighborhood. It was one of those fresh, cloudless spring days that felt wide open, like anything could happen. As we climbed the Cooper River Bridge, "Slow Ride," by Foghat was playing on the sound system.

I kept going back over what the figment of my imagination who looked like my mother had said Saturday morning. Was it possible that wasn't some sort of wishful vision on my part? Was it possible Liz Talbot had retired from being a PI because she'd developed hallucinations? Come down with some flavor of crazy?

Three things, Momma'd said. One was that she was sorry—but what in this world for? She'd been the best mother anyone could ever hope for. Two was "help her," and I was thinking then this could only have meant Bridget. And that made sense, because my instinct had been that Momma would've come down on the same side of this as Gavin—put Cash first. So it was plausible she felt she needed to let me know this was an exception to her rule.

Sweet mother of pearl.

I was clearly losing my mind.

Nothing about any of this was remotely plausible.

Was it?

That third thing was an echo of what Liz had said her friend Colleen told her—that Momma wasn't supposed to be there. She'd broken rules to reach me. It had to be something vitally important to her, but that made no sense at all. Unless it was all about Bridget.

I was so busy brooding about all of this, I nearly missed my turn. Fortunately, there was no one close behind me when I had to execute a fast turn off Maybank Highway down Howle Avenue, a long straight road with no cross streets. Scarlett Hathaway lived in a renovated brick ranch a few houses from the end of the street. I was early, so I turned around in the cul-de-sac, drove back down to Maybank Highway, and took a spin down the next road over. It was good to know what Scarlett's house backed up to.

The next street held a mix of service businesses, apartments, and a few homes. Satisfied I had the lay of the land, I parked in a gym parking lot and waited until five till three. Then I drove back to Scarlett's house and parked in her driveway by a large magnolia tree.

I climbed out of Jolene and made my way down the walkway towards the front porch. A deeper porch than original to the house appeared to have been recently added, with a metal roof. The stained wood shutters looked freshly installed. The yard was tidy but not elaborate, with traditional planting beds around the house featuring azalea bushes dripping with bright pink blooms. Two pots brimming with purple petunias flanked the steps.

Scarlett must've been watching for me. As soon as I stepped onto the porch, the door swung open.

"Ms. Cooper?"

She looked exactly like her driver's license photo—porcelain skin with a dark glossy bob. Her makeup was carefully applied, but her eyes were troubled. In tailored black slacks and a bright blue silk blouse, she appeared ready for a day in the office.

"Please call me Hadley. Thank you for seeing me on such short notice."

"Come in." She laid a hand on my arm and gave me a look that implied she had important things to tell me. "I've made us some iced tea."

I followed her through a small foyer into a living room with cream-colored painted beadboard walls and pale hardwood flooring. Two cream-colored sofas faced each other at right angles to a fireplace. Everything in the room was some shade of solid-colored neutral, accented with natural baskets and wooden bowls. The effect was soothing. Everything was impeccably clean.

A tall contraption with multiple carpeted levels, platforms, ramps, boxes, and hammocks sat by a tall window overlooking the side yard. From the top level, a mottled orange tabby with a torn ear and a white patch under his chin hissed at me. Then he scampered down the tower and ran off towards the back of the house.

"Don't mind Huckleberry," said Scarlett. "He doesn't generally take to strangers."

"What happened to his ear?" I asked.

"A youthful misadventure involving a fishing pole. Please, have a seat." Scarlett poured tea from a cut glass pitcher on the coffee table into matching glasses. "I'm still in shock. I can't believe someone would hurt Patricia. And in her own home—where I worked every day for nearly ten years. It's disturbing on so many levels. But...I am completely focused on manifesting a good outcome for your investigation."

"I appreciate that," I said, accepting the glass with a smile and resisting the urge to raise both my eyebrows. What did that entail, this manifesting? I vaguely recalled hearing the word tossed around. "You worked with her a long time. You were happy?"

Scarlett sank into the sofa across from me. "Very. Oh, Patricia had high standards. Very high. But she was fair. She treated me very well." She dabbed at her eyes with a tissue. "She paid me more than most executive assistants make, and I got to travel with her occasionally, to New York, Paris once...places I'd never been before."

"You were close?"

"As close as you can be with someone like Patricia." Scarlett's voice softened. "She wasn't warm, exactly, but she trusted me and I trusted her."

"Anything in particular she trusted you with that you think I should know?" I tried to sound casual.

Scarlett's eyes narrowed slightly. "I signed an NDA when I first went to work for her. I take that seriously."

"Understood." I nodded slowly. Why would Patricia Gaillard need employees to sign a nondisclosure agreement? "I'm just trying to find out who killed her, so I appreciate anything you could tell me that might be helpful...I mean...you don't think Bridget actually did this...?"

"Oh, good Heavens, *nooo*. I can't believe they arrested her. That poor girl. I honestly don't have any idea who would've done such a terrible thing. But the one thing I'm certain of is that the last person it would be is Bridget."

"That was my take on it too," I said.

"I hope you can help her—no—I mean, I'm certain you can. I'm going to create a vision board."

What the heck was that? I nodded. "Just so I can

check all the boxes, would you tell me where you were between 11:00 p.m. on Thursday, March 23 and 1:00 a.m. on Friday, March 24?"

"I was right here," said Scarlett.

"Were you alone that evening?"

A huffy expression slid over her face. She raised her chin and looked at me down her nose. "As it happens, a friend stayed the night."

"Could I have that friend's contact information, please? It's simply to rule you out as a suspect."

"I shouldn't think that would be necessary. How exactly am I a suspect to begin with?"

"Technically speaking, *everyone* in Patricia's life is a potential suspect. It's easier if I rule out the people I'm sure were not involved first. It's just for the paperwork." I waved dismissively.

"Fine, whatever. His name is Brett Campbell. I can text you his phone number."

I rattled off my number, and she sent the text. "Thank you. Now...what were your normal hours, in your job with Patricia Gaillard?"

"It varied. I was typically there between 9:00 and 5:00 weekdays, sometimes later. Frequently I worked part of the day on Saturdays, if Patricia had an event—there was always something that needed doing—and when I did, she gave me time off during the week. I didn't typically work more than forty hours, sometimes less."

"Is that what happened on the morning of March

24? You came in late because you worked on a Saturday?"

"I'm sorry?" She gave me a look that was a mixture of annoyance and confusion.

"Bridget found Patricia at 9:15 and called 911. I don't recall her mentioning you were there at the time."

"Oh, well, I...I overslept Friday morning. I arrived right after EMS. It must've been around 9:20, 9:25?"

"Well, that explains it then." Was she shook up remembering the trauma of that morning? Patricia being found dead and EMS arriving? Or was there something else? Perhaps she was embarrassed that her overnight company made her late.

"You mentioned Patricia having 'events' on the weekends...what sort of events?"

Scarlett gestured with an open palm. "Charity benefits, concerts, plays, parties...*social* events."

"Did she typically have escorts for this type of thing?"

"Occasionally a friend would accompany her. But no. There hasn't been a man in Patricia's life since Chalmers passed, if that's what you're asking."

"What can you tell me about the people closest to Patricia?"

She gave me a skeptical look. "You don't seriously suspect the family? These are not the sort of people to resort to violence. The Gaillards and the Pinkneys—you *do* know Patricia was a Pinkney? These are well-established Charleston families."

I had no idea what to say to that. If only "better families" didn't commit murder. "I guess Patricia's closest relative was her sister, Corinne. Were they close?"

"I suppose, in their way. They didn't spend a lot of time together. They had different interests. Patricia was heavily involved in charities that benefit children. She loved kids, but couldn't have her own, so she did everything she could for other people's children. Corinne was busy with her own girls."

"I saw Patricia was on the board at Neighbor to Family," I said.

"That's right. They work to keep siblings together in foster care. Patricia was passionate about that. Neighbor to Family and Charleston Studios—that's an after-school music program for kids. Those were the two organizations where she spent most of her time. But she gave money to several other children's charities as well."

"Sounds like Patricia was good people," I said.

"She was. That's why it's so difficult to imagine someone wanting to hurt her. You know, I've been thinking...and I'm just speculating here, mind you..."

I leaned forward, curious. "What's your theory?"

Scarlett lowered her voice to a conspiratorial whisper. "I think it might have been one of the Pinkney spirits."

I blinked. "I'm sorry—what?"

"The Pinkney spirits—ghosts." Scarlett nodded solemnly, her eyes wide. "Patricia's house has been in the Pinkney family for generations. It was built back in the 1800s. That's the house she and Corinne were raised in. Patricia inherited it, and she loved it so that Chalmers agreed they would live there. He spent truckloads of money renovating it exactly like Patricia wanted. Of course that was before my time, but I understand the spirits did not care for all that hullabaloo one bit. Anyway... everyone knows the house is haunted.

Today was my day to reckon with ghosts.

Scarlett chattered on, "There's the Lady in Lavender who supposedly died of a broken heart in 1883, and Colonel Beauregard Calhoun who was courting one of the Pinkney girls. He was killed in a duel over a gambling debt right there in the gardens—where the pool is now. Those are just the two I know by name. I'm certain there are more. You can just tell that house has seen things."

I struggled to keep my expression neutral. "And you think... one of these ghosts killed Patricia?"

"It makes perfect sense." Scarlett tapped her perfectly manicured nails against her glass. "Two weeks ago, Patricia hired a company to remodel the master bath—again. She wanted a bigger tub and one of those showers with all the heads that spray you from every direction? The contractors tore down a wall the week before Patricia was killed, and the very next day, every clock in the house stopped at exactly 3:17 a.m."

"Could have been a power blip, I guess?" Surely there was a rational explanation.

"No." She shook her head. "When I say the clocks *stopped*, I mean they stopped and did not start back. We had to replace several alarm clocks and a coffee maker and call an appliance repairman for the ones in the ovens. Nothing else was impacted as far as we could tell."

Okay, that was strange, I'd give her that.

"Then," Scarlett continued, her voice rising with excitement, "the day before she died, Patricia told me she heard someone in military boots marching up and down the hallway all night. No one else was in the house."

"So you believe Colonel Calhoun was... upset about the renovation?" I asked, trying to keep the skepticism out of my voice.

"Precisely!" Scarlett pointed at me and nodded. "The police are looking at people with pulses when they should be investigating the supernatural angle. I've watched enough of those ghost hunter shows to know that spirits can manipulate physical objects when they're angry enough."

I took a long sip of tea, using the moment to compose myself. "That's certainly... an interesting suggestion." Not to mention completely crackers.

"This is Charleston, after all," Scarlett said. "Ghosts are hardly rare here."

So it would seem. I'd had a close encounter recently myself. *Did not.*

"What's the name of the company doing the renovations?" I asked. Could one of the workers have gotten into an altercation with Patricia?

"Reid Historic Solutions. They specialize in renovating historic homes, so you'd think they'd know how to avoid upsetting the spirits."

"You would think." I nodded. Had Patricia known Scarlett had an overactive imagination? Wait...was it possible there *were* actual ghosts in the house? I wasn't entertaining the idea they'd killed Patricia, mind you. Homicidal ghosts had never been a thing as far as I knew. But based on my recent personal experience, I had to leave room for the possibility that there were actual ghosts in the house. I shook my head to clear it. In all my years as a private investigator, I had never had a case where someone suggested a ghost was to blame for a crime. "Back to Corinne, for just a minute...was there any drama between the sisters? Old hurts, that kind of thing?"

An odd look crossed Scarlett's face. "Nothing that comes to mind."

I waited while she seemed to wrestle with a decision. Then she smiled and said, "Everyone with a sister has a story...some sort of trauma, I imagine."

"That's what I hear." There was something Scarlett wasn't telling me. "Was Patricia close to her nieces, Emerson and Everly?"

"Not especially," said Scarlett. "Corinne has always had her girls on the debutante track. Of course, both Corinne and Patricia were debutantes themselves. But Patricia really didn't put much stock in all of that. I imagine Corinne planned to marry them off by now, but neither girl is married. My understanding is that they're both in DC. Everly's going to law school at Georgetown, and Emerson is some sort of aide to a congressman. Last I heard they were roommates."

"Did Patricia ever discuss her estate with you?" I asked. "Who would benefit in the event of her death?"

"To some degree," said Scarlett. "I know she had generous bequests for the charities she supported. But as far as who inherits the rest, I would guess Corinne, but that's just a guess."

"Did she get along well with her husband's son? Chalmers Gaillard III?"

Scarlett laughed. "Everyone loves C. J. He's such a happy-go-lucky soul. You have to work hard at it to not get along with him."

"But his father—"

"Yeah, he was the exception. I doubt Chalmers Junior would've even recognized him as his son, but Senior did, so Junior didn't really have a choice. There was drama there for decades, but none of it really had to do with Patricia. She stayed above the fray. That was her policy in most instances."

"Would C. J. expect to inherit any of what was his father's estate when Patricia died?"

"I doubt it. Junior's will—he absolutely hated being called Junior, but how else do you keep them all straight?—left everything to Patricia with no strings. She was free to do whatever she liked with the whole enchilada. But Senior took care of C. J., set him up a trust fund. The two of them are a lot alike. Both of them live to play golf."

"Interesting...Senior must be getting pretty...senior...by now."

"He's an inspiration. He's pushing eighty-five, living in one of those active adult communities in Summerville, playing golf every day, drinking bourbon, and chasing women."

"Good for him." I chuckled. "Switching channels a bit...did Patricia spend a lot of time in Nashville? I understand she had a college friend who lives there?"

"Right...Uma Jennings. Patricia went to see her a couple of times a year. Uma came to Charleston occasionally. They chatted on the phone frequently."

"Any drama in that relationship?" I asked.

"No, none at all."

Interesting. Scarlett had a direct answer to this question when we were talking about Uma, but not Corinne.

"Do you know if Bridget ever approached Patricia about her husband Arlo?"

"I'm sorry?" Scarlett squinted at me.

"My understanding is that Uma's husband is a record executive. Did Bridget try to get Patricia to speak to him on behalf of her ex-husband, Arlo Donovan? Apparently, he's a musician."

"That's the first I've heard of any of this, so I'd have to say no. Bridget didn't talk much about her personal life, except her kids. She did talk about them. But I could not have told you her ex-husband's name on a bet. I don't think she ever mentioned him at all."

"Is there anyone you can think of Patricia had a recent disagreement with?"

"No." Scarlett's voice was firm.

"Okay, well...I'd like to create a timeline of her movements over the last couple of weeks of her life. Do you have access to her calendar?" I asked.

Scarlett raised an eyebrow. "Naturally, but the police took her computer. Everything is on that."

"Did she by chance use a cloud-based calendar?"

"Ahhh," said Scarlett. "She did. Everything is on the iCloud."

"Would you happen to have the login credentials?"

"Nearly everything is shared. I log in to her account with my own password."

"Could we take a look at the last few weeks? See if there are any clues?"

"I don't feel right about that," said Scarlett. "It feels like an invasion of her privacy. And then there's my NDA..."

"Do you think Patricia would want you to do whatever was necessary to help find whoever killed her?" I asked.

"Well, I suppose so..."

I raised my eyebrow and lifted a shoulder, flashing her an expression that said, *well let's get on with it.*

"I'd like to consult with Kootálá."

"Is that your attorney?" I didn't recognize the name.

"Oh no." She shook her head. "He's my spirit guide. He's an ancient Hopi warrior."

I nodded slowly and scrambled for a response. "Okay then."

"Oh, I can't do that with *you* here. No. I need absolute quiet. I meditate first, to open myself up to communicating with Kootálá."

This nuttery might work in my favor. "How about if you go into your bedroom and I promise to be absolutely still? I will sit here quietly and not move a single muscle."

She made a face and shook her head. "I just don't see him being receptive to that."

"I think you're selling yourself short." Lord forgive me for indulging this poor soul's crazy. "If you are sincerely seeking his guidance, I bet he will respond."

"You really think so?"

"I do." I gave her my sincerest look. "Look, we have nothing to lose. Why don't you just try to reach him?" This was wrong on so many levels. I opened my mouth to say *never mind, and maybe we should talk about this whole spirit guide thing—*

"You know, I think you're right." She stood and walked to the bookcase to the left of the fireplace and took something from one of the wooden bowls. "I'll use the amethyst." She held up a purple rock to show me.

"Great idea." My head just kept on bobbing up and down. I had no idea—nor did I want one—how rocks entered into this nonsense.

Scarlett headed towards the hallway. "Back in a bit. Wish me luck."

I waited a ten count after I heard the door close behind her, then tiptoed over to the desk situated in front of a large double window between the living room and dining room. Easing into the chair, I picked up a small spiral notebook. I leafed through the pages and picked one at random. This was Scarlett's personal calendar. I snapped photos of January through April and then set it back precisely where I'd found it.

The writing desk had only three drawers, one left, one right, and one center. The top right drawer held office supplies and a stack of business cards from a plumber, an HVAC repairman, a pool service, and the like. In the organizer tray in the center drawer, I found what I needed: an index card with all of Scarlett's—and a few of Patricia's—passwords. I snapped a photo, then flipped the card over to find the keys to Patricia's kingdom: the gate code, the alarm code, the login, the all-clear and panic words, and one other six-digit code that wasn't labeled. Thank you, Scarlett. I'd no sooner snapped the photo and eased the drawer closed than I heard a door open down the hall. I sprang up and darted to the center of the room.

"It's no use—" Scarlett stopped at the end of the hall and eyed me accusingly. "I guess I know why I can't focus. You were supposed to be still and quiet."

"I know." I gave her a sheepish look. "I'm so sorry. I needed the powder room."

"Second door on the left." She stepped aside and waved an arm at the hall.

I scooted into the bathroom. After a gander at the medicine cabinet yielded nothing of interest, I flushed the toilet and ran the water for a couple of minutes. When I returned to the living room, Scarlett waited by the front door.

"I'm afraid there's nothing else I can tell you today," she said.

"You've been very helpful—thank you."

"The more I think about it, the more I just don't think I can let you see Patricia's personal calendar. When I reach Kootálá, I'll see what he says, but..."

"I understand. Here's my card. If you think of anything else that might be helpful, please give me a call."

"I hope you'll consider what I said about the spirits. And please know that I will continue to manifest a positive outcome." She laid her hand on my arm and leaned in with her sincere expression. "Would you like a crystal? Here, let me get you one. I wonder which would be best?" She consulted the ceiling.

"Oh, my goodness, look at the time." I glanced at my watch. Three-forty-five. I shook my head. "Thank you so much. I'm late for my next appointment. Bye now." *You poor confused woman.*

A feeling of relief washed over me as the door closed behind me. I hoped not to have to come back. With any luck, I had everything I needed from Scarlett. It was hard for me to regard her as anything other than an unreliable witness at best.

Or was it possible she was pretending to be crazy because she was guilty? Was this an elaborate ruse to deflect suspicion?

As I pulled out of Scarlett's driveway, "Hold on Loosely," by 38 Special played through the sound system. I was looking forward to happy hour and my prickly pear margarita. My anxiety level was rising, and not because of Scarlett's nonsense. I hadn't heard from Cash all day, which sometimes happened when he had a big case, of course it did. That's all it was. I was sure of it.

That's what I was telling myself, anyway.

Chapter Eight

The Sullivan's Island Supper Club was an eclectic, multigenerational circle of women bound together by food, laughter, and a knack for finding themselves in the middle of one dust-up or another. On the last Saturday of the month, we gathered around the table to share a meal and, inevitably, a few secrets. I'd been invited to join a couple of years ago, back when I was still the new girl on the island, and what started as a standing dinner date quickly grew into the kind of friendship I'd always hoped to find: steady, forgiving, and loyal. These women had become my confidantes, my partners in mischief, and my family by choice.

The group held an informal, come-if-you-can happy hour weekdays at five p.m. Most days it was a few of the ladies plus Fish, the official bartender. For a long time after our friend Eugenia, God rest her soul, first started the tradition, happy hour was held on the beach under a large sunshade. I think Eugenia liked the feel of the sand between her toes.

Eugenia left her beachfront house—which was a few houses down from my house—to Fish. Soon after Tallulah and Fish married, they'd put Tallulah's house on the market and consolidated their households into the house that had been Eugenia's.

Recently, Fish and Tallulah had moved happy hour to their pool deck, which was only a few steps off the beach. They'd added a few lounge chairs on the ocean side of the pool deck and installed a pergola for shade to create a permanent happy hour spot. This was surely an easier arrangement. No cabana to set up every day, no cooler to tote to the beach—just serve from the pool house bar. Fish also reasoned it was easier this way to keep us warm, with patio heaters during winter months. And, as Camille liked to remind us, we weren't flouting the law against alcohol on the beach this way. Eugenia'd had a bit of a rebel spirit and may've enjoyed getting away with something.

I came through the gate into the backyard, called out a hello to Fish as I passed the pool house, and stepped under the pergola. "Hey, happy Monday."

Sarabeth, Tallulah, Birdie, and Camille looked up from their loungers and responded with a chorus of hellos. One of the most remarkable things about our group was that our age ranges crossed several generations. Fish, Tallulah, Birdie, and Camille were in their sixties. Sarabeth was somewhere in her fifties, at least that's what she told us. To look at her, with her smooth skin, easy grace, trim figure, and energy level, you would've never guessed it. Libba and Norah, who were elsewhere that Monday, were in their forties like me. And Quinn, also absent, was the baby of the group in her mid-thirties. The thing was, we all felt like we were Quinn's age inside.

"Your usual, Mademoiselle." Fish grinned as he approached with a tray and handed me a clear insulated tumbler with a familiar pink drink.

"You are a prince among men, Hamilton Alexander Hughes Fisher Ravenel Aiken. I need this today more than usual."

"Long hard day of skulking about?" asked Tallulah.

"It's been a long hard year since sunup Saturday," I told her. "Sarabeth threw me to the wolves."

"I did no such thing." Sarabeth was all innocent indignation.

"Did you, or did you not, give my name to Carolyn Talbot and tell her she should call me because she needed a PI?"

"Well, okay, I did that. But she did need a PI, and you are very good at your job. I don't understand how that constitutes throwing you to the wolves."

"Did you somehow not know that was Cash's case?" I asked.

Sarabeth blanched and raised a hand to her chest. "Oh, Hadley...I *didn't* know that. I am so, so sorry. Oh, my stars! Please forgive me."

I waved a hand at her. "It's fine. Well, I think it will be. Eventually. Hopefully."

"I will just never forgive myself if this causes problems for y'all," said Sarabeth. "It's just...poor Bridget needed someone in her corner. And I don't know any other private investigators. Surely you can refer her to someone else?"

"It's not that simple," I said. "I was kidding, Sarabeth. Please don't worry about it." I was worried enough for both of us. Anyway, I was committed to the cause now, and there was no point in Sarabeth beating herself up.

"Tallulah, do we know any other private investigators?" Birdie squinted.

"If we do, I've forgotten," said Tallulah.

"What about the folks that live on Stella Maris? What's the name of that agency?" Fish looked up like he was consulting the clouds. "It'll come to me."

"Talbot & Andrews," I said.

"That's it," said Fish.

"They transitioned into another line of work about seven years ago," I said.

"There has to be someone else who can handle this," said Camille. "Good men are too hard to find. You don't want to screw things up with Cash."

"Why didn't you tell me you'd given her my name?" I asked Sarabeth.

"I meant to, and then we had a tumultuous uproar at home and I forgot all about it. I am telling y'all...the Lord has such confidence in me."

"Everything all right?" asked Birdie.

"Yeah, everything's fine," said Sarabeth. "Tucker and Deacon were butting heads. I love my son, don't get me wrong, but Deacon is just so danged hardheaded. You know, I should call up one of those places where they study the whole 'Nature versus nurture' quandary. I have the answer to that, and his name is Deacon Ford Dawson. Tucker and I raised that boy together from the time he was six years old. The sperm donor had nothing to do with it. But Deacon is exactly like Bobby Earl Dawson, no two ways about it."

"I didn't know you'd used a sperm donor," said Camille.

"Oh, we didn't, honey. That's just what I call Bobby Earl—my first husband—because his involvement with child raising ended at conception."

"He should be shot." Camille had suffered several bad experiences with men, one fairly recently. "Let me know if you need my help with that."

"Oh, no," said Sarabeth. "That was for the best. Deacon is so difficult as it is. Just think if he'd had Bobby Earl's example to study on top of all those unfortunate genes."

"If you don't mind my asking," said Birdie, "what became of the girls' mother? Were they married?"

When Deacon, Sarabeth's only son, had moved in with her and Tucker, and not for the first time, he'd brought with him his two teenage daughters, Lennox and Calliope—along with various pets.

"Deacon was married to their mother for about

fifteen minutes," said Sarabeth. "I'm joking. They got married right before Lennox's first birthday. A couple of months before Calliope was born. Their mamma's not much more involved in child raising than the sperm donor was with Deacon. She turns up occasionally to take the girls to do something fun."

"That's too bad," said Tallulah. "At a certain point, wives are supposed to take over the task of civilizing men from their mothers."

"Exactly," said Sarabeth. "What I need is a new daughter-in-law. One who loves teenagers. I'm thinking about running a notice in the church bulletin that I'm taking applications."

"Does Deacon go to church?" asked Camille.

"Not often," said Sarabeth.

"Well, he'll never know then, will he?" said Birdie.

"That was my thought exactly," said Sarabeth.

Tallulah turned to me wearing a concerned look.

"Hadley, are you absolutely positive there's no one else who can handle this case? Because it seems to me there's no way you can possibly win this."

"What do you mean?" I asked.

"Well, if you try to help this young mother, and you can't, you'll always wonder if someone else—perhaps without the distraction of a personal involvement with the SLED agent in charge—might've been able to accomplish what you couldn't.

"On the other hand," continued Tallulah, "if you do find proof that someone else did this thing—that your client is innocent—you've proven Cash arrested the wrong person. Men don't like to be proven wrong, in my experience. That might be something Cash has a hard time getting past."

"Now don't sell Cash short," said Fish. "I don't think his ego is so tender that he couldn't bear being wrong."

"Fish, could I have another drink, please?" I asked.

"Of course. Anyone else ready for another?"

"Yes, please," said Sarabeth. "It's a good thing I walked down the beach this afternoon. I'd have to leave my car here if I'd driven. Goodness gracious what a mess I've made."

"It's not your mess," I said. "I agreed to take the case after I promised Cash I wouldn't take any more of his cases. This is on me."

For a few minutes, we all sat and watched the waves chase each other in. A flock of seagulls flew by in V-formation, squawking at each other about something.

"Some days I'd like to migrate," said Sarabeth.

"*What*?" I flashed her a skeptical look. "I thought this was your dream, living on Sullivan's Island."

"It is." She sighed. "But the reality is somewhat more stressful than my dreams. Some days I think a tiny house someplace less expensive would be better for Tucker's sanity." Sarabeth and Tucker had dealt with a long list of expensive home repairs for items the inspector missed. Their financial security had taken a hit.

"I'm just being silly," she said. "Hey...so what've you got planned for tomorrow? Can I tag along? No—

wait. Not tomorrow. I need to take Calliope shopping after school for a few things. How about Wednesday?"

Oh. I drew a deep breath. I adored Sarabeth. But I'd never had anyone along while I worked before—well, okay, except North once or twice. But that was different. Somehow... "Sure." I forced enthusiasm into my voice. "I'll need to leave around six a.m. I want to get an early start."

"I can do that. I'll be at your house at five thirty. I'll bring breakfast."

"You don't have to do that. You know I'm a high maintenance eater."

"Nonsense. You make your own coffee. I don't have any of that odd stuff you put in yours. But I'll bring us some breakfast. So...what will we be doing?"

"Surveillance," I said.

"Oh, yay! I'm so excited," said Sarabeth. "This is exactly the kind of thing I need for my book."

"Yay." I hoped I wasn't going to regret this.

"Are you writing a book about a private investigator?" asked Tallulah.

"Not exactly. My main character is an author, but she keeps getting tangled up in these murders and has to investigate."

"Sounds like 'Murder She Wrote,'" said Birdie.

"Oh no, my character is *muuuch*...well, come to think of it, she's actually not all that much younger than Jessica Fletcher. But the character is completely different. Trust me."

"Does she happen to find a dead body in her front

yard?" I asked. *Like you did?* Sarabeth had had a traumatic experience a while back, but that's a whole nother story.

"Maybe." She lifted her chin and adjusted her sunglasses.

"Now there's the answer, right there," said Tallulah. "Get Sarabeth a private investigator's license, and she can take the cases that involve Cash."

If only that were a quick fix.

"Say," said Tallulah, "did y'all hear any more about that baker who was killed over in West Ashley?" She shook her head. "Broad daylight, practically. Stanley something—he made the most divine sourdough. Such a shame."

"That's Cash's case too," I said.

"What is this world coming to?" Tallulah just kept shaking her head.

Cash did call me, later on that night, to check in and to tell me that he'd rebooked our Maison reservation for Thursday evening at 6:00.

"They didn't have a table on a Friday or Saturday for a few weeks," he said. "I hope Thursday's okay."

"It's fine. I'm looking forward to it," I said. "How was your day?"

This was a safe question for me to ask him. His work on Bridget's case was all over until it was heard in court.

"Fine. Busy, so it went fast...I have a new case. Identity theft."

"Identity theft. Okay."

"Yeah, it's a nice change of pace. Nonviolent. So far, anyway."

"Good, good."

He hesitated, I knew, because he couldn't let the conversation veer into the details of my day. This effort to keep things superficial was awkward and felt wrong.

"I hope your day went well," he said—a statement, not a question.

"It did, thanks. Well...I guess I'd better go. Time to tuck the kitties in."

"Still no word from their owners, huh?"

"Not a peep."

"You'll hear from them soon. Well...good night."

"Good night." Tears welled up in my eyes. I could feel the distance between us growing. Still, in the deepest part of me, I knew that if I didn't help Bridget, she would go to prison—or worse, death row. Her children would be left to her ex-husband's parents, and someday, if the truth finally surfaced, Cash would have to carry the guilt of helping condemn an innocent mother.

There was no decision to make. The stakes were too high, the price too unbearable.

Chapter Nine

Tuesday, April 4, 2023

Patricia Gaillard's house was a charming Queen Anne Victorian on Logan Street, between Broad and Tradd. Logan Street was a narrow, one-way lane, and given the fact that on any given day *someone* would be renovating their historic home, requiring large trucks and possibly dumpsters in the street, I parked on Broad Street, a block away from the intersection with Logan, just past the Cathedral of Saint John the Baptist. I swiped my handy pre-paid parking card and headed towards Logan just after 9:00 a.m. that Tuesday morning.

While I had all the necessary codes—and a handy lock pick set—I needed more information before using them to let myself into Patricia's house, like which of her neighbors had cameras that captured people coming and going from the Gaillard home. This information would serve two purposes: it would inform how I approached getting inside, and with any luck it might give me an alternate suspect.

For today's purposes, I wasn't in disguise. I needed to play the PI card and look like my photo ID. To increase the odds of getting folks to answer the door, I dressed nice, in a floral print midi-length skirt and silk shell. I was aiming for a realtor-like look. It wasn't unheard of for realtors to cold call homeowners with fabulous offers in hand. Most people would want to at least hear the offer, even if they hadn't planned on selling. And if they looked at the camera and saw me and assumed I was a realtor, well, mission accomplished.

First, I walked Patricia's block. Neighborhoods always look different on foot than by car. You notice things on foot that you don't when you drive through, like exactly how buckled and uneven the sidewalk is, how it's a patchwork of slabs of slate, brick, and sections of concrete. You need to watch where you're going, or you'll trip for sure. Especially in the sandals I was wearing with my realtor outfit.

I turned around at Tradd Street, where Logan dead-ends, and walked back up to Patricia's neighbor to the right as you're facing the house. According to the property records, a widow named Florence Nelson lived in the yellow brick house with brown shutters. I smiled wide for the camera and rang the bell. She must've thought about it for a while, because I'd almost given up when a petite woman of Asian descent wearing a yellow warm-up suit answered the door.

"Hello, can I help you?" she asked.

"Mrs. Nelson?"

"Yes. And you are?" She lifted her chin and raised her eyebrows expectantly.

I opened my leather ID wallet, showing her my PI license and my driver's license. "My name is Hadley Cooper. I'm here about your neighbor, Patricia Gaillard." I glanced at the house next door.

"Oh?" Mrs. Nelson gave me a quizzical look. "I thought they arrested the maid."

"Yes, ma'am. They did. But it turns out she's innocent. I've been hired to investigate."

"Is that right?" she asked. "Well...I can't say I'm surprised. I've said from the beginning it was very likely the illegitimate son. Did you know Chalmers Gaillard had an illegitimate son?"

"Yes, ma'am. Is there a reason you suspect him?"

She made a scoffing noise. "The money, of course. Isn't it always about the money?"

"Very often it is, I'm afraid. Do you know if he stood to benefit from Mrs. Gaillard's death?"

"Well, I should certainly hope so," she said. "Even if he was illegitimate, he was a Gaillard."

"Did you notice anything unusual the night Mrs. Gaillard was killed?"

"Not a thing. I go to bed at ten o'clock sharp. My bedroom is on the opposite side of the house."

"Did you know Mrs. Gaillard well?" I asked.

"Not particularly." She sniffed and lifted her chin. "Mr. Nelson and I bought this house fifteen years ago. He became sick soon after. He passed away three years later. I've kept to myself since then. Patricia came by a few times. She invited me to this or that. By the time I was ready to face the world again, she'd given up. I think she was a kind lady. I was sorry to hear what happened. And it scares me, to be truthful. Ordinarily, I would invite you inside and offer you refreshments. You don't look like a homicidal maniac. Many of them don't." Her eyes opened wide in an expression that carried fear.

"It's better to be safe," I said. "I see that you have a doorbell camera. Does your security system have other outdoor cameras as well?"

"One for each side of the house." She nodded. "The police have already been by. They downloaded all the videos."

Of course I'd known this would be the case. But the thing about downloading was that it didn't automatically delete the original video. "How long does your system keep recordings?"

"They're automatically deleted after thirty days unless I save them. But...there's a stray cat in the neighborhood that keeps activating the backyard camera. It goes off a hundred times a day if it goes off once. It's a nuisance. My storage gets full, and I have to delete some of the videos or buy more storage. So, I stay on top of keeping those cleaned up. I typically delete everything after a week. After the police downloaded what they needed, I didn't see a reason to keep it."

"I see. That makes sense. Well, thank you for your time."

"Remember what I said about the illegitimate son. It's always about the money."

"Yes, ma'am. Thank you."

I had better luck at the cream-colored Charleston single house directly across the street from the Gaillard home. Mr. Oscar Gregory, who was pushing ninety if I had my guess, blushed and looked sheepish in his bowtie and suspenders. "Yes, ma'am, ah...I do have a security system, with several outdoor cameras, none inside the house, mind you. But I don't much like dealing with the police, to tell you the truth. It's possible I wasn't able to get to the door when they came by."

Why on earth would this sweet old man be shy of the police? "Understandable." I nodded, in an effort to be supportive. "Do you still have the videos from March 23 and 24?"

"I guess I do," he said. "I don't know how long they stay in the system. You're welcome to check." He opened the door and stepped back to invite me in.

I hesitated a moment, Florence Nelson's words echoing in my ears. Oscar Gregory didn't look anything like a homicidal maniac. Also, he was a couple of inches shorter than me and likely weighed less. I had pepper spray in my bag if I needed it.

"The computer is in my office. It's right through here." He looked at me through guileless eyes.

I smiled and followed him. He was probably a lonely soul. "Thank you. I appreciate your help."

He led me down a hallway, past the living room, and into an office that had so many stacks of magazines, file folders, and books that it crossed my mind he might be a borderline hoarder.

"You can sit in my chair." He gestured to the desk, moved a stack of something from one of the visitors' chairs, and sat down. "My computer is already on."

He was awfully trusting. I slid into his chair and opened the app for his security system. After scanning the files, I said, "It looks like you have everything for this month and last month. It's set to delete last month's files at the end of this month."

"Well, good then. You have what you need. Do you think whoever killed Patricia is on my video?"

"It's possible." I popped a thumb drive into one of the ports. "I'll scan the videos later. That will take a while. I don't want to take up your entire morning. Did you know Patricia Gaillard well?"

"Please. Take up my morning. You can have my afternoon too if you need it. Yes, I'd say I knew Patricia well. I've lived across the street since before she was born. She was a nice lady. She's checked on me at least once a week since Margaret—my wife—passed away. That's been more than three years."

"Someone suggested Mr. Gaillard's son might be responsible for Patricia's death."

"C. J.? Oh, that's just ridiculous." He waved dismissively. "First of all, he's just not the type to resort to violence. But secondly, what possible motive would he have? It wouldn't be money. I'm not saying Patricia didn't leave him anything. Maybe she did. Who knows? But it certainly wouldn't be something he was counting on. Besides, his grandfather made sure he was taken care of. As far as I know, C. J. and Patricia never had much interaction. No, if you're looking for someone close to her, someone who maybe had an ax to grind or what have you, it wouldn't be C. J."

"You don't think maybe he was angry because Patricia inherited all of his father's money and he didn't get any?" I asked.

"The way I hear it, C. J. got as much from Senior as Junior did. I suspect that's partly why Junior never did warm up to C. J. He became a pawn in a war between Junior and Senior."

"That's sad," I said.

"It really is. Some people don't appreciate the family they have."

"Do you have a big family?" I asked.

"My, yes," he said. "I'm a great-grandfather. Margaret and I had three children, and they all have children. I have eleven grandchildren. Most of them are married now, and my oldest granddaughter just had a baby."

"How exciting. Have you seen the baby yet?"

"Oh, no. My granddaughter lives in Seattle with her husband. All of our family is spread out. None of them live around here anymore. My daughter keeps trying to get me to move to be close to her. She lives in Atlanta. But all of my memories are here in this house. Margaret and I lived here together for sixty-five years. How can I leave?"

My heart hurt for him. "Wouldn't you take your memories with you if you moved?"

"I suppose so," he said. "But...and you'll think I'm a crazy old man when I tell you this, but I can live with that. You see, Margaret is still here."

"I'm sure it must seem that way."

"Her spirit never left this house after her body passed away."

Again with the ghosts.

"I've heard the Gaillard house is haunted," I said. "Apparently it's a common thing here."

"Oh, it is indeed. But I wouldn't say Margaret haunts me. She just keeps me company. A lot like she did before she passed. To tell you the truth, not much has changed. The grocery bill has gone down. She did tell me there were several ghosts in the Pinkney house. That's what we call it. There were Pinkneys living there when we moved in."

I pulled out the thumb drive. "I have what I need. Thank you so much." I was all done with talk of ghosts.

"My pleasure," he said. "What's that?" He looked towards the second chair in front of the desk, the one occupied by a cardboard box filled with who knew what. "Very well then..." He turned to me. "Margaret wanted you to know that Patricia's spirit was lingering as well. Apparently, there's one more ghost across the street than there used to be."

Thanks to my cursory review of the neighborhood, I knew the family who lived to the left of Patricia Gaillard was a young couple with school-age children. If one of the parents were at home that morning, they were unswayed by my realtor outfit. No one came to the door. But across the street, the hospitality door stood open on the cheery yellow Charleston single house, a sign the residents were receiving. As I crossed the street, I admired the double piazzas and the window boxes overflowing with purple and red impatiens and several varieties of greenery.

I stepped through the doorway and climbed a short flight of steps to the lower piazza. When I rang the bell, a dog went to barking inside the house. Moments later, the door swung open. If I'd had to guess, I'd've said the polished lady in the expensive-looking navy pantsuit standing in the doorway was a member of Tallulah's generation—somewhere in her sixties. There was something vaguely familiar about her.

"Petunia, that's enough now." She gave the English bulldog beside her a quelling look, then turned back to me, a hint of recognition in her eyes. "Hello." Her honeyed drawl was unmistakably native Charlestonian.

I showed her my ID. "Hey there, I'm Hadley Cooper—"

"Of course. You're Swinton Legare's daughter. Please come in." She stepped back and opened the door wide.

"I'm so sorry—have we met?" I stepped into the foyer, then followed her into the elegant but comfortable living room to the right.

"Actually, I don't believe we've been formally introduced. I'm Josephine Huger, but I suppose you must know who you called to see. I attended your brother's birthday party—my goodness, that's been nearly two years ago now, hasn't it? His mother, Judith, and I are old friends. I confess I am quite curious what's brought you to my front door today."

"Well, it's lovely to finally meet you. I thought you looked familiar."

"Please have a seat. I'll get us some iced tea. Petunia, sit."

"Please don't go to any trouble—"

She was already gone. "Nonsense. We need to stay hydrated," she called from somewhere towards the back of the house.

Petunia sashayed over to a tasseled cushion by the fireplace, situated herself, stared at me, and panted. I perched on one of the tropical-print side chairs across from the flax-colored sofa.

Moments later, Josephine reappeared and set a glass of iced tea on a coaster atop a side table next to my chair. Then she took a seat on the sofa. "So you're a private investigator. I imagine that's a fascinating career."

"Some days it is."

"Tell me. What brings you by?"

"I'm here about your neighbor across the street, Patricia Gaillard."

"Of course. But haven't the police arrested someone?"

"They have. I've been hired to investigate further."

"I see. How can I help?"

"Did you know Mrs. Gaillard well?"

"I suppose so. We weren't close friends, but we were good neighbors, if you know what I mean. We would pick up packages from the porch if needed or check on things for each other when we were out of town...that sort of thing."

"Do you have a security system that might've recorded someone coming or going at her house?"

"The police came by and asked about that. As a matter of fact, it was Special Agent Reynolds with the South Carolina Law Enforcement Division." A mischievous smile played at the corners of her mouth. "I believe you know him quite well, don't you?"

"Yes, ma'am, I do." I felt myself blush. How much did this stranger know about me?

"I imagine that's a stressful situation, both of you working on this case. In any event, Arthur—my husband—he downloaded the video from the security system and gave it to Special Agent Reynolds. But Arthur looked at it himself later on, and he said there was nothing of any help. The angle of our cameras is wrong. I'm afraid he deleted it. He typically deletes things older than a week or so. Something about the storage."

Hopefully I had something helpful on the footage Oscar Gregory had given me. "I understand a lot of folks do that. Did you notice anything out of the ordinary during the week or so before Mrs. Gaillard's death?"

"Hmmm...well, I'm not saying this has anything to do with Patricia's death, mind you, but if you ask me strictly about unusual things, I'd have to tell you that Patricia's sister Corinne was here that very afternoon and they must have argued about something because Corinne was agitated when she left. I was out walking Petunia. We were just coming back down the street, and Corinne came storming down the front steps. Patricia followed her out to her car. I couldn't make out what they were saying, even though their voices were raised. But I will say this: they were clearly having a disagreement about something. And that is unusual. I've never known them to argue in the street before. Their mother raised them better than that."

Interesting. Scarlett had known more than she'd told me about the relationship between the sisters. "Do you know Corinne?"

"Not well. We're acquainted, is all. The only other thing out of the ordinary is that several times recently, one of our neighbors who drives a brown Subaru Forester has parked on our end of the street. Parking is often an issue for us. Of course we pay for residential permits, as does everyone else on the street. But when neighbors have guests, well there just aren't enough spaces on the street for everyone. Arthur had to park several blocks away. Now, I do recall specifically that happened the night Patricia was killed. But it also happened one other evening that same week, and two or three other times recently as well."

"So a guest parked on the other end of the street, and the person who drives the Subaru was displaced and he parked where your husband normally does?"

"That's right."

The question was, who took the Subaru's spot?

Chapter Ten

As usual, I let Dana choose the restaurant where we'd meet for lunch. And as usual, she chose a barbecue joint. She was already in line at Lewis Barbecue on Nassau Street when I arrived.

"You're gonna love this," she said.

"Oh, I bet." Dana knew full well I ate plants, and only plants, typically anyway. I did make the occasional exception for fish, or some dish with cheese or eggs. But that was rare. I'd started eating this way when Momma was first diagnosed with ovarian cancer and read a book about how eating plant-based can help a variety of health problems, including cancer. We figured it couldn't hurt. I couldn't say whether it made a difference for her, extended her life at all. But I'd been eating this way for so long it was simply my preference, and you couldn't argue with my annual blood test results. I was freakishly healthy.

"I'm serious," said Dana. "You like beans, don't you?"

"I love beans."

"Their Cowboy Beans are vegan."

"There is something vegan in this shrine to all things meaty?"

"Yes, indeed, there is. But don't think for a second that's what I'm having. I've been thinking about a pile of brisket all morning. Mmm-*mmm*."

"I know this will shock you, but I harbor no illusions about converting you to a plant-based diet. It's not like my mission in life or something to get people to eat this way. It's just my preference. I'm not on a soapbox here."

"Yeah, whatever. And you oughta try that corn pudding, even if it does have a little bit of cheese and maybe an egg or two. It's not going to kill you. And the collard greens? Mmm-mmm—outta this world. They say they're vegetarian, so they're definitely not seasoned with pork. I can't think of anything else you'd add to collard greens that would make them vegetarian, but not vegan, can you?"

"I cannot. The beans and the collards sound good. Nice pick, Smalls."

"Thank you. Get yourself some of that corn pudding too now, you hear me? 'Cause if you don't, you're gonna be wantin' some of mine, and that ain't happening."

We chattered about food and whatnot while we waited to place our orders. Dana ordered a brisket sandwich along with her corn pudding, and I got a pint of the Cowboy Pinto Beans and a side of collard greens. We settled into a table by a floor-to-ceiling window and dug into our lunch. The beans and the collards were both excellent, and I have to say, I was tempted by Dana's corn pudding, but I would never tell her that.

A few bites in I asked, "Have you seen Bridget yet?"

"Of course I saw her." She pulled back and stretched out her lips in an expression that inquired what was wrong with me. "I saw her Sunday afternoon. That was the quickest I could get in."

"How's she doing?"

"Oh, she's doing fine now. Your friends at that fancy foundation took care of her half-a-million-dollar bond. She'll be going home in a few hours, soon as the paperwork is processed."

"Oh, thank goodness. That's such good news. Will she have to wear an ankle monitor?"

"Yeah, but that's still way better than staying at that jail. She can look for a job, take her kids to daycare, and whatnot. She has a seven p.m. curfew, which is workable. You found anything yet that'll help *keep* her outta jail?"

"Nothing solid, but I have a few leads."

"You'd best get them solidified quick like. Her ex-in-laws have gotten themselves an attorney and asked for an emergency hearing about the kids."

"But with Bridget free and able to care for them,

surely the Donovans can't take them from her, can they? Grandparents have no direct legal rights, do they?"

"Family court is different. If the Donovans can convince a judge the kids are better off with them? That Bridget is even potentially a violent person? Maybe. Maybe not. As long as there's a possibility Bridget is going to prison, I wouldn't bet against it. Especially if Mamma Donovan can get her son back here from Nashville. Until Bridget is exonerated, the children's future is in jeopardy."

"I'm on it." I was certain Bridget was innocent. And I was sure as sunshine going to prove it.

Chapter Eleven

I didn't want to leave Big Kitty and Tiger Kitty alone so much, so I decided to work from my home office that afternoon. It had been four days. The kitties' family must be worried sick. I'd asked North to put up some fliers I'd made with their picture—and getting that picture had been a challenge, let me tell you. Big Kitty and Tiger Kitty made it clear they did not care to share their personal space for the length of time it took to snap a picture. Treats had been required.

The staircase in my house is a work of art—and I can take no credit for this. The house was built for me, but without my input, which is a whole nother story. The stairs look like someone carved them out of a single block of some sort of exotic wood. The left side of the steps curves upward, forming a wall that flattens into the landing above. The kitties followed me as I climbed the stairs and headed into my bedroom, which is on the far right corner of the second floor. I changed into my favorite soft grey comfy clothes—the ones that could easily be mistaken for pajamas—and my slippers, and padded towards my office.

I'd only taken two steps when Tiger Kitty pounced on my right bunny slipper. Then Big Kitty swatted my left bunny slipper with his paw.

"Cut it out, you guys." I picked up Tiger Kitty—she hissed at me—and moved her off my foot. She immediately re-pounced. After playing this game a few more times, I slipped off my bunny slippers and put them away in my closet, replacing them with fluffy socks the cats had no interest in, thank goodness.

My home office was on the opposite side of the second floor and had floor-to-ceiling windows overlooking the ocean on two sides. Every time I worked from home I questioned the decision to acquire office space. On the one hand, at home I had a fabulous view of the Atlantic to the front and all the way up the beach to Breach Inlet to the left. On the other hand, these beautiful views could be a distraction. And then there was the matter of meeting with clients.

My first order of business was viewing the video I'd gotten from Oscar Gregory, the mere presence of which was already twisting my stomach into knots. Technically speaking, I was potentially in possession of evidence in a homicide investigation. And not just any homicide investigation, but one of Cash's. If I actually found anything remotely relevant, the first thing I'd have to do is hand it over to him. But then wouldn't there be a chain of custody issue?

Yes—I believed there would. In fact, now that I stopped to think about it, I was reasonably certain that if there were exonerating evidence on the video, it would be inadmissible. Oh, good grief. I had royally screwed up. I should've called Cash and had him come download Oscar's videos while I kept him company and soothed his nerves. I should've thought about that earlier, but I didn't, so here we were. Where were the Tums? I grabbed my backpack and dug around until I found a bottle and chewed three.

I took a deep, cleansing breath, then settled in at my desk, which was situated catty-cornered in the glass corner on the front left side of the room, and watched the waves roll in and slide out for just a moment before inserting the thumb drive into one of the ports on my computer and loading the video. Big Kitty curled up under my desk at my feet, but Tiger Kitty insisted on sitting on my lap. I was skeptical of this arrangement at first, but after a few minutes, I caught myself stroking her neck with the front of the fingers on my left hand while using the mouse with my right. It soothed me as much as it did her. Soon we were both purring. Could cats lower your blood pressure?

I had taken all the video clips from March and the first few days of April—all the history Oscar had—but started with the night Patricia was killed. The videos were a series of motion-activated clips. I scanned the evening of March 23 and found twenty clips during the window from 5:00 p.m. to 3:00 a.m. on the 24th.

None of the videos showed anyone coming or going to Patricia's house during that time—that would've made things too easy. Most of the clips were taken due to cars passing. One was cat-related, causing Tiger Kitty to *raaooowww* at the screen. I had a partial view of the back side of the brown Subaru Forester that had so upset Josephine Huger. Someone backed it into the parking spot just to the left of the Huger front door, in front of a crepe myrtle tree, at 5:15 p.m. I could only see the last two characters of the license plate—PX—and the driver was never in the camera's view.

The final clip during the 11:00 - 3:00 window was taken at 11:15, when someone got into the Subaru and drove away. Now why would Josephine's neighbor be leaving at that hour? And if it actually was Josephine's neighbor, why hadn't he walked past Oscar's house—coming from the other end of the street near the intersection with Tradd? Josephine lived in the last house on Logan that faced Logan. The single house to her left was situated facing Broad Street, with the long backside of it facing Logan Street, and the piazzas facing a courtyard on the other side of the house. More to the point, that home had ample off-street parking beside said courtyard. There would be no need for those particular neighbors to park on Logan, ergo, it must be someone who lived between Oscar's house and Tradd Street. There could easily be a simple explanation. But I wouldn't be satisfied until I heard it.

Next, I loaded the clips from the afternoon before Patricia was killed and watched the argument between Patricia and Corinne. Josephine had described it accurately: Corinne tore out the door, her expression telegraphing that she was angry. Patricia was fast on her heels and followed her out to her car. The sisters were definitely having a heated discussion. They simmered down as soon as they noticed Josephine approaching with Petunia. Then Corinne just drove away. Neither of them appeared to say goodbye, and there was no friendly waving. This was not a typical Southern goodbye with lingering hugs.

I didn't find the most compelling thing on the video until I went back to the clips from the Wednesday morning before Patricia was killed. Bridget arrived for work at 8:45. As soon as she climbed the porch steps and went inside, a silver Buick Enclave rolled by slowly. The driver had shoulder-length dark blonde hair, and her head was craned in the opposite direction—looking at Patricia's house—until the very last second, she was in the camera's view. I pressed pause as she glanced towards Josephine's house.

It was Mary Ellis Donovan.

Why was she following Bridget?

Later the same day, Mary Ellis made another pass by the house at five o'clock. Then, five minutes after Bridget came out at 5:10 and left in her older white Dodge Caravan, Mary Ellis pulled into the same parking spot. She got out of the car with a blue hydrangea bush, made her way to the front porch, and rang the doorbell. Scarlett must've gone for the day as well, because Patricia answered the door. Mary Ellis handed Patricia the plant. They chatted for a few minutes. It was impossible to see either of their faces as Mary Ellis stood close to the doorway, in front of Patricia and had her back to the camera. Finally, the door closed. When Mary Ellis turned around, the expression on her face was stricken. As she headed down the front porch steps, the look hardened into anger. What on earth was happening here?

Now I was curious. Had Mary Ellis ever been to Patricia's house before?

I started with March 1. It was a tedious process, with numerous short clips triggered by cars, pedestrians, and the occasional bicycle. But I only had to go as far as Monday, March 6 to find Mary Ellis again.

Her Buick rolled slowly by the house at 5:05, then returned at 5:11—right after Bridget left, just like in the video from Wednesday, March 22—and parked in the spot Bridget vacated. This time, she reached into the back of the SUV and pulled out a large cardboard box and a small brown box that looked like it was covered in alligator skin or some such thing. It had a large brown bow.

Mary Ellis craned her neck to see around the huge cardboard box as she carefully approached Patricia's porch and navigated the steps. She set the boxes down to ring the bell. Because the boxes were in front of the door, with Mary Ellis behind and slightly to the left, I could see Patricia's face. She smiled like she was greeting a friend.

Did these women know each other? It surely appeared that they did. But Patricia didn't invite Mary Ellis in, so perhaps not well. Patricia listened as Mary Ellis spoke and gestured for a minute or so. Then Patricia smiled warmly and mouthed the words, "thank you so much." They spoke back and forth for a few minutes, then Mary Ellis picked up the smaller brown box with the bow and handed it to Patricia. Her face registered delight. She thanked Mary Ellis profusely.

And that's when Mary Ellis reached inside her purse and pulled out something small and bright blue. She reached over the big box and handed it to Patricia, all the while continuing to talk and gesture. Patricia nodded, gesturing with the hand that held the little blue thing I was betting was a flash drive. It sure looked like she'd agreed to something—likely to send that flash drive to her friend in Nashville. It would appear that Mary Ellis gave up on convincing Bridget and somehow made a connection with Patricia.

Interesting. Very Interesting.

I scanned through the rest of the video clips and found nothing more of interest except a couple of more appearances of the brown Subaru Forester that reportedly belonged to Josephine's neighbor. I sighed with relief. There were a couple of things that made me curious on the videos, but nothing Cash would consider evidence, at least not at this point.

Next I turned my attention to verifying Scarlett's alibi, so I could check *someone* off my list. But the number she gave me rang and rang. No one answered and voice mail never picked up. I'd try again later.

I pulled up Patricia's iCloud calendar and looked at her pattern for the last several months. There was nothing unusual in the weeks before her death. No mysterious meetings. No new names. Just her typical volunteer hours at Neighbor to Family and Charleston Studios, her standing lunch with Corinne on Thursdays—their argument must've happened after lunch the day Patricia was killed—and occasional evenings at the Charleston Symphony, the Gaillard Center, or the Dock Street Theatre. Did she go to these events alone? There was no indication on her calendar of anyone else accompanying her.

Her calendar was empty after lunch on Thursday, March 23—the evening she was killed. By all appearances Patricia was home alone—except for Scarlett and Bridget—after Corinne left.

I went back to the photo of all the passwords I'd taken at Scarlett's house and found the login for Patricia's account with her security company. Cash had mentioned early on—before I took this case—that there were four exterior cameras, but no helpful footage. Just to dot my i's, I logged in and pulled up the history—or tried to.

There were no saved video clips until the morning after Patricia was killed. The sensitivity filters on the cameras were apparently set up so that small animals and passing cars didn't trigger them—only people coming and going. One camera covered the front door, and there was one on each of the three remaining sides of the house. When Bridget arrived for work the morning she found Patricia's body, the front door camera recorded her coming in, then the police arriving at 9:18. After that there were tons of clips of people coming and going.

I checked the settings and verified that all four cameras were set to record when their motion detectors activated. The system worked fine, and was set up to delete recordings more than thirty days old unless they were saved. It appeared that someone had manually deleted all of the history up until after Patricia's death. Only Patricia herself or someone who set out to cover their tracks would have done such a thing.

Frustrated, and after being inside most of the afternoon, I needed some fresh air. Mary Ellis and her hydrangea had reminded me mine needed deadheading. I set Tiger Kitty off my lap, petted both kitties, told them where I was going, and went outside.

My mother had loved pink hydrangeas. I suppose I picked that up from her. I had a row of them along the fence in the backyard where the house shaded them from the afternoon sun. I'd been snipping the spent blooms for ten minutes or so when North joined me.

"Everything okay?" he asked.

"Yeah, sure. Why do you ask?"

He shrugged. "You don't work from home much now that you have the fancy new office."

"I worry the kitties aren't used to being alone so much."

"I've always heard cats were pretty independent. How's the case going?"

"Okay, I guess. I'm still in the more questions than answers phase."

"Anything I can help with?"

I studied him. He had helped me from time to time with cases, usually with technical things. Once or twice, he'd helped with logistics when I needed to be in two places at once.

"Actually, that would be fabulous. I could use an extra pair of eyes and fingers on the keyboard. I've got a partial license plate on a brown Subaru Forester that was parked diagonally across the street from Patricia's house the evening she was killed. I'm told it belongs to one of the neighbors, but someone left in it at 11:15 p.m., which is in the window of time when Patricia died. It has piqued my natural curiosity, though the driver isn't on video coming out of Patricia's house."

"People who know there are cameras can find a way to avoid them."

"Exactly. Would you see if you can work some geek magic and track down who owns the car?"

"I'll do my best."

"Oh—and I could really use a magnetic sign for my Honda that says 'Lazy Days Pool Service.' They're a company based in North Charleston, but they service

the entire area."
"On it."

Chapter Twelve

Wednesday, April 5, 2023

The next morning, Sarabeth arrived at my house at 5:25 a.m. carrying a small cooler.

"I made chia seed pudding parfaits with fresh berries, homemade granola—not a single drop of oil—and a mixed berry compote. It's a copycat recipe of that A.M. Superfoods Bowl at First Watch—you know that breakfast place over at Mount Pleasant Towne Center?" She unpacked the cooler on my kitchen island.

"That sounds delicious. You need coffee?"

She winced at me. "I *doo*...I left mine sitting on the bar. I like cream and sugar...what is it you put in your coffee again?"

"I promise you will love it. I sweeten mine with

date syrup and use an oat milk caramel macchiato creamer. I'm going to make you a to-go cup just like mine."

"All righty then." Sarabeth smiled wide, her voice overly bright, betraying her apprehension. "Thank you so much."

When we were settled at the bar with our coffee and parfaits, she took a hesitant sip, then raised her eyebrows. "That's actually not bad. So. What kind of surveillance are we doing today?"

"The usual kind. We're going to continuously observe a suspect."

"Ooh, like a stakeout? I've never done a stakeout before." Sarabeth grinned and lifted her shoulders like a gleeful shiver of excitement ran down her spine.

"Yes, like a stakeout."

"Do we need disguises?"

I glanced at the navy blue Medical University of South Carolina sweatshirt I was wearing. "This is actually part of my disguise."

"Is what I'm wearing okay?" asked Sarabeth.

"Actually, no. That athleisure look screams middle-aged matron. We need you to look like a grad student. I told you to wear jeans or leggings."

"Hadley, I hate to disappoint you, but I am *way past* the middle-aged matron phase and on into 'woman of a certain age.' There's no way on God's green earth I'll pass for a grad student."

"So maybe you had a few gap years, all right?"

"I just think we should have realistic goals." She

sighed. "I brought a pair of jeans. They're in my bag. But they won't be nearly as comfortable on a stakeout as my Pure Jill organic cotton warm-up suit."

"There's a lightweight College of Charleston hoodie on the table. Put that on with your jeans. We don't need anything more elaborate than that in the car. But if we follow her on foot, I'll do something with my hair. Unless you're planning to come to work with me every day, you probably don't really need a disguise per se. You just need to lend authenticity to mine. The point of disguises would be to keep her from noticing she saw us in multiple places on different days. That would likely make her suspicious."

"Well I might tag along with you a few more days. I better have a disguise too. Do you have a wig?"

I smiled and shook my head at her enthusiasm. "I have several. And hats. You'd be amazed what a pair of big sunglasses will do."

Sarabeth disappeared into the guest room and returned minutes later transformed, her honey blonde waves cascading over a well-worn College of Charleston sweatshirt paired with slim-fitting jeans. She was one of those enviable women who aged so gracefully you couldn't quite pin down her years—somewhere between forty-something and none-of-your-business. Because she was so young looking, the clothes really did make all the difference.

"You said we didn't want 'her' to notice we were following her," said Sarabeth. "Who exactly is 'her?' Who are we surveilling?"

"Mary Ellis Donovan. Bridget's ex-mother-in-law."

"Seriously? I've studied everything that's been in the papers. There hasn't been any mention of her at all. Now, mind you, I'm not a fan of Mary Ellis Donovan. She's a bona fide piece of work. But why on earth would *she* have killed Patricia Gaillard?"

"I'm not sure yet. Maybe to frame Bridget?"

"Well, that would surely make it easier for her to commandeer the children. She annoys the pure-T fire out of Bridget, but she didn't have a legal leg to stand on before Bridget was arrested. If she were convicted of murder that would certainly change things. Goodness, I hope Mary Ellis isn't that diabolical."

"*Someone* was diabolical. They killed one woman and framed a single mother," I said.

"Yeah, but Mary Ellis is those kids' *grandmother*. The idea of a homicidal grandmother is just a whole nother level of disturbing."

"Right now, she's one of several suspects, in my book, anyway. But she's up to something. She was on some video footage dropping in on Patricia a couple of times, which is odd."

"That is very strange. The two of them don't exactly travel in the same circles."

"Anyway, I just need to figure out what was going on between her and Patricia. At the moment, Mary Ellis is the only person connected to the case who's behaved suspiciously. Also, she's hired an attorney to try to take the kids, so if she is up to something nefarious and I catch her in the act, that may help Bridget hang onto her kids."

"Unbelievable. Poor Bridget," said Sarabeth. "That woman is a constant source of aggravation and worry."

"We'll start at the Donovan house and if Mary Ellis leaves, we'll follow her wherever she goes. Just be prepared for a lot of waiting. Surveillance is mostly boring."

We polished off the last bites of breakfast, snagged our still-steaming coffee mugs, and clattered down the stairs to the garage. Sarabeth made a beeline for Jolene.

"Seriously?" I laughed at her. "The idea with stakeouts is to blend in, not stand out." I pointed towards the white Honda Accord I had bought for the sole purpose of surveillance.

"Now looky there," said Sarabeth. "You've already taught me something. But dang, riding around in Jolene sure would be a lot more fun. I was looking forward to putting the top down."

I threw a duffel in the back seat, and we climbed into the Honda and backed out of the garage. The automatic gate swung slowly open, and we pulled onto Marshall Boulevard. It was a beautiful spring day, with a bright blue sky that held only a few puffy clouds. I pressed play on my favorites playlist and "Call Me the Breeze," by Lynyrd Skynyrd sang out of the sound system. Sarabeth smiled and tapped along.

Forty minutes later, we were parked down the street from the Donovan home in Ladson, with a clear view of their house. It was a solidly middle-class neighborhood of homes built in the 1980s and 90s with roughly half-acre lots, sidewalks on both sides of the street, and mature trees, mostly pines and crepe myrtles with a few oaks and palmetto trees sprinkled in.

"I'm not trying to tell you your business," said Sarabeth, "but this is one of those neighborhoods where a car parked in front of someone's house is bound to be noticed."

"You're absolutely right. Which is why I picked this particular house." I pointed to the mottled brown brick house we'd parked in front of. "Someone in this house runs a CPA business. Which means the neighbors are used to people coming and going."

"What about the people who live here? Won't they come out and ask what business we have parked in front of their house?"

"They might," I said. "Which is why you're going to go ring the doorbell and tell them we're having car trouble, but Triple A is on the way."

"Fun." She gave a little squeal and fluffed her hair. "I'll be right back. Wait now. It's just six forty-five. What if they're not up yet?"

"Then the doorbell will wake them. But it's better to disturb their beauty rest than risk them knocking on the window at an inopportune moment."

"Right." Sarabeth hopped out of the car and sashayed towards the front door.

The Donovans' red brick ranch sat across the street and down the road just a bit, nestled among tall pines. It looked peaceful in the early morning light. No movement yet, but my gut said that Mary Ellis was an early riser by habit. Although she and George had an empty nest these days, surely her mission to "save" her grandchildren got her out of bed early.

Sarabeth climbed back into the car. "That poor woman has three wild boys between five-ish and eight-ish, plus a baby on her hip. It's a madhouse in there already this morning, getting ready for school. She couldn't care less if we sit here all day or set up a circus tent in her front yard."

"Perfect."

"So that's where the mother-in-law from Hell lives." Sarabeth whispered, following my gaze.

"Former mother-in-law. Arlo and Bridget are divorced, remember?"

"I don't think Mary Ellis recognizes her change in status. You know, most ex-mothers-in-law have to go through their kids to see the grandkids. But with Arlo in Nashville...Mary Ellis should be thanking her lucky stars. A lot of young mothers wouldn't put up with her shenanigans." Sarabeth shrugged. "It's a nice house. Very well-kept."

I nodded, conceding her point, and we settled in to wait. Sarabeth practically vibrated with excitement beside me while I focused on the house, wondering what Mary Ellis had on her agenda today. I hoped for something more revealing than spring cleaning.

At 7:10, one of the garage doors rumbled open at the Donovan house, and a white Chevrolet pickup truck backed out of the driveway.

"That's George Donovan," I said. "He's likely on his way to work. He's been the manager at the Ladson Piggly Wiggly for more than a decade. Worked his way up."

"I've never met him. He looks like a nice man."

"How can you tell from here?"

"Well, he keeps his house and yard nice. He's worked at the same job a long time to provide for his family. He's steady. Steady men are often underrated."

George waved at us and smiled as his truck passed by.

"And look at that," said Sarabeth. "He's friendly. I bet Mary Ellis browbeats him."

"I wonder how he feels about taking his grandchildren away from their mother," I said.

"I bet you a hundred bucks that's all Mary Ellis," said Sarabeth. "I would not be one bit surprised to find out she holds something over him—like maybe he has a floozy on the side, or a gambling problem, and he's afraid the people at church will find out and that's the only reason he goes along with her."

"You know, if I didn't know that you wrote fiction for a living, I'd figure it out pretty fast. You do have an overactive imagination."

At 7:15, the other Donovan garage door opened, and a silver Buick Enclave backed out with Mary Ellis at the wheel.

"Showtime," I said.

"She's leaving bright and early," said Sarabeth.

"Which makes me hopeful she's going somewhere

interesting. Let's find out." I waited until Mary Ellis had turned at the end of the street before starting the Honda, turning around in the CPA's driveway, and following at a discreet distance.

The morning traffic worked in our favor, providing plenty of cars between us and Mary Ellis's SUV. She drove with purpose, making her way to Highway 78 and taking the back way into Summerville, avoiding morning traffic on I-26. I hung back, careful not to get too close.

"You're good at this," Sarabeth said, leaning forward in her seat. "I'd be right on her bumper, trying not to lose her."

"And that's exactly how you'd get spotted. The trick is to keep them in sight but not get too close."

When we got to Main Street in Summerville, Mary Ellis turned left on South Main and went around the block. She pulled into a parking spot on West Richardson Avenue near Hutchinson Square.

"Keep your eye on her." I made a quick left at the light, looped back down Little Main, turned right on West Richardson, and then found a space across the street from Mary Ellis and a few storefronts down.

"Did you see where she went?" I asked.

"Cafe de Fleur."

"Maybe she's meeting someone for breakfast."

"I have been wanting to try that place. I've heard they use local ingredients and make everything from scratch. The cinnamon bun danish is supposedly to die for."

"Well, today's your lucky day." I reached into the backseat and grabbed the duffel bag I'd packed. I pulled out a pair of fake reading glasses, a couple of ponytail scrunchies, and a baseball cap and oversized sunglasses for Sarabeth. "Put your hair in a low ponytail and put on the sunglasses. I'm going to do a messy bun."

We both opened the mirrors in our sun visors and went to work.

"Wow. I do look different," Sarabeth said with delight as she settled the cap on her head. "Tucker couldn't pick me out of a lineup."

"Remember, we're just two friends having coffee. Don't stare."

"Got it. Operation Coffee Shop Surveillance is a go."

I swallowed a smile as we exited the car. "Just follow my lead."

As we jaywalked across West Richardson, I scanned the area, then faked an earring drop next to Mary Ellis's car, and attached a GPS tracker to her back right wheel well.

"You find it?" Sarabeth helpfully asked.

"Yep. All good."

When we walked into Cafe de Fleur, the aromas of fresh-baked pastries and coffee wrapped around us like a warm hug. The space was cozy but modern, with white walls, and black-framed windows and doors.

Mary Ellis sat at the table by the front window with a woman whose short brown hair looked like it had been tightly rolled, then teased within an inch of its life, sensible chunky white tennis shoes, and the outfit I'd made Sarabeth take off. I smirked at her.

"Oh, for goodness' sake," she muttered. "It's the sum of the parts. There's not a thing wrong with that outfit."

The cafe was small, with only three tables in a tight row. If we sat too close to Mary Ellis and her friend, it might make them hesitant to speak freely. Time to formulate a quick plan B.

We stepped up to the counter and ordered an oat milk chai latte for me and a caramel latte for Sarabeth.

"I'm going to get a cinnamon roll danish for us to share, just to try it," said Sarabeth.

I smiled and widened my eyes in an expression meant to communicate *would you please focus*?

She wrinkled her nose and squinted at me, then turned to finish placing her order. We moved to the side to wait.

I pulled a listening device the size of a quarter with museum putty stuck to the back from my purse. "Follow my lead," I murmured to Sarabeth.

"I'm sorry, what?"

"Help me create a diversion." I turned and walked towards the door. When I was next to Mary Ellis's table, I "tripped" over my own foot, landing in the floor right in front of the door.

"Oh my stars. Are you okay?" Sarabeth hustled over.

"Are you all right?" Mary Ellis stood and knelt beside me.

Her friend rose and hovered above me.

"I think so," I said. "I just twisted my ankle."

"Well here, let me help you." Mary Ellis offered me a hand.

"Oh, no," I said. "Thank you. I'm fine." Wobbling, I pushed myself up. I looked at Sarabeth like, *get with the program*.

"Maybe we shouldn't move you?" Sarabeth said. "Are you sure nothing's broken?"

I "slipped" and sank back to the floor. "Nothing is broken. I just need to sit down for a minute."

The door opened and two twenty-something women stopped in the doorway and stared at me.

"I've got it now." I started to rise again. "I just need to get to a table outside, where there's some fresh air."

Sarabeth squinted at me. "I'll hold the door."

The twenty-somethings stepped back onto the sidewalk. Sarabeth grabbed the door and held it open. For a brief moment, Mary Ellis and her friend looked towards Sarabeth, and as they did, I staggered up and grabbed Mary Ellis's arm to steady myself with my right hand.

"Thank you." I smiled at Mary Ellis. "I'm just clumsy this morning. Stayed up too late studying."

"Here, I'll help you outside," she said.

"I've got it, thank you." I hobbled outside and sat at the sidewalk table on the opposite side of the doorway. This way, we wouldn't be just on the other side of the glass from Mary Ellis.

Sarabeth brought our order outside and sat across from me. "Are you all right? What exactly happened there? And why are we outside? I thought the idea was to eavesdrop?"

"I'm fine, and it is," I said. "I stuck a very small listening device under their table. We're in range, but not so close we make them nervous."

"How do we hear what they're saying?"

"It streams to my phone." I handed one earbud to Sarabeth and put the other in my ear.

Her eyes grew round.

Over Sarabeth's shoulder, through the window, I could see Mary Ellis leaning in to speak and gesturing. "...the whole reason I volunteered at Neighbor to Family. Patricia was running a clothing drive. That's why I asked y'all to donate children's clothing."

"So you could get on her good side?" The woman with the teased hair asked.

"Well, I had to do something."

"Of course. It worked, I gather?"

"Up to a point," said Mary Ellis. "I mean, she sent the flash drive thingy to her friend. She said she did, anyway. But when I asked her about it, she said Trevor Jennings was a busy man, and she didn't know when he'd have time to listen to Arlo's music. She made out like I was being unreasonable."

"Why, just because you asked a question?" said her friend.

"Well, exactly," said Mary Ellis. "And now, I just worry this opportunity died with Patricia. There's no way for me to follow up with these Jennings people. How do I even know Patricia really sent it? She could've just told me that to get me to shut up and leave her alone."

Sarabeth made a face that seemed to agree that was a distinct possibility.

"I wonder if they're related to Waylon Jennings?" said her friend.

"Now how would I know that, Marcia?" Mary Ellis's tone was testy.

"I just thought maybe Patricia mentioned it, is all."

Sarabeth popped a bite of cinnamon bun danish in her mouth, made a face that said *this is the best thing I've ever eaten,* and pushed it towards me. I shook my head.

"She was all sweetness and light when I dropped off those kids clothes," said Mary Ellis. "And then, later, when I asked if she'd sent the flash drive, she got downright patronizing. I despise being patronized to. Snooty woman. God rest her soul."

"I'm sure Arlo's CD or whatever is fantastic and the people in Nashville will be in touch," said Marcia. "They won't want to miss out on such a talented new artist. And if not, well you didn't mention this to Arlo did you?"

"Of course not. He would *not* be happy with me. Arlo wants to do things for himself, which I understand, but everyone needs help on occasion."

"That's good then. If the Nashville people don't get in touch, he'll never know the difference. At least he won't be disappointed. How did you find out this was a record company he hadn't spoken to before?"

"What do you mean?" asked Mary Ellis.

"I mean, you wouldn't want to send them his CD if he'd already spoken to them and things didn't work out. That might embarrass him."

Mary Ellis was quiet for a minute. I couldn't see the expression on her face from that angle.

"I didn't mean to upset you," said Marcia.

"If it ever comes up, I'll tell him Bridget must've given the flash drive to Patricia."

"There you go. Blame her. It doesn't matter if he's mad at her anymore," said Marcia. "Now, tell me…how did George's canoe trip down the Edisto River go? Did they have a good time?"

"He said he did. That's the longest we've been apart in nearly thirty-five years of marriage. It was heavenly." They both laughed.

"You know I love George," Mary Ellis continued. "But it was real nice to have time to myself. I had myself a day of beauty on Saturday and ate cheese and crackers and grapes for dinner. It was glorious."

"I'da thought you'd've gone out and had a nice dinner maybe—someplace George didn't care for. That's what I'd've done."

"Oh, no. I don't like to eat in restaurants by myself. I just focused on some 'me' time. I don't think I saw another soul the entire time they were gone, which suited me just fine. And I didn't cook a single thing from the time George and the boys left that Thursday morning before dawn until they got home late Sunday evening. Now, I did cook them Sunday dinner, mind you. A nice pot roast."

"I bet they appreciated that," said Marcia. "So all the boys went—aside from Arlo, I mean."

"They did. I was surprised Adam took the time, to be honest. He's so busy with Meredith and the kids—and his job. He's a consultant now. I mean, he's still a mechanical engineer. But he consults with other companies. Anyway, he stays real busy. He didn't think he was going to get to go. He had a work conflict. But George changed the whole thing from March 16th to March 23rd so Adam could go. I think that meant a lot to Adam."

Sarabeth's eyes went wide. Our eyes met and locked. She nearly choked on a sip of her latte.

Mary Ellis didn't see a soul from Thursday March 23 before dawn until Sunday the 26th at dinnertime. Patricia was killed around midnight—an hour plus or minus—on March 23.

Mary Ellis had no alibi.

The downside to placing the listening device under their table was that we had to wait until Mary Ellis and Marcia left to retrieve it, which meant we'd have to catch up to them. Once we were in the car, I opened the app that communicated with the tracking device I'd attached to her car.

"It looks like she's on her way home." I headed towards Ladson. "Keep an eye on her and let me know if she changes direction."

"Aye aye. Roger. What do PIs say for 'okay?'"

"Okay."

"Well that's not very colorful. We should come up with something better than that," said Sarabeth. "Mary Ellis might need to go meet with her accomplice this afternoon. You never know."

"What accomplice? There goes your imagination again. I'm thinking if she did this, she did it alone."

"What makes you say that?"

"Just a feeling. She strikes me as someone who holds her cards close to the vest."

"So, intuition is important to your job," said Sarabeth.

"Intuition yes. Imagination, not so much. But we learned a few facts this morning."

"We know how Mary Ellis sucked up to Patricia," said Sarabeth.

"...and that she was angry when Patricia couldn't give her an update," I said. "I saw the look on her face when she left Patricia's the afternoon of March 23. She was angry, for sure. But most importantly, we learned that Mary Ellis does not have an alibi for the night of the killing because George and all three of their local sons were on a canoe trip."

Mary Ellis went straight home. I parked at an

apartment complex a few streets over, and we waited to see if she would leave again. At four o'clock, we'd gone through our snacks and drink supply—and appealed to the kindness of strangers once already to use the facilities in the office of the apartment complex, pleading a car breakdown.

"Let's call it for the day," I said. "If she leaves the house I'll know it and can see where she goes. We may have learned all there is to learn by following her around."

"What else can you do to figure out if she's the killer?" asked Sarabeth. "I mean, unless she spontaneously confesses, like people seem to do on television?"

"Well, we've established that she had a motive—possibly two…"

"Increasing her odds of getting custody of her grandkids, and possibly anger or revenge, depending on how the situation with Arlo's album played out," said Sarabeth.

"Exactly. Since Patricia was killed with her own gun, anyone at the scene during the time she was killed had the means and the opportunity. I need to either tie Mary Ellis to the crime scene or catch her or her car in that neighborhood that night. Neither of those things by themselves would be conclusive. She likely has a good explanation ready. But it would go a long way towards constructing an alternate theory of the crime and raising reasonable doubt."

"Do you really think she did it?" asked Sarabeth.

"Maybe. On the one hand it's unlikely she'd kill the woman who promised to help her. But on the other, she's dead set on getting custody of Bridget's kids...If Patricia somehow didn't follow through, or if the music producer passed on Arlo's album and Patricia said something that sent Mary Ellis into a fit of rage...then maybe it occurred to her she could take care of two birds with one stone."

"But she told her friend Marcia the Nashville music producer hadn't listened to Arlo's music yet."

"If Mary Ellis is capable of murder, she's certainly capable of a lie. There's a narrative she's telling herself. And whatever that is, that's what she tells other people too. Besides, what is it they say? Hell hath no fury like a mamma bear defending her cub."

Chapter Thirteen

Thursday, April 6, 2023

My phone rang before eight the next morning. I was out on the pool deck and had just finished my smoothie. A glance at the screen told me the caller was not in my contacts, but was *maybe* calling from Talbot & Andrews Foundation.

Interesting. "Hello?"

"Hadley, hey, this is Liz Talbot. I hope I'm not calling too early."

"Not at all."

"I wondered if you might stop by the foundation today? If you're going to be in Charleston, that is. I wanted to update you on Bridget's custody case."

"Sure. I have some work to do South of Broad. Is 9:00 too early?"

"That's perfect," she said. "See you soon."

Big Kitty and Tiger Kitty rubbed themselves against my legs. I'd noticed they seemed to expect treats when they did that. Or maybe it was just my response. I got them each a PurrrFeast Morsel organic, cage free chicken liver treat and bent down to scratch their heads.

"Why didn't she just update me over the phone?" I asked.

"*Raaooow.*" Big Kitty was the more talkative of the two felines.

My phone dinged. I glanced at the screen and saw a text from Sarabeth.

> Hey, what are you up to today?
> Can I tag along?

There was simply no way I could let Sarabeth come with me that particular day.

> I wish. Would love the company. But today will be too risky.

> Now I REALLY want to come! ☹

> You say that now, but you'd be sorry when Tucker had to come bail you out of jail.

> I'm intrigued...but yeah, Tucker doesn't need any more stress. Call me if you need me to bail YOU out.

> Will do—thanks!

The Talbot & Andrews Foundation was housed in a large brick converted home near the intersection of King and Broad Streets—between the John Rutledge House Inn and the Archives & Records Management offices of Roman Catholic Diocese of Charleston. Luckily, I snagged a nearby parking spot on Broad Street.

I climbed out of the Honda and just stood there for a second, slack-jawed. There are so many lovely historic homes in Charleston, I guess I'd never paid this particular one much attention. The place was a stunner. Built in 1763 by a Johns Island planter—yes, I Googled that—the three-story brick mansion rose up on a high basement and sprawled over more than 10,000 square feet. Don't ask me what architectural style it was—some kind of fancy—but it had quoins and brickwork so detailed it looked like a work of art. One of the skinny ends faced the street, like the old single houses downtown.

A tall brick wall wrapped around the entire property, with a wrought-iron gate that teased a view of the courtyard inside—green and shady, with the music of a water fountain coming from somewhere beyond the gnarled limbs of an ancient sprawling live oak. Wide, double-stacked piazzas hugged the first and second stories of the house overlooking the courtyard. Charleston green shutters flanked the windows, and cream-colored trim paint framed the piazzas in crisp lines.

As I approached the hospitality door, Liz opened it and waved, her smile wide and welcoming. "Come on in," she called.

She must've been watching for me. "Good morning." I smiled back at her and stepped through the door, climbed the steps, and followed her across the piazza to the front door, which sat squarely in the middle.

"This place is just gorgeous," I said.

"Aww—thank you. Well, we can take no credit, of course. We do our part to preserve it."

"It's amazing."

"Would you like a tour?" Liz asked.

"If you're sure you have time. Maybe just a quick one."

She led me through the first floor, with its wide-planked wood floors, intricate woodwork, and arched doorways. "We've tried to make it functional without losing any of the historical spirit and beauty. The dining room and the breakfast room are still used for meals, but also as conference rooms. The living room

—which is not much smaller than the ballroom—and the drawing room have desks for our staff, but also comfortable sofas and chairs. The ballroom we use only for events."

I admired the woodwork on the wide archway leading to a room I didn't have a name for. Its purpose seemed to be housing the wide, sweeping curved staircase made from a dark stained wood with a cream and gold runner.

"Nate and I have offices on the second floor, as do two program directors," said Liz. "We also have a bedroom on the second floor for times we need to stay over in Charleston. The last ferry to Stella Maris leaves Isle of Palms at 11:30 p.m., which means we need to leave downtown no later than 11 to make it. Sometimes that's just not possible. This saves us packing a suitcase and grabbing a hotel room."

We made a brief stop in each room. Somehow the whole house looked like we'd stepped back in time but also like it held all the modern comforts and conveniences. The gleaming hardwoods and elaborate moldings and woodwork continued throughout the house.

"There are three more guest bedrooms with baths on the third floor, plus a storage room," said Liz, but she didn't head up the stairs.

Instead, she turned back down the hall. "Have you had any breaks in Patricia Gaillard's murder?"

"Not really," I said. "I have a couple of suspects, but more questions than answers at this point."

Liz pushed open the door to her office and walked through.

I felt like we'd stepped inside an issue of *Veranda* magazine. Soft light poured in through tall windows dressed in creamy drapes with a subtle floral pattern. A soft rug in muted tones covered the honey-toned wood floors. The room had this calm, polished air about it, like it had been spritzed with magnolia perfume and good judgment.

Built-in bookshelves painted a soft dove grey with just enough crown molding to whisper "good taste and old money" lined the wall behind her desk. A few hardcover detective novels were tucked in amongst the professional books, along with family photos in silver frames, sweetgrass baskets, and glass bowls of sand dollars and shells.

The desk was a French antique, or a really good reproduction—light wood with carved legs and just the right amount of patina. A fresh bouquet of white hydrangeas rested near the corner. Liz perched on one end of the ivory tufted sofa with thick fringe around the bottom that was situated in front of the windows.

"Please have a seat wherever you like," she said.

I settled into one of the blue and ivory print side chairs, the one directly across from her. She put her feet up on the ottoman between us. "Bridget is home with her kids, right?"

"She is. Thank you so much for arranging bail."

"Of course," said Liz. "I'm happy we could help. That's one of the advantages of giving up PI work and setting up the foundation. It's rewarding to be able to help when someone needs help."

"Interesting," I said. "That's why I became a PI—to help people who needed help."

Liz nodded slowly, a wistful look on her face.

"Anyway," I said, "I'm hoping that with Bridget home, her mother-in-law's schemes will be thwarted."

"About that. We've hired Rutledge & Radcliffe to shut that down. They're very good. Hopefully they can get the Donovans' request for an emergency hearing quashed, at least for now. I'll let you know if they run into a problem."

"That's wonderful. I know Bridget will be relieved."

"The main thing is we have to figure out who really killed Patricia Gaillard and get these charges against Bridget dismissed."

The way she said "*we* have to..." did not go by me. I just smiled.

"I wanted to show you the electronic case board I mentioned."

"Oh—right. That sounds like something I could really use. Sometimes my handwriting is illegible."

"Mine too. That chair swivels, by the way." She hopped up and crossed the room. I spun the chair around to see the technical demonstration. She must've pressed a button or something. A pair of large seascape oil paintings on the opposite wall slid apart revealing what looked like a hundred-inch square iPad. When she touched the screen, it woke up. A much neater version of my case board came to life. Clearly, Liz Talbot had been working this case on her own.

"Who are your top suspects?" she asked.

"Apparently the same as yours," I said. "Mary Ellis Donovan and Scarlett Hathaway."

"Have you interviewed her? Scarlett Hathaway?"

"I have, yes."

"What was your impression of her?" asked Liz.

I tried and failed to suppress a snort of laughter. "I'm sure it's a sign of a character flaw of my own, and I feel badly about it, but I think she's a quack."

"Why on earth would you feel badly about that? A quack is a quack. What kind of quack?" She squinted and raised her chin.

"I try so hard not to judge. She's into...crystals and such. She has a spirit guide—and not one she knew while he was alive. It's an ancient Hopi warrior, she says. She was talking about 'manifesting a positive outcome.'" I shook my head. "Oh—and she thinks these ghosts from the Civil War era that live in Patricia's house killed her. It's really hard to communicate her level of crazy without sounding judgy. That's why I feel badly about it. But I know crazy when I see it."

"Homicidal ghosts?" Liz looked skeptical.

"That's what I thought."

Liz cocked her head and stared sternly at the cream-colored leather office chair behind her desk, like she was calling it down. It was spinning, slowly at first, then faster and faster, like someone sitting there was feeling playful. Liz made an expression that might've meant *give me a break.*

"I guess Colleen wants you to notice her," said Liz. "She says ghosts can't kill people. She should know... yes, I know you're not a ghost."

A chill traveled up and down my body and I felt vaguely nauseous. "Your friend who died...she's here?"

"Yes. She often is. The thing about guardian spirits—and ghosts as well, she tells me—is that they never age. She will forever be seventeen." Liz raised an eyebrow. "And she was a bit immature before she passed away."

I didn't know what to say to that.

"Hell's bells, Colleen, are you trying to run her off?" asked Liz.

The chair abruptly stopped spinning.

"Sorry about that," said Liz. "She enjoys messing with me a little too much. Things have been too quiet for us since I changed careers. I think she's excited to have a case to think about. Although, she's part of the reason I gave it up."

"I'm still getting used to the idea of guardian spirits, or ghosts, or whatever you want to call them," I said. "Assuming we're not both crazy and we actually have both seen dead people, I don't understand why Colleen seems to be a part of your daily life, but my mother isn't allowed to speak to me."

Liz was quiet for a minute, then said, "It's all tied to their mission. Colleen's is preventing overdevelopment on Stella Maris. There's a huge potential for disaster if the island population gets too large to safely evacuate. She basically uses me to carry out the things she needs done.

"Your mother's mission apparently involves something not directly connected to you. And actually, Colleen isn't allowed to contact family members either. As I understand it, these spirits can easily get too involved in their family's lives, which is problematic on two fronts: it distracts from the mission, but more importantly, it impacts a person's free will. If you could consult your mother, who knows things mortals do not, you might make different life choices. Free will's a funny thing. It stirs up an awful lot of heartache and trouble, but take it away, and the choices we make are meaningless."

"Wow." I felt my eyebrows slide up my face. "That's a lot."

"I know. It took me some getting used to, I'll tell you that. But think how fortunate you and I are to have witnessed absolute proof of the next world. I don't know about you, but it makes things more clear for me. Colleen's gone by the way. For now. She'll be back to harass me after you leave. So...back to our case board..."

"Could I have a glass of water, please?" Our case board. She said *our case board*.

"Of course." Liz darted over to a wet bar, opened a small refrigerator, and pulled out a pitcher of water with berries and some sort of herb floating around it. She poured me a glass and walked over to hand it to me. "I really do apologize about her. I meant what I said. She's still a teenager. She has poor impulse control."

I attempted a smile and sipped the water for a few minutes. "It's fine. What about the case board?" There was no margin in refusing to discuss it with her. A fresh perspective might benefit Bridget.

"You were saying that Scarlett was one of your top suspects. She doesn't have an alibi?"

"Well, she offered me one. I just haven't been able to verify it. She said she had overnight company, gave me a name. But the cell phone just rings and rings. Voicemail isn't set up on the account. It's strange. I've tried all times of day and night."

"Maybe he's just not answering because he doesn't recognize your number."

"Yeah, I thought about that. I've spoofed a couple of different businesses. So far nothing has worked."

"You want me to have a crack at it?" Her face brightened with a hopeful expression.

"You really miss this job, don't you?" I asked.

"I really do."

"Okay. I appreciate the help."

"Really?" She sounded positively gleeful.

"Sure. The name she gave me was Brett Campbell. I'll text you the phone number." I copied the number from my call history and did a quick paste and send.

"Good morning, ladies."

We both turned towards the door, where a tall man

with dark blond hair and startlingly blue eyes stood. His warm smile lingered on Liz.

"Sweetheart, come meet Hadley," said Liz. "Hadley Cooper, this is my husband, Nate Andrews. Nate, Hadley."

"A pleasure." He approached my chair as I stood, and we shook hands.

"Nice to meet you," I said.

Nate turned to stare at the case board and raised an eyebrow. "Slugger, what are you up to?"

"I'm just tinkering," said Liz. "Nothing for you to be concerned about."

"Uh-huh." He eyed her suspiciously. "So, Hadley, do you work alone, or do you have a partner?"

"It's just me so far. I hope to have some associates at some point, but I haven't been able to pull that off yet."

"I can't imagine working a case without Nate," said Liz.

"And yet, apparently you've been doing just that," he said with a teasing smile. "It is good to have someone to bounce things off of."

"And someone to divide things up with," said Liz. "We used to divvy up the suspects when we were gathering alibis. And then there were the operations neither of us could've run alone. You always need a lookout."

"Yeah, I can see where that would come in handy," I said. "I have a friend who's helped me out a time or two. And when I was training, I worked with my mentor, Joe Vincent."

"Joe's a good guy," said Nate. "Excellent detective."

"The best," I said. "I was just admiring Liz's fancy case board." I crossed the room to get a better look. But as I approached the screen, my gaze ran across a small console table to the right. A collection of framed photos were arranged across the top.

The one that caught my eye had me in it.

I stopped and stared for a minute. Then I reached out and picked up the frame. A handsome man roughly my age who I'd never met was in the picture with me and two small children, a boy and a slightly younger girl.

I turned to Liz, but couldn't articulate a question.

"That's Poppy," said Liz. "My sister-in-law, with my brother, Blake, and their two children."

"I think I need to sit down." I took the picture with me and went back to my chair.

"The resemblance is startling," said Nate.

"This is why you and your mother kept looking at me oddly." I turned to Liz. "And both of you asked me about my family, rather pointedly, as I think about it."

"Well," said Liz. "Can you blame us?"

I stared at the photo and shook my head. "No. We could be twins. I literally thought I was looking at a picture of myself, with people I've never met. It's very disorienting."

"I can imagine," said Liz. "It's a bit disorienting for me. I keep wanting to call you Poppy."

"Well." I shook my head to clear it. "I guess I have a doppelgänger."

"I couldn't decide whether to say anything or not," said Liz. "Even Mamma wasn't sure what to do, which might be a first. We were still trying to figure it out. I guess I should've put that photo away. Then again, I think part of me figured if you saw it, well, I wouldn't have to worry about whether to say anything or not anymore."

"I've heard everyone has a doppelgänger somewhere," I said. "It's just a really big coincidence mine is right here in the Charleston area and married to your brother."

Liz and Nate were both quiet, like there were things they were thinking but hesitated to say.

"I need to stay focused right now on Bridget's case." I nodded, the conviction sliding into place. "It's uncanny, the resemblance. But uncanny things happen, right? I need to stay focused."

"Please let me know if you want to talk about… this," said Liz.

"I've got a meeting to get ready for." Nate pulled Liz in for a hug and a kiss that was quick but not one bit perfunctory. "Behave yourself."

"Naturally," she drawled.

He shook his head slowly and gave her an affectionate but exasperated look. "If I thought for a second you'd pay me the slightest bit of attention, I'd tell you to stay out of Hadley's case." He headed towards the door. "Nice to meet you, Hadley."

"Nice meeting you." I managed a little smile and wave. I had so much to process.

"So..." Liz gave me a mischievous look. "What's on your agenda for today?"

"I'm going to search Patricia Gaillard's house this morning. This afternoon I have an interview with her sister, Corinne."

"You're going to search her house in broad daylight? That's how I'd do it, too, though plenty of PIs would do it at night."

"I prefer midday for searches," I said. "You don't have to worry about the neighbors noticing lights on, or a flashlight beam."

"Exactly," said Liz. "Plus, fewer neighbors are even home during the day. And the ones who are are less suspicious. How are you planning to go in?"

"Through the back door in the courtyard."

Liz gave me a quizzical look. "That courtyard looks inaccessible to me other than the gate at the end of the driveway."

"It is." I nodded. Clearly, she'd been thinking about having a look around herself. "There's a six-foot wall around the entire backyard with a thick hedge that's taller just inside the wall, with palm trees every ten feet or so. I could get over the wall easily enough, but the hedge makes it unworkable. I'll have to go in through the driveway."

"So you'll use a pretext?"

"I may have photographed Scarlett's calendar, which has all the household stuff on it. The pool company typically comes on Thursday mornings. I impersonated Scarlett and canceled this week. I told them the pool deck is being deep cleaned and it can't be walked on. Then I went to Target and bought a T-shirt the same color as their technicians wear—there's a picture on the website of a crew cleaning a pool. I ironed on the company name—it's not the same as theirs, but it's close enough, I think. Luckily, their service techs don't drive vans. They all drive their own cars with magnetic signs. A friend borrowed some of those for me."

Liz smiled and nodded. "Good plan. I'm impressed. No one will give you a second glance... What would you say to me coming along to Patricia's? A second pair of hands might come in handy...that's a big house... And you never know when you might need a lookout."

"Well, I only have the one T-shirt, but if anyone asks, I can tell them you're a trainee. Sure." I shrugged. "But just so you know, if my client asks me if you've been tagging along, I'll have to tell her the truth."

"Well, we'd better do it quick then." Liz grabbed a handbag from a drawer behind her desk. "As soon as it occurs to her, Mamma will forbid it."

Chapter Fourteen

If I'm perfectly honest, I was happy to have company going into Patricia Gaillard's house. I'm not saying I bought into Scarlett's theory about the ghosts killing Patricia. But I couldn't completely discount the idea that there were ghosts in the house, either, given my recent close encounter, and I wasn't eager for alone time with anyone from the spirit world who I hadn't known while they were alive.

I pulled as far into Patricia's driveway as I could. The lot was long and narrow, and the Honda—with not one, but three Lazy Days Pool Cleaners signs: driver's door, passenger door, and back window—was screened by Patricia's house on one side and the neighbor's hedge on the other. Only someone looking directly down the drive would ever see the car.

"This far in, we're probably out of range for security cameras across the street," said Liz.

"We are. I scanned more than a month's worth of footage from the house directly across. The camera only reaches as far as the edge of Patricia's house."

"But what about your license plate? Surely someone's camera picked it up?"

"Maybe," I said. "But the neighbors are expecting the pool cleaners today. We check that box. There's no reason for anyone to make a note of my license plate or sound the alarm."

"You're right." Liz nodded. "It's hard for me to swallow, but I might be the teensiest bit skittish. It's been a long time since I've done this."

I checked my reflection in the mirror on my sun visor. We'd both changed into jeans. I wore my teal blue fake Lazy Days Pool Service shirt, and Liz wore a pink T-shirt from a Stella Maris diner called The Cracked Pot. Ponytails, ball caps, big sunglasses, check.

"Ready?" I asked.

"One sec." Liz pulled an automatic pistol out of her purse.

I recoiled against the driver's door. "*What are you doing?*"

"What do you mean? I'm putting Sig—my weapon—in my ankle holster." She smoothed the leg of her jeans over the top of the ankle holster. "What kind do you carry?"

"I don't carry a gun. At all. Ever. I don't like guns. And why on earth would you think we need a gun to search an empty house?"

"Because there's no guarantee it's going to stay empty until we finish searching it. I always carry my weapon. This job is unpredictable. Like I told you, I've had a few close calls. I like to be prepared."

"I just don't see the need for lethal firepower to do a simple search."

Liz shook her head. "And I don't understand how you can do this job without personal protection."

"Oh, I have protection." I let her know with a look I had things well covered.

"Like what?"

"First line of defense—strategy."

"Strategy?"

I nodded. "Yes. It's basically called 'be elsewhere.' I avoid dangerous situations. If one's unavoidable, I remove myself from harm's way. Reflexes." I shifted, demonstrating my lightning-fast reflexes.

"Seriously?"

"Absolutely. I train with a punching bag and a video game." I didn't care one bit for the smirk on her face. "And if all else fails, I am heavily armed."

"With what?"

"A stun gun, bear spray, a tactical pen—"

Liz's eyebrows rose. "Did you say a tactical pen?"

"Yes."

"*Hell's bells.* What are you going to do, ask a shooter for his autograph?"

"Don't mock the tactical pen. It's multifunctional. A tactical pen—"

"I know what tactical pens are used for. I just think we should defend ourselves with the best available tools."

I shrugged. "You do you. But keep that thing away from me."

"Oh *puh-leeze*."

We pulled on gloves and hopped out of the car. I made quick work of keying in the gate code I'd memorized. In seconds, we were inside a secret garden, surrounded by a tall, lush green hedge. The pool was the centerpiece of the courtyard, with multi-level patio areas, some brick, some a cream-colored travertine, for sunning, eating, and socializing. The backyard was narrow, but thankfully none of the neighbor's windows had a view.

We made our way to the back of the house. Liz slid a file through the door crack and lifted the bar-style lock on the screen door, then we slipped through the screened porch to a set of double glass doors. Liz picked the lock and pushed the door open.

Somewhere, an alarm system started beeping slowly, counting down to when it would trip. The door opened into a family room. I went in first, moving quickly, looking for the alarm panel.

I scanned the walls, then moved to the kitchen.

No sign of a key pad.

It must be in the foyer, near the front door.

The beeping got faster.

I dashed through the dining room, down a short hall, and into the foyer.

Beep-beep-beep-beep-beep-beep-beep!

I keyed in the code and the beeping stopped, with possibly a second to spare.

"Whew." I took a deep breath. "I am *really* grateful not to have to explain this to Cash."

"Eh, we would've been long gone before the police got here," said Liz.

"Maybe so," I said, "but when they looked at the footage from the security cameras on the back and side of the house, I'm thinking he would've recognized me."

"Yeah, that could get messy. I'm glad Nate's never been in law enforcement. That arrangement must be really stressful for you. Have you seen the security footage from the night of the murder?"

"There wasn't any," I told her. "It looks like someone deleted it all."

"Interesting. Are you thinking it was a Wi-Fi jammer? If I'd known this morning before I left home we'd need it, I could've brought our jammer."

"You have a Wi-Fi jammer?" I asked like, *you have got to be kidding me*.

"Of course. I'm surprised you don't. Why shouldn't the good guys have the same tools as the bad guys—or better?"

I shrugged like, *you make a fair point*. "Someone might've used a Wi-Fi jammer the night Patricia was killed. But all the videos from the last thirty days were missing, so my guess is someone deleted it all."

"Someone with her login..." Liz mused.

"Exactly. And whoever killed her was either let in or used a key. There was no sign of forced entry. I learned that before the Chinese wall went up." I raised my nose and sniffed the air. "Smells chemically."

"Yeah, it does."

"We'd better get to work. I'll take upstairs and you take down?"

"Sounds like a plan."

I climbed the front stairs and did a quick walk-through to see which rooms were where. The same golden, wide-plank, heart-of-pine hardwood floors that covered the entire first floor were everywhere upstairs except the bathrooms. The primary suite was on the back of the house, overlooking the pool. Patricia's office—with an extra desk for Scarlett—was on the front of the house overlooking Logan Street. Two other bedrooms were situated along the hall between them, with each bedroom opening onto the upper piazza, and each having a private bath.

I started with the office. The number one thing I wanted to find today was a copy of Patricia's will. Knowing who stood to benefit financially from her death would no doubt narrow down my list of possible suspect and motive combinations.

Patricia Gaillard's home office looked way too pretty to be functional. Tall, narrow windows along the front and doors down the side offered a two-sided view of the deep, L-shaped upper piazza with its haint blue ceilings. Muted pewter damask drapes framed white sheer curtains that diffused the generous slants of Charleston sunshine just enough to give everything a soft glow.

I sat behind her antique desk, which looked like it might've belonged to Marie-Antoinette—large, curvy, and cream-colored with carved legs. The polished surface was spotless, except for a thick crystal lamp, a vase of white orchids that looked real but must've been silk, a framed photograph of Patricia and Chalmers Gaillard at a black-tie event, and a crystal paperweight. No overflowing letter tray. No laptop—of course the police had taken that. No tangled cords. Not even a stray paperclip.

Methodically, I searched the drawers, but found nothing remotely interesting. I turned to the matching credenza and went through the file drawers. After finding nothing helpful there, nor in Scarlett's writing desk, I sat back in Patricia's buttery leather office chair and perused the room. Where would I keep a copy of my will?

The walls were painted cream-on-cream with full-wall wainscoting. Tasteful, muted oil paintings—a marsh at sunrise, a courtyard garden, and a view of the Battery—accented three walls. A matching settee and Louis the something or another armchairs flanked a small table stacked with artsy books. The room was coordinated and curated to the point of being cold. Was there a safe hidden somewhere in this elegant chamber?

I stood and walked around the room, checking behind each painting and the oversized drapes. It wasn't going to be that easy. I opened the closet and switched on the light. Shelves and drawers held the typical office supplies and no evidence of a safe or hidey hole. As I turned to switch the light off, my gaze caught the tail end of a register receipt lying on the floor, partially beneath a shelf.

I knelt, slid it out from beneath the shelf, and picked it up.

It was a receipt from a UPS Store in West Ashley from March 7, stapled to something that looked like a shipping label, but specifically stated that it was not. It was a shipment receipt, for a package sent to Uma Jennings from Patricia Gaillard on March 7.

This was the day after Mary Ellis had given Patricia the flash drive—she must've sent it on to Nashville. I slid the receipt into my crossbody bag, flipped the light switch, and closed the closet door.

After exhausting the possibilities that came to mind for a location for a safe, I meandered down the long hallway to the owner's suite.

A chill ran down my spine as I stood in the doorway. A small sitting room with two comfy chairs and footstools served as a hub, with the bedroom beyond, and access doors to the bathroom and closet on the opposite wall. I stepped into the bedroom. This was where Patricia had been killed, two weeks ago tonight. Did she know the person who'd ruthlessly snuffed out her life?

Had the crime scene been released? Had someone cleaned? This information was now on the other side of a Chinese wall, but there was no discernible bloodstain on the hardwood floor or the sandy-toned area rug, and no signs of forensics processing the scene. You would never know this serene suite was a crime scene. It was spotless, and the chemical smell was stronger in the bedroom—it had to've been cleaned.

I began combing through it step-by-step. Searching through someone's personal belongings feels like a violation. It's also quite tedious.

I started with the small bedside chest on the left. You'd be surprised what you might find in some people's bedside drawers. In Patricia's case, the top drawer was for charging electronics—hers, of course, having been removed by the police leaving just the cords. The middle drawer held an assortment of the usual things: hand cream, nasal spray, eyedrops, a book (she was reading *Lessons in Chemistry*, by Bonnie Garmus) reading glasses, et cetera. The bottom drawer was empty. Is this where she'd kept the gun that had been used against her and planted in Bridget's car?

I moved to the other side of the king-sized bed, with its layered fluffy bedding in tones of cream, sand, and pale blue. The right bedside chest also had wires in the charging drawer. Had she never removed her husband's charging cords?

I pulled open the second drawer and found a current issue of *Men's Health*, a Lee Child paperback that Cash had also read, and I knew was more recent than Chalmers

Gaillard's death, reading glasses, three cough drops, a pair of heavy, yellow gold Cartier cuff links, and a small pill box. I slid the pill box open and found a half dozen little red pills with flames on them. My Rx app identified them as a combination drug made up of Viagra and Cialis.

Patricia Gaillard had clearly been keeping company with *someone*.

Up until that point in the investigation, no one had suggested Patricia had a significant other—not since her husband passed away in December of 2021. Scarlett had specifically denied it. Maybe she simply didn't know.

Whose things were these?

I took a photo of the drawer's contents, then closed the pill box.

Inside the bottom drawer was a small fingerprint controlled gun safe. There must've been a matching setup on Patricia's side of the bed. Cash's working theory of the crime was that Patricia heard the intruder—Bridget, in his misguided opinion—and took her gun out of the safe only to have it taken away and used against her.

And I'd bet good money he considered the bruises on Bridget's arm evidence of that struggle.

I flattened myself on the floor and checked under the bed. Nothing there. I checked between the mattress and box springs, and felt around the inside of the bed frame. Again, nothing. I stood and turned slowly around, perusing the room. It was small as primary bedrooms went. The only other furniture in the room was a small chair.

I moved on to the large walk-in closet, which had one of the systems with built-in shelves, drawers, and racks. In addition to Patricia's extensive, tasteful wardrobe, there was quite the collection of lingerie—the kind designed more for show than comfort. Her dressing table occupied most of the back wall, with floor-to-ceiling mirrored accessory cabinets to the left and right. But there were no men's clothing at all.

As I meandered into the bathroom, I remembered what Scarlett had said about the remodeling. It appeared the construction company had finished. This bathroom was crisp and elegant, with a glass-enclosed walk-in shower, an oversized freestanding tub, a sleek white double vanity with a wide mirror that reached the ceiling, and white tile with mosaic accents in shades of grey. Had Patricia even gotten to enjoy one bath in her new tub? Her medicine cabinet held the typical over-the-counter remedies along with two prescription drug bottles, both in her name, one for blood pressure and one for acid reflux.

I'd finished in the master suite and moved on to one of the guest rooms when Liz climbed the stairs.

"Nothing remotely of interest downstairs," said Liz. "But Bridget is an excellent housekeeper."

"Agreed. I haven't seen a single dust bunny. Does it seem strange to you how quickly this crime scene was released? Someone other than Bridget, obviously, has cleaned since Patricia was killed. This place is immaculate."

"Seems quick to me too."

"I'm down to these two guest rooms." I told her about Patricia's apparent overnight guest and the UPS receipt. "The funny thing is, Scarlett must've sent that package. If she knew what was in it, and surely she did, it seems like she would've mentioned that when I asked her about Bridget's ex-husband."

"Maybe her spirit guide advised against it."

"Yeah, maybe."

"I'll check the room next door."

"Don't shoot anything."

I didn't look but felt her roll her eyes at me.

The guest room closest to the primary suite was pretty basic: a queen-size bed, flanked by round tables with no drawers, a chest, and a storage bench. The closet held only a dozen empty hangers, and the chest was empty, but the storage bench held stacks of albums, boxes of photos, and other mementos—greeting cards, handwritten notes, play programs, and the like.

I pulled the top album out of the stack and sat on the floor to flip through it. It was possible a clue was hidden somewhere in these memories, but it would take days to look at them all. I'd scanned several volumes, Patricia's life passing before my eyes, when I reached her high school years.

She was a graceful, willowy teenager. I scanned a few pages of beach days, boat days, and barbecues. A few photos around holidays had both Patricia and

Corinne. If memory served from my profile work, Corinne was five years older than Patricia. She was likely in college at this point.

Who was the wiry young man who appeared with Patricia in so many of the photos?

He was tanned and fit—not classically handsome, but attractive, and he exuded confidence. There was something familiar about him. His eyes...

As interesting as Patricia's high school years were, the answers I needed were far more likely to be found among more recent memories—which were most likely digital. I made a note to check her iCloud Photos and put everything carefully back the way I'd found it.

From the next room, I heard knocking. When I rounded the doorway, Liz was staring at the wall.

"Find anything?"

"Not a thing," she said. "But I was thinking one of these panels might hide a secret compartment. I've knocked on and pressed against every section. If there's one here, the opening mechanism is more high-tech."

"Huh. There's this same kind of molding-trimmed panels in Patricia's office. I think I'll try in there."

Liz followed me down the hall.

"I'll start over here." I scanned the wall to the right.

Liz went to tapping on the wall to the left of the door, and we worked our way around the room. Most of the exterior walls were either windows or doors.

When I pulled back the heavy drapes to examine the wall between the two front windows, I hit pay dirt. The wall sounded different when I tapped it. I pressed the panel, a pressure latch released and the section swung open to reveal a wall safe.

"Sweet Lady Gaga." I stared at the open wall.

"Well done." Liz crossed the room and joined me in the staring. "Any ideas on the combination?"

"Not a—*wait*. Yes!" I pulled out my phone and navigated to the photos. I scrolled to the one with the alarm codes and so forth from Scarlett's desk. There'd been one code without a label. "I bet this is it. 8-3-9-1-7-4."

I keyed in the code and the lock sang out a happy tune and disengaged.

Wide-eyed and hopeful, I swung it open.

Inside lay a stack of papers, half a dozen jewelry boxes, and four stacks of cash. I snapped a picture of the contents, then eased out the documents and moved them to Patricia's desk.

Flipping through the documents, I stopped when I came to a folder from Middleton, Bull, & Vanderhorst. I flipped it open to find Patricia's will.

"Bingo."

"I'll put the rest back in the safe." Liz gathered the remaining papers.

I opened the document scanner app on my phone and started scanning. When I had the document fully loaded and saved to my iCloud folder, I started reading. And my stomach sank.

"Oh no."

"What is it?" Liz came to look over my shoulder.

"Patricia left Bridget and Scarlett each $100,000."

"Well, if she knew…"

"But the assumption will be she did, even if she says she didn't."

Liz pointed at the first paragraph. "But Corinne gets millions—and this house. Her daughters get a cool million each. And what about these charities? We should check out every one of them to see if they're in financial trouble. These gifts are not insignificant. Bridget and Scarlett are the smallest bequests."

"But still…to someone on Bridget's budget, $100,000 is an awful lot of motive."

"This doesn't change anything," said Liz. "Our job is still to find out who really did this."

"My money is still on either Mary Ellis or Scarlett. Corinne is already well off, as are her daughters…but wait a minute…" I set the will down and squinted at the safe. "Patricia clearly kept her expensive jewelry in the safe. Why would Bridget—and by that I mean of course whoever was trying to frame Bridget—take one necklace and leave six more and a stack of cash? Why would a cash-strapped single mother take a necklace that would no doubt be hard to sell and leave all that cash?"

Liz crossed to the safe and fanned through each of the stacks. "Four stacks of twenties. That's eight thousand dollars."

And that's when we heard the alarm system announce "front door open."

I stuffed the will back in the folder and laid it on

top of the documents stack in the safe. Then I swung the door closed and pressed Lock.

Liz pushed the panel shut and pulled the drapes back over it.

Someone was coming up the steps.

I motioned to the doors leading to the piazza and she nodded.

We scooted across the room.

The door creaked as Liz opened it.

I eased out the door, and she followed and pulled the door closed behind her.

We darted over to the section of wall between the sets of doors and put our backs against it.

"Any idea who that is?" Liz whispered.

"Probably Scarlett?" Maybe she'd come to clear her things out now that the crime scene had apparently been released.

I crouched low and peered around the edge of the drapes into Patricia's office.

No one there.

Staying as low as I could, I scooted down the piazza to the doors that opened into Patricia's bedroom.

A tall, bald-headed man wearing a business suit stood on the far side of the bed in front of the bedside chest with his back to me. He leaned over and appeared to be fiddling with the drawers. He put something in his jacket pocket, tucked something under his arm, then turned around and walked towards the sitting area.

Porter Barnwell.

Corinne's husband.

Those eyes.

I had a really good idea what the sisters had been arguing in the street about.

I felt more than saw Liz hovering above me.

Porter passed out of view.

I twisted around and sat on the porch and Liz eased down beside me. We waited until we heard the front door open and close, then moments later a car door close.

"I wasn't expecting that. How about you?" I asked.

"Me either, but I got a picture of him."

"That was pretty brazen. He could've seen you—seen us both."

"What was he going to do? If he called the police, he'd have to explain what the heck he was doing here."

"If he killed his sister-in-law, what would've stopped him from killing us both?"

"I guess your tactical pen and my Sig 9."

I rolled my eyes at her and pushed myself up. "I want to see what all he took."

We went back in through Patricia's office and made our way down the hall. When I pulled out the drawer, the magazine, the paperback, the cuff links and the pill box were gone.

"How did the police miss that stuff to begin with?" Liz asked. "Looks like that would've been taken as evidence."

"Somebody didn't do their job," I said. "I guess

whoever searched that drawer was thinking this was a burglary gone wrong and didn't see the significance."

"Sounds right. They already had a theory of the crime, and Patricia having a lover was probably seen as salacious and irrelevant."

"And as soon as the house was released, Porter high-tailed it over here to collect his belongings before Corinne came to go through her sister's things and pack up."

"What do you want to bet his wife gave him those cuff links?" Liz asked.

"I would not bet against it. Come here, I want to show you something else." I headed back to the guest room and pulled Patricia's teenage photo album out of the bench.

I turned to one of the closeups of Patricia with her high school sweetheart. He stood behind her, his arms wrapped possessively around her. They both smiled happily for the camera. "Look at the eyes."

Liz looked at the photo, then pulled out her phone and navigated to the photo she'd just taken of Porter Barnwell.

"The hair throws you off. But that's definitely him," she said.

"I'd like to amend my bet in light of new evidence," I said. "Corinne is my new favorite, with Porter a close second. But I still don't think we can rule out Scarlett or Mary Ellis."

Now I was the one saying "we."

I'd had no idea how much I would like working

with a partner until I'd had one two days in a row. Granted, Sarabeth hadn't been so much a partner as an observer. And I did wish Liz had left her gun in the car. But still, it was nice to have someone to bounce things off of...nice not being alone when things went sideways.

I slid the photo out of the album and into my purse.

Chapter Fifteen

Liz would've loved to've come with me to interview Corinne Barnwell, but she had meetings that afternoon she couldn't get out of. As I left the Charleston peninsula, my head was spinning, both from what we'd found at Patricia's house, and from the discovery of my lookalike. I couldn't get the image of my mother out of my head. The way her lip had quivered when she said, "I'm so sorry. Please forgive me." My gut insisted this had something to do with Poppy Talbot. Or maybe I'd lost my mind.

I forced myself to set my personal crisis aside and focus on my upcoming interview with Corinne—as soon as I had sustenance. Was it the stress making me so unusually ravenous? Corinne and Porter Barnwell lived on Sullivan's Island, which made it convenient for me to pop home for some lunch.

Staring into the refrigerator, it occurred to me how

much easier lunchtime was for omnivores. They could just make a quick sandwich from some sliced turkey or whatever. I had to wash and chop vegetables and whip up a batch of homemade hummus—store brands used added oil—to make my veggie sandwich. Eating a whole food plant-based diet was time consuming.

As soon as the hummus was ready, I pulled out some baked pita chips and carrots, slid onto a stool at the island, and dug in. I'd have to work in some more veggies later. There was no time for all the washing, peeling, slicing, and chopping.

Thirty minutes later I'd finished lunch, freshened up, and was on my way to the Barnwells' house, which was almost to the other end of Sullivan's Island, near Station 10. As Jolene and I rolled down Middle Street, I reflected on why Corinne had agreed to speak with me at all. It was curious. She was under no obligation, of course. I'd expected her to be "unavailable." From her perspective, the police had arrested her sister's killer. Unless of course she knew they'd arrested the wrong person.

As I pulled into the pebble-covered driveway, I wondered if Corinne was simply a grieving sister who had no idea her sister had betrayed her, or if she was a cold-blooded killer who was playing with me to see what I might know or suspect.

I climbed the steep steps to her raised two-story beach house to find her on the wide wrap-around porch in a padded chaise lounge. With her pale creamy skin and delicate features, she resembled Patricia, but

Corinne's hairstyle was short and fluffy and advertised an expensive salon blowout. In every photo I'd seen of Patricia, her hair was long and straight. Corinne's orange silk outfit was from someone's luxury resort wear line, her chunky gold necklace and earrings a tad dressy for porch sitting. I counted four rings on her hands.

"Good afternoon," she said. "You must be Hadley Cooper." Her honeyed drawl sounded like old Charleston money.

"I am. Mrs. Barnwell?"

"It's Corinne, please. Have a seat." She gestured to the lounge chair on the other side of a small table holding a tray with two glasses of iced tea. "I hope you don't mind speaking out here. It's nice today. And indoors, my two goldendoodles will be all over you. They're quite friendly."

"This is fine." Were there other reasons she didn't want me inside her house? Was this an excuse to wear large, dark sunglasses while we spoke? This made reading her reactions to my questions much more difficult. I left my sunglasses on to keep us on an even footing.

"The tea is unsweetened. I hope that's all right."

"That's my preference, actually."

She picked up her glass and made a little toasting gesture. "You're a private investigator? How very progressive. Tell me, what can I help you with?"

"As I mentioned on the phone, I've been hired to look into your sister's death."

"As I understand it, the maid killed Patricia." Her

voice sounded quite cold to my ear. We were discussing her sister, after all.

"Have you ever met Bridget?" I knew the answer to this question, of course.

"I have. She seems like a nice young woman. But regrettably, circumstances sometimes cause people to act out of character."

"That is *so true*." I gave her a sympathetic smile. "And I am just so sorry to bring up unpleasant memories, but would you tell me what you and Patricia were arguing about the afternoon before she was killed? In front of her house?"

Corinne's smile froze into a brittle little thing. "Someone has given you bad information, I'm afraid."

"Sadly not. I've seen the video from the neighbor's security camera. If you'd like, I can turn it over to the police, and they can come ask you about it." I kept my smile and my voice sweet, and shrugged, like *it's your call*.

She hesitated, likely weighing if the police would be interested, given that they'd already made an arrest. "It has nothing whatsoever to do with Patricia's death. It's private. Irrelevant. Something between sisters."

"All the more reason you might not want to discuss it with a SLED agent..." who I would absolutely tell straightaway should this line of questioning prove to be relevant after all.

Corinne sighed deeply. "Very well. Patricia and I had lunch together at Chez Nous. It is our habit to have lunch on Thursdays. Over lunch, I said something careless...something that brought up an old hurt. We quarreled. And yes, we took our quarrel into the street, like common rabble. I'm not proud of it and neither was she. There. Are you happy?"

Not quite. I slid the photo out of my purse and held it up for her to see. "Is this what that old hurt was all about?"

Her voice dropped to a stage whisper. "Where did you get that picture?"

"You'd be amazed what you can find online these days." I certainly wasn't about to tell her the truth.

Her face creased in confusion.

"You didn't answer my question," I said. "Were you and Patricia arguing over Porter?"

She seemed to be calculating whether it was in her best interest to answer or not. Her shoulders squared. "Fine. All right. Yes. Patricia dated Porter in high school—eons ago. He was already in college—he's four years older. She was smitten. But then she went to school in Nashville. Porter and I had graduated college and come back to Charleston. Patricia didn't come home much her freshman year. Porter was focused on his job at his father's shipping company. They decided to take a break. Porter and I kept running into each other at events and so forth. Charleston is a small town in a lot of ways. One thing led to another. I believed Patricia was over Porter—that she'd moved on.

"Porter and I eloped the spring of Patricia's junior year. I don't think she ever really forgave me for that. She said I should've known he was her one true love. It was all quite dramatic. She married Chalmers Gaillard as soon as she graduated. He was ten years her senior and desperately in love with her.

"At lunch that day, I said I thought things had worked out for the best for all of us—that she'd had a happy life with Chalmers. He positively doted on her. That was the wrong thing to say. I should've let that bit of history lie. I thought we were all past it. Apparently not.

"But the salient point here is that I did *not* kill my sister because she got angry at me over a thoughtless comment. For goodness' sake."

Once I asked her about the affair, the interview would be over. I had a couple of other points to cover first. "Thank you for sharing that with me. I'm terribly sorry to have to ask about it. I understand the house on Logan is your family home."

"That's right. It's been in our family for generations."

"I imagine Patricia left the house to you?"

"Well certainly she did."

"I could recommend a company to help you with setting things to rights when the police are finished… it's never easy after something violent happens in a home…"

"Thank you, but that won't be necessary. I was worried we'd need paperwork or some such thing from the house, and I just couldn't face seeing it… seeing everything the way it was the night Patricia died. It was just too horrible. I asked Porter to have it taken care of, and he did. Porter insisted they allow us to have it cleaned at the earliest possible moment. Between you and me, he went over a few heads on that one. Porter is a personal friend of the police chief. A top-notch cleaning crew came in just yesterday."

No doubt Porter was as eager to have it done as Corinne. I could've told her they did a great job but probably didn't use environmentally friendly products. The house would need a good airing to get rid of that chemical smell.

"I have one more question, strictly as a formality—so I can check the box. Where were you the evening Patricia was killed?"

"I was right here. In my bed. As was Porter. You can ask him. Now if you will excuse me—"

I smiled and slid my feet off the lounger, like I was leaving. "Oh...just one more question."

"I've answered all the—"

I held up my phone. "Do you recognize anything in this photo?"

She stared at the phone, curiosity outweighing her desire for me to be gone. "As a matter of fact, I do. I paid nearly four thousand dollars for those cuff links for our twenty-fifth wedding anniversary. They're Cartier, solid gold. Porter lost them a month ago. That's his pillbox as well. Where exactly did you get that picture? Where are they?"

I truly did not want to do this. I had no desire to hurt her. I kept my voice gentle. "This picture was taken at the crime scene—Patricia's bedroom. It's the contents of the bedside table drawer."

"*How dare you?*" Her face paled, her hand clutched her chest.

I wished I could've seen her eyes to be certain, but she surely looked shocked.

"Did you know Porter was having an affair with Patricia?"

"*Get off my porch this instant.*"

I left my card on the table and obliged her.

Driving home I turned it over in my head. My gut said Corinne didn't know about the affair, ergo, she had no known motive to kill her sister.

And what a screwed up relationship these sisters had. I couldn't shake the image of Corinne's face when she talked about Patricia...the ice in Corinne's voice. And it was odd...Corinne was the one who'd betrayed her sister so badly all those years ago, and yet she seemed resentful of Patricia. Had Corinne always felt like Patricia was Porter's first choice? Had Corinne been playing second fiddle to her sister all these years? Had Porter let her know she was a consolation prize? That would surely be hard.

Corinne came off as brittle...as if decades of resentment were layered over what had probably once been love. Was that what happened to sisters who let secrets fester? I thought about the woman in Liz's photograph, the one who looked so much like me. What would it have been like to have a sister to share everything with? To be there to hold my hand when

Momma got sick...? A sister should be a built in best friend, not a romantic rival. How had these sisters gotten so off track? I couldn't imagine ending up like Corinne and Patricia. Did either of them really know where Porter's true allegiance lay?

Porter...

Porter had a potential motive, if Patricia had threatened to tell her sister...maybe after all these years she was pressuring Porter to choose her. A divorce would mean giving half his assets to Corinne, the mother of his children and wife of twenty-eight years.

But Corinne had just confidently cited him as her alibi, which in turn alibied him. Would she retract that after further consideration? Either way, he certainly had the resources to hire someone to do his dirty work if he wanted to.

As did she.

Chapter Sixteen

I took my time getting ready for dinner with Cash. We ate a lot of takeout, but it wasn't often we took the time to have a date night in a nice restaurant. He'd made an effort to have a special night, and I'd canceled last minute. I wanted to make it up to him.

When I first moved into my house, I couldn't use my bathtub—it completely freaked me out. The tub is gorgeous—one of the deep oval freestanding kind? But it sits in front of a huge floor-to-ceiling window that has a view of my front yard. It took a while for me to trust that the window is made with a special finish that allows me to see outside, but no one can see in. It helps that there's a huge live oak tree in front of it, but still.

I tried to soak the stress out of me, then did all the primping things before sliding into the little black dress I'd bought just last week for the occasion. Sleeveless, with a V-neck and fitted waist, its swing-style skirt hit a couple of inches above the knee. It was the kind of designer dress I'd never in a million years splurge on except at my favorite consignment store, where I got it for a steal. I spritzed citrusy perfume on my wrists and dotted it behind my ears, then carried my black purse and strappy black sandals downstairs.

Cash rang the bell at 5:15.

When I opened the door, I think I gasped a little, he looked so handsome standing there in his grey plaid blazer, crisp slate shirt, and dove grey slacks. I stared at him for an impolite amount of time, then realized he was staring too.

Our eyes locked for a long moment.

"You look amazing," he said.

I felt myself blush. "So do you."

He escorted me to the back seat of an Uber, opened my door, and helped me inside, then walked around and climbed in the other door. We may or may not both drink that evening, but this way, it wasn't an issue for either of us.

Having a perfect stranger in the driver's seat doesn't exactly encourage intimate conversation, but beyond that, we were suddenly shy with each other and didn't talk much on the way into Charleston. But there was an electric charge zapping around the car. We grinned at each other a lot.

As we climbed the Cooper River Bridge, I gazed out the window at Charleston, shimmering across the water in the late afternoon light, thinking how fortunate I was to live in this magical place. How blessed I was to have this kind, handsome, upright man holding my hand. I turned to smile at Cash to find him watching me. Something unreadable flickered in his eyes.

I tilted my head at him with a look that asked *what's up?*

He just smiled and squeezed my hand, then turned to take in the view from his window.

Maybe that was the moment I started suspecting he had something serious on his mind.

From the outside, you might not guess Maison is a chic French bistro. It's in a purpley-blue building on upper King Street—maybe a little further up than some folks think of as "Upper King," actually. We walked across the patio, with the mural of the Eiffel Tower, and then through the door, where a hostess greeted us. We followed her down a narrow alley between the grey marble bar and a row of caramel-toned leather booths lining the front wall, to a corner café table with rattan bistro chairs. It was cozy and tucked just enough out of the way to feel intimate. Aside from the booths and the stained wood tabletops, most everything in the restaurant was in shades of grey or black and white, from the chair coverings, to the floor tile, to the large framed black-and-white photographs that graced the walls.

A waiter introduced himself and left us with menus to consider and thick blue glasses filled with water. The hum of conversation, the clink of cutlery, and faint notes of music floating through the air provided a background soundtrack that was perfect for quiet conversation.

"Do you feel like a cocktail?" asked Cash.

"That sounds lovely." I perused the cocktail menu.

When the waiter came back, I ordered the L'ouvrier—a mezcal concoction—and Cash the Parisian Negroni. We studied the menu, chatted about food—I was taking the evening off diet-wise and would not fret at all over the ingredients—and by the time our cocktails arrived, we were ready to order.

When the waiter stepped away, Cash raised his glass. "To the loveliest woman I've ever seen."

I blushed again. "You're very kind," I murmured. "Thank you."

"Kindness has nothing to do with it. I'm an objective observer."

Earlier in the day, I'd worried it would be hard to stay in the moment, given the tension over the case and everything else I had on my mind. But the evening was nothing short of magical. We chatted about the upcoming Blessing of the Fleet, what dish to take to supper club, a Boz Scaggs concert at Charleston Music Hall we were looking forward to, and how we need to do this more often.

Our appetizers arrived—the Onion Soup Croquette and the mushroom leek ravioli—along with glasses of a rich, smooth red blend. Both the small plates were divine. We continued the light-hearted chit-chat, neither of us wanting to venture into heavier topics. We had so needed this kind of evening, and we were both relaxed and carefree.

When our entrees were delivered—Steak Frites for Cash and the Flounder Grenobloise with Carolina gold rice for me—we each sampled our own, then shared a bite. Okay, I didn't have a bite of Cash's steak, but I did have one of the frites dipped in béarnaise aioli, which was delicious. We were devouring our food, chattering away, and having such a good time, when, mid laugh, I looked up and saw the hostess leading two couples to one of the booths.

My smile froze and my eyes bulged.

It was Corinne and Porter Barnwell with a couple I didn't know.

A bolt of lightning seared me to the spot.

Good grief Charleston was a small town.

And weren't those two grieving?

I took a deep breath and gulped my wine.

"Everything all right?" Cash asked.

I tried to form words.

"Hadley?" He followed my gaze.

The Barnwells had spotted us. They whispered to each other.

Why? Of all the restaurants in Charleston...they'd

burst the bubble we'd been floating in all evening. And things had been going so perfectly.

Porter Barnwell stood and walked in our direction.

Oh my stars. Surely I was not going to be in the middle of another scene at a high end Charleston restaurant. I would be banned. Banned from all nice restaurants in the county. My picture would be behind the bars and at the hostess stands with signs that said "Do not seat or serve."

"Cash—" I said.

"I'll handle this." He stood.

Porter stepped in close.

"Mr. Barnwell," Cash said, like *fancy seeing you here.*

"Agent Reynolds," Porter ground out like he was Cash's superior officer or something.

Of course Cash had interviewed the Barnwells at some point over the last two weeks.

Porter's voice was low enough that no one else could hear him. "I'm at a loss, I confess. I don't know your companion's name. But what I do know is that you have engaged in a disgraceful breach of protocol and likely broken the law."

"I beg your pardon?" Cash's face screwed up into an incredulous expression. "I don't have a clue what you're talking about. Regardless, this is not the time or the place for this discussion. If you'd like to speak with me, call and make an appointment."

"You sent your girlfriend *to my home* to harass my wife, who is grieving the loss of her sister."

"I did no such thing."

"I have no need to speak with *you* further on the matter. I will take this up with your superiors. First thing tomorrow morning." He glared at me, turned on his heel, and stalked back to their booth.

Cash sat and downed his water.

Corinne said something to Porter, and he nodded, then helped her out of the booth. The couple with them followed as they hustled out of the restaurant.

I glanced around the room. Thankfully, it seemed no one else was aware there'd nearly been a scene.

"Cash, I—"

"Wait. Please. Let me think about this for a minute."

After a minute, he said. "Okay. I'm guessing you interviewed Corinne Barnwell. A natural step to take. She's the victim's sister." He shrugged and made a face like, *no big deal*.

"This afternoon." I nodded. "I upset her, I'm afraid. I know we have a Chinese wall, but given what just happened, you might want to know what that was all about. I gather seeing us together made them think you were somehow behind that. I'm so sorry."

Cash massaged his left eyebrow. "Okay. All right. I guess you'd better tell me."

"I uncovered evidence that Porter was having an affair with Patricia."

"*What*? What evidence?"

"You don't want to know what the evidence is, because then I'd have to tell you how I came by it.

You're better off not knowing that. You have plausible deniability. Porter and Patricia actually dated when Patricia was in high school. They rekindled their romance sometime...okay, I don't know when it started, or how long it's been going on, but it was going on at the time of Patricia's death."

"You're absolutely certain of this?"

"Yes. And I showed Corinne proof today. She's the one who told me about their earlier romance. Reading through the lines of her self-serving version, I suspect that Corinne basically wooed Porter while Patricia was away at school. The sisters had a big fight over it the day before Patricia was killed."

"Wait...did Corinne know about the affair?"

"I don't think so. She seemed shocked."

Now Cash rubbed both his eyebrows. "Porter Barnwell's sordid affair aside, he and Corinne alibi each other, Hadley."

"That may be the case, but spousal alibis are not all that reliable. And either of them certainly have the resources to hire someone to take care of their dirty work."

"Look, I don't want to debate alternate theories of the crime with you. And you shouldn't want to either. Because at some point, you and I are going to be witnesses in a courtroom, on opposite sides of this case. And those alternate theories are very likely going to be presented to a jury. You don't want to be telling me in advance what they are. That's not in your client's best interest."

"I know. I just...I'm hoping to prove one of them before it ever gets that far. Don't you think he reacted like a man with a guilty conscience?"

"Can we just try to rewind to before that jerk came over here? Let's enjoy our dinner, okay?"

"Okay." I nodded, knowing that would be impossible. Had I caused so much trouble for Cash he was going to be fired? This looked really bad. Would he be able to explain? Would anyone want to listen?

We picked over our entrees until finally we both gave up and the waiter cleared our plates. The mood of the evening was ruined.

I excused myself to go to the ladies' room, and when I was on my way back, one of the waitstaff was standing by our table with a bucket of champagne. Cash was talking to him, and the waiter was nodding. Then he tilted his head, and said something that looked like, *I'm so sorry, sir.* Then he whisked the champagne away.

I slowed my step.

Had Cash preordered that champagne?

He stood as I approached the table. "Would you like anything else?"

"No, thank you. I'm starting to get a tension headache. I think we'd better go."

What sort of celebration did Porter Barnwell ruin?

Did Cash want to celebrate some sort of everyday good news—a personal best time on his morning run? an atta boy at work? a winning scratch-off ticket?

...or was this meant to be a big night for us?

I heard Gavin's voice in my head saying, "After a couple a years of smooth sailing, you and Cash might be thinking about the future a bit."

Oh no.

Was that just Gavin's wishful thinking, or did he know something I didn't?

Chapter Seventeen

I barely slept at all Thursday night, tossing and turning and twisting my sheets up so badly the cats didn't even try to get in bed with me. My mind kept whirling between Cash being in jeopardy of losing his job—and it being all my fault—Cash and the aborted champagne celebration, my mother apologizing for something that brought her to tears *right before* I discovered I had a doppelgänger, and poor Bridget, who was depending on me to stay focused and deserved better than what she was getting from me.

Finally, at four a.m., I gave up trying to sleep, got dressed, and left early for my morning bike ride. I flew along my usual route, pedaling hard as I hashed out my game plan for the day.

As I watched the sunrise over Breach Inlet, I kept hoping my mother would show up so I could ask her a few questions—mostly just the one. There was no sign of her, of course, because the whole thing was a figment of my fevered imagination.

I took my morning smoothie, my coffee, and an extra thermal French press and mug outside to the pool deck in hopes North would join me. He sometimes had a sixth sense about when I needed him. I closed my eyes and let the music of the surf wash over me, my body relaxing in sync with the crash and retreat of the waves.

I may have been in a trance when North called out, "Good morning."

I opened my eyes to find him crossing the terrace from the direction of the dunes, hair tousled, bare feet sandy, and looking relaxed and cheerful. Living at the beach was good for him. I sent up a prayer of thanks.

"You have breakfast?" I asked him.

"I grabbed a protein bar and a banana before my morning walk."

"Want some coffee?" I nodded towards the French press like a drug dealer offering the good stuff.

"Thanks." He poured himself a cup and settled into a lounger beside me. "How's your case going?"

I shook my head. "Too many plausible scenarios and not enough evidence. Also, my insistence on taking this case may cost Cash his job." I told him what had happened the night before.

"That was just abysmally bad luck," said North. "Running into the Barnwells when the two of you were together? Figure the odds…"

"You know I don't believe in coincidences. It's all part of a pattern."

"What do you mean? You think the Barnwells were tailing *you*?"

"No—" I squinted at him. "Well, maybe. Based on what I know of them so far, I wouldn't put it past either of them. But what I meant was that it feels like someone or *something*...some force in the universe...is conspiring to keep Cash and me apart."

"Hmm...how can I help?"

"Help me close this case. Did you find anything on the brown Subaru?"

He nodded. "About that—"

"You *did* find something?" So much hope rose in my chest. I could seriously use a break in this case.

"Yes and no. That particular Subaru does *not* belong to one of Patricia's neighbors. There *is* a neighbor who drives a very similar car, but their car is a fancier model—the "Touring" version—there's a plate on the back of that trim package that's missing from the image you got off the security video. *That* Subaru is the "Limited" model. Only the Limited and the Touring models come in "brilliant bronze metallic," which is Subaru speak for brown."

"So who does the one parked in front of Josephine Huger's house belong to?"

"No way to know," said North. "The plate must've been switched. It's definitely a South Carolina tag. It has the blue bar at the bottom, and you can see the 'NA' in the video. But there is no Subaru Forester registered in the state of South Carolina with the last two plate digits 'PX.'"

"Well that's plenty fishy. That car left at 11:15 p.m., right in the window of when Patricia was killed, and it had a stolen plate? Would you crosscheck everyone on my case board with the list of owners of brilliant bronze metallic Subarus in South Carolina?"

"Sure thing."

"I'll stop by my office and take a picture and text it to you."

I flew through my morning routine, showering and slathering lotion on my arms and legs, then topping it with a layer of sunscreen before slipping into a blue-and-white-striped sundress and a pair of flat sandals. At my dressing table, I applied the face serums and creams I hoped would keep the wrinkles at bay, followed by a bit of tinted sunscreen, a few swipes of mascara, and some lip gloss. I was ready for whatever the day might bring. I hoped.

As soon as the clock struck 8:00 a.m., I called Scarlett and asked her if I could drop by for a few followup questions. She seemed *really* eager, which did not bode well. What new and even more outlandish theories did she have to share?

I fed the kitties, changed their water, and had a talk with them about keeping an eye on things. They were feeling chatty that morning, and seemed to imply they'd expect treats in return for their guard-cat services. I'd need to pick up another bag of those treats if their people didn't show up soon. How else could I try to reach them? These fine kitties had to belong to someone on Sullivan's Island, right? Their little legs were pretty short. Surely they couldn't've wandered far from home. I petted them goodbye and headed down the steps into the garage.

The forecast for the day was mild, with a high around seventy-two. It was shaping up to be a perfect day for a convertible in Charleston. I climbed into Jolene, started the engine, and pressed the switches to put the top down and open the garage door. We rolled into the shady front drive.

Ninety-nine times out of a hundred, I turn left out of the driveway. But that particular morning, as I waited for the automatic gate to open, I noticed a truck with a load of building materials was taking up most of Marshall Boulevard to my left, so I turned right out of the driveway, went down to Station 29 Street, and made a left. That's where I ran into Sarabeth on her bike.

She stopped, stepped down off the seat, and waved with both hands. "Hey," she called. A broad smile lit her face.

I cringed a little bit inside. I loved my friend a lot. But I had very mixed emotions about her coming with me to work. I pulled to a stop. "I thought you and Norah were walking in the mornings."

"Oh, we walked earlier. I just popped down to remind the Johnsons' cute little house sitter that trash cans don't go out to the curb on Fridays until after Memorial Day. I noticed he'd rolled it out, but it was too early to knock on the door."

"Where are the Johnsons?" I asked.

"There is no telling. They're on a six-month trip around the world. I thought you knew."

I shrugged. "I don't really know them that well."

"I know them from church," said Sarabeth. "I promised her I'd keep an eye on things. I think she found this house sitter through some sort of online service. She was kinda nervous about it. But he's as cute as he can be and sweet as sugar."

"That's good. Well—"

"Where are you off to?" she asked in an eager voice.

"I've got some followup interviews to do with Scarlett, Patricia's secretary, and then Bridget." I waited, feeling in my heart how much Sarabeth wanted to climb in the car.

"Dangit. I wish I could come along," she said. "I've got an appointment with a landscaper this morning. Tucker wants a quote on redoing the front beds. Our bushes are probably the original ones planted after the house was built, and they're scraggly."

"Well, this will probably be boring anyway," I told her.

"Maybe tomorrow?" She looked hopeful.

"I'll know what I'm doing tomorrow after I see how today goes."

"Well, let me know."

"I will. *Hey*...do the Johnsons have cats?" Maybe that was why I hadn't heard from the kitties' family—they were out of town. A house sitter wouldn't be plugged in to the island forums...

"No, they had a German shepherd but they lost him last year. Laura said they decided against getting another dog because they wanted to travel a lot over the next few years and it wouldn't be fair to a pet. Oh... I see...no. The two lost kitties don't live at the Johnsons' house."

"Ah, well...see you later."

I waved goodbye and rolled down the street. The Johnsons' house occupied the corner of Station 29 and Brownell. Their trash can was still out, clear as day.

In the interests of trying to eliminate one of my potential suspects from the list, on the way across Ben Sawyer Bridge, I called Uma Jennings. I just couldn't believe Mary Ellis Donovan would've killed Patricia as long as she thought there was any chance she might help Arlo. I was hoping Uma could shed some light on where all that stood. That said, I was surprised when she answered the call.

"Good morning, Ms. Jennings, my name is Hadley Cooper. Thank you for taking my call. I'm investigating Patricia Gaillard's murder. Would this be a convenient time for me to ask you a few questions?"

"It's Uma, please. Poor Patricia. I still can't believe this is real. I was under the impression there'd been an arrest..."

"There has, yes. But we still need to dot all the i's. I've been hired to investigate."

"You're a PI?"

"That's right."

"So you're working for the defense?"

"I'm just working to find the truth, ma'am. I'd like to find out for sure who killed your friend. I believe Bridget Donovan was framed."

She seemed to consider that for a moment. "What did you want to ask? I don't know what I can tell you, really. I hadn't seen Patricia since February, when we went to Naples for a girls' weekend."

"She recently sent you a package, didn't she?"

"Well, yeah…back in early March. It was just a pound cake—Trevor adores Patricia's lemon blueberry pound cake—and a flash drive with an album she wanted him to listen to. As a matter of fact, it was her cleaning lady's husband's. I remember her saying that now."

"Ex-husband, actually." Lemon blueberry pound cake, *yummy*. My favorite. Gavin made a vegan version with "cream cheese" frosting every year for my pre-birthday.

"Anyway, Trevor said the young man had a decent enough voice, but there was nothing compelling that made him stand out. He didn't light a fire under Trevor to sign him, and really, that's what it takes. You have no idea how competitive the music industry is."

"I can imagine. Did you tell Patricia that?"

"I did. Seems like it was a couple of days before she

was killed. Surely you don't think this had anything to do with it? I can't imagine..."

"I'm just checking boxes. It's probably not connected."

"*Surely* no one would kill the messenger over a thing like that...I mean, if Patricia told her cleaning lady her husband wasn't star material...I would hate to think Trevor's *opinio*n got Patricia *killed*."

"It was actually the mother, not the ex-wife, who gave Patricia that flash drive," I said. "Do you know of anything or anyone that troubled Patricia recently, any issues at all?"

"Not that she mentioned to me."

"Do you know if she was seeing anyone...romantically?"

"Patricia hasn't shown any interest in a man since Chalmers passed."

I supposed that much was true. Patricia was keeping her "interest" in her sister's husband as quiet as possible, as one would.

Scarlett met me at the door and led me back to her cream-colored sofas. I sat in the same spot I'd occupied on Monday and hoped for minimal crazy.

"Have you figured out who killed Patricia?" She leaned towards me and spoke in a conspiratorial tone.

"Not yet. I've been trying to reach your friend."

She squinted at me like she was bewildered.

"The gentleman you entertained the evening Patricia was killed."

"Oh. Brett. Really? You haven't been able to get ahold of him? Well, let *me* try." She swiped and tapped and put her phone up to her ear. After a minute she lowered the phone. "He must not have voice mail set up. I'm sure it's just an oversight. When he calls me, I'll ask him to call you."

"How long have you known Brett?"

"We only just met. At a bookstore, actually. We were both browsing the cookbook section. We ended up going for coffee and we just hit it off."

"And when was this?"

"That same evening. The evening Patricia was killed."

"Have you heard from him since then?"

"Well, no…but it's only been two weeks ago yesterday. I'm sure he's busy with work."

"What did you say he did?"

"I don't think I mentioned it. His job is highly confidential."

Poor Scarlett… If she hadn't heard from Brett in two weeks, it seemed unlikely she ever would. His "highly confidential" career sounded suspiciously like some sort of pickup line. "Right. When you hear from him, please let him know I need to speak with him."

"Of course. I'm sure I'll hear from him soon. We really hit it off. He's a cat lover just like me—Huckleberry ate right out of his hand if you can believe that.

And you know, Brett was *very* interested in Kootálá—in connecting with *his* spirit guide."

Somehow I doubted that. "So, I do have a few more questions...were you aware that you are a beneficiary of Patricia's will?"

"*Whaaat*?" She drew back her chin, looking genuinely shocked.

"I'll take that as a 'no.' She left you and Bridget each a hundred thousand dollars."

"Well, what do you know about that? I had no idea," said Scarlett. "And I'd bet money Bridget didn't either."

"I'm sure Patricia's executor will be in touch." I gave her a look that I hoped communicated *this next part is serious business*. "Did you know Patricia was having an affair with her sister Corinne's husband?"

Scarlett took a deep breath, stared at the ceiling for a moment, and rubbed her lips together. "I would never have told you that in a million years. As I said, I signed an NDA. But since you've found out, I will confirm it."

"How long had that been going on?"

"I don't really know. I found out about it around Valentine's Day. Porter had a fancy meal delivered to Patricia's house on the thirteenth. I guess he celebrated with his wife on the actual day. Anyway, the delivery person was early—apparently, she was swamped with meals for the next day as well and got an early start. I was on my way out around five fifteen, and I answered the door. Apparently, Porter planned to be there by six, which is when the food was supposed to arrive.

"It was very clear it was a romantic dinner for two—chocolate dipped strawberries and the whole nine yards—*and* his name was on the paperwork. Patricia was upstairs in her bathroom getting ready. I put the perishables away and left. The next day, Patricia swore me to secrecy, and reminded me of the nondisclosure agreement I'd signed. She was very upset."

"Do you think Corinne ever found out?"

"No." Scarlett shook her head. "There would've been *big* fireworks."

"Were you in the house the afternoon of March 23, when Patricia and Corinne came back from lunch?"

"I was. Corinne followed Patricia inside. They were arguing about something Corinne had said at lunch, something Patricia took the wrong way. She was upset. I didn't hear the whole thing, but Patricia made some comment about how sisters were always able to hurt you the worst. But I guarantee you Corinne did not know about the affair. The last big argument they had—it was years ago—some offhand comment Chalmers made at dinner offended Corinne and turned into a big hullabaloo between the sisters—Corinne threw an expensive artsy vase and shattered it all over the kitchen floor."

"Corinne has a temper."

"Yes she does. If she'd known about the affair… there would've been damages."

"So she didn't *know*, but maybe she suspected?"

"That's possible, of course. It's also possible she suspected Porter was having an affair but never dreamed it was with Patricia."

"I wonder if that 'insensitive comment' she made was her attempt to bait Patricia…see how she would respond?"

"That could be, I suppose."

"Tell me about the diamond necklace that was stolen and planted in Bridget's car…"

"It's a Cartier diamond and platinum necklace… the kind with diamonds that go all the way around, like a tennis bracelet for your neck? It has sixty-four oval-cut diamonds. The total carat weight is more than twenty-three carats. Chalmers gave her that necklace for their twenty-fifth wedding anniversary."

"Do you know what it's worth?"

"More than $250,000. It was her nicest piece."

Good grief. How could anyone walk around with something that valuable around their neck? I'd be scared to death. "I'm thinking she kept that somewhere secure?"

"Of course. All of her expensive jewelry stayed in the safe when she wasn't wearing it."

"And where is the safe?" Better to play ignorant here.

"In Patricia's office."

"Who all has the combination?"

"Only Patricia and me," she said. "At least that's what Patricia told me."

"Do you have any theories about how the necklace came to be out of the safe on a random Thursday evening with no fancy parties on the calendar?"

Scarlett slowly shook her head. "Not a one. I know I didn't take it out, so Patricia must've, unless someone cracked the safe. Now..." She pointed at me and nodded. "...like I was telling you, ghosts can move objects. It's true. It's entirely possible one of them watched Patricia open the safe and remembered the combination. I bet they can whirl that dial with telekinesis."

Helen of Troy. "What else is in the safe?" Of course, I knew the answer to this, but I needed Scarlett to tell me, so I had a plausible explanation for knowing. Also, I needed to quickly get her off the subject of ghosts.

"Papers—her will. Her other good jewelry, maybe half a dozen pieces. A few were inherited from her mother, and the rest were gifts from Chalmers. And cash. Patricia always kept emergency cash."

"How disciplined was Patricia about keeping her expensive jewelry in the safe? If she wore a piece, did she take it off and put it away immediately, or did she sometimes leave it on her dressing table?"

Scarlett tipped her head left and right, weighing the question. "It's hard for me to say, really. She typically wore her good jewelry to black-tie affairs in the evening. Bridget might know better than me. I worked in the office mostly. She would be the one making up Patricia's bedroom the day after a gala."

"Did the police ask you to open the safe?"

"No… I'm not sure they know there is one. It didn't come up in the questions they asked me."

How was that even possible? Why would Cash not be looking for a copy of the will? Had someone volunteered one?

"Okay…last question for today…pivoting back to Bridget's husband, Arlo, and his dreams of being a country music star…" I might've been a little OCD about this package. Uma had already told me what was in it. But I had a pressing need to connect all the dots. "I asked you if Bridget had ever mentioned Arlo to Patricia, in terms of getting Uma Jennings' help, and you said you didn't think so, and that's the first you'd ever heard of Bridget's ex-husband."

"That's right. I didn't even know his name until you said it."

I showed her a photo of Mary Ellis. "Have you ever seen this woman?"

Scarlett peered carefully at the photo, squinting. "I think she volunteers with Patricia. I can't remember which charity. She came by the house one day and dropped some children's clothes off."

"Right. *That* is Arlo's mother, Mary Ellis Donovan."

"Oh…Patricia never mentioned it." Scarlett shook her head innocently. "I had no idea."

"Mary Ellis gave Patricia a flash drive to send to Uma Jennings with her son's music on it."

"This is the first I've heard about that."

I pulled the UPS receipt out of my purse. "Did you not ship this package?"

Scarlett took the receipt from me and studied it. A confused look washed over her face. "That's the UPS store I ship from. I set up an account there for Patricia. But I haven't shipped anything to Uma recently. Tuesday, March 7—let me check that date."

She swiped and tapped on her phone for a minute. "Oh. That's the week I was out sick. I had the stomach flu, and I was absolutely miserable. Patricia wanted no part of any stomach virus. She insisted I stay home the entire week. I probably could've worked Thursday and Friday."

"I gather she took the package to the UPS store herself, then?"

"That is typically my errand. I don't recall Patricia ever going herself, but I suppose she must have—unless she sent Bridget. Is this important?"

"Probably not. But I can't stand loose ends. They make me itch."

"Well, I'm curious now," said Scarlett. "I'm friendly with the folks who work there. The sweetest couple own it—Ignacio and Mariposa Garcia. Bonita Diez is the clerk who usually waits on me. I'll just call and see if she remembers Patricia coming in."

She swiped and tapped and then put the phone to her ear. After a moment she said, "Hey, Mariposa? This is Scarlett Hathaway. How are you?...I'm fine. I just had a quick question...Do you know if Bonita helped Patricia with a package back in early March? On March 7? Did she by chance—"

Scarlett's face turned white. Her hand went to her chest. "Oh…Mariposa…I'm just in shock…I don't know what to say…I'm so sorry…I wish I had known…" Her eyes filled with tears. She looked at me and shook her head.

"Please let me know if there's anything I can do." She ended the call and turned to me. "That's just so sad. Bonita was diabetic. She went into a diabetic coma and passed away a couple of weeks ago. I had no idea. I wish they would've called me. I would've gone to the service. Oh…I'm afraid I got distracted and forgot all about the reason I called to begin with."

"I'm so sorry to hear about your friend," I said. "Don't worry about the package. I'll check with Bridget. If you didn't drop it off, and neither did Bridget, it must've been Patricia. It didn't walk to the UPS store because it took a notion. I know Uma received it. She said it had pound cake in it."

"Oh, well that explains it," said Scarlett.

"It does?"

"Patricia made fabulous lemon blueberry pound cake. Trevor and Uma loved it. If Patricia baked pound cake, she would've wanted that to go out right away, while it was fresh. She wouldn't've waited until I was back. She must've dropped it off herself."

Or sent Bridget. But what had Patricia told Mary Ellis? Did Patricia share everything Uma told her about Arlo not being star material? Mary Ellis told her friend

Marcia that Patricia said Trevor Jennings had been too busy to listen to the album yet. Was Patricia trying to save Mary Ellis's feelings, or did Mary Ellis tell Marcia the version of the story she liked better?

Did Mary Ellis kill Patricia in a fit of rage and blame Bridget so she could get custody of her grandchildren?

Or...had Corinne somehow discovered the affair?

Or...had Porter been covering his tracks?

Or...was Scarlett lying? Was this Brett person a figment of her imagination just like Kootálá? She had the combination to the safe...Did she know about the $100,000? And did she have a pressing need for money? Nothing had popped on her financials, but there were a number of disasters that might not turn up right away on a credit report.

Porter, Corinne, Scarlett, Mary Ellis.

That was my ranking of my prime suspects as I drove across the T. Allen Legare Bridge over the Ashley River that morning. The song changed, and "Sharp Dressed Man," by ZZ Top played over the sound system. The image of Cash at my door the evening before popped into my head. He surely was dressed sharp...so handsome. What sort of day was he having?

I sent up a prayer that whatever trouble Porter Barnwell made for Cash would not be a threat to his career. And that he would forgive me for taking this case to begin with.

Chapter Eighteen

I drove slowly through Bridget's two-street neighborhood of low-slung, ranch-style duplexes, taking it in. Tucked behind a row of aging strip malls, fast food joints, and auto repair shops just off Ashley Phosphate Road in North Charleston, it was the kind of place where every house looked like a cousin to the next one, dressed in slightly different shades of faded brick. The grass growing in the small yards might not have a pedigree—it appeared to be a mix of some sort of wide blade variety, clover, and dandelions—but it was neatly mowed.

There were trees and streetlights and the occasional basketball goal. Each half-house unit had its own short concrete driveway and a backyard just big enough for a swing set, a sandbox, or a plastic slide that had faded from red to coral in the sun. Bridget and Imani occupied opposite ends of a modest grey brick house with black shutters. Pink, yellow, and orange zinnias sprouted cheerfully around the mailboxes out front, a bright little rebellion against the asphalt and heat.

Two thoughts struck me as I parked behind Bridget's minivan and crossed the cracked concrete to knock on the door. First—this place wasn't fancy, but it had heart. Second—I remembered all too well how high rent was in Charleston County, even for a modest apartment. I had no earthly idea how Bridget pulled it off on a maid's salary.

She offered me a weak smile as she pulled the door open. "Welcome to my humble abode. It's nice to see you under better circumstances."

"Yes it is." I smiled back at her and followed her inside. The two-bedroom apartment was small—no more than nine hundred square feet altogether—with vinyl plank flooring, low ceilings and not nearly enough windows. "Kids at school?"

"They are. Please, have a seat."

I stepped from the small entryway into the living room and settled into a moss green upholstered side chair. To my left, a tweedy-brown sofa anchored the room, with a Victorian-looking loveseat covered in a Bohemian print fabric completing the opposite side of the U-shaped sitting area. A wooden trunk with leather straps served as a coffee table. Scattered accent pillows, throws, and an abstract rug tied everything together. The space was eclectic and homey, and smelled like lemons and clean, crisp linen.

"I'll be right back," said Bridget. "You take lemon in your tea?"

"No, thank you. Please don't go to any trouble on my account."

She stepped into the galley kitchen. A pass through over the sink opened into the living room, so she could talk to me while she filled our glasses.

"It's no trouble at all. I appreciate you coming. I received a notice about an emergency hearing. Mary Ellis is doubling down on her efforts to take my children, apparently." She looked up from what she was doing, her big eyes roiling with anxiety.

"Someone from Rutledge & Radcliffe—that's the attorney's office I told you about?—should be in touch. If they're not able to get it quashed, they'll be in court to argue on your behalf." I could not imagine the amount of stress this poor woman must be under.

She walked back into the living room and handed me a glass of tea and a napkin. "I hope to hear from them soon. This is nerve-wracking."

"I know it must be. Rutledge & Radcliffe is top tier. You're in good hands."

Bridget sat on the end of the sofa closest to me. "This all feels like a nightmare and a miracle at the same time. I could never afford to hire you, let alone these expensive attorneys. I'm just so grateful for everything everyone is doing."

"The important thing to remember is you're not in this alone. You have the folks at Talbot & Andrews behind you. And of course, Carolyn Talbot. It all started with her. She's a force to be reckoned with—and me. I will do my dead-level best to figure out who really killed Patricia. And you couldn't have a better advocate in the courtroom than Dana Smalls. Do you mind helping me out with a few questions?"

"Of course not." She looked at me with an expression that said, *I'm an open book. What do you need?*

"I understand there's a safe in Patricia's office. Do you know the combination?"

"No, there was never any need."

I looked at her for a long minute. My manure meter did not alert. "The necklace that someone so kindly left in your car, that typically was kept in the safe, right?"

"That's right—Patricia kept all her really valuable pieces there."

"Was she vigilant about putting those pieces away right after she took them off, or did she leave them out until it was convenient?"

Bridget gave a little shrug. "Sometimes the morning after an event, the jewelry Patricia wore the night before would be on her dressing table, or on the chest by the bed. But then she'd put it away that day. She didn't just leave the good pieces out indefinitely."

"When was the last event she attended when she would've worn the diamond necklace?" I asked.

"Oh, gosh..." Bridget looked at the ceiling, thinking. "There was a benefit gala for one of the local cancer charities in March...Patricia wore the diamond necklace then. That's the last time I saw that piece. It was on her bedside table when I first went upstairs the next morning to make the bed and straighten. But the next time I went back into the bedroom, to replace a blanket I'd washed, the necklace had been put away."

"Okay, this may be difficult, and I'm so sorry to ask, but I need you to think carefully about the morning you found Patricia...before the police got there. Close your eyes and try to visualize the room. I need to know what it looked like before it was cleaned."

She winced, then closed her eyes. "I'll do my best... Patricia was on the floor...it was pretty clear she was gone...I can't..."

"That's fine. What was she wearing?"

"A black...negligee. That's what my mother would've called it."

"You mean a sexy nightie?"

"That's right. There was a matching peignoir over the chair."

"Was the room a mess...did it look like it'd been ransacked?"

"The lamp on the bedside table—on her side, closest to the door—was knocked over."

"Okay...what else was on the bedside table? Was there a glass in the room—like she'd had a drink?"

Bridget's forehead creased. "No, and that's unusual. She always had a glass of water and a small carafe by the bed." She opened her eyes. "I hadn't thought of that before. There's a pale blue glass carafe with a matching tumbler. I keep it in the cabinet by the sink.

She filled the carafe with chilled, filtered water every night at bedtime. I would take it downstairs in the mornings and wash it and put it away."

"Is there anything else you can think of that stands out?"

Bridget shook her head. "No."

"You did Patricia's laundry, right?"

"I did."

"What can you tell me about the black nightgown? Is this typical of what she slept in?"

"Actually, no. She's more of a cotton pajamas type typically. The silky nightgowns were a once or twice a week thing."

"Do you think she was in a relationship?"

Bridget nodded and rolled her lips in and out. "I do. I've suspected it for a while…six months, maybe eight?"

"Do you have any idea who with?"

She shook her head. "Not a clue. Whoever it was, she kept a really tight lid on it."

"On the nights she appeared to be entertaining, would you typically find wineglasses or cocktail glasses in the bedroom or in the kitchen sink? Was there any other evidence someone else had been there?"

"Typically, there would be either wine or champagne glasses in the dishwasher. Once or twice they were in her bedroom, and I brought them down."

"But that particular morning, there were no glasses in the bedroom?"

"No. I hadn't opened the dishwasher yet, so I

couldn't tell you if there were glasses there...wait a minute... Back in February, there was a night when Patricia had company—it was a black nightie evening—and the next morning, that necklace was on her dressing table. I think she wore it with the lingerie."

"If she did that the evening she was killed, it would explain the necklace being out of the safe." For whoever killed Patricia, it was a convenient, highly identifiable piece of evidence they could plant in Bridget's car.

"Do you think her lover killed her?"

"It's possible. But it's also possible someone else arrived after her guest left."

"I don't understand why whoever all came and went weren't captured on video. There are cameras on both doors, the driveway, and the far side of the house. But I guess they weren't working, or I wouldn't be in this mess."

"They were working fine. Someone deleted the videos. Do you know if Patricia had the security app on her phone?"

"She did...she could log on from her desktop too."

Just like I had. Anyone with the password or access to Patricia's cell phone—and the logged in app—could've deleted the videos.

"Do you remember if Patricia's phone was by the bed?"

"It was on the floor near her. I called 911 from the landline. There's a phone on the credenza in her office."

Patricia's cell phone was no doubt in the police

evidence storage facility. "Patricia and Corinne had lunch the day Patricia was killed…"

"Right. They did most Thursdays."

"But that particular Thursday, they came back to the house and had an argument. Did you happen to hear what they were arguing about?" I was looking for confirmation of what Scarlett had told me, or perhaps a piece of the conversation Bridget overheard that Scarlett didn't…or maybe didn't want to share.

"No." She shook her head. "I must've been upstairs cleaning the bathrooms. I clean with my earbuds in."

"Okay…switching channels here…did you know that Mary Ellis Donovan was volunteering at one of Patricia's charities?"

"*What?*"

"I'll take that as a 'no.'"

"The nerve of that woman. No doubt she was sucking up to her so she could beg her to pitch Arlo to Trevor Jennings. She tried for the longest time to get me to ask Patricia to send Arlo's demo album, but I wanted nothing to do with that. Arlo abandoned his kids to chase his pipe dream. He's on his own as far as I'm concerned."

"Yeah, I think that operation had moved from the sucking up to the begging phase. I have Mary Ellis on video handing Patricia a flash drive."

"Unbelievable."

"So I guess you didn't go to the UPS store back in March—the week Scarlett had the stomach virus—and ship a package with pound cake and said flash drive to Uma Jennings?"

"No...I remember Patricia being in the kitchen all morning one day the week Scarlett was sick making her lemon blueberry pound cake. And as soon as it cooled, she wrapped it up and took it to the UPS store. I had no idea there was also a flash drive in that package."

"Last question for today. Did you know Patricia left you something in her will?"

"No. I had no idea. What, you mean like a memento of some sort?"

"She left you and Scarlett each a hundred thousand dollars."

Her eyes grew, shock and fear radiating from them. She covered her mouth. "That was amazingly generous of her. But that's not good news for me right now, is it? I swear I didn't know."

A hundred thousand dollars would no doubt make a huge difference in Bridget's life...maybe a nice down payment on a house for her and the kids...a buffer between them and life's calamities. I just had to solve Patricia's murder before a district attorney had the opportunity to paint Bridget's windfall as a motive.

Chapter Nineteen

Big Kitty and Tiger Kitty rubbed themselves against my legs, tunneled between them, and *raowwwed* at me while I put together my lunch—hummus and veggies again, though I did throw in a couple of pickles to mix things up. Finally, I got the kitties each a PurrrFeast Morsel so I could eat my lunch in peace. I mulled the case for a full thirty seconds before Liz texted me:

> On my way home from Mount Pleasant. You home? Okay to stop by?

Had I told her where I lived?

> Sure.

I figured she'd ask if she needed the address or directions. Apparently, she did not. I texted her the gate code. Ten minutes later she rang the doorbell.

The kitties trailed me to the front door, something I hadn't noticed them doing before. When I pulled it open, the large golden retriever Liz had on a retractable leash started barking.

The kitties hissed territorially and stood their ground.

"Rhett, hush up," said Liz. "Sorry—I had taken him to the vet for a well-doggy visit. I should've mentioned it."

She was color-coordinated from head to toe, her necklace, earrings, sandals, and crossbody bag complementing her pink and white floral sundress. I was glad I'd taken time to primp that morning and had put on a sundress.

"No worries," I said. "Feel like a walk on the beach?"

"Perfect."

I gestured. "Follow the path to the right and I'll meet you out back."

When I closed the door, the kitties went back to rubbing against my legs, clearly lobbying for another treat. Because I figured they'd been traumatized by the large dog, I complied.

"We can't make a habit of this," I told them. "Too many treats will affect our youthful figures." Technically, I was pretty sure a vet would tell me they were both already way overweight, but that was a problem for their people. I just needed to keep the kitties safe and happy until their people came.

I headed out the sliding door and down the steps to the pool deck where Liz and Rhett waited.

Rhett started towards me, a friendly, sloppy grin on his face.

I raised my palms in a stop gesture and took a step back. "I'm so sorry. I'm very allergic to dogs. Their dander, sure, but mostly their saliva."

"Oh, no. Would you rather I take him home?" Liz reeled in his retractable leash.

"No, it's fine as long as he doesn't lick me and we're outside."

"Mind your manners, Rhett," she said as she urged him down the path.

He *woofed* and romped towards the beach.

"He's a gorgeous dog," I said.

"When he was a puppy, I wouldn't've been able to keep him off of you. But he's well past middle age, and a perfect gentleman most of the time."

We left our sandals at the gate, made a right on the beach, and walked towards the lighthouse. It was a postcard-perfect spring day, with only a few wisps of clouds in the bright blue sky. The gentle breeze off the ocean tossed our hair and fluttered the hems of our dresses. Gulls cried overhead, and happy children squealed and laughed as they sloshed around a large tide pool.

Liz gave Rhett plenty of line. He trotted ahead,

stopping occasionally to check out a piece of driftwood, a shell, or a jellyfish, then racing to catch up.

After a few moments, Liz said, "I wanted to let you know...I felt like I had to say something to Poppy. She's my sister-in-law, and we're close. I didn't feel right..."

"It's fine," I said. "I mean, I figured you would. I'd like to meet her...see if we can figure out...we must be related somehow." My mind reeled just thinking about it.

"I'll text you her phone number," Liz said.

"Thanks."

"I have other news. Case-related news."

"Oh?"

"Nothing major, but maybe it'll help. I hope you don't mind me sticking my nose in..." She gave me an apologetic look.

"Not at all. I appreciate the help." That was the truth, just not all of it. If I was fully honest, I felt anxious, like the case was veering off course and I had lost all control. That was likely a sign of some sort of personal defect I needed to address.

"Nate and I used to divvy things up...have one of us work on knocking out the long shots —checking off their alibis so we could pare down the suspect list. Truthfully, I usually asked him to do that, and he always did. He knew I couldn't wait to dig into our prime suspects."

"He sounds like a great partner."

"He was—he is. You ever think about partnering

with Cash? I mean, he's a trained investigator. Seems like it would simplify your life a lot."

"Honestly, it never occurred to me he'd even consider such a thing. He was a Charleston Police detective before he went to work for SLED. He's pretty dedicated to law enforcement. Me, I'm more focused on helping people who are in a jam. Our perspective on cases is completely opposite..." Anxiety gnawed at my stomach. I still hadn't heard from Cash. I was terrified he'd lost the job that meant so much to him because of me. "So, what about the case? Who can we check off the list?"

"I had a PI friend in Nashville check out Arlo Donovan's whereabouts for March 23rd and 24th. He was on stage in a dive bar both nights, two sets. There's no way he could've killed Patricia. He has no means to hire anyone, and no motive I've been able to figure."

"That's one down—thanks. Oh—to check off most of the rest of the Donovan family, George Donovan and Arlo's brothers Adam, Aaron, and Andrew were on a canoe trip down the Edisto River from Thursday to Sunday. Honestly, the only motives I could see for Arlo's brothers were far-fetched anyway. But the menfolk's weekend away leaves Mary Ellis without an alibi."

"So she moves up the list... We can check off Emerson and Everly Barnwell, Corinne's daughters. They were both at a black tie event in DC the night of March 23 that lasted until after midnight. I don't see them hiring someone to take out their aunt for an early inheritance. They both have trust funds and no pressing financial needs."

"Ah—thanks. I haven't had a chance to delve into the nieces yet."

"Well, they were low priority, for sure," said Liz. "But now you can erase them altogether."

"That is truly a satisfying feeling." I couldn't wait to update my case board.

"My pleasure." She gave me an apologetic little wince. "I actually have a couple of more...Chalmers Gaillard I and III were in Scottsdale Arizona playing golf the entire week. I actually spoke to Chalmers III, and I have to say, he's as happy-go-lucky a guy as I've ever run across. Neither of them had an ax to grind with Patricia—Chalmers II, yes. But he's unavailable as it were."

"You've been busy," I said.

"Not as busy as I'd like. I just made a few phone calls." Her voice was wistful.

"Well, I appreciate it. Anything on Scarlett's alibi? She tried calling him this morning, but he didn't answer for her either."

"And there's a very good reason for that," said Liz.

"Do tell."

"That phone number she gave you rings to a pay phone in a parking garage on Horlbeck Alley."

"I forget those things are still around."

"There are a handful in Charleston. And I think this one's also been used by some phone scammers. It's been reported a number of times."

"Interesting. Now the question is, did Scarlett make this Brett Campbell up out of whole cloth and give me that number to make him seem legitimate, or does he actually exist, and she met him just as she said, and he gave *her* a fake number because he's a total jerk?"

"So far I haven't found any evidence of a Brett Campbell who lives in the area, but it's possible he's a recent transplant and his electronic footprint hasn't caught up to him yet."

"I'm inclined to be slightly more suspicious of Scarlett," I said. "But I still think it's more likely Porter or Corinne."

"Honestly, I think it's a toss-up between the four of them—Porter, Corinne, Scarlett, and Mary Ellis. Which makes it harder to decide who to focus on."

"Well, we know Porter was there the night Patricia was killed." I filled her in on Scarlett confirming the affair and what Bridget had told me about Patricia being dressed to entertain the evening she was killed.

"My working theory is, I'm thinking Porter and Patricia spent some quality time together, and then *either* she made demands on him and he got angry and killed her, *or* he left and someone else...most likely Corinne...came in and killed her shortly thereafter. When Patricia became aware she was in danger, she opened the gun safe at her bedside and took out the gun, which someone struggled with her over, ultimately taking it from her. Patricia wore the diamond necklace with her lingerie, and whoever killed her took the opportunity to plant the gun and the necklace in Bridget's car."

"That tracks," said Liz.

"About Corinne and Porter," I said. "I have a plan."

"Do tell," said Liz.

"You know how all the security footage from Patricia's house was wiped?"

"Regrettably, yes."

"Well, suppose the security system company had backups, or a way to recover the deleted videos."

Her head jerked towards me. "Do they?"

"No. Well, Patricia's company doesn't, anyway. Once the customer wipes them, they're gone forever."

"Ah...you're going to set a trap," said Liz.

"Precisely. I'm going to call Corinne and Porter separately and tell them I've found a way to restore the videos and I want money. They're to bring me a hundred thousand dollars in a duffel bag and leave it in a recycling can at Waterfront Park at 10:00 p.m."

"Brilliant," said Liz. "But why not include Scarlett and Mary Ellis too?"

"Only because neither of them has enough money to be blackmail targets."

"Maybe ask them for less money...an amount they could get their hands on. Tell them it's a down payment. But throw it out there to all four of them. Even if they can't come up with the money, the guilty party will show up to try to bargain with you—or kill you."

She tilted her head and gave me a look that said, *this is about to get dangerous.*

"I like that idea—not the killing me thing. It's one of the four of them. It has to be."

"Of course in Porter's case, he has an affair to hide," said Liz. "Him showing up wouldn't *necessarily* mean he killed Patricia."

"Yeah...about that...his wife knows about the affair, and I'm thinking he knows she knows." I gave Liz the condensed version of my conversation with Corinne and the scene at Maison, leaving out all the personal stuff. "He's got nothing left to hide unless he's the killer."

Liz gave me a sympathetic look. "What horrible luck."

"Or something. Anyway—I think 10:00 p.m. is late enough. It won't be deserted, and that's a good thing."

"Agreed. You'd better make those calls soon. Our perpetrator will need to get to the bank this afternoon."

"Good point." We'd reached the lighthouse, and I was just about to ask if Liz was ready to turn around when I saw Sarabeth striding towards us waving.

"Hey," she called out, a big smile on her face.

"That's my friend, Sarabeth." We waved back.

When she was in range, Rhett pulled at his leash and woofed, his tongue hanging out.

"Rhett." Liz reeled him in.

"Oh, he's fine." Sarabeth petted Rhett and baby talked to him while he wagged his tail.

I made the introductions, and we all said hey and all that, then Sarabeth said, "So did you learn anything new this morning, Hadley? I can't wait to hear."

"Nothing that wraps the case up for me with a bow. The most significant thing I learned is that Porter Barnwell was at Patricia Gaillard's house the evening she died." I turned to Liz. "Sarabeth is a mystery author. She's been doing research by following me around."

"How fun," said Liz. "You know, we could use some help this evening."

"We—what? What we? We who? Are you planning to come with me tonight?" I squinted at her.

"Of course I am," said Liz. "I can hardly let you go on your own to meet a murderer when you bullheadedly refuse to carry a gun."

"But I—" This was about to spiral out of hand. I could feel it in my bones.

"And I'm thinking a third pair of eyes would be ideal," said Liz.

"Count me in for sure." Sarabeth's eyes sparkled with excitement. "Now what are we doing?"

"We're going to trap us a killer," said Liz.

Chapter Twenty

After Liz left, I went upstairs to my office to make the calls. I opened my spoofing app and started with Mary Ellis. I typed in her number and the number I wanted to appear to be calling from—that of Middleton, Bull, & Vanderhorst. I reasoned all four suspects would answer for the prominent attorney's office, if for different reasons. Porter, Corinne, and Scarlett might anticipate something to do with the estate. Given Mary Ellis's ongoing crusade to take Bridget's children, I was betting she'd be plenty curious about any attorney's office that appeared on her caller ID.

Using a voice filter, I made my voice male—okay, maybe this is sexist, but guys sound more threatening, right?—and gave it an Australian accent.

When Mary Ellis answered the phone, I said, "I have the restored video footage from the security system at Patricia Gaillard's home. I know what you did. Bring a good-faith down payment of a thousand dollars in a duffel bag to Waterfront Park at ten o'clock this evening. Take the brick walkway to the right of the Pineapple Fountain. Walk to the first recycling can, just past Middle Atlantic Wharf. Put the money in the recycling can and walk away. If you don't show, I will give the video to the police."

"Who *is* this?"

"The person who holds your future in the palm of her—his—hand." I ended the call and rolled my eyes at myself. That last part was a little theatrical, even before I botched it.

Okay…I rolled my shoulders, shook out my arms, stretched my neck left and right. *I can do better.*

I selected a male Irish accent, rang Scarlett, and repeated the script.

"*Who is this?*" she demanded, her tone indignant.

"I'm the person in possession of evidence that will send you to jail." Was that better? I wasn't sure. Blackmail was definitely not my strong suit.

For Corinne, I used a male New York accented voice and upped the ante to $100,000. I needed the amount to be believable, but also one she could get in cash on short notice. Porter got the male Proper King's English version. I have to say, the two of them used way more colorful language when they asked the question, "*Who is this?*" Their mothers would've washed their filthy mouths out with soap for sure.

Once I'd called them all, I was at loose ends. Sarabeth and Liz would be here at eight. We wanted to allow plenty of time to get in place before ten o'clock. But it was just now quarter to three. There wasn't really anything else I could do until time to leave.

Okay, so I'm not proud of it, but I gave into temptation and used the handy app North had designed for me and pulled a profile on Poppy Talbot—maiden name Oliver.

Her birthday was February 14, 1981—Valentine's Day. She was not quite four months older than me, and born at MUSC—Medical University of South Carolina University Medical Center—the same hospital where my half brother J. T. and I were born two days apart. I couldn't see an image of Poppy's birth certificate, but I could access most of the data.

Poppy's father, Jason Oliver, was in the Army, and they'd moved to California in June, just a few months after she was born. Sadly, he died in a training accident when Poppy was only two. Jane Smith Oliver returned to Charleston with Poppy, where they lived in a West Ashley neighborhood. Poppy's mother died of breast cancer in 2008. She'd lost her mother to cancer just like I did, but ten years later.

Poppy was the only child of two only children. All four grandparents were deceased. There was literally no one I could ask about her background except Poppy.

I picked up my phone and tapped the number Liz had given me.

Poppy answered on the first ring. "Hi."

Were we on the same wavelength? She even

sounded like me. This was all so unnervingly odd. "Hi. Hello...I guess Liz told you that you have a lookalike?"

"Yeah, she mentioned it," said Poppy like *that's all I've heard about for days.*

"That would be me. I'm Hadley Cooper. I wondered if we could meet sometime..."

"Would three-thirty be convenient? I had just picked up the phone to call you when you called me. I had an errand in Charleston, so I'm nearby."

Wow. Okay. We were doing this right now. "Ah, sure. Of course. Where did you have in mind?" I asked.

"Wherever you'd like."

"Would you like to come to my house?"

"That sounds great. Liz gave me the address. I hope that's okay."

"Of course," I said, and gave her the gate code. "I'll see you soon."

I watched for Poppy out the window by the front door and pondered my mother, and what the figment of my imagination had meant when she said she was sorry. The kitties had protested, but I'd sequestered them in the laundry room, not knowing how Poppy felt about felines. I watched her open the door of the large burgundy Subaru SUV and step out. She took a minute to study my house, then walked towards the steps. It was such an odd feeling—watching myself climb my front steps.

I opened the door as she reached the landing.

The mirror image of me stopped in her tracks and stared slack jawed. "Wow." Even our dark brown hair was worn the same—long and straight.

"I know. Crazy, right?"

We both tucked our hair behind our right ear at exactly the same moment, then got the giggles.

"Liz tried to tell me," Poppy said. "But to be honest, I thought she was exaggerating."

"Please...come inside." I stepped back and waved my arm in a welcoming gesture. "I poured us some iced tea."

She followed me inside and through the foyer, then stopped when she caught sight of the aquarium. Poppy gasped and crossed the room to get a closer look. "This is amazing. I love aquariums."

"Me too. For a long time I thought fish were the only pets I could have. I'm allergic to dogs, and I always thought I was allergic to cats, but recently I've learned I'm not."

"I have a cat," said Poppy, not taking her eyes off the aquarium. "Ruffles...she's a mix of something and Selkirk Rex. She has ruffly fur."

We watched the brightly colored fish swim by for a few moments, each getting our bearings.

Finally, I said, "Would you like to sit down?"

"Of course." She followed me into the living room.

I waited for her to pick her spot on one of the camel-colored leather sofas, then sat in a side chair to her left. The iced tea I'd prepared was on a side table between us at the end of the sofa.

"You're thinner." She smiled.

I shrugged. "I'd say I'm maybe too skinny."

"I didn't think anyone could be too skinny."

We both sipped our tea. I was so eager to know everything about her, but felt awkward. Who were we to each other?

"We have to be related," I said. "I just don't have any idea how. Both my parents were only children. They never married...well, that's a whole nother *long* story. I have a half-brother, J. T. He and I have the same father—and we both favor him quite a lot." All kinds of possibilities danced in my head. My parents' story was complicated enough already. Surely there wasn't another wrinkle...another woman. *Oh my stars*.

"My parents were only children too," she said. "To be honest, I don't look a thing like either one of them. Of course I've only seen pictures of my dad. He died when I was two."

"What would you think about taking a DNA test?" I asked.

Poppy nodded. "My husband, Blake, suggested that. I didn't know how you'd feel about that...they can tell from a cheek swab if we're related, and how closely."

"Exactly. That's the sensible thing to do. Once we know if there's a connection—and surely there must be—and how close it is, hopefully that will give us some clues where to look in our family trees."

Poppy smiled, opened her eyes dramatically wide, and blushed. She pulled two small boxes out of her very large purse. "I'm glad you feel that way. I was hoping I didn't overstep. I went to a lab in Charleston. They can turn around a test in two to three days. We just need to swab our cheeks." She passed me one of the boxes.

"All right then."

We each opened our boxes, read the instructions, and did the swabbing. I sealed my envelope and handed it to her. "When will you drop them off?"

"As soon as I leave here." She put both of our thick white envelopes in her handbag and pulled out an ivory one made of fine stationery and laid it on the end table. "I brought a copy of my birth certificate. Liz suggested that might be helpful. I had the impression she was struggling to resist the urge to ask me for a copy herself."

"Thanks," I said. "I'm sure we'll figure this out."

Poppy gave me a wry smile. "I'm pretty sure there's a simple explanation. Probably involves shenanigans on the part of two of our parents."

I smiled back at her. The simplest explanation was that we shared a father who had relationships with three women in 1980. But that wouldn't account for what my mother was sorry for, not without another piece of the puzzle, anyway.

"Hey," I said, "would you mind if we took a selfie?"

"Of course not," said Poppy.

I slid beside her on the sofa and we both leaned in and smiled as I snapped a few shots.

"Send me one of those, would you?" she asked.

I selected the one I liked the best and texted it to her. "Let me know as soon as the results are in."

"I think we should open them together," said Poppy.

"Do you really think we're half sisters?"

"I'd bet on it," she said.

I'd been an only child for so long, then found out I had a half brother—J. T.—when I was sixteen. Could it really be that all along I'd had a half sister too?

We hugged at the door before she left. I stood at the door and watched her go, waving as she pulled out of the drive.

There was a time I would've been easily convinced my father—Swinton Legare—was a philanderer capable of three virtually simultaneous relationships. But now I knew I'd judged him far too harshly most of my life. I believed he was deeply in love with my mother and married Judith, J. T.'s mother, only after my mother rejected him, which was a whole nother sad story.

I couldn't shake a conviction there was something much harder to explain that accounted for my doppelgänger. If Dad and Judith weren't in Italy on vacation I'd take these photos of Poppy and me together and show them to him and see what ideas *he* might have on the subject.

All my personal records were upstairs in a safe inside the media closet in my office. I picked up Poppy's birth certificate and headed upstairs. I opened the safe and flipped through the file until I found my birth certificate and took it to my desk.

With the two documents side by side, I easily found what I was looking for. The same doctor delivered us both, Dr. Margaux Albright. I recognized the name. Dr. Albright had seen my mother occasionally as far back as I could remember—right up until she was diagnosed with cancer. After that, it was all oncologists, surgeons, and radiologists.

A quick search told me that Dr. Albright had passed away in 2014.

Sensing I was on the verge of discovery, I dug into her practice, which had been taken over by two partners. I called and spoke to the office manager, who told me Dr. Albright's nurse had finally retired five years ago, but still lived in Mount Pleasant. Her name was Linda McMurtry.

Why did that name ring a bell?

When I plugged her name into the profile app, I found an address on Simmons Street, two blocks over from Gavin—from the house next to him that I grew up in.

I headed towards Gavin's house.

"Bonjour, bitch," Rudi, Gavin's foul-mouthed military macaw, squawked as I walked through the door. This was the technicolor menace's customary greeting, though he had called me much worse.

I waved dismissively at him as I passed through the living room. "Pipe down, Rudi."

"State your business," said Rudi. "Semper fi."

"Gavin?" I called.

No answer.

I knew he was here. His truck was in the driveway and so was Joe Vincent's. After a quick search, I found them on the covered patio out back having a beer.

"Twinkle." Gavin grinned from ear to ear. I never had to wonder if he was happy to see me.

"Good. You're both here," I said.

"It's good to see you, darlin'." Joe climbed out of the turquoise metal chair.

I gave them each a quick hug. "I need to talk to y'all."

"Sounds like you got a bee in your bonnet. What's up?" Gavin settled back into his chair.

I slid into the metal sofa glider, suddenly at a loss for words. First things first. "Have either of you spoken to Cash recently?"

Gavin and Joe exchanged a glance, then both flashed me innocent looks.

"Let's see..." Gavin looked up like he was maybe asking God to refresh his memory.

"Not that I recall," said Joe. "But you know, my memory isn't all that reliable anymore."

"*Gavin*..." I raised an eyebrow at him.

"What?"

"What was all that you were trying so hard not to tell me Monday when you came by my office?"

"I don't know what you mean," said Gavin.

"Gavin, I think things got messed up last night. I need to know *what* exactly got messed up."

"Messed up how?" He frowned at me.

"It's complicated. We ran into a couple of suspects while we were out to dinner."

"So you had your fancy dinner?" asked Joe.

"What do you know about that fancy dinner?" I lowered my forehead and stared up at him.

"Joe, don't say a word," said Gavin.

My head spun towards him. "Gavin, *please*..."

"Twinkle, don't ask me questions I've promised not to answer," said Gavin.

"So he did talk to you."

"I never said that," said Gavin.

"But clearly he did. What, did he ask the two of you for my hand?"

They both looked everywhere but at me.

"That must be it." The Barnwells had submarined what would've been a romantic proposal. Were there signs Cash was thinking about marriage? How had I missed them? Did I want to get married?

Maybe I did.

I loved Cash.

We were surely old enough.

We were both well established in our careers.

Careers which carried with them occasional conflicts.

"Surely he would've spoken to your father about such a thing," said Joe.

"Maybe," I said. "But the two of you have been in my life a lot longer than he has, so I'm guessing Cash, being the considerate guy that he is, covered all the bases."

I wasn't going to get Gavin or Joe to admit it, but it was clear to me that's exactly what happened. And given the way things turned out, would Cash try again? Or had he changed his mind? I needed to think all this through. In the meantime, I had other business with Gavin.

How to ask this? I pursed my lips and rolled them in and out. Then I pulled out my phone and showed him one of the photos I'd just taken of me with Poppy.

Gavin squinted at the screen.

Joe ambled over to have a look over Gavin's shoulder. "What, you been playing with some new software? That some sort of computer-generated nonsense?"

"No. That's me with Poppy Oliver Talbot. We just met. She was born four months before me at the same hospital. The same doctor—Dr. Albright— delivered us both. Her nurse, Linda McMurtry, lives two blocks away. Wasn't mom friends with her?"

Gavin went still and closed his eyes, his lips screwed up in a bitter expression. After a minute, he opened his eyes and stared across the yard like he was pondering something heavy.

Joe and I both watched and waited.

In a quiet voice, Gavin said, "Excuse me. I'll be

right back." He rose and lumbered inside, shoulders sagging.

Joe and I exchanged a glance. *What in this world?*

Long moments later, Gavin stepped out the back door holding an ivory envelope. He walked over to the glider and held the envelope out to me but didn't let go. "Your mother gave me this for you before she passed. She said I might not ever need to give it to you, and I shouldn't unless it was absolutely necessary. She said I would know if the time came. I think this is it. Hope I'm right."

I took ahold of the end of the envelope.

Gavin's troubled eyes held mine for a moment, then he let go of his end but didn't move.

I stared at my name in mother's handwriting, pressure building in my chest and climbing up my throat. For days I'd wondered what she could possibly be sorry for. The answer was inside this envelope, I knew that.

"Maybe Joe and I will head inside..." said Gavin. "...give you a moment."

I nodded slowly. It felt like I was watching myself in a dream.

Gavin patted my shoulder, then looked at Joe and gestured towards the house with his head. Joe shot Gavin a look of annoyance and heaved a deep sigh, like he wanted his objection noted, but wasn't going to argue the point. Joe climbed out of his chair and moved over to pat my other shoulder. They glared at each other, a silent argument playing out across their faces as they patted and rubbed. Finally,

Gavin jerked his head towards the house again and headed inside. With a long-suffering sigh, Joe followed.

When the door closed behind them, I slid my finger under the seal, carefully opened the envelope, and removed a single sheet of ivory paper. The letter was handwritten:

April 8, 1998

My Sweet Hadley,

If you're reading this, I've gone on to the next great adventure and the hardest decision I ever made has somehow come to light, or Gavin suspects as much. I should clarify—he doesn't know what I've done. I couldn't bring myself to tell him, or anyone for that matter.

You know how tight money was when you were growing up. I barely kept you fed, though I tried not to let you see how dire things were at times. There was so much I wanted to give you but couldn't. From the moment I found out I was expecting, I always knew we'd struggle on a waitress's salary. But I desperately wanted you and was determined to take as good a care of you as I possibly could.

And then I learned there were two of you. I knew I could only manage to raise one child. That was my reality. Taking care of two of you was just never a possibility, and I was afraid that if I tried and failed, I risked losing you both, either to social services or to your father.

I only told one person, my friend Linda McMurtry, that I was having twins. Gavin never knew. Please don't blame Linda. She helped me when I was desperate. She is a nurse, and was there when you and your sister were born. She made sure your sister was adopted by a loving couple who were desperate for a child but unable to have one. I'm not certain the adoption was a hundred percent legal. Linda had to take some liberties with the paperwork. I know your sister's birthdate was altered. I beg you not to make trouble for Linda.

I understand the couple who adopted your sister moved to California soon after you were born, so it's unlikely your paths will ever cross. If you're reading this, I guess I was wrong about that, and you have found your identical twin sister.

I pray that you can both forgive me. I did what I thought was best for you both.

So much love,

Mamma

I took slow deep breaths.
I have a sister.
An identical twin.
On some level, I think I knew Poppy was my twin from the first time I laid eyes on her picture in Liz's office. But I just couldn't believe it.

Oh good grief...I need to tell Dad he has another daughter.

And J. T. has another sister.

I have a sister.

I have a sister!

I fumbled for my phone, then froze.

How would Poppy receive the news that Mamma gave her up at birth? How would I feel if that had been me?

I slid my phone back into the side pocket of my backpack.

Maybe I should fully digest this news before I shared it.

Chapter Twenty-One

Water soothes me, and I really needed soothing, so as soon as I got home, I put on a swimsuit, grabbed a towel, and headed for the pool. After a few laps, I climbed on my blue foam float and closed my eyes, drifting and listening to the waves crash on the beach.

I still hadn't heard from Cash, and it was after six p.m. It had been nearly twenty-four hours since the debacle at Maison...since I'd almost gotten engaged, and that horrible man, Porter Barnwell, had made an awful scene and threatened Cash.

And, apparently, I had a twin sister my mother had given away at birth in an illegal adoption scheme. The DNA tests would be back in less than three business days, and I was the only person available to explain what had happened to my sister, who was likely to be very upset about the whole situation—I would be.

I needed to get my head straight. In less than two

hours, Liz and Sarabeth would be here and we'd head into Charleston for the sting operation I'd set in motion. With any luck, I'd wrap up my case that evening.

And if I could hand it to Cash all wrapped up with a bow, with incriminating evidence against the true perpetrator—which, logically was probably Porter Barnwell, even though my gut currently leaned towards Scarlett Hathaway, though I couldn't put my finger on exactly why—maybe Cash could take the evidence to his boss and he would be so thrilled he would forget all about Porter Barnwell's tirade against Cash, because after all, Porter Barnwell was a murderer and no one cared anymore if he was angry, and he just needed to be thrown under the jail.

These were the things I was thinking as I rolled off the float and relished the weightlessness of floating directly on top of the water. In my defense, I was trying to fully decompress…to relax and clear my head.

And this was one way I did that…floating in the pool, face down, holding my breath, with my arms, legs, and entire body completely relaxed like a rag doll. Drifting…fully relaxed…all the tension released from my body…floating…letting all the stress sail away on the breeze…

"*Hadley!*"

I had no time to respond before the surface of the water exploded.

Strong arms wrapped around my waist, flipped me over, and towed me towards the shallow end of the pool.

"*Cash!*" I kicked and sputtered. "Wait. I'm fine. *I'm fine.*"

I wiggled and kicked and managed to get my feet under myself.

Cash staggered backwards—I might've accidentally pushed him—and fell. It took him a minute, in his drenched Levi's and button-down to pull himself to his feet.

"Are you all right?" He wiped the water from his eyes and slicked his hair back.

"I'm fine," I said. "That's a relaxation exercise."

"I thought you'd drowned." He closed his eyes and grabbed the side of the pool.

"I'm sorry I scared you."

"You nearly gave me a heart attack."

I sloshed over to the side of the pool. "Thank you for saving me."

"Anytime." His voice was almost curt. He didn't pull me to him. There was too much space between us.

"Is everything okay?" I searched his eyes.

He looked away. "It will be. I hope."

"Did Porter Barnwell make a stink like he threatened?"

"I would say it was worse than advertised."

I winced. "I'm *so* sorry."

"I've been told in no uncertain terms that you *cannot* work this case."

"I'm sorry, *what*?"

"It's a conflict."

I bristled. "Is there some law, some regulation, that I'm unaware of to that effect?"

"Not that I know of."

"Then what the heck?"

"My work on the case is all but done, otherwise, they'd simply pull me off of it. Believe me, they'd really like to do that. But they can't at this point. I have to testify. But you working this case...it makes the division look bad."

"I know you know this, but your boss can't actually tell me what to do."

Cash shook his head. "You're right. He can't. And that *really* frustrates him."

"So he's just going to make *your* life miserable?"

"That's about the size of it."

"Look...I think this case will be wrapped up soon. It's Friday evening. By Monday, when you see him again, hopefully I'll be looking for a new case anyway." Please, God, let that be the way things worked out.

He pulled back and gave me a look that asked all sorts of questions, like *What are you up to?* and *What do you mean, exactly?*

"Chinese wall." I shook my head.

He closed his eyes and looked like maybe he was doing a self-soothing exercise. "We have seriously got to figure out a way to keep this from ever happening again. A way we can both stick to. Otherwise, I'll end up getting fired."

"I know." But how? How could we make sure it never happened again?

"Do you mind if we get out of the pool? These clothes are starting to be really uncomfortable." He trudged up the steps.

I wrapped myself in a towel and curled up in a lounger, listening to the surf while Cash went inside to change. When he came back out, he perched on the end of my pool chair.

For a long moment, he watched me watching the ocean.

"Is something else bothering you?" he asked. "Something besides this case? You seem like you're a hundred miles away."

Where to start? "It's been a crazy week...and speaking of crazy..." I chose my words carefully, leaving out the incident at Breach Inlet—the one starring my mother—and went straight to how I'd met Poppy, ending with the letter Gavin gave me.

"The handwriting in the letter is definitely your mother's?" His face crinkled with skepticism.

"Yes. And honestly, it never occurred to me to question it. *Gavin* gave it to me."

"Of course. Sorry. That's just—"

"Crazy. I know."

"There are two of you?"

"You will never believe how much she looks like me. I'm a little thinner...that's the only difference."

"You haven't spoken to her since you read the letter?"

"No. I wanted to process everything a little more. And I thought I should tell her about the letter in person. She lives on Stella Maris...Cash, she has two kids. I'm an aunt."

He grinned. "That's amazing. Wow...your biological family just more than doubled. I'm happy for you."

The happy wasn't making it all the way to his eyes.

"What else is going on?" I asked.

"Nothing else...nothing we need to talk about anymore today. You've had shocking—but wonderful—news. You need some time to absorb that, I know."

"Cash, what is it?"

"It will wait." He looked away.

"I don't want it to wait. Talk to me. Please. You know I hate it when you start to tell me something and then clam up."

He sighed. "Fine...it's just what we were talking about earlier."

"When you jumped in the pool with your clothes on?" I gave him a teasing smile.

But his expression stayed serious.

"The case thing?" I squinted at him.

"Yes, of course the case thing. We had an agreement. And your...commitment to helping people in trouble—which is a beautiful quality—trumped our agreement. This case may—or may not—be wrapping up, but what about the next case? I haven't heard anything that makes me think you wouldn't do the exact same thing again... and again and again. It's like we both want the truth, always, but you visualize us on different sides somehow."

"I think we *are* on different sides sometimes."

"How does that work, exactly, given that we both want the same thing—justice for everyone involved?"

"You see everything through the lens of punishing the guilty, and I see it through the lens of helping people."

"That's absurd. How am I not helping people if I lock up the criminals who hurt them?"

"Maybe sometimes you're a little too quick to lock people up." That came out way harsher than I'd meant it to, but sadly, this was honestly how I felt.

"How can you say that? It's not like I enjoy throwing people in jail. But that's how victims get justice, and how we keep people safe so there aren't *more* victims. Criminals should go to jail, Hadley."

"Bridget Donovan is not a criminal. She's a single mother who someone went to a great deal of trouble to frame."

"I understand you have a soft heart and you want to believe that. But the evidence says otherwise. It's my job to follow the evidence."

"I follow the evidence too."

"Only if it's evidence you like."

"That's neither true nor fair."

"Look...I did not want to get into this thing this evening. But since you insisted, the bottom line is we had an agreement. One we both felt like was in the best interests of our relationship. And the first time that agreement ran contrary to you taking a case you really felt strongly about, the agreement went right out the window."

"I just couldn't turn my back on Bridget. I didn't have it in me."

"And I didn't want to fight with you, so I convinced myself we could get through it by not discussing the case at all. But that blew up in my face last night, didn't it? How can we make this relationship work if we don't both make each other—and agreements between us—a priority?" His voice got soft. "I don't feel like your priority, Hadley."

A fat tear rolled down my face. The truth was I loved Cash, and he was my priority. But he wasn't my only priority...and he was right...I couldn't argue that I hadn't gone back on our agreement the first time I felt like a client needed me and I thought I was the only one who could help. Was that just my hubris?

Cash stood. He looked at me like he was hoping I would argue with him.

He walked away while I frantically searched for the right words.

Chapter Twenty-Two

We all rode in Liz's van, an old white panel model that she'd stuck a Lowcountry 24-HR Plumbing Solutions sign on. Maybe I needed an old white van. Out of necessity, I was long in the habit of not spending money unless I absolutely had to. But I could see where a van like this would make surveillance and pretexting so much easier. I rode shotgun, with Sarabeth behind me, leaning in with her head between the seats. She wasn't going to miss a thing. For my part, I was happy to have a distraction from my imploding love life.

We'd no sooner left my house than my phone vibrated. It was on silent, but as I raised the screen, a voicemail notification flashed across my screen. It was Scarlett. I'd missed her call.

"We've heard from one of our suspects." I tapped the voicemail icon and put it on speaker.

She spoke fast, her voice almost giddy. "I wanted to

let you know Brett came to see me this evening, out of the blue. He said he's so sorry for missing our calls. He's been real busy at work. We're actually on our way out to grab a bite. He's the sweetest thing—he's taking me to The Rooftop at the Vendue. I've been craving one of their lobster rolls. In any case, I told him to call you, and he said he'd be sure to do that tomorrow, since we're busy this evening. I gave him your number. Bye now."

"Well, well. That's interesting," said Liz. "The Vendue is only two blocks from our drop point."

"I would've bet good money she'd never hear from him again," I said. "*If* he is actually a real person to begin with, which I'm still not convinced of."

"I won't be the teensiest bit surprised if she turns out to be our culprit," said Liz.

"So y'all are thinking she made this Brett person up to give herself an alibi, and she's just continuing to make things up about him to make Hadley believe he's legit?"

"It's entirely possible…" I said, "…and she might've used the Vendue in her story to give herself a plausible reason to be in the area."

From its spot in a dashboard mount, Liz's phone sang out "Shake Ya Tailfeather," from the Bad Boys II Soundtrack. She swiped the slider to answer. "Hey, Mamma."

My head swiveled towards her.

A smile played at Liz's lips as she listened through Bluetooth earbuds. "I'm sorry, Mamma, but I have something I need to take care of this evening...no, it's work-related...Mamma, I know it's Good Friday... Nate's at home...Yes, by himself on a Friday night, Mamma...No, Mamma, he has something for dinner... yes, ma'am...I will...of course...Mamma, I said I would...I promise...I have to go now...bye now...love you too...bye bye now."

Liz's shoulders rose and fell in a sigh.

"Your *mother's* ring tone is "Shake Ya Tailfeather?" I felt my face squinch. "Care to explain that?"

Liz grinned. "Mamma loves Jazzercise. As far as I know, that's not one of their dance tunes, but I tease her about going to "shake her tail feather."

"Does she know that's her ringtone?" I asked.

Liz laughed. "No, and she would not be amused. I guess you have something on me now. She wants you to come for Easter dinner on Sunday, by the way. Bring Cash with you."

"Ahh—"

"You've met Mamma," said Liz. "You know very well she will have her way, if she has to send Blake, Nate, and Joe after you. Resistance is futile."

"I can't intrude on your family time," I said.

"Oh—I'm so sorry," said Liz. "What on earth was I thinking? You likely have a family get together of your own to attend."

"Well..." Gavin and Joe *had* asked me to go with them to Halls Chophouse for the Sunday Gospel Brunch, but their reservations were for 11:00, and I wouldn't be out of church until noon.

"So you don't?" Liz glanced at me, then back to the road as we approached the Cooper River Bridge on Coleman Boulevard.

"I thought your daddy was in Italy," said Sarabeth. "And your brother was on a private island somewhere with that woman who's been chasing him for years... what was her name? Alex something..."

I flashed her a *pipe down* look, then smiled at Liz. "Thank you so much—please thank your mother for me. But—"

"Poppy and Blake and the kids will be there, of course."

"Poppy...and the kids..." She was offering me the opportunity to spend Easter with my sister and a niece and a nephew I'd never met.

"Who's Poppy?" asked Sarabeth.

"It's a long story," I said. "I'll tell you all about her later."

"And Merry and Joe and Nate and me. Normally Mamma's whole side of the family—the Moores—would be there on Easter too, but they're all headed to Orlando to see about Uncle Cecil. He's having a hard time because his albino boa constrictor's gone missing? He reported it kidnapped, but there's no ransom demand so far. Anyway, it'll be a smaller crowd than usual. Mamma has already been cooking for days. Her Easter feast is better than Thanksgiving, I kid you not."

"Well, I—"

"I think my daddy's cousin Ponder will be there, but really, he's the only one besides our immediate family, so, a small circus, rather than the full three rings."

"I'd love to, thank you," I said when I could get a word in.

"Your family certainly sounds entertaining," said Sarabeth.

"Would you like to join us?" Liz's eyes brightened. "Mamma's happiest when she's feeding a crowd. And honestly, we'll be eating leftovers for days unless we can recruit some more folks."

"Thank you so much," said Sarabeth, "but my family is expecting us at the circus in Florence."

"Another time." Liz smiled at Sarabeth in the rearview mirror.

We rode in silence for a while. I was convinced Porter was the most likely suspect. But something about Scarlett and her possibly made up boyfriend made my shifty meter ping.

Right at eight thirty, Liz pulled the van into the driveway of a building under construction on Prioleau Street, then hopped out and placed an orange cone behind it.

"Now tell me what that's for," said Sarabeth as she climbed out of the van, a confused look on her face.

"It makes us look more authentic," said Liz. "Ever notice how often work trucks have these cones around them?"

"Ooohhh." Sarabeth nodded. "That's smart. I'm learning so much from y'all."

The knots in my stomach tightened. I didn't feel

one bit good about bringing Sarabeth along to a potentially dangerous operation, but after Liz brought it up, I was hard pressed to convince my friend who'd been chomping at the bit since Wednesday to stay home.

We'd all dressed as if we were out to exercise: I was in black leggings paired with a thin T-shirt; Liz wore grey exercise capris and a matching tank; and Sarabeth wore her navy Pure Jill organic cotton warm-up suit. We all had on our tennis shoes. If we needed to move quickly, we were ready. We walked to the nearest corner, made a left on Exchange Street, crossed Concord Street, and climbed the shallow flight of steps into Waterfront Park. As we turned left and headed down the brick path, the set of trash and recycling cans I'd directed our suspects to came into view.

We sat on the park bench next to the cans and waited.

"Okay, it's clear now for a minute." As planned, Sarabeth watched for foot traffic approaching from the direction of Public Pier. At nearly nine p.m. on a Friday night in April, there were still plenty of locals and tourists meandering along the paths at Waterfront Park.

"Good this way." Liz kept watch towards the Pineapple Fountain.

Couples, families, and groups of teenagers strolled along the path by the Cooper River, but they all gazed out across the water. None of them were looking in our direction.

I pulled the fake rock with the hidden camera out of my backpack and darted over to the live oak behind the recycling and trash cans. With a glance over my shoulder, I placed the "rock" at the base of the tree.

Moving quickly, I pinched a bit of putty from the pocket of my capris and stuck a tiny camera onto the large concrete pillar nearby. Next I took a dime-sized camera with a pushpin back and stuck it onto a tree across the walkway. Then I slid back onto the bench between Sarabeth and Liz.

I opened the app on my iPad and pulled up the feed for all three cameras. "All set."

"Everyone got their earpiece in?" asked Liz.

"Yes," I said.

"Roger." Sarabeth grinned.

"Everyone see us all in Where's Everybody?" I asked. We'd created a special circle in a tracking app so we could find each other if we somehow got separated.

"Check," said Liz.

"Roger," said Sarabeth.

I navigated to photos. "Here's a recent photo of Porter..." I swiped left. "And Corinne...and Scarlett...and Mary Ellis. Just so everyone knows who we're looking for." I knew Liz had researched all these people enough to know what they looked like, and of course she'd seen Porter. But Sarabeth had only ever seen Mary Ellis as far as I knew.

"Okay...we should get in position. I'll be directly across, by the river..." I pointed to another bench along the waterfront path. I'll be watching the realtime camera footage on my iPad. Liz, you'll be just on the other side of the Middle Atlantic Wharf entrance to the park, also with your back to this spot..."

"Check," said Liz. "The reflector on the back of my cap has a camera I can monitor on my phone.

"And Sarabeth, against my better judgement, you'll be on a bench by the Pineapple Fountain, facing this way."

"Check." Sarabeth smiled wide and gave a giddy little shiver.

"If anything goes sideways, we meet at the van," I said. "Y'all ready to get your props?"

"I guess we'd better," said Liz.

"This is so exciting," said Sarabeth as they stood and hurried off towards the van.

At nine thirty, an older woman hunched over a walker waddled by, her hair in a bun, wearing large, thick glasses. Sarabeth lifted her nose and pointedly ignored me as she passed.

Five minutes later, a mother sporting a ponytail and a pink ball cap power-walked by pushing a baby stroller. Liz settled on a bench beyond the Middle Atlantic Wharf park entrance.

I took my backpack and crossed the park to a riverfront bench directly in front of our target recycling can. I pulled out my iPad and opened the camera app. I pressed a button hidden under my shirt near my collar bone. "Video is live. We're on go."

"Check," said Liz. "Mamma is rocking the baby."

"Roger," said Sarabeth. "Granny is waiting for the grandkids."

Porter Barnwell would no doubt show up soon—I was convinced of it. He was our culprit. Nevertheless, I opened the GPS tracking app on my phone. The tracker I'd left on Mary Ellis's car registered as a blinking red light on my screen.

I pressed my mic button. "Well, well. Ladies, it looks like Mary Ellis may be on her way to us. Her car is on I-26 heading towards Charleston."

"Well, I'll be," said Sarabeth. "Here I am expecting Scarlett."

"My money is on Scarlett," said Liz. "I-26 goes lots of places. Mary Ellis could be on her way to meet her hot Italian lover."

"I'm laying my bets on Porter," I said. "Wait... Mary Ellis got off on Ashley Phosphate. Is she headed towards Bridget's apartment? I better call her."

Bridget answered on the second ring. "Hey, Hadley."

"I'm not sure, but I think Mary Ellis may be on her way over. Any idea what she's up to?"

"It's not her week to have the kids—they're asleep. She well knows it's past their bedtime. Most likely she's checking up on me. Occasionally she drives by to see if I'm home, if I have company, if I'm throwing a wild party—I've never even been to a tame party. I'm more the watch-a-movie-in-my-jammies type."

"Let me know what's going on if she shows up."

"Will do."

I turned my attention back to the camera feeds. The occasional couple or family passed by the drop-off. It was almost ten o'clock.

"I don't know who this guy is," said Liz, "but he's passed by three times now. He's dressed oddly for this time of year—has on a hoodie. He seems to be looking for someone. Might be unrelated."

"Did you get a picture?" I asked.

"Yeah, I don't know how good it will be in this light."

A guy in a grey hoodie passed by the cameras. "I see him. Look at the camera, mister." He kept his face pointed straight ahead. The one angle we didn't have was facing down the pathway towards Exchange Street. Oh well, he was probably just a random guy looking for a friend.

"No sign of anyone we're looking for by the fountain," said Sarabeth.

We waited.

Five minutes later, Liz said, "'Lonny the Loiterer' circled back. He's on the inside brick path at the end of Concord. Headed your way, Sarabeth."

A minute later, Sarabeth said, "I've got him. He's headed back your way now. I took a fake selfie and snapped a picture of him, but he wasn't looking my way."

"I wonder if he was sent by one of our suspects," I said. "Maybe one of the Barnwells hired someone."

Liz said, "Well, if they hired him to make a drop, he's not doing his job."

"I'm guessing if he's a hired hand, he was hired to find out who made the call," I said.

"And likely to neutralize the threat," said Liz.

He passed by the cameras again, but still didn't glance at the cans. This time, he made a u-turn onto the waterfront path, because moments later, he passed in front of me.

"Excuse me, sir?" I reached into my backpack and pulled a random bill out of my wallet and folded it twice.

He stopped on the path a few steps past my bench. Slowly, he turned towards me, but he didn't speak. He was caucasian, with medium brown hair, of average height, and average build. In addition to the grey hoodie, he wore a black T-shirt, jeans, and tennis shoes. He was basically average all the way around, with no distinguishing features, no face tattoo, no nose ring.

"Did you drop this?" I smiled warmly and handed him the folded bill, which turned out to be a twenty.

"Thanks." He took the money, but didn't return the smile. His eyes held an expression I couldn't read. He turned and continued down the path.

What was his deal?

When he was out of earshot, I pressed my mic and said, "Let's retreat to a spot we can pick him up from and tail him when he gets tired and leaves. Sarabeth, you first. Head back to the van, get inside, and make sure the doors are locked. In two minutes, Liz, you head out. Get to the roof of the parking garage on Prioleau, between North and Middle Atlantic Wharf. See if you can spot him when he leaves and let me know where he's headed."

"Roger that," said Liz.

"Roger," said Sarabeth.

I stayed put. He didn't pass by me again, but he did pass the cameras. It was nerve-wracking not having other sets of eyes on him, wondering if he'd left, what he was doing. Foot traffic in the park thinned.

Ten minutes later, Sarabeth said, "I'm in the van. Doors are locked. I can see Prioleau in the sideview mirror in case he passes this way."

A couple of minutes after that, Liz said, "I'm on the garage roof."

I waited another five minutes, then put my iPad in my backpack and strolled up to the Pineapple Fountain. Where was he?

"I've got him," said Liz. "He just passed between the City Gallery and the condo building. He's coming up on Prioleau and North Atlantic Wharf."

I hustled around the fountain and down the walkway between the buildings. He'd gotten a good look at me earlier. As I walked, I pulled a lightweight yellow jacket out of my backpack and slipped it on. Then I popped on a baseball cap and tucked my hair underneath it.

When I reached the intersection of Prioleau and North Atlantic Wharf, I could see him ahead of me on the left sidewalk on North Atlantic Wharf heading towards East Bay.

"Heading down North Atlantic Wharf," I said into my mic.

"I see you," said Liz.

"Tracking you," said Sarabeth.

Our quarry crossed East Bay and cut through a parking lot to State Street. I tailed him, ducking behind the occasional tree, car, or building, then hurrying to catch up. With me in tow, he crossed State and made his way down Chalmers to Meeting Street, where he crossed the street, then made a left.

I followed him several blocks down Meeting Street. Just past Nathaniel Russell House, he ducked down Price's Alley. I hung back. There's no way "Lonny the Loiterer" wouldn't spot me on that narrow passage that ran between two rows of homes over to King Street. I waited until I thought he'd had time to clear the other end, then dashed down Price's Alley, passing under live oak branches, along courtyard walls, and by brick driveways and planting beds.

I looked both ways on King Street.

There—he'd gone left and was half a block away.

He crossed King Street, and I stayed on the left-hand sidewalk.

A few blocks down, right before Ladson Street, he darted down a driveway between two houses. I sprinted down King Street and followed him down the brick drive, but it gave way to a walled courtyard. There was no sign of our target.

Could he have scaled the six-foot brick wall?

He must have—but in which direction, left, right, or center?

The backdoor of the home opened, and a man stuck his head out. "Can I help you?"

"Oh! I'm so sorry," I said. "My dog ran down your driveway, but I don't know which way he went. Charlie? Here boy."

The man stepped out on the porch and scanned the yard. "I don't see him. Are you sure he came down our drive? He couldn't have gotten out of the backyard if he did."

"Well, I sure thought so." I shrugged. "I guess it must've been your neighbor's. Sorry to have troubled you." I smiled and waved as I jogged back to King Street.

"I lost him," I said into my mic.

"We'll pick you up at King and South Battery." Liz's voice came through my earpiece.

"Roger that."

I headed down King Street. Where had "Lonny" gone? He must've realized I was following him. Dejected, I waited on the corner of King and South Battery.

Which way would Liz and Sarabeth be coming from? I could open Where's Everybody on my phone or iPad and see, but I glanced up and down South Battery.

That's when I saw the brilliant bronze metallic Subaru parked three cars down to my right on South

Battery. Was that *the* Subaru? I jogged down the sidewalk. The license plate read 2348PX.

Frogs raining from the clear blue sky.

This was the brown Subaru that had been parked across the street the night Patricia was killed.

I snapped a picture of the plate and looked up and down the sidewalk.

A couple walking a labradoodle approached from the direction of Legare Street. Beyond them, I caught a glimpse of a grey sweatshirt.

I ducked down a path between two large double-porched houses and hid behind a riotous Lady Banks' climbing rosebush that spilled over the fence. I fumbled in my backpack for my phone.

Peeking out from the yellow-bloom-festooned branches, I watched as "Lonny the Loiterer" scanned the street, one hand on the door handle of the Subaru.

I snapped his picture just as he looked my way. He froze, and I knew he was staring right at me.

After a three count, he climbed into the Subaru.

Weak with relief, I sank to my knees. He must not've seen me.

He started the car, and pulled onto South Battery.

Chapter Twenty-Three

"Hadley, what's going on? Where are you?" Liz asked through the earpiece.

"Here." I scrambled up, darted out from my hiding place and ran to the van sitting at the corner of King Street and South Battery.

As I climbed in, I shouted, "*Go.*" I pointed down South Battery. "He's in the brown Subaru. He just pulled out."

Liz rolled forward, gradually picking up speed. Taillights glowed ahead of us. Just as we approached Council Street, we got close enough to recognize the car. "There he is."

"He went over a garden wall on King Street," I said. "I thought I'd lost him. And then there he was, parked three cars down from the spot you picked me up at."

"That's amazing." Sarabeth hung between the

front seats. "Who do y'all think this guy is? I mean...he wasn't carrying a duffel bag full of money, so he wasn't here to pay off a blackmailer..."

"I think he's the person who killed Patricia, probably paid by Porter Barnwell, who also paid him to show up tonight," I said. "At a minimum, he was sent to figure out who the blackmailer is."

"*Sonavabitch.*" Liz banged the steering wheel. "I guess my instincts are rusty. I really thought it was Scarlett. Wait—they could still be in this together."

I said, "*Dangit*, I wish I'd been able to get a tracker on that car. He nearly caught me taking a photo of the plate."

"Did you run it?" Liz looked both ways, then followed the Subaru across Tradd Street and headed up Chisolm.

"I'm doing that right now." Impatiently, I waited while the system searched, the circle spinning on the screen of my iPad.

Liz lingered at the stop sign and let a Camry between us and the Subaru before turning left on Broad Street.

"That car belongs to Michael and Lauren Spencer," I said. "They live on Limehouse Street. Wait—no. The *tag* is registered to them. But it belongs on a Lexus."

We followed him to the end of Broad Street and around the curve onto Lockwood Boulevard, then left on 17 and over the Ashley River Memorial Bridge. When he went left towards Folly Beach, the

Camry went right to stay on 17. We were right behind him.

"Lonny" moved into the right lane to turn onto Maybank Highway. Liz poked along, allowing room for someone else to slide in between us, but no one did.

"Oh no." In the pit of my stomach, I knew where we were headed. "He's going to Scarlett's house. She lives on Howle Avenue. Hang back a little more."

Liz slowed the van.

I called Scarlett.

"Lonny" put on his left turn signal.

"Turn left on Fleming," I said. "Scarlett lives towards the end of Howle. It's a dead end with no cross streets."

Scarlett's voicemail picked up. "She's not answering." I didn't bother with a message. What could I have said anyway? Were they co-conspirators, or was she his innocent victim?

"Are you sure that's where he's going?" asked Sarabeth.

Liz made the turn.

"Positive. I haven't worked out yet how it all fits together, but I think 'Lonny' is actually Scarlett's boyfriend Brett."

"But she was with Brett this evening," said Sarabeth. "I thought they were going to The Rooftop at the Vendue."

"There's a collision repair shop on the right on down a ways. It backs up to Scarlett's yard." I turned to Sarabeth. "I know that's what her message said. But I've got a bad feeling about this."

Liz turned into the collision repair shop, which was deserted on a Friday night. She cut the lights and pulled around back.

"Scarlett's house is on the other side of this row of trees. If it were daylight, we could see it through the trees." I pulled a pair of cargo shorts out of my backpack and slid them over my leggings.

Liz turned to me as she secured a holster over the waistband of her leggings at the small of her back and pulled her tank top over it. "Please take my extra weapon."

"I've never even held a gun," I said. "I have a can of long range pepper spray." I slid it into a side pocket.

Liz closed her eyes, shook her head, then opened her eyes and sighed. "What's the plan?"

I stared through the trees. "I can't see his car from here. But I know he's there."

"Hang on." Liz unbuckled her seatbelt and stood.

Sarabeth slid back into her seat to let Liz pass as she climbed into the back of the van. She returned moments later with a fancy pair of binoculars. "Try these."

"What are these, government issued super secret spy goggles?" I asked.

"They're Amazon issued night vision binoculars," said Liz.

"Really? You have the coolest toys."

"Nate is forever buying gadgets, some of which I've never even used. But these come in plenty handy."

I scanned Scarlett's backyard, then zoomed in on the driveway at the right side of the house. "Oh, yes. He's there all right. The Subaru is in the driveway."

"Should we call the police?" asked Sarabeth.

"We don't have enough evidence yet to go to the police, at least not on Patricia's murder. If they pick him up now, we tip our hand. But we need to make sure Scarlett is okay, and figure out exactly what her role in all this is. He's seen me—knows I was following him. He will probably recognize Liz from the park."

"I can fix that." Liz climbed back to the back of the van.

"Excellent," I said. "Then you go to the front door. Say you're visiting from out of town at the neighbor's house, and your sister told you that Scarlett has some fabulous crystals and you really need one to contact your spirit guide."

Liz stopped mid-motion, just as she poked her head through a sundress. She looked at me like I'd lost my mind. "Are you smoking mushrooms right now?"

"Trust me," I said. "This will make it believable. I will try the kitchen door. If I can't get in there, I'll try the windows. Keep him occupied as long as you can. I'll find Scarlett. As soon as I know she's all right, I'll let you know and we'll clear out. If I find her and she's not all right, or if anything goes sideways, Sarabeth, one of us will say 9-1-1... and you call 9-1-1 STAT. Say you're the neighbor and someone with a big gun broke in at Scarlett's house, you heard gunfire, and you believe she's been injured." I gave her Scarlett's street address.

Liz pulled her hair out of the ponytail and fluffed it. Then she reached into a rubber tote, pulled out a burner phone, and handed it to Sarabeth. "Use this if you need to call 9-1-1."

We all popped our earpieces back in. I handed Sarabeth the binoculars.

"Ready?" I asked.

Liz nodded.

"Sarabeth, lock the doors as soon as they close behind us," I said.

"I will." Her face creased with worry. "Y'all, please be careful."

Liz opened the back doors and we climbed out.

She eased the doors closed and we waited until we heard the click on the other side that let us know they were locked. Then we ran towards the tree line.

As we cleared the uneven patch of mature pine and oak trees, we could see that Scarlett's backyard was bordered by trees on both the right and left side. From the right side of the yard, we could see lights were on in the living room/dining room combo. I jerked my head left, and we followed the tree line on the left up to the corner of the house.

Liz motioned towards the front. I gave her a thumbs up and she darted around the side of the house. I crept over to the small back porch off the kitchen, climbed two steps, and crouched low to the right of the door. The back door had a window in the top. When I heard the doorbell ring, I counted to three, then raised my head just high enough so I could see into the house.

Light spilled into the kitchen from the great room. I could see straight through to where "Lonny" stood by the front door. He pulled it open. I could hear Liz talking, but I couldn't make out the words. I couldn't see Scarlett, but I didn't have a view of the entire room either. But if she were able to answer the door in her own house, surely she would have.

I tried the doorknob. Locked.

I scurried down the steps and along the back of the house to the corner, where I calculated Scarlett's bedroom was. I tried the corner window, but it was locked, and the curtains were pulled shut.

As I rounded the corner of the house, I sent up a prayer for an open window. I tried the first one I came to, and it was locked as well, but the curtains were open. I pulled out my iPhone and turned on the flashlight. Shining it into the window, I swept the room from left to right.

There she was, sprawled sideways across the bed in the dark like she'd just dropped there.

My flashlight landed on a large pair of eyes and I jumped.

Huckleberry, her cat, was curled up beside her. He hissed at me.

Maybe it was just a headache. Or maybe something wasn't quite right.

I tapped softly on the window.

No response from Scarlett, but Huckleberry hissed again.

I moved the light around the bed and spied a prescription bottle lying beside Scarlett on the bedspread with the cap off.

What had she taken?

Did she take it of her own free will?

When she left the message, just after 8 pm—less than three hours ago—she was excited about going to dinner with Brett. They were on their way out, she'd said.

I pushed my mike button. "I have eyes on Scarlett. She's unconscious. May have been given an overdose. 9-1-1. 'Lonny' is inside the house."

"Roger," said Sarabeth.

A few moments later, Liz said, "I'm out."

I waited until I saw her coming around the side of the house, then jogged over to the wooded area. She joined me and we hightailed it across the yard, staying as close as possible to the shelter of the trees.

When we were almost back to the van we heard the sirens.

"Should we leave before the police arrive?" Sarabeth asked as we climbed in and closed the doors.

"No," I said. "I want to be sure he doesn't somehow talk them into this is a false alarm. I'm almost positive she needs immediate medical attention."

"He definitely wasn't about to let me through the

door," said Liz. "But he did hand me a quartz to get me to leave."

We all ducked as headlights cut through Scarlett's yard.

"I think he's leaving," said Liz. "He must've heard the sirens."

"Good grief, what is wrong with me?" I shuddered in frustration. "I can't believe I didn't get a tracker on that car—again."

"We had other priorities," said Liz.

"Lonny"—or Brett—shot out of the driveway and sped away.

"You want to follow him or stay with Scarlett?" asked Liz.

"We have to stay with Scarlett," I said.

"Agreed," said Liz.

Apprehension clutched at my stomach. "She was out cold. Whatever she took or was given, it happened earlier. He's only been back a few minutes. Pills wouldn't act that fast. Maybe we should go give her CPR."

"EMS will do a much better job of that if it's necessary," said Liz. "They'll be here before we could possibly break into the house—there are smart double deadbolt locks, the kind that auto lock a few seconds after the door closes. I scoped them out while I was chatting with him about crystals and heard them engage as I was leaving. Plus, if we did that—if we're there when the police arrive—we're going to have a lot of explaining to do, probably at the police station.

That could seriously hamper our efforts to track this guy down."

Moments later, Scarlett's yard lit up with emergency vehicles: a fire truck, an ambulance, and two police cars. By the headlights and flashing lights, we watched as police officers and EMTs climbed out of their vehicles and dashed towards the front door.

"I wonder why he came back here," said Sarabeth. "'Lonny,' I mean. Brett. Whoever he is. It doesn't make any sense."

"I'm thinking he came back to get rid of Scarlett. He must've given her something fast acting...or if he gave her an overdose earlier, maybe he wanted to make sure she was gone." I sent up a prayer that she would be okay.

"Probably that," said Liz. "Or maybe he remembered something he needed to wipe his prints off of. Hey, there's a regular pair of binoculars in the glovebox if you need them, with all those lights."

I pulled them out. "Yeah, that's better." We waited until we saw the EMTs roll the stretcher out. "I see the IV bag. She's alive. Oh, thank Heaven." Relief washed over me. "I'd like to go to the hospital. Do y'all need to go home?"

"I planned to stay at the foundation tonight," said Liz. "I figured I'd miss the last ferry. I can go with you to the hospital."

Sarabeth's eyes were huge. She looked like she felt queasy. "I can Uber home from there. Tucker will be worried about me. I mean...it's past my bedtime. Do y'all think Scarlett will be okay? I sure hope so. Y'all keep me posted, hear? I cannot believe he nearly killed her. *Oh my stars, y'all*! What if we hadn't followed him?"

Sarabeth continued chattering like a magpie all the way to the hospital, while we searched for a parking place, and as we waited with her for the Uber. As the driver pulled to the curb, she chattered while she called Tucker. After checking the license plate on the Honda CR-V, Sarabeth climbed into the car. "Sweetheart, you will not be*lieve* what happened this evening...I can't talk right now, but I'll tell you everything as soon as I get home..." She closed the car door and waved as the car pulled away.

"She seems very...animated," said Liz. "You think she'll ever ask to come to work with you again?"

"She'll either never mention it again, or she'll be waiting on my front porch every single morning. It could go either way."

Chapter Twenty-Four

Although we weren't family, Liz and I were the people there for Scarlett that night. Still, what with privacy laws and whatnot, the doctor and nursing staff were annoyingly tight-lipped, though not unsympathetic. We had to resort to eavesdropping—one of our most reliable skills—to learn Scarlett had ingested Lorazepam and alcohol, what could've been a lethal dose, but thankfully, she'd gotten help in time. They were cautiously optimistic that she would be fine.

We weren't allowed to see her—the doctor said she wasn't awake and likely wouldn't be for a while. He told us to go home and come back later in the day.

I knew from doing her profile that Scarlett didn't have any local family. I called her parents, who lived in Chattanooga, and they said they'd get here as quick as they could. Only because neither Liz nor I had the first idea where to look for "Lonny," we called it a day. She dropped me off at my house just before 1:00 a.m.

It felt like that Friday had lasted forty days and forty nights. I was exhausted, but way too wired to sleep. How was I going to find the man who I was now convinced must be Brett Campbell?

And why on earth would this person who hadn't shown up anywhere in Patricia's family, friends, or associates want to kill her unless he'd been hired? And he must have, though I was far from being able to prove it. Or could he possibly be that hardest of all killers to catch—a psychopath who killed randomly for the thrill? If so, how had Patricia crossed his path?

My rapidly evolving theory of the crime was that this Brett had followed Scarlett to the bookstore and chatted her up. She was lonely...he probably poured on the charm and suggested they have dinner. He followed her home and things progressed from there. Sometime during their evening together, he must have drugged her, then left to go kill Patricia. He probably got the codes the same way I did—from Scarlett's desk drawer—and borrowed her key to Patricia's house as well.

Scarlett, unaware she'd been drugged, assumed he'd just gotten up early and left. She was late to work but chalked it up to a late night and maybe too much alcohol.

I thought I understood the how...I just had no idea of the why, nor how to find the *who*.

I had his car on video, leaving the area around the time of the murder.

He'd tried to kill Scarlett, presumably because she was the link between him and Patricia...

That was my theory, but I needed *proof* he'd killed Patricia, especially given I hadn't established a solitary connection between the two of them. I felt it in my bones that he had, in fact, killed her. But I needed more than my conviction to help Bridget.

First things first, I needed to tie that car to him. *Oh good grief*. I had asked North to run everyone on my suspect list against the list of brown Subaru Forester owners in South Carolina, and then I'd gotten wrapped up in talking to Uma Jennings on the phone and completely forgotten to stop and take a picture of the case board for him. Maybe a company in Porter or Corinne's name owned that car...Brett had likely swiped a random tag to avoid having the real tag traced back to the owner...

I needed that list of suspects for North, and yes, I could've recreated it, but I was just *sooo* antsy...I needed to do *something*. So, before I even climbed the stairs after Liz dropped me off, I hopped in Jolene and drove over to my office in Mount Pleasant to snap that promised photo. Here is where a pair of those fancy electronic case boards would have come in really handy...one for my home office and one for my Mount Pleasant office...

As I walked back to my car in the parking lot behind the one-story commercial building, a red BMW convertible passed along Pherigo Street. It caught my eye because traffic was light at that time of morning, and because I'd often admired a similar car owned by one of my neighbors. It was a jaunty little ride, and I appreciated it—though no convertible would ever take Jolene's place, of course.

When the same BMW convertible pulled in two cars behind me at the light on Coleman Boulevard, I squinted at it in the rearview mirror and wondered if it actually *was* the one that belonged to someone in my neighborhood. The top was up, and I couldn't see the driver. Not that I had any idea specifically *who* drove the car I was familiar with. I'd just seen it around Sullivan's Island often enough to assume it was a local, but for all I knew, it could've belonged to a serial daytripper with good taste in cars.

By the time the car turned left to follow me onto Marshall Boulevard, I was thinking, *At this hour, surely this is a neighbor driving home. The sporty red car must belong to one of my neighbors further down Marshall Boulevard.*

It was late, and I was tired to the point of being bleary-eyed and giddy.

At the end of my driveway, I waited for the gate to open and then pulled into the drive. I raised a friendly hand to the driver I couldn't see on the dark street, like neighbors do. The convertible passed on by.

With Jolene safely ensconced in the garage, I started towards the steps.

A noise I couldn't identify came from somewhere outside.

What was that clanging? It sounded like maybe someone was pounding the steel fence with a hammer.

What in this world?

Did the gate malfunction when I came in? Was it somehow banging against itself? I pressed the button to open the garage door. As soon as the door was high enough, I ducked my head and started to step outside to see what was going on.

Then everything happened at once.

The clanging abruptly stopped.

A stiff burst of wind blew me back into the garage, knocking me on my rear end.

Crack. Crack. Crack.

Something whizzed over my head.

Gunfire?

Heaven help me.

In a motion somewhere between a crab-crawl, a roll, and a dive, I scrambled behind the concrete pillar between the garage doors. Peeking out, I scanned the driveway, the gate, and my small front yard with the huge live oak. Outdoor lights with motion sensors and timers had been triggered when I pulled in, and still brightly lit the stamped concrete drive.

Everything appeared completely normal.

What in the name of sweet reason and sanity was going on here? I sent up a silent thank you for the rogue wind gust that may well have saved my life.

I hopped up and dashed to the wall at the bottom

of the steps, where the switches were mounted. I hit the first button to close the door and knelt back down.

Was that really gunfire?

I *might've* confused the sound.

It could've been firecrackers—except for the things that came zipping over my head.

Mother of pearl. It was definitely gunfire.

Once the garage door was all the way down, I pressed the lock button, scrambled up the stairs, and keyed in my code to unlock the door and disarm the security system. I bolted the door behind me and had my hand poised to set the security system to "stay" when I heard the knocking.

Someone tapped urgently on glass.

I stuck my head in the living room. No one at the sliding doors.

No one at the dining room doors.

I dashed to the kitchen.

North.

Oh, thank goodness. Relief flooded through me.

He stood on the other side of the sliding door, peering in. He stopped knocking when he saw me.

I shot across the room, unlocked the door, and slid it open.

"Are you all right?" asked North.

"I think so. Did that sound like gunfire to you?"

"Yes, it did. Call the police." He backed away. "I'm heading out."

"Wait." I needed a moment to process everything. If the police came, they would likely search my property for whoever fired the gun. They wouldn't skip over North's outdoor sanctuary. There would be questions...it would be obvious someone lived in my garden. This would raise law enforcement eyebrows. North would be on their radar ever after. They'd dig into his background. This would no doubt make him anxious, and he'd been doing so well lately. This could be a setback.

Whoever fired that gun was likely gone by now.

Somehow, it had to be "Lonny" or Brett or whatever his name was. Had he gone to the hospital to try to finish Scarlett off? Fear sliced through me. Was she still okay?

Had Brett seen us at the hospital and followed when Liz brought me home? Or had he somehow tracked me down from my name and phone number, which Scarlett had given him? Could that have been him in the red BMW?

Who was this person, and what sort of resources did he have?

Poised to run, North's anxious eyes were glued to mine, waiting for a decision.

"There's no point," I said.

"We need to make sure the house and yard are safe."

"There's no way he could've gotten inside the house—"

"He? Do you know who this was?" asked North.

"I'm reasonably certain it was the guy who killed Patricia Gaillard. He tried to kill Scarlett Hathaway this evening. I'll explain everything later. Look, the house is safe, I'm sure of it. The security system is state of the art. But he could have gotten over the fence. Would you consider sleeping in one of the guest rooms just for tonight? It's just a few hours till daylight. Then we can make sure the premises are secure." I couldn't let North sleep outside tonight. "Please."

He swallowed hard and looked away. "I won't leave you alone." He nodded. "Okay."

I stepped back and motioned him inside and locked up, then went back to the panel and reset the alarm.

We settled North into the guest suite on the far side of the living room. With two sets of sliding doors and three windows, like the rest of the house, it felt almost like being outdoors. If not for North and his damaged psyche that couldn't tolerate closed spaces, I would've closed the metal hurricane shutters. The entire house wrapped itself up like an armadillo at the flip of a switch.

"Will you be okay?" I asked.

North stood by the door staring out at the night, kneading the muscles in his neck. Tension radiated off him. He turned to me and nodded. "I'll be fine. Try to get some rest."

"I will. I'll be right upstairs if you need anything."

I scurried up the stairs, but before heading to my room, I scanned as much of the yard as I could from every second floor window. I found both the cats in the media room, sitting on the window seat, staring out into the front yard. I sat beside them, scrutinizing every inch I could see of the driveway, yard, and street.

Everything was quiet. No sign of anyone, or that anything had happened.

Oddly, not a breath of air stirred the palm fronds, the tree branches, or the wind chimes. It was completely calm. A million stars glittered in the narrow swath of sky I could see overhead. The night was clear. The wind gust that saved me seemed to've been an isolated blast. Very strange.

A Sullivan's Island Police cruiser rolled slowly by. Someone else must've reported hearing gunshots. I waited, and the white Ford Explorer with "Police Sullivan's Island" in blue and yellow on the side came by a second time. Marshall Boulevard appeared to be sound asleep. With no signs anything was amiss, the police officer went to patrol another part of the island, or perhaps return to the police station. The noise would likely be written off as fireworks.

I opened the security system app on my phone. There were no video clips from the evening except those of Liz, Sarabeth, North, and me. Several backyard cameras were turned off for his privacy, but the shots had come from the front of the house. The shooter must've been standing beyond the motion detector and camera range, likely outside the five-foot tall black metal picket fence. If he'd been inside the fence, one of the cameras on the front or sides of the house would've picked him up. I hadn't figured on shooters when I'd decided on the coverage perimeter. Note to self: increase security system range.

"*Raaaooowww.*" Big Kitty turned his large green eyes on me, as if to ask a question.

"I think he's gone," I said. "But he knows where I live."

Both cats bristled and hissed.

Chapter Twenty-Five

I didn't sleep at all that Friday night. Neither did North.

When I left at five a.m. on my bicycle, he was still dressed and awake, the bed undisturbed. He strenuously objected to my going out but quickly gave up that fight. With little sleep over the past forty-eight hours, it's possible I was ornery and mulish. To ease North's mind, I took the pepper spray with me. He said he'd check the yard as soon as the sun was up.

I didn't ride my usual route. Instead, I did a grid search of the northeast end of the island, from Breach Inlet to Station 26, looking for a red BMW convertible or a brown Subaru Forester. If either vehicle was in the area, it was tucked away inside someone's garage.

Before I spread my beach towel on the sand at Breach Inlet, I carefully scanned the area. Satisfied I was the only soul stirring, I settled in to watch the sunrise.

That morning, I was in the midst of a crisis of confidence, I guess you'd call it. It had clearly been plain old pride...conceit...arrogance that I thought I was the only one who could help Bridget. I was failing her spectacularly. Anybody's meemaw with a clipboard could've done a better job.

Let's face it...I had no idea who this Brett person was, or why he might want to kill Patricia. I *speculated* Porter Barnwell—or possibly Corinne—hired him, but I had nothing but a half-baked hunch to base that on. To be perfectly honest, it was a guess based solely on the fact that they were the only ones connected to this case with a motive who could afford a hired killer. What the heck kind of investigator was I?

I was nowhere near solving this case. I was clueless...floundering...incompetent...

And but for the grace of God, I'd be dead this morning.

Had I somehow been protected? Or was Brett Campbell just a bad shot?

Did my mother have something to do with me surviving that ordeal?

Did she send the gust of wind that knocked me down right at the precise moment he fired at me?

Was she in trouble for saving my life?

Would I ever see her again?

Had I somehow accidentally ingested psychedelic mushrooms?

Good grief...

...and you know what else? Liz was absolutely right—I needed a partner. Having her around had shown me how badly I needed the "& Associates" part of Hadley Cooper & Associates.

Maybe she was right about the gun thing too...or maybe I just needed to find a career I was actually good at. Because if I had to learn to shoot a gun, something inside me would shrivel up. I was just not a gun person. But clearly, this job required better personal protection than I was currently carrying.

And on top of everything else, I was losing Cash, a man I truly loved, even if I often disagreed with him... Who was I kidding? I wasn't *losing* Cash...I'd almost certainly well and truly lost him for good this time... and for what? I was no help whatsoever to Bridget...

These were the things I was telling myself.

I was in a bad place, is what I'm saying. A dark place.

And then the day broke in quiet drama, the sun low and glowing like a hot coal, turning the thin stretch of clouds across the horizon a blazing tangerine. Wisps fanned out above like brushstrokes, scattering gold, peach, and rose across the sky. The inlet lay nearly still—so calm it mirrored the blaze above like the good Lord had poured fire on glass. Overhead, the clouds gave way to a sky so achingly blue it brought tears to my eyes. Beneath it all, the wet sand—etched with fresh tidal ridges—set off the whole spectacular show.

That sunrise took my breath away. I knew I was witnessing something holy, could feel God's presence.

And I knew in that moment, no matter how hard it might be, I was on the right path.

And that gave me peace.

Chapter Twenty-Six

For breakfast, North and I had brain smoothies—the smoothie I'd concocted over the years with a long list of things that are good for your brain, like wild blueberries, kale, and cacao—and coffee at the table near the outside kitchen on the pool deck. I seriously needed all the help with thinking I could get.

"Thank you for humoring me and staying inside last night. I know that was hard for you," I said.

"I managed," he said.

"I was thinking...let's just call that bedroom yours. You don't have to sleep in it, but it's always there if you want to...if it's too cold or too hot or there's a bad storm...for whatever reason."

"That's kind of you," he said. "I don't see me making a habit of it... So...I examined every inch of the yard. There's no evidence our shooter came inside the fence."

"That's comforting."

"A five-foot fence isn't that easy to climb over on the spur of the moment," said North. "It has those spikes on top to discourage people from trying that... but he might be back after he's had a chance to plan better."

"I need to make sure he's arrested before that happens."

"I also found the remnants of two bullets in the garage. Looks like they bounced off multiple concrete support columns and landed on the floor. The third one is probably lodged somewhere, but I couldn't find it."

My stomach lurched. Someone really did shoot real bullets at me. I should've called the police, but I knew how much that would've traumatized North, and I also knew I'd err on the side of protecting him again, every time.

"I need to find Brett Campbell," I said. "Did you have a chance to dig into the Barnwells' finances at all?"

"I did. They really should have a more secure home network. If either of them paid someone to kill Patricia, they paid the hit man from the cash they keep buried in the backyard. There's no electronic record of any transaction more than a thousand dollars in the last three months."

"*Dangit.*"

"And that's not all...their security system footage verifies they were both home the night Patricia was killed. Corinne got home before six, and Porter arrived around ten thirty. Neither of them went back out after that until the next day."

"The earliest Patricia could've been killed is eleven. He would've had to have left her house by ten after ten. Their alibis are solid." *Dangit, dangit, dangit.* I was reasonably certain at that point Brett was our guy, but that theory depended on the Barnwells paying him. Otherwise, he had no apparent motive. And if neither Porter nor Corinne had paid him, they'd been my runner-up suspects. If Porter had been captured on video coming in late and looking guilty, that would've made my job easier. He could still have paid Brett to stake out Waterfront Park and find out who had tried to blackmail him...

"I wish I had some good news to offer after that, but I wasn't able to sleep last night, so I took the opportunity to look for a connection between anyone connected to the case and the brown Subaru."

"And?"

"Nothing. Porter's company owns several vehicles, but they're all some variety of Chevrolet. The only vehicles I could tie either of them to aside from that are the Cadillac sedans they drive. Nobody on your case board has any connection I can find to a brilliant bronze metallic Subaru."

"Well." I drew a long, slow breath. "I guess that means it's either his car, or he borrowed it or stole it. This guy...he's like...Jell-O...I can't seem to pin a single thing down about him."

"I don't think that's true, Hadley," said North. "One thing you know for sure is that he sees you as a threat. Otherwise, why turn up last night at Waterfront Park at all?"

"Scarlett must've told him someone attempted to blackmail her. He showed up to see who it was…"

"Exactly. He might not have known who you were before then, but he knew the blackmailer was a threat. And he knew Scarlett kept insisting he contact you—supposedly to provide *her* with an alibi, but surely he realized he was also a suspect. Then, after he scrolled through Scarlett's phone and found your number, he staked out your office, probably never dreaming you'd turn up there so fast. And then he followed you home. Why would he take the risk of shooting at you on a public street? Only because he believes you're closing in. Which means you very likely are, whether you realize it yet or not."

Chapter Twenty-Seven

Someone had brought Scarlett a pair of pink polka dot pajamas. She looked pale, but otherwise seemed to be rallying. Sitting up in the hospital bed, sipping iced tea from a Styrofoam cup with one hand and gesturing dramatically with the other, she answered my questions.

"I called you from my bathroom," she said. "I was touching up my makeup because he said we were going out. He didn't have any idea I'd called anyone."

"But then he changed his mind? About going out, I mean?" I asked.

"*Well*, of course he never intended to take me out at all. Lord, I see that plain as day now. I wish I could go back in time and slap the naive fool I was silly. Told me to go get *gussied up*—like we were headed to the Harbour Club for cocktails. Hah! He just wanted me out of the room long enough to whip up my exit elixir and hemlock hors d'oeuvres with a side of treachery. When I came out of the bedroom, he had champagne chilled like we were celebrating something—what, I couldn't tell you. He'd brought some sort of sad little cheese puff appetizers from the freezer section...he must've put something in those. The doctor said it was Lorazepam...Ativan. I *do* have a prescription for that, but I'm scared to death of it. I filled it, sure, but I practically keep it under lock and key. I rarely take it, and I'm so careful of it. And you *never* mix Ativan with alcohol. My doctor told me straight up that would kill me."

"I think you're smart to be wary of prescription drugs."

She nodded emphatically and pointed at me with a fuchsia-tipped finger. "That's what Kootálá always says..."

Kootálá and the kook...

"The cheese puffs actually weren't all that bad," she continued, "and Brett kept making toasts...I was such a dingbat. He toasted me over and over and I fell for it...my eyes, my lips...you get the idea..." She blinked back tears. "I was eating the cheese puffs because I was drinking too much champagne on an empty stomach, and I didn't want to get all loopy that early in the evening. I thought it was going to be a special night."

I just felt so badly for her. Bless her kooky little heart. "Do you think he drugged you the night Patricia was killed too?"

Her eyes fluttered and she gave me a look that said that thought hadn't occurred to her before. Then she nodded and pointed at me. "He very well may have... yes. I think he probably did." Her voice trailed off. She continued nodding for a moment, then covered her face with her hands.

"The night you met him, he followed you home from the bookstore, right?"

She raised her tear-streaked face and sniffed. "That's right."

"What was he driving?" I asked.

"A brown Subaru."

"This 'highly confidential' job of his...did he tell you what that was?" I asked.

"He *said* he was a postal inspector...and that his job isn't what most people think, that he was a law enforcement officer, and he investigated all sorts of things like mail fraud, identity theft, and weapons smuggling. He also said he was in town undercover on a top-secret case."

I winced. "Whatever he does, I'm guessing it's not that. Have the police been by to talk to you?"

"Yes, a couple of detectives came by. Now, that did raise my spirits. Both of them were ridiculously handsome, and apparently single. Neither of them was wearing a wedding ring. One of them was a Ravenel... Sonny Ravenel was his name. I bet you anything he is related to those people on *Southern Charm*, although I did ask him that and he told me no. But that's what he would say, isn't it? The other one was every bit as handsome...Agent Cash Reynolds..." Scarlett's dreamy look got dreamier.

Cash was awfully handsome, I had to give her that. I cleared my throat. "Did you tell them all about Brett...how you met the night Patricia was killed...the whole story?"

She nodded. "I did. I made sure not to leave out a single thing. Let me tell you, I was in no rush for them to leave, no ma'am. Oh...and I did bring up Patricia's safe. I told them you'd asked about it, though they never did, and I wanted to make sure they knew all about it, and what Patricia kept in there."

"Oh?" Something tightened in my chest. I hadn't expected her to leave my name out of it altogether, but did she really have to throw gasoline on the bonfire of my love life by pointing out I'd spotted something they'd missed?

"Yes, and they said they already knew about the will. But when I mentioned how strange it was that Patricia's necklace was out of the safe, you could see plain as day that was news to them."

Well, maybe that would light a fire under them. Surely they'd want to talk to Brett Campbell. And once they discovered he was a ghost, that ought to make them plenty suspicious.

"When is the hospital going to discharge you?" I asked.

"This afternoon, I hope."

"Do you have a friend you can stay with?"

"Oh, honey, Huckleberry and I are going straight

back to Chattanooga with my mamma and my daddy and my sister. They'll be here any minute and they'll go with me to pack a suitcase and gather up Huckleberry and his things. I'll call a realtor from the safety of Tennessee. There's nothing for me here anymore...I don't have a job, and I'll never feel safe in that house again."

I was nervous Brett might try again to kill Scarlett—she was the link between him and Patricia. So I stayed and listened to her go on about all manner of nuttery until her parents arrived with her sister, Sharon. They seemed like normal people to me—they were quite lovely, actually, and couldn't stop thanking me for waiting with Scarlett. Hopefully, being closer to her family would help Scarlett get her head screwed back on straight. Then again, there were people who were convinced I was a nut because of the way I ate, so who was I to judge?

Chapter Twenty-Eight

Limehouse Street runs between Tradd Street and Murray Boulevard. Before I headed home, I drove through the neighborhood looking for the Lexus Brett had swapped tags with. It would've been helpful to find it parked on the street with a tag registered to Brett Campbell, but no such luck. Michael and Lauren Spencer, the owners of the tag on the Subaru Brett was driving, didn't answer when I rang the doorbell on the mustard-colored historic home with rust-hued shutters and a deep double front porch.

I walked the length of the porch and looked over to the driveway. The house had off-street parking, but no garage. A silver Land Rover and a golf cart under a cover occupied the short strip of concrete. There was no Lexus in sight.

As I walked down the steps and crossed the front

walk to the gate of the white picket fence, a lady dressed for exercise, who was maybe somewhere in the neighborhood of sixty-five-ish, approached from the direction of Tradd.

"Good morning," she called with a friendly wave. Her smile was wide and genuine. The yellow sun visor she wore matched her outfit.

"Good morning." I smiled back at her.

"You looking for the Spencers?"

"Yes, ma'am." I swung open the gate and stepped onto the sidewalk.

She gave me an assessing look. "You're not selling Amway or anything, are you?"

"No, ma'am."

"Not selling your take on God?" She squinted at me.

"No, ma'am. I was hoping the Spencers might be interested in selling their house. I have a client who's in love with it." I hadn't dressed the part of a real estate hustler, but maybe I could still sell the pretext.

"*Reeeally*? Well, how about that. Come stand in the shade." She stepped beneath a crepe myrtle. "Their house is gorgeous. They just completely renovated it a few years back. They're actually in New York. I'm Clarissa Carmichael. I live over on Lenwood Boulevard."

I joined her under the tree and held out my hand. "Marybeth Gibbes." People found familiar names comforting. Gibbes was on a nearby street, a museum, and a historic home. "So nice to meet you."

She pulled a phone from a side pocket in her capri-length leggings, tapped in a password, and did some scrolling. "I think I have Lauren's phone number in here somewhere. Here it is..." She rattled off a number and I typed it into my phone.

"Thank you so much."

"They may well decide to sell. Michael's in banking. He has a new job in New York. They're up there indefinitely. I think once he's gone through training or what have you, he can work remotely, but Lauren did mention they were thinking about moving."

"I'm delighted to hear that," I said. "My clients are super-motivated. They are in love with this house—they've seen the renovations. And they go on and on about how they simply must have off-street parking. Several houses they've looked at don't, and that's a deal breaker for them. This house has enough room for two cars, which is ideal for them."

"Hmmm...well, Michael and Lauren have two cars and a golf cart. I think they probably *could* get both cars in the driveway. That's Michael's Land Rover. Lauren drives some sort of Lexus SUV. She generally parks on the street, I believe, because of the golf cart. I know she has a permit because we were talking about how we both really like the digital permits—they just scan your plate now to verify it. Anyway, they drove her car to New York so they'd have it if they needed it."

"How long have they been gone?" I asked.

"Let's see...they left on a Tuesday...it was about two and a half weeks ago?"

Did they know the plate had been stolen? Had it been reported? Or had they somehow not noticed? "Well, I'll give Lauren a call. Thank you again for sharing her phone number."

"Oh, you are most welcome. So, what demographic are your clients? Can you say? Are they retired? Some of us get together for bunco..."

"They are indeed. If the deal goes through, I'll put her in touch if you'll give me your number too."

Clarissa called out her number and I typed it in. "I like Lauren and Michael just fine. They're younger, you understand, mid-forties. I have to say, it would be nice to have another couple closer to our own age nearby. Things have a way of working out, don't they? Lauren was so upset when they couldn't find a house sitter. They could be in New York for as long as a year before Michael can work from home along with some travel. She really didn't want the house empty that long. That's when she started talking about maybe selling. Maybe they're meant to be in New York after all."

I called Lauren Spencer on my way home but got voicemail. I left a message asking her to call me back regarding an urgent matter. When I pulled into my garage and hit the button to close the door behind me, I shuddered. Was he out there? Was he inside my garage? I scoured every inch I could see before I unlocked my doors and climbed out.

I hated how I was letting this clown make me into a Nervous Nellie.

My phone dinged with a text from North.

> Cash is in the living room. NOT happy.

My heart sank.

Of course he'd heard. The local law enforcement community had a very active grapevine.

I found Cash standing by the fireplace in the great room, hands on his hips, jaw tight. He didn't smile when I walked in.

"Hey," I said. "I'm so glad to see—"

"Someone shot at you." His voice was flat. Controlled. But his eyes blazed. "Three times. *In your own front yard.* And I had to hear about it from Sonny Ravenel, who heard about it from a buddy on the Sullivan's Island force."

My stomach flipped and roiled. "Cash, I was going to tell you—"

"When?" He dropped his arms and took a step towards me. "After the funeral? After I spent the rest of my life wondering why you didn't trust me enough to pick up the phone?"

"It's not about trust—"

"Then what is it about, Hadley? Because from where I'm standing, it looks like you'd rather handle everything yourself than let me help you. Even when your *life* is in very literal mortal danger."

"I didn't want to make things worse for you! You're already under review because of Porter's complaint. I thought if I told you, you'd feel like you had to get involved, and it would only—"

"Only what? Only make me look like a law enforcement officer who actually cares when someone tries to murder his girlfriend?" His voice cracked on the last word.

I stared at him. I'd never seen Cash this angry. Frustrated, yes. Disappointed, plenty of times. But this was something else. This was ice-cold fear dressed up in white-hot fury.

"I'm so sorry," I whispered. "I was wrong."

He stood there, breathing hard, looking at me like he was trying to decide something. Then he shook his head slowly.

"I can't do this, Hadley. I can't be with someone who shuts me out when it matters most." He held up a hand before I could speak. "I'm not saying we're done. I'm saying I need some time to process all of this. Us. I need to process what we really are—what I am to you and what I'm not and never will be. About what I'm willing to live with."

The tears came before I could stop them. "Cash—"

"I'll call you." He walked past me towards the front door.

I didn't follow him. I just stood there, listening to his footsteps, the door opening, the door closing, and then silence.

TROUBLE'S TURN TO LOSE

I sank onto the sofa, pulled a throw pillow into my lap, and cried.

Chapter Twenty-Nine

I couldn't tell you why I'd never taken the ferry over to Stella Maris before that Easter Sunday. I just… hadn't. As soon as Pastor Ben finished the benediction at Isle of Palms First United Methodist, I drove straight to the marina. There was something mildly fantastical about rolling Jolene aboard the 12:30 ferry—like we were off to Neverland, Narnia, or Oz. The sky was that dazzling Carolina blue you almost can't believe is real, and the salty breeze carried a whiff of pluff mud and possibilities. Across the water, a bank of dark clouds crouched low on the horizon. I sent up a silent prayer that whatever was brewing out there wasn't headed our way.

Twenty minutes later, Jolene and I rolled off the ferry and onto Stella Maris. I took my time winding through the tree-lined streets of the business district, past shops with cheerful awnings and overflowing window boxes and a park straight out of a storybook—complete with an old-fashioned bandstand. I hadn't even parked yet and already knew I'd be back to visit this magical town. At the far end of the park, we veered right, and after a couple more turns, I pulled into the driveway of the Talbot home.

Carolyn and her husband, Frank, lived just two blocks from the beach, a little north of the lighthouse, in a mature neighborhood with eclectic homes and large yards, the kind people took a lot of pride in, but not because there was an HOA. Their two-story Lowcountry-style house sat back from the road behind a wide green lawn, bordered by beds exploding with hot pink azaleas. Two ancient live oaks flanked the house, their gnarled limbs sweeping low like they were bowing to the porch. The house itself was painted the color of wet sand, with muted teal shutters that actually worked—not just the ones for looks. As I walked up the front steps, the row of rocking chairs and the porch swing all but said, *Come on up and sit a spell.* This wasn't just a house—it was a home, and it oozed hospitality.

I rang the bell and waited.

When the door jerked open, laughter and animated conversation spilled out. From the photos I'd seen, I knew the man at the front door in pressed slacks, a white button-down shirt with the sleeves rolled up, and a necktie that had been loosened was Blake Talbot.

He scowled at me. "If I'd known you were going to

change, I would've asked you to bring me some shorts. Where are the kids?" He winced and shook his head. "They ran straight to the backyard, didn't they?"

I started to giggle. "I don't think we've met—"

"Very funny. Listen, Mom's about to lose her ever lovin' spit because once again, Dad has the crazy dial on full throttle with these dang chickens and Liz's new friend is coming for lunch. I don't have time for games, woman." His language was somewhat more colorful. He pecked me on the forehead, spun away, and darted down the hall.

I shrugged, followed him inside, and closed the door.

I followed the sounds of happy family down the wide front hall and to the right. Another short hall led me into an enormous kitchen with a breakfast area and a keeping room with a fireplace and comfy furniture.

Liz and a woman who must've been Merry stood next to a butcher-block island wearing mischievous grins.

Carolyn Talbot stood by a large stove that looked like it belonged in a restaurant stirring a cast-iron pan full of gravy. She laid her spoon down and rushed over to give me a hug. "Hadley, darlin'. I'm so happy you're here. Please forgive me for not raising my daughters better. I tried my best."

"Thank you so much for having me." Through the French door, I watched as Blake crossed the large screened porch, opened the screened door, and stepped into the backyard. "I think we have a misunderstanding..."

Liz and Merry burst out laughing.

"Yes," said Carolyn. "The girls thought it would be amusing to send their brother to the door. Poppy went by the house after church and Blake came back with us to help Frank with his most recent episode of insanity. She'll be along shortly."

"Is there anything I can do to help?" I asked.

"Not a thing," said Carolyn. "We'll be ready to eat as soon as Poppy and the children arrive."

Liz leaned in for a quick hug. "Hadley, this is my sister, Merry Talbot-Eaddy. Merry, Hadley Cooper."

We both said hey and all that.

"I'm so sorry," said Merry. "We couldn't resist."

"So Blake doesn't know..." I squinted at them.

"Oh, we tried to tell him," said Liz. "He just didn't believe us when we told him how much like Poppy you look. He said we were exaggerating as usual. He was cocky. It had to be dealt with."

The front door opened and the sound of running feet preceded two blonde children into the kitchen. "Hey, Gammie," they called as they made a beeline towards the French door.

"Hold up a minute." Poppy hurried behind them. "Say hello to Hadley. Hadley, this is Frankie and Emma Rae."

My niece and nephew were adorable. My eyes glistened. Not wanting to traumatize them, I refrained from wrapping them up in a hug and squeezing them tight. I might be their aunt, but no one else here knew that yet. "Hey there," I said.

"Hello," they called over their shoulders as Frankie opened the door. Then they both stopped and stared at me.

"Tell Poppaw lunch is ready," said Carolyn.

The kids kept staring, their eyes big and round and full of wonder.

Then they looked at Poppy.

"Go," said Carolyn. "Lunch is getting cold."

They scampered out the door.

"So, your husband thinks I'm you..." I said.

"You want to do the swap thing? You run after the kids for a few days and I stay at your house? I'm thinking we could get away with that. I could feed the fish and the cats...swim...maybe catch up on my reading..."

"You might have trouble getting me to switch back. Those are adorable kids."

"Aww, thanks. They both look just like Blake." Poppy stepped over to the door and looked outside. "So, there are actual chickens now, in the Poultry Palace?"

"Twelve of them," said Carolyn. "Frank brought them home yesterday. This morning half the neighborhood called to complain. Sunrise turned into a full-blown barnyard opera. As it turns out, Frank's 'hens' included four roosters, all with something to prove. They started crowing at 4:45 a.m."

"Aren't they baby chicks?" Poppy looked confused.

"No," said Liz. "Full-grown birds."

"I understand the customary thing is to buy chicks," said Carolyn, "so, naturally, Frank did something entirely different and brought home a mature flock. He says this way we'll have eggs immediately."

"What do you mean, 'in the palace?' Are they indoor chickens?" I asked.

"Have Frank take you on a tour after lunch," said Carolyn. "It's a sight in this world."

"Daddy had an 'intelligent coop' installed," said Liz. "According to the company's advertising, it's the future of backyard chicken keeping. He'll tell you all about it. Just try to stop him. We all call it the Poultry Palace."

"I think it's wonderful he's found a new hobby," said Merry.

"If only he could find one that didn't involve livestock." Carolyn finished pouring the gravy into a tureen and set the pan back on the stove. "Liz, put this on the table, would you?"

"Of course, Mamma." She picked up the large china bowl with its matching under plate and backed into a swinging door that must've led to the dining room.

The kids came bursting through the back door, followed by Blake, Nate, and three other men.

"Frankie, Emma Rae, let's get washed up." Poppy took Emma's hand, put a hand on Frankie's shoulder, and steered them down the hall.

Blake stared at me, a stupefied look on his face. He ran a hand through his hair.

"Hadley Cooper, this is my brother, Blake Talbot," said Liz, "and my Dad, Frank Talbot, my brother-in-law, Joe Eaddy, and Daddy's cousin, Ponder Talbot. You remember Nate."

"Yes, of course," I said. "It's lovely to meet everyone. Good to see you again, Nate."

Everyone said their hellos and pleased to meet yous.

"Hadley..." Blake shook his head. "I'm so sorry—"

"No apologies necessary." I smiled at him.

"Frank, have you opened the wine?" asked Carolyn.

"Two reds and a white—they're on the liquor cabinet down by my chair, ready to go."

Liz looked at me. "Daddy's favorite sport is aggravating Mamma. He's just trying to get her attention. He knows full well she hates it when he calls her 1930s mahogany beverage server a liquor cabinet."

Carolyn made a face that might've meant *I adore the man but he drives me stark raving mad*. "Everyone head to the dining room. Lunch is buffet style today."

For the next few minutes, there was bustling, clattering, and mild pandemonium as the last few serving spoons were ferried to the dining room and hand washing, drink pouring, and what-all ensued. Carolyn showed me to the dining room and pointed out a seat in the middle of a long table set for thirteen. "I thought your young man was coming with you."

Emptiness ached in my chest. "I'm sorry, he couldn't make it." I hadn't spoken to Cash since Friday night. How was he spending Easter?

"Another time." Carolyn patted me on the arm and quickly removed the extra place setting.

I was reasonably certain that was never going to happen, but it wasn't the time to tell her that I was hopeless at maintaining a romantic relationship because I apparently suffered from poor judgement. Also not the time to mention how I should've stuck to my guns and not taken the case she brought me.

When everyone was gathered, standing behind their chairs, Carolyn raised her hands and took Liz's on her right, and Emma Rae's on her left. We all joined hands and Carolyn said grace.

"Heavenly Father, thank you for this beautiful day, for your love and mercy, and for sending your Son into this fallen world to save us. Thank you for the blessings of family and friends gathered around our table, and for the food before us. Bless it to our use and us to thy service. In Jesus' name we pray, Amen."

We all said Amen, then all eyes turned to the food.

The Easter buffet at Carolyn Talbot's house was a full-tilt production, a spread that might've appeared in the *Southern Living: Holiday Issue*. Most of the food lined the mahogany sideboard that matched the long dining room table. Everything was artfully arranged on platters—some multi-tiered, some footed, some rectangular, and some oval. The scent of baked country ham, fried chicken, and yeast rolls hung in the air like sweet perfume.

Poppy and Blake went through the buffet line first to fix plates for the kids, then we all took our heirloom china plates from the table and piled them high with the meats and every side dish imaginable: Charleston red rice with shrimp, macaroni and cheese, mashed potatoes, lady pea salad, tomato pie, lima beans and corn, squash casserole, roasted asparagus, cucumber and tomato salad—I couldn't get some of everything on my plate.

When I set my overflowing dish on the table dressed in pressed linens, silver, candles, and fresh hydrangeas, I saw there was still more food over here: two baskets of biscuits, the tureen of gravy, and enough deviled eggs to feed the entire congregation at a church potluck.

I slid into my chair and stared at my plate.

What on earth had come over me?

The thought of choosing only the plant-based options had never even entered my mind. I'd cheerfully followed the crowd, caving to peer pressure without a whiff of resistance. The last time chicken or ham had crossed my lips, I'd been sixteen years old. I stared at the two golden, crispy wings on my plate. When I was a child, I'd loved country ham. The slice on my plate made my mouth water.

"Biscuit?" Nate handed me the basket of butter-glazed decadence. The aroma was the final straw.

"Thanks." I smiled, took a biscuit, and passed the basket to Joe.

Seconds later, when Nate handed me the gravy, I ladled two brimming spoonfuls onto the biscuit I'd split in half on my bread plate.

I was all in. Life was short. Carolyn's biscuits and gravy were more temptation than mere mortals could resist.

Everyone was quiet for a few minutes as we tucked into our plates.

Oh my stars. I closed my eyes as I savored the first taste of biscuit and gravy. The fluffy, buttery, savory combination was out of this world. When I opened my eyes, Poppy grinned at me and nodded from her spot across the table, between Emma and Frankie. "I remember my first meal at this table like it was yesterday."

"This is amazing," I said. Truly, Carolyn Talbot missed her calling. She could've been a famous chef with her own restaurant, TV show, and line of cookware. Paula Deen and Ree Drummond surely had nothing on Carolyn.

"Well, thank you, Sugar," said Carolyn. "It's nothing fancy. Are you sure you have everything you need?"

"Oh, I have way more than I need," I said.

"That's a requirement," said Blake. "Mom's not happy unless every single one of us is tick-full and miserable."

We all stuffed ourselves silly. I enjoyed every bite of

my chicken and my ham and went back for seconds on the tomato pie and lady pea salad. I freely admit I had a second biscuit smothered in that decadent, velvety elixir from the gods. The guys all went back multiple times. Everyone was smiling, making appreciative noises, and complimenting the chef. Carolyn beamed. Peace, harmony, and goodwill reigned in the Talbot dining room.

"Did anybody hear if they ever caught whoever killed that baker in West Ashley?" asked Ponder. "Terrible business."

Carolyn turned to Ponder and gave him a look that might have meant *let's not discuss unpleasantness at the dinner table.*

"Oh, ah...sorry, Carolyn," said Ponder. "My apologies." Eyes wide, he stuffed a bite of biscuit in his mouth.

Blake cut a look at his mother, then cleared his throat. "Actually, I'm glad you brought that up. Everyone needs to be more aware of their surroundings when you're out shopping or running errands or whatever, especially if you're off the island. They have *not* made an arrest, and muggers are very seldom once and done criminals."

Carolyn gave Blake the same look she'd given Ponder but turned up the volume and maybe added a threat.

"Mom, I'm only concerned about everybody's safety," said Blake.

That was Cash's case. For everyone's sake, I

hoped he made an arrest soon. Was that what was keeping him occupied right now? Did he have a suspect? Was he on a stakeout? Was he just too busy to call?

"Evil roams around," said Frank. "Sometimes it's just a body's bad luck to cross its path. Blake's right. Best we all stay alert. Forewarned is forearmed." He glanced at the phone lying by his plate. Something must've caught his eye.

"Frank? Sweetheart?" From her seat at the end nearest the kitchen, Carolyn raised an elegant eyebrow at her husband, who sat at the opposite end of the table.

"Carolyn, I'm just checking on them, now." He delivered a bite of ham to his mouth.

Carolyn's tone hardened. "You're setting a bad example for the children, Frank. We don't bring our phones to the table."

"Right...let me just..." He continued staring at the screen as he picked up the phone and slid it onto the beverage server behind him. "There we go. All set. Poppaw just had a small emergency."

"Emergency? What kind of *emergency*?" Carolyn glared at him.

"No, now...that's not what I meant. I meant this was an exception to the rules...just this one time. Frankie, Emma Rae, we don't bring our phones to the table. It's very rude. But we just got the chickens home yesterday, and Poppaw has a responsibility to make sure they're settling in all right."

"Cuz, you want me to run check on 'em?" asked Ponder.

"Nah, that's why I have the Intelli-Coop," said Frank. "Smartest investment I ever made."

"What's an 'Intelli-Coop,' if you don't mind me asking?" I took a bite of tomato pie and suppressed a joyful moan.

"It's the future of backyard chicken keeping." Blake smothered a grin.

"It's a smart home for chickens," said Frank. "...a *coop de luxe,* state-of-the-art poultry compound, complete with fans, an auto-feeder, and daily updates on flock activity, including individual bird recognition. Even has a motion-sensor water mister to keep 'em cool and happy. The coop sits inside an oversized smart run, and the entire shebang is monitored by an AI guardian. It's got automatic doors, an egg counter, and Cluckwatch predator detection with an automatic SOS that scares off varmints with barking dog noises and flashing lights. And 24/7 live streaming of the coop cam to the app on my phone. It's the solution to high-priced eggs, I'll tell you that right now."

"Yes," said Carolyn, "as soon as we recoup the ten-thousand-dollar investment, all our eggs will be free."

Thunder rumbled nearby.

"At the price they're getting for them at the store these days, that won't be very long, now, will it?" said Frank. "Not to mention, the quality of the eggs is far superior."

"These are *blue* eggs." Liz nodded with big eyes.

Merry scowled at Liz. "They're a heritage breed, right, Daddy?"

"That's right," Frank said. "These are not your average backyard hens. They're Cream Legbars. The fella I bought 'em from said they lay blue eggs and have the temperament of golden retrievers."

"Golden retrievers, really?" said Nate, in a voice as dry as a perfect Bombay gin martini. "Will they fetch?"

Frank raised his open palms and tilted his head. "Maybe so. I didn't ask the fella I bought them from about that."

"If only they would lay golden eggs," said Carolyn.

"Are these chickens you can fry?" Joe grinned.

"Well, I reckon you can." Mischief twinkled in Frank's eyes. "I bet Carolyn could pluck a couple of them lickety-split."

"Really, Frank?" Carolyn smiled sweetly. "Rest assured, should I feel the urge to snatch something bald, it won't be a chicken."

"Speaking of alligators," said Ponder, "did y'all see that TikTok video? Bunch of kids from off came over here last week in a Scooby-Doo van hunting for Old Herschel."

"Were we?" Nate looked perplexed. "Speaking of alligators?"

"Who's Old Herschel?" I asked.

"The Marsh King." Merry said it like I should've known. "He's this legendary gator that lives in the marshes on the back side of the island. Been spotted for decades. People say he's a hundred years old and sixteen feet long."

"Fourteen feet long," said Blake.

"Twelve," said Frank. "Fourteen's an exaggeration."

"You've seen him?" I looked from Blake to Frank.

Frank and Liz exchanged a look I couldn't quite read.

"Anyway," said Ponder, "these influencer kids were wading around out there with their cameras, trying to get him on video, and one of 'em found a bone. A hand bone, they said. Posted it right there on the internet for the whole world to see."

"A human hand bone?" Poppy's fork stopped halfway to her mouth.

"Well, now, nobody knows for sure what era it's from," said Ponder. "Could be ancient history."

"A hand bone?" Frankie's eyes went wide. "Like from a dead body?"

"Eat your dinner," said Poppy.

"But Mom—"

"Blake?" Liz squinted at her brother.

Blake sighed. "We're looking into it. It does appear to be human, but that doesn't mean it's recent. There was a lot of military activity in these waters during the Revolutionary War. Could be a soldier who never made it home."

"A Revolutionary War soldier?" Frankie's eyes grew wide with wonder.

"Or a pirate," said Merry, scrolling on her phone

under the table where Carolyn couldn't see. "The comments on that video are something else. Somebody said maybe it's Jimmy Hoffa."

"Could be D.B. Cooper," said Joe. "Man's gotta be somewhere."

"Somebody thinks it's a Swamp Squatch," said Merry.

"A what?" Nate looked at her.

"You know, like Bigfoot, but for swamps. There's a whole Reddit thread."

"It's a marsh," said Frank. "And there's no such thing as a Marsh Squatch."

"That's exactly what someone who'd seen a Marsh Squatch would say," said Joe.

"I wanna see Old Herschel," said Emma Rae. "Can we go look for him after lunch, Poppaw?"

"Absolutely not," said Poppy and Carolyn in perfect unison.

"But what if there's a skeleton out there?" Frankie bounced in his seat. "What if the gator ate somebody and the bones are just lying around in the marsh?"

"That is a disturbing thought, son," said Blake. "I think you've been watching too much TV."

"Humphrey Pearson told me he saw Old Herschel drag a whole deer under last summer," said Ponder, warming to his subject. "Said it took about three seconds flat. Just—" He made a violent yanking motion with his hands.

Emma Rae's eyes got huge.

"Ponder." Carolyn's voice could have frozen the gravy.

"I saw a video once where a gator did a death roll," said Joe. "That's where they grab onto something and spin around and around until—"

"Joseph Andrew Eaddy." Carolyn set down her fork with a decisive clink. "We are not going to discuss death rolls, human remains, or legendary reptiles at my Easter table. It is the Lord's day. We have children present. And I have worked entirely too hard on this meal to ruin it with talk of carnage."

Silence fell over the table.

"Yes, ma'am," said Joe.

"Sorry, Carolyn," said Ponder.

Frank studied his plate with great interest.

"I'd appreciate it if everyone stayed away from the marsh for a while," said Blake, in the careful tone of a man trying to wrap up a conversation his mother wanted ended. "Until we figure out what we're dealing with. These TikTok people have stirred up way too much interest."

Carolyn picked up her fork. "Thank you, Blake. Now then. Hadley, would you like some more tomato pie? How about some lady peas?"

Thunder rumbled from one end of the sky to the other.

A sharp, loud crack boomed overhead as lightning hit nearby.

The lights went out.

The sky opened, and rain hammered down on the roof and pinged off the gutters.

From outside, a dog howled piteously.

"Chumley." Merry hopped up and dashed through the swinging door to the kitchen.

"Nobody panic." Frank raised his voice to be heard above the roar.

The lights flickered back on.

"I'm so thankful for that generator," Carolyn said loudly.

Frank grabbed his phone from the beverage stand.

"Frank, really," said Carolyn.

"Carolyn, I've got to make sure my hens are all right." He scowled at the screen. "The picture won't come up. What's the matter with it?"

"The Wi-Fi probably went down when the power blipped," said Blake. "It'll be back on in just a minute." Everyone was practically shouting now.

"That little circle is going round and round and round..." Frank made a spinning motion with his finger and stared at his phone.

As abruptly as it had started, the rain stopped.

From the kitchen, Merry cooed, "Poor sweet Chumley. Let's get you dried off."

Chumley woofed in reply.

"How did my hound dog get left outside in the storm?" Frank stood, confused indignation on his face.

"You were preoccupied with your poultry," said Carolyn. "The dog comes and goes as he pleases these days anyway."

Frank hurried from the room and Ponder followed.

"What kind of dog is it?" I asked.

"A spoiled rotten basset hound," said Liz. "Daddy somehow persuaded Mamma to let him have a newfangled doggie door installed in the mudroom. It's designed to keep random critters from inviting themselves in. When Chumley approaches, this stainless steel panel slides up and lets him inside. It's activated by a sensor in his collar...or the app. But it does not call him to come in out of the rain."

A mournful howl issued from the kitchen. Then Chumley went to woofing.

Merry squealed. "*Joe!*"

Beside me, Joe hopped up and dashed out of the dining room.

"Shoo, shoo." We heard Frank's voice, low and urgent, as the door swung shut.

A shriek—sharp, startled, and *definitely* avian—echoed from the back of the house.

Carolyn's eyes grew large and round.

Nate looked at Blake. "Is the Poultry Palace plugged into the generator?"

Blake bolted up. "That dog door is on the Wi-Fi."

Nate was right behind him.

They both dashed into the kitchen.

That's when the crowing started.

The roosters were clearly on the other side of the swinging door staking out territory.

"Frank Talbot, I will draw and quarter you and

feed you to the alligators." Carolyn stood and spun towards the kitchen in horror. But she didn't make a move, seemingly frozen by the images conjured by her imagination.

"Mamma," said Liz gently. "Let's just sit back down, why don't we? Whatever is going on in there, we don't need to see it." She stroked her mamma's arm.

"My kitchen," said Carolyn numbly. "There are *roosters* in my kitchen."

"I'll go make sure everything is okay," said Liz. "You have a seat and finish your wine, okay? Nothing good will come from you going into the kitchen right now." Liz grabbed the bottle and put it where her mamma could reach it.

Carolyn nodded numbly, returned to her chair, and downed her wine. Then she refilled her glass.

The crowing continued. Emma and Frankie looked at each other, then jumped up and darted towards the kitchen.

"Frankie! Emma! Come back here!" Poppy followed them through the swinging door.

Liz went around the other way—through the front hall—with me on her heels.

The scene in the kitchen was surreal. The chickens had fully breached the perimeter. Birds perched atop virtually every surface.

They were pretty chickens, I'll say that much—an interesting mix of black, white, shades of grey, and tan. From the top of a refrigerator, one of the roosters crowed. Another challenged him from the back of the sofa in the keeping room. Then all four roosters crowed, one right after the other, on repeat.

The chickens were everywhere, squawking, shrieking, clucking, and crowing like a barnyard flash mob.

A plump hen waddled by like she owned the place and two more followed. One reared up and flapped her wings furiously from the pass-through to a back hallway.

Emma Rae screamed with delight. In her yellow smocked dress and Mary Janes, she chased the flapper like it was the Easter Bunny.

Frankie hollered, "Let it be, Emma Rae! You're 'bout to get pecked." He flung a dinner roll like a fastball at the chicken's head as it reared back in indignation.

The roll went wide.

Nate ducked.

Blake scooped up his daughter.

Ponder crouched and waddled behind a rooster until it turned and charged him, then he jumped up and yelled, "Consarnit, Frank, I told you that coop needed backup power!"

One of the hens flapped her wings and hopped up on the counter by the sink.

"This is way better than the Easter egg hunt!" Frankie hollered. "Look, Daddy—they can fly!"

By the fireplace, Merry sat dazed with Chumley on her lap, both of her arms wrapped around him as he howled pitifully.

Nate clutched one of the chickens to his chest. "I'll

get this one outside and secure the pen. Somebody get that dog door shut."

"I'm on it," hollered Joe.

One of the hens flapped her way to the light fixture over the breakfast room table. Emma and Frankie broke into peals of delighted laughter.

Poppy cooed at a hen on the island as she wrapped her arms around it. "I got one." She headed towards the back hallway.

Liz crouched down and scooted after one of the chickens, but it squawked at her and flew up onto the stove.

Frank disappeared and came back moments later with a fishnet on a long pole. He stalked a rooster like Elmer Fudd trying to trap Bugs Bunny.

Blake hustled the kids back into the dining room.

One of the chickens perched on the island—calm, collected, and eerily poised. As Blake came back through the swinging door, it made eye contact, flapping its wings like it was issuing a challenge. Blake charged it, arms wide. The bird hopped and landed square onto his shoulder, flapping madly and squawking like he was preaching a sermon.

Blake reached up and grabbed the hen and dashed towards the back door.

I was still rooted to my spot near the pass through to the front hall. As Frank scooped up a rooster in his net, another came charging my way. I shooed it back towards the kitchen. I was too intimidated to try and catch one of the creatures, but I could help contain them.

Nate and Joe came running back in, grabbed a couple of roosters like footballs and scrambled back outside.

When all the birds were back in their pen, we all stared at the destruction. Feathers floated in the air. Gravy tracks were splattered across the stove and counter. Everything sitting on counters had been knocked over. Somehow, a blob of what might've been squash casserole was slowly sliding down the front of the stainless steel refrigerator. It appeared the chickens had a food fight.

Liz said, "Poppy, would you check on Mamma? Hadley, if you don't mind going with her? Merry...I bet Mamma needs one of her little yellow pills. No—wait. She's had wine. Get her some more. I'll get everything in here cleaned and sanitized."

"I'll help," said Nate.

"Cuz, why don't we make sure that pen is good and secure?" said Ponder.

"Good idea." Frank clapped him on the shoulder and they started towards the hallway that led to the back door. "We need a backup latch, don't we?"

"That thing needs a lock on it. Maybe some zip ties will get us through till we can get to the hardware store. You got any zip ties?" asked Ponder.

The door closed behind them.

Thirty minutes later, we were all seated back in the

dining room, enjoying coffee and the best coconut cake I've ever had in my life.

It was almost like it had never happened, except for the glazed look in Carolyn's eyes and the way Frankie kept replaying the action and making Emma dissolve into giggles.

"Well," said Carolyn, "at least this time the wildlife didn't make it to the dining room."

"See there, everything's fine now," said Frank. "All that carrying on for nothing."

"Frank." Carolyn raised both eyebrows and leaned towards him. "If ever another farm or woodland creature crosses the threshold of my house, I will move you out so fast you'll think I did it with mirrors. Perhaps there's room for a sleeping bag in your chicken coop."

Poppy's eyes got big and round.

Joe leaned over and whispered, "Get someone to tell you about the goats."

Chapter Thirty

I found Poppy on the screened porch, swaying gently in the swing and sipping what looked like a generous pour of something brown and medicinal.

"Mind if I join you?" I picked a piece of chicken fluff from my dress.

She nodded towards the cushion beside her. "You survived your first Talbot holiday. Need a drink? Frank has a well-stocked liquor cabinet."

I settled onto the swing. "No thanks. Y'all sure know how to celebrate the resurrection."

"We try," she said, lifting her glass in a toast. "Frank's projects always reach some kind of crescendo during family gatherings. Last Fourth of July he installed a homemade fireworks launcher in the backyard. It took out a rain gutter and nearly set Ponder's Buick on fire."

"I was told to ask about the goats?"

"Yeah…that was the first night I came here for dinner. Liz invited me. That's the night I met Blake. Carolyn made my favorite—country-style steak and gravy. Frank had bought three goats to manage the brambles and weeds and such in the woods around the perimeter of the yard. This was at the same time the swimming pool was being installed. Ponder and a man named Ray Kennedy were working on it. Anyway, somehow the goats got in the house and ended up on the dining room table. Liz can tell the story better. Poor Carolyn…she spent the night at Liz's house."

"And I thought the chickens were bad."

"Give it a few days and the stories will be hilarious. We cope with chaos by embellishing it and entertaining each other with it for years to come."

I looked out over the lawn, where Emma Rae and Franklin Jr. were chasing bubbles, seemingly unfazed by the day's poultry panic. "Your family is something else."

"They're a lot," Poppy agreed. "Messy, loud, opinionated, a little crazy—but I adore every nut in the bunch. I wouldn't take anything for them. For the longest time I didn't have any family at all."

For a minute we just listened to the rustle of the breeze and the laughter of happy children.

It was time.

I reached into my purse and pulled out the copy I'd made of Momma's letter.

"Poppy," I began. "I wanted to talk to you earlier, but, well, this is the first chance I've had…"

The air between us changed—tightened, like a thread being pulled.

"I'm not sure there's a right way to say what I'm about to," I said. "But I'm afraid you wasted your money on the DNA tests."

"What do you mean?"

"I need you to read this, please."

She took it from me, her brows knitting together as she unfolded the letter. Her eyes scanned the page—once, twice. Then she looked up at me. Her face went still, the way water does when the wind stops.

"This...this is from your mother?" she asked, voice barely above a whisper.

I nodded. "She gave it to someone for safekeeping before she died. It only found me a couple of days ago."

"But this says..." Her voice broke off. "It says we're—"

"Twins," I finished. "Identical twins. Separated at birth. By luck of the draw, you were adopted. Mom wanted us both, but she was a waitress. Money was ridiculously tight. She knew she couldn't afford to raise us both."

She blinked, lips parted in silent shock. "I think I knew it was something like this. Well, I suspected our dad was a ladies' man..."

"Yeah, I used to think that too. He's not. He's the best. And the good news is, he's alive and well, just in Italy right now."

"So they never got married?" Poppy scrunched her face at me.

"No...and that's a really long and complicated story. Maybe one better for another day. Oh—you'll love our half-brother, J. T."

For a long moment, neither of us spoke. Then she reached out—slowly—and took my hand.

Her eyes filled, but she smiled. "I've always wanted a sister."

"Me too." Tears spilled down my own cheeks. "I've always felt like something was missing."

At the same moment, we pulled each other into a hug and held on.

"Well," she said, voice thick but steady, "I guess we just found out what that was. We have a lot of catching up to do."

"You're not mad?" I asked.

She pulled back to look at me. "Why on earth would I be mad?"

"Well, I got Mom..."

Poppy shook her head. "It's not like you got a vote. And it's like you said...luck of the draw. I had parents who loved me. Well...I never really knew my dad. He died when I was two. But I had an amazing mom. She never thought to mention I was adopted, so there's that. But also not your fault. And now we both get whole new wings of our family—me, Dad and J. T., and you a niece, and a nephew, and this whole crazy Talbot clan."

We sat on that swing, rocking back and forth until

the sky turned lavender and the stars blinked on overhead.

Finally, Blake opened the back door. "Pop, you ready to head home?"

"Yeah...but come say a proper hello to your sister-in-law first."

Chapter Thirty-One

We waved goodbye to Poppy, Blake, and the kids as they drove out of the driveway. I was just about to say my goodbyes when Liz turned my way and said, "Are you feeling peckish? I was thinking about grabbing a ham biscuit."

Was she serious right now? "I may never be hungry again."

Liz shook her head and grinned. "We have got to build up your stamina. How about a walk? That will help."

"That sounds good, actually. How do you people eat that way and not weigh eight hundred pounds?"

"We don't eat like *that* every day. Nate and I actually eat pretty healthy most of the time. We try to pace ourselves for the once or twice a week we eat with Mamma and Daddy. I guess we've all developed strong metabolisms."

We walked the two blocks to the beach, left our sandals at the end of the path, and turned left on the sand, heading towards the north point of the island. It wasn't completely dark yet, but the moon rose over the water, ripe with ivory light, casting a shimmering path across the waves. The breeze carried the scent of rain-washed air and the tang of salt, and the soft ebb and flow of the surf smoothed the edges off the day.

"Someone shot at me last night," I said, apropos of nothing.

Liz turned to me, her face screwed up in an expression that might've shouted *what the actual heck*? "*What*? When? Where? Who? *Why* in the name of sweet reason are you just now telling me this, oh so casually?"

I winced. "It didn't seem like appropriate holiday meal conversation... So, I ran back out to the office after you dropped me off to take care of something. There was a red BMW that might've been following me. I can't be sure. Anyway, after I got home and pulled into the garage, someone made a noise to draw me out into the front yard. Right as someone fired three shots, out of nowhere, this huge gust of wind knocked me down. I think it probably saved my life. I think the shooter was probably Brett. Scarlett gave him my name and number. He must've looked up my office address. It was a fluke that I went back there last night. If I hadn't, maybe he'd've broken in? I'll never know..."

"First of all, I'd lay odds that 'gust of wind' was one

of our departed friends. Maybe your mamma...possibly Colleen."

"I thought that too. I'm pretty convinced of it, in fact. Have you ever had anything like that happen?"

"Many times. Colleen always looked out for me because I was critical to her mission. I'll see what she knows about this next time she pops in."

Liz stopped walking and grabbed my arm. "Does Cash know?"

I kept my eyes on the horizon, where the last streaks of pink were fading to purple. "He found out yesterday. Sonny Ravenel heard about it through the Sullivan's Island police grapevine and told him." I tried to keep my voice steady. "He showed up at my house. He was...furious doesn't quite cover it."

"Oh, Hadley."

"He said he can't be with someone who shuts him out when it matters most. He said he needs time to think about us." My voice cracked on the last words, and I pressed my lips together.

Liz pulled me in for a hug. "I am so sorry."

"The thing is, he's not wrong." I pulled back to look at her. "I *should* have called him first thing. Part of me was trying to protect him—protect his career. But part of me..." I hesitated. "How in the heck was I supposed to explain that a ghost knocked me down right as someone fired three shots at me? I haven't told Cash about seeing Momma. He's a very facts, figures, and cold hard evidence kind of guy. How do I tell him my dead mother might have just saved my life?"

Liz nodded slowly, understanding in her eyes. "Oh boy, I remember those days. It's complicated. For the first couple of years after Colleen first appeared to me, I couldn't tell Nate about her. It's against the rules, apparently. It was only after we were married he could see her too. It's different for you, though...your mother was going rogue when she popped in. There were so many times early on when I just knew Nate was going to wash his hands of me because he must surely have thought I was nuts."

"How did you handle it?"

"Honestly? I just acted like I didn't know what he was talking about. Swept the whole thing under the rug. But that's because Colleen told me in no uncertain terms I *couldn't* tell him about her. And honestly, I was afraid that would make things worse. That he'd be even more convinced I was crazy." She gave me a rueful smile. "I know...honesty is important in relationships. But...with you, I don't think this is going to be a recurring problem. Maybe you should tell him the truth and let him think you imagined it if that's what he wants to think. What would that hurt?"

"Momma's only appeared to me the once, and I think maybe that was an emergency..." I sighed. "It couldn't possibly make things worse to tell him, could it? The whole thing may be moot at this point."

"Give him time," Liz said gently. "And give yourself some grace. You're navigating something most people never have to deal with. He'll come around.

And when he does, you'll know what to say and what to let go."

We started walking again. The surf rolled in and out, filling the silence.

"I hope you're right." But hope felt like such a fragile thing just then, easily shattered.

We walked in silence for a moment, listening to the surf. "You know, when Momma first appeared to me, she said, 'Help her.' I assumed she meant Bridget—and now I'm convinced she did. But I can't decide if she purposely pointed me in that direction because she knew exactly what would happen—that Bridget's case would lead me to you and ultimately to Poppy—or if she struggled with that decision. Because sending me down that path would uncover her most closely held secret, and she was afraid Poppy and I might both judge her harshly." I shook my head slowly. "Did she tell me to help Bridget because it would lead me to Poppy, or in spite of that?"

Liz smiled softly. "Guardian spirits can be sneaky that way. Sometimes it's a matter of working within the rules. Or finding ways around them."

"Sneaky." I laughed, though my eyes burned a little. "Momma's definitely capable of being sneaky."

"Are you ready to shop for a gun now? I'll go with you to the range..."

"The thought crossed my mind," I told her. "But honestly, it would make me so nervous, I'd be so worried about it accidentally going off, I wouldn't be able to think straight. I'm afraid of guns. And I could never bring myself to shoot anyone. I would hesitate right at the critical moment. It would be pointless for me to carry a gun. Trust me. Just...please...help me think through all of this." I brought her up to speed on Scarlett, what I'd learned from her, and the latest on the tag Brett swiped.

"Did you call the Spencers in New York?" Liz asked.

"I did. I'd left a message, and Lauren called me back last night. She said they'd parked their car in a garage in New Jersey because parking in Manhattan is so ridiculously expensive. They were going today sometime to check to see if the tag had been switched, though she said they hadn't noticed it on the trip up."

"I imagine they had a lot on their minds, moving, new job, et cetera. It would be an easy thing to miss," said Liz.

"Agreed. If she can just get me the number of the tag that's actually on their car, we can run it and get an address on Brett."

"Well, theoretically."

"More and more I'm thinking Brett is some sort of random psycho killer," I said. "He didn't show up in Patricia's background at all, and if I'd missed him, surely Scarlett would've mentioned it. She's worked for Patricia long enough to know everyone in her orbit."

"Do you think it's possible he's a serial killer?" asked Liz.

"Maybe so. Maybe Patricia was his first, who

knows? If he'd succeeded in killing Scarlett too, he'd be well on his way to being a serial killer."

"But somehow, Patricia crossed his path...what did Scarlett say he did for a living?" asked Liz.

"He told her he was a postal inspector, working here undercover on some top-secret case. It's a safe bet that's made up."

"Okay, so we don't have enough information to figure out *his* routine, but what about Patricia's routine in the last days and weeks of her life? What was unusual? What was a departure from her routine? That's a place to start, anyway..."

"I've gone over her calendar, spoken with Bridget, and with Scarlett...snooped through her desk...I've done everything I know to do. And the only anomaly is a trip she took to the West Ashley UPS store to ship some homemade lemon blueberry pound cake and some of Arlo Donovan's music. At first it kinda felt like something...I had this feeling..."

"Always trust those feelings."

"Right? I typically do...but this was just a dead end. I thought it had something to do with a motive for Mary Ellis...like maybe Patricia told her what this Nashville record producer really thought about Arlo's music—he's not the reincarnation of Merle Haggard, as it turns out—and it made Mary Ellis so angry she flew off the handle and killed Patricia."

"Is there any connection between Mary Ellis and Brett?"

"Not that I've found," I said.

"Did you talk to the people at the UPS store?" asked Liz.

I shook my head. "No...I decided Porter and Corinne were stronger leads and focused on them."

Liz shrugged. "So maybe tomorrow go talk to the UPS folks. See if they noticed a strange man in the store that day. Maybe it's as simple as he was mad they waited on Patricia before him. You never know what sets lunatics off. I'll go with you if you like."

"I'd like that. Oh—the woman who actually waited on Patricia was diabetic and she passed away recently. But the owner of the store was there too. I have her name in my notes."

"All right then. First thing tomorrow."

"First thing tomorrow." I smiled, trying to work up some enthusiasm. Honestly, at that point, going to the UPS store felt like an exercise in futility, but I needed to do something. Maybe overnight a better idea would occur to one of us.

Chapter Thirty-Two

Mariposa Garcia and her husband, Ignacio, owned The UPS Store on Savannah Highway in West Ashley. They were both behind the counter that Monday morning when Liz and I arrived a little after ten. We'd apparently gotten lucky and hit a lull. There was no one else in the store.

"Do you remember the day Patricia Gaillard came in herself to ship a package?" I asked.

"Oh, yes." Mariposa's kind eyes grew round. "Nacho and I were just talking about that. It's so strange." She glanced at her husband.

Nacho must've been her nickname for Ignacio.

"Strange that she came in herself?" Liz asked.

"Well, yes, that too," said Mariposa. "We'd never met her before. Scarlett always came to do her shipping. Patricia was a nice lady. They both are."

"What else was strange?" I asked. "Was there anyone else in the store that day?"

"Yes." Mariposa nodded. "Several people. They were all standing around discussing the lemon blueberry pound cake. Stanley was a baker, and he was very interested in Patricia's recipe. He was thinking he might make that for the bakery."

"And now he will never have that chance." Ignacio shook his head.

"Wait." I scrunched my face up. "Are you saying that nice baker who was mugged and murdered recently was in the store that day?" I asked.

"Yes," said Mariposa. "Stanley Mahaffey. Such a nice man. He came in to ship a loaf of bread to a customer. He did that sometimes if he missed the pickup time. His sourdough is amazing...*was* amazing."

"Do you know they found him in a patch of woods near his bank branch not more than a mile from here?" asked Ignacio. "An animal did this."

"It's just so sad..." said Mariposa.

Liz and I exchanged a look. I was not a fan of coincidence and guessed she wasn't either.

"I heard about that," I said. "Was there by chance a younger man in the store that day as well? Maybe in his thirties or forties? I have a picture...it's not a very good one, but maybe..." I tapped my phone to pull up the photo I'd taken of Brett at Waterfront Park.

Mariposa and Ignacio both looked at my phone, then at each other and shook their heads. "No."

"I've never seen him before as far as I can remember," said Mariposa.

"He doesn't look familiar to me either." Ignacio shrugged. "But a lot of people come in here. It's impossible to remember everyone."

"But at that particular moment," said Liz, "when Patricia Gaillard and Stanley Mahaffey were discussing the pound cake, he wasn't here then?"

"No." They both shook their heads.

"It was Stanley, Patricia, of course Bonita, who waited on both of them, and the young lady with the will. And me." Mariposa smiled. "And a couple of older ladies, but I don't remember their names. They were interested in the cake recipe too."

"I'm sorry, who? What about a will?" I asked.

"There was a young lady who came in to have her will notarized that morning. Bonita was a notary. Patricia and Stanley happened to be here in line, and the young lady asked them to be witnesses. They were happy to help, of course. Patricia advised her to have an attorney help her with that, but she said she couldn't wait, she was heading out of the country soon. She was a nurse...one that goes to foreign countries to volunteer for relief work."

A strange look came over Liz's face. "Do you happen to recall her name?"

"No," said Mariposa, "but it will be in Bonita's journal. Notaries have to keep a record."

"Would you mind checking?" I asked.

"Not at all," said Mariposa. "We're happy to help if we can."

She searched under the counter, moving things and walking a few steps left and right as she looked. Finally, she pulled a logbook out and flipped through the pages, then ran her finger down a list. "Dana Clark. I have her address and phone number if you need to speak with her."

Liz's breath caught. "*Hell's bells*. I actually know her. Unless there are two Dana Clarks who are relief nurses in the area. I think that's highly unlikely."

Mariposa spun the journal around for us to take a look.

I took a picture of the woman's address and phone number.

Liz studied the notebook. "No...that's the same Dana Clark."

"And the woman who notarized her will and both witnesses are now dead." My eyes locked onto Liz's.

"It's all just so terribly sad," said Mariposa.

Chapter Thirty-Three

We drove back to Liz's office so we'd have a quiet place nearby to process everything we'd learned at The UPS Store. We'd no sooner settled in, Liz on the sofa by the window and me in the same blue-and-white chair I'd sat in the first time I'd visited, when my phone rang.

"Hey, Lauren," I answered before the phone rang a second time and hit the speaker button.

"I just wanted to let you know you were right," she said. "I meant to call you back last night, but we got tied up with the police. We had to report our tag stolen, and it was a mess because we assume, based on what you said, that it was stolen in Charleston before we ever left."

"Do you have the tag number that was left on your car in its place?" I asked.

She read off the series of letters and numbers.

"Thanks for letting me know, Lauren." We said our goodbyes and ended the call.

Liz moved to her computer to run the tag and I stood behind her chair and looked over her shoulder. Seconds later, the name Corey Brett Clark popped up, listed at a Taylors, South Carolina address.

Liz pulled up Corey Brett Clark in one of the databases she had access to. "Taylors is near Greenville," she said. "Dana grew up there...and yes, Corey Brett Clark from Taylors has a sister named Dana." A better picture of the man we'd encountered in Waterfront Park occupied the top left corner of her display.

"There's not a more recent address?" I stared at the screen. "This says he's a receiving coordinator at Southern Building Supplies in North Charleston."

"Maybe he just moved down here," said Liz. "We need to talk to Dana."

"Agreed...I'm thinking she's in mortal danger." My stomach clenched.

Liz tapped her phone and put Dana on speaker.

"Well hey there, Liz," said a pleasant voice. "It's good to hear from you."

"Dana, I'm so sorry to be short, but where are you?" ask Liz.

"I'm in the Atlanta airport," she said. "You caught me between planes."

Liz and I locked eyes and breathed a deep sigh of relief. Dana should be safe from Brett there, at least for the time being.

"Are you on your way home?" Liz asked.

"I am. I'll arrive this afternoon around three thirty."

"Do you mind me asking how long you've been gone?" asked Liz.

"Not at all. I left Saturday, March 11. I was actually supposed to fly the next day, on Sunday, but there was weather moving in, and I ended up changing my flight to get out ahead of it."

"This will sound like a barrage of strange questions. I'm here with a colleague, Hadley Cooper. She may have questions too."

"Hey, Hadley." Dana still had a smile in her voice.

"Hey, nice to meet you," I said.

"Dana, I understand you had a will made out before your trip," said Liz.

"Well, yeah, I did," said Dana. "I was on my way to South America. The world being what it is, I just thought I should have the paperwork in place. You and I haven't spoken in a while...James gave me a very generous severance package and helped me invest. I have the kind of money I never dreamed I would. But I had been neglectful of some of the things I should've taken care of, like a will."

"Hadley, Dana used to work for James Huger, a well-heeled local businessman."

"I'm familiar with the family." I nodded. "And you had a woman at the West Ashley UPS store notarize your will, and two other customers witnessed it?"

"That's right." Dana's tone shifted. "What's going on?"

"Dana, who benefits from your will?" asked Liz.

I could hear the confusion in Dana's voice. "Well, every bit of it goes to charity...hunger relief, the medical relief organization I volunteer for, and my church. Why do you ask?"

"Humor me just a minute," said Liz. "Who *would* have benefitted if you passed away and did not have a will?"

Dana sighed. "That would be my brother, Corey. He's the only family I have left."

"And under your new will?" I asked.

"Like I said, it all goes to charity. Having that much money would not be a good thing for Corey. He'd very likely end up dying of an overdose of something...drugs, alcohol, sex, or some unholy cocktail of all three—probably on a rented yacht with a herd of Instagram models and a mechanical bull."

"Apologies for what must sound like a random question, but could you confirm what Corey drives?" I asked.

"Sure, it's a brown Subaru Forester."

Liz's voice took on a layer of regret. "Dana, I hate like anything to have to be the one to tell you this, but the woman who notarized your will and both witnesses have all turned up dead since you've been away."

"I'm sorry...what?"

"You had your will notarized on a Tuesday and left town the following Saturday," said Liz. "Less than two weeks after you left, both witnesses to your will were murdered, and the notary died unexpectedly."

"I don't understand," said Dana.

"It appears Corey may be involved," said Liz.

"I talked to Corey a couple days before I left," said Dana. "I mentioned I had drawn up a will. I did *not* tell him anything at all about what was in it, and I certainly didn't tell him who notarized or witnessed it."

"What's your relationship with your brother like?" I asked.

"Strained..." she said. "Corey's resented me my entire life. He twists everything in his mind to paint me as evil. And he really resents that I have money now and he doesn't—not that he's ever worked for anything. Years ago, while I was in nursing school, I lived in a...well, a *boardinghouse* downtown that had a... let's just say it had a colorful history. James Huger—he's a very successful local venture capitalist—was a friend of the owner, and I worked for him during school, as an assistant of sorts. When I finished school, he gave me a generous severance package for my years of service and taught me how to invest it. Corey's convinced there was something sordid going on between James and me. There wasn't—James is completely devoted to his wife. But Corey believes what he wants to believe, and nothing I say will change his mind. Sorry...I went off on a bit of a tangent."

"Would he likely guess that any will would not be to his benefit?" Liz asked.

"Well...yes. Probably." Dana sighed.

"Is there a copy of your will in your condo?" Liz asked.

"Yes, and there's one in a safety deposit box at my bank."

"Does Corey know that?" I asked.

"I didn't mention to him that I planned to put one in the safety deposit box. It didn't seem relevant at the time," she said. "He would naturally have assumed that I'd have a copy at home."

"Where is it?"

"I have a small safe in my office," said Dana.

"Does Corey have a key to your condo? Alarm codes?" I asked.

"He does." Dana's voice sounded tired, older. "I was trying to build bridges…I don't know what I was thinking. Anyway, I decided to get the locks changed and change the codes when I got back."

"My guess is that he let himself in, checked to see what was in the will, made note of the witnesses and the notary, and probably destroyed it," said Liz.

"Well, he couldn't have destroyed the one in the safe deposit box," said Dana.

"But he doesn't know that," I said.

"And y'all think he killed all these people?" Dana's voice was filled with dread.

"Well, we can tie him to one death and an attempted murder. We need more time to investigate the others, but it seems likely. Do you think that's something he's just not capable of?" asked Liz.

Dana hesitated. "I would sure hate to think that he could…I…I just don't know."

"We know for certain he tried to kill one woman, but we intervened," I said.

"We think his next move is to try to kill you," said Liz.

"Oh, dear Lord," said Dana.

"Of course we're not going to let that happen," said Liz. "But we do want to give him the opportunity to demonstrate his intentions. Does he know you're on your way home?"

"Yes. Well, I haven't spoken to him recently, but before I left I told him I'd be back on April 10," said Dana.

"Where is he living right now?" I asked. "The address we found was Taylors, South Carolina."

"Right," said Dana. "That's where we grew up. But we sold our parents' house years ago. Corey's lived in the Charleston area for a while. He works at Southern Building Supplies in North Charleston. He's a receiving coordinator. He doesn't have a permanent address. Corey is a serial house sitter. He finds gigs in this Facebook group, and goes from one house to another. Right now he's staying on Sullivan's Island, up towards Breach Inlet."

Something sucked every molecule of air right out of my lungs, as if a ravenous boo hag—one of those Gullah-Geechee spirits that steals your breath while you sleep—had ahold of me. My hand shot back to steady myself against the bookcase behind me.

"Dana, is your car at the airport?" Liz asked.

"No, I Ubered."

"We'll pick you up," said Liz.

When she ended the call, I said. "He's staying in the Johnsons' house, right around the corner from me. Sarabeth told me they found a house sitter on Facebook...a stranger, and they wanted her to keep an eye on things. What do you want to bet they own the red BMW convertible?"

"We need thinking food," said Liz.

"You're right. But first we need to call Bridget."

Liz squinted at me.

"The Wednesday before Patricia was killed—before Scarlett met 'Brett' in the bookstore, some jerk came on to Bridget on the cereal aisle in Harris Teeter. They went for coffee, and when he came on too strong she pulled the plug. He didn't take that well, and left bruises on her arms. She said his name was 'Corey something.'"

Liz sucked in air. "He tried to pick Bridget up first, struck out, then tried Scarlett two days later."

I nodded slowly. "If Bridget had let him take her home, he would've planted the evidence in Scarlett's car, and she'd be in jail right now."

Chapter Thirty-Four

Liz picked the Swig & Swine on Savannah Highway for lunch. I had no idea why every other professional woman I met craved barbecue, but apparently it was a thing. One whiff of that brisket, though, and I was done for. Whatever switch Carolyn Talbot had flipped in me had unleashed my inner carnivore, and she was eating with wild abandon.

"That looks really good." Liz eyed my brisket grilled cheese.

"It's sinfully good," I said. "You know this is all your mother's fault."

"I'm sorry?"

"Before I got involved with her? I was a *vegan*. Well, not a vegan exactly—I ate a whole-food, plant-based diet. Most days, anyway. That all ended yesterday."

Liz laughed. "Yeah, Mamma could probably tempt

anyone off a healthy diet. Heck, she does it to me every week. Every Monday, I start over on a Mediterranean diet. Then on Wednesday night, we eat at their house, and it's fried something with gravy and eleven side dishes with butter or cheese or both. I do understand the problem."

We clinked our Cheerwine bottles.

"What are you thinking we're going to find here, exactly?" Liz asked. "I mean, I'm not opposed to a little B&E in the name of justice, as you're well aware...but Bonita's death was ruled natural—diabetic complications."

I'd parked Jolene in Bonita Diez's driveway. Her painted brick West Ashley bungalow sat deep in a quiet neighborhood less than a mile and a half from the UPS Store where she'd worked.

"I know in my bones this Corey clown murdered Bonita too," I said. "I just want to look around and see what we can see. It's not like we've got anything else to do until time to pick up Dana."

"True enough." Liz shrugged. "And for what it's worth, I agree—he probably did it. We may never be able to prove it, but there's absolutely no harm whatsoever in taking a peek."

We scurried around to the backyard so as to be less conspicuous while breaking in during broad daylight. We both donned gloves, Liz picked the lock on the back door, and we slipped inside. Thankfully, there was no alarm system.

Someone—maybe Mariposa, maybe family, maybe a service—had thoroughly cleaned the house recently. The place smelled like Pine-Sol. Not a single thing was out of place. Fifteen minutes after we arrived, we both shrugged and agreed there was nothing to be found. We were on our way to the door when I saw the photo on the mantle of Bonita with her cats.

"I don't believe it." I picked up the frame.

Liz looked over my shoulder. "Those cats look a little like your cats."

"No," I said, shaking my head.

"What do I know?" She shrugged. "I'm not a cat person. They look similar to me."

"What I'm saying is they don't *look like* the cats at my house. These *are the same cats.*"

"What?"

I dropped onto the sofa.

"He must've killed Bonita, then realized she had cats. While he had no sympathy whatsoever for the *person* who lived here, he didn't want to leave the cats unattended, not knowing how long it would be before someone came to check on Bonita."

"You're thinking a murderer was so worried about the cats he took them with him?"

"Yep," I said. "Scarlett said he was a cat lover. And then somehow they got out of the Johnsons' house. Corey's not in any of the local Sullivan's Island Facebook groups or forums, so he hasn't seen the notices about them online. Either he missed the flyers or he was too scared to come forward and claim them. But those cats are proof he was here."

Liz bent down, picked up a photo album from the table by the recliner, and flipped through it. "Several pictures of the cats in here...look—here's one when they were kittens."

She handed me the album. Two adorable kittens stared back from separate snapshots—one smoky grey with green eyes, the other a golden-eyed brown tabby with a white chin. Their names were written in fancy lettering beneath the pictures.

The grey kitten's name was Goose.

His brown striped friend was Nala.

Chapter Thirty-Five

Dana Clark—in my head, she was always Dana Clark, never just Dana, because plain old *Dana* would always be Dana Smalls the public defender—lived in a condo building at the edge of the Cooper River, not far from the South Carolina Aquarium. Her two-story penthouse was a showstopper—an airy, light-drenched space that framed expansive views of the Cooper River through a wall of floor-to-ceiling windows. The whole place was done up in what I was sure the decorator called something like *Coastal Reverie*—mostly tans and foggy greys, with carefully placed bursts of blue in several shades that looked like they'd been chosen by someone with one of those fancy fat color sample fan decks and a lot of opinions.

Dana's two-story living room was divided into two seating areas by a floating staircase with rich wood treads the same shade as the hardwood floors. She and

I were curled up, her on a plush sofa and me next to her in a swivel chair, both of us with comfy throws and a glass of wine on a side table.

"You ready?" I asked her.

"Ready as I'll ever be. This is nerve-wracking."

"He should be here any minute. We'll know soon enough for sure what's going on."

As soon as I'd arrived, Dana had called Corey and told him she was back…just checking in…and she mentioned she'd gotten a call from a private investigator who was on her way over to ask her some questions. When he'd asked, she told him she had no idea about what, but that the PI told her she was in danger. Corey had made a show of brotherly concern before Dana told him she had to go.

The doorbell chimed.

"Here we go." Dana slid out from under her blanket and went to answer the door.

"Hey, I didn't expect to see you tonight." Her tone was natural and easy. She was good at this.

"Well, I was worried after what you told me," said Corey. "Maybe I should stay in the guest room tonight."

Dana closed the door behind Corey. "Do you really think that's necessary?" She returned to the sofa and quickly arranged the throw back around her.

Corey followed her from the foyer into the living room. He had a gift bag in his hand.

"Hadley, this is my brother, Corey. Corey, Hadley Cooper."

His eyes were stone cold, without a flicker of recognition, though of course he knew exactly who I was.

"Hello." I smiled sweetly. I could take this charade as far as he could.

He raised his chin an inch in acknowledgement. "This looks more like a hen party than an interview."

"I was ready to unwind," said Dana. "Travel today was a bear. My first flight was delayed and I almost missed my connection. Hadley kindly agreed to join me."

"I brought a bottle of champagne and some snacks," said Corey. "I thought we'd celebrate you being home."

"How sweet," said Dana. "You know where everything is." She looked towards the wet bar in a nook under the stairs.

Corey nodded and stepped over to the mirrored cocktail station. "What's this about Dana being in danger?"

"Several people have been killed lately in Charleston," I said. "The only connection between them is that they notarized or witnessed Dana's new will."

"That's some crazy coincidence," he said. The cork popped on the champagne.

"Oh, I don't think it's a coincidence at all," I said.

"Really?" He paused for a minute, then carried three champagne glasses towards us, two in his right hand and one in his left. "How could it be anything else but a coincidence?" He set a glass by Dana and one by me.

"Apparently, someone wanted to make sure there was no evidence anywhere that a new will had been drawn up," I said.

Corey stepped back over to the wet bar and returned with a plate of cheese puffs.

"Isn't that the first will you've ever done?" Corey looked at Dana.

"I just never got around to it before." She shrugged.

"Well then, it's not like someone was disinherited, is it? Pardon me for being blunt, but this sounds like a pretty harebrained theory to me."

"Corey, switch glasses with me," said Dana.

"What?" He gave her a look like *what's the matter with you*, but his delivery was brittle, overdone, and obviously fake.

"Switch glasses with me." Dana smiled at her brother.

"Why?"

"Humor me."

"I don't think so." He shook his head at her in a fake teasing way. "Now, I'd like to propose a toast—"

"I'm not toasting anything until you switch glasses with me," said Dana. "Neither of us have had a sip. What's the difference?"

"It's ridiculous," said Corey.

"Aren't they exactly alike?" asked Dana.

A sour look washed over his face. "What has she told you?"

"That this champagne is likely drugged," said Dana.

"And you believe that?" He screwed up his face and shook his head.

"I didn't want to," said Dana. "I really hoped you'd just switch glasses with me."

Corey set down his glass and pulled a gun from his jacket pocket. He gave me the evilest look imaginable. "You've made a big mistake coming here."

"Corey, what in the world are you doing?" asked Dana.

"I'm cleaning up loose ends," said Corey.

"Is that the gun you used to shoot at me last night?" I asked.

"Yes, actually," said Corey.

"Why would you shoot at her?" asked Dana. "Have you lost your mind? Corey, put that gun away this minute."

"Afraid not, Sis. Now we can do this the easy way, or the hard way. It's up to you ladies. If you'll just drink your champagne like good girls, you can drift off to sleep. Otherwise, I'll have to shoot you."

"What have you turned into?" Dana looked anguished.

"*Me*? Oh, you're a good one to talk...always Miss Perfect." Sarcasm dripped from his words. "Everything was always so easy for you, the golden child...everything was handed to you your whole life—just like that money. It's not like you worked for it."

"Of course I worked for it," said Dana.

"You should've given me money when I needed it. I'm your only family. And it's not like you didn't have it."

"If I'd given you money every time you asked for it, we'd both be broke now," said Dana.

Corey's face contorted with rage. "You left me no choice. It's your fault three people are dead. That's on *you*."

"*Me*?" Dana squealed in indignation.

"You're the one who decided to get cute and draw up a will. Every last penny to charity. Not one cent for your own brother. You didn't care if I starved."

"Oh please," said Dana. "Someone you owed money to, or a jealous husband would've killed you long before *you* could ever have collected from *my* will."

Corey smiled evilly. "That's where you're wrong, Sis. I would've taken care of you before you left the country if you hadn't changed your flight at the last minute. Imagine my surprise when I showed up and you were already gone. Good thing you told me about the will, though. I took it out of the safe, burned it, and flushed the ashes down the toilet. But not before I made a note of the witnesses and the notary. I took care of those loose ends waiting on you to get back... and fantasized about which way I wanted to kill you the second you showed back up in Charleston."

Dana's face turned white and she looked like she might be sick.

"I have a question," I said. "Just, you know, out of curiosity. Corey, why did you take Bonita Diez's cats?"

He scowled. "Who would leave two cats alone to starve? I tried to take Scarlett's cat with me too, but he had other ideas."

"So you did kill Bonita Diez?" I asked.

He shrugged. "I helped her on her way. She was diabetic, overweight, and she liked her wine. I doubt she would've been around much longer at the rate she was going."

"So you, what, gave her way too much insulin and set it up to make it look like she drank herself to death?" I asked.

"No, no, no...she was drinking wine all on her own. I did give her an insulin shot. Okay, first a little chloroform, then an insulin shot... And yes, I got the rest of the wine in her after she was out cold. That's harder than you might imagine...I had to practice that little maneuver. The idea for sleeping pills and wine that I eventually used on Scarlett actually came to me while I was waiting for Bonita to drink her wine. She was so slow about it, and I'd already been there two hours, hiding, waiting on her to down it."

"And Stanley Mahaffey?" I asked. "You tried to make that look like a mugging...it was smart not to kill them all the same way."

He nodded smugly and tapped his temple. "It *was* a mugging. It was just a mugging with an additional motive."

Dana was staring at her brother with a horrified expression. "What happened to you?"

"Oh please," said Corey. "You're not exactly Saint Dana. I'm not the one who lived in a whorehouse for years. You earned that money on your back."

"That's a despicable lie." Dana spat.

What was he smoking? Dana was a nurse who volunteered in Third World countries. Where on earth had he come up with that bizarre accusation? Who cared—it was irrelevant. "So, I do have one more question...about Patricia...why did you park on the street so early? And how did you get into the house without being picked up on one of the neighbor's cameras? That backyard wall is pretty well impenetrable unless you skydive in."

"Ah," he said. "I parked there early so I'd be sure to have the car nearby when I was ready to leave. Then I just went to grab some dinner and came back later. There's one spot where you can climb from the yard next door into the driveway. It's out of the sight range for the cameras across the street—right in front of the gate. And I had the code for that. Now, if I've satisfied your curiosity, please, drink up. I don't want to have to shoot you, but as you know, I will if I have to."

He looked from me to Dana, and when he turned his head, I pulled the bear spray out from under my blanket, aimed, and fired.

"*AAAAAHHHH!!* What the heck?" His language was much more colorful than that.

He pointed the gun at Dana, or tried to, but his eyes were squeezed closed.

I swiveled in my chair, jumped up, and lunged at him.

He fired the gun, continuing to yell like a banshee.

Dana screamed.

Liz, Nate, and the huge guy that works for them named Bart came running down the stairs, guns drawn.

Bart tackled Corey, then wrestled him over and put zip ties on his wrists. "That'll be enough out of you."

"Everybody okay?" asked Nate.

"I'm fine." I reached for my phone to call Cash.

"Well, I'm not shot," said Dana. "It'll be a while before I'm fine."

Chapter Thirty-Six

"Hadley, what is this?" Cash stared at his plate.

"It's a rib-eye steak with mushrooms in mustard cream sauce. Medium rare."

It had taken me until Wednesday to work up the nerve to call and invite him to dinner. Now it was Friday night, and we sat at a table on my pool deck. I'd gone all out—lit the tiki torches and everything. He seemed in a remarkably good mood, all things considered.

Of course it helped that he and Sonny Ravenel had closed the books on three murders and three attempted murders—no long, expensive, messy, unpredictable trials required. With his confession already on tape and several witnesses backing it up, Corey Brett Clark had admitted everything. All charges against Bridget were dropped, and the Talbot & Andrews foundation had offered her a job and a college scholarship—an opportunity she'd been overjoyed to accept.

"Mine is a filet," I said. "But I thought...the butcher advised me to get you a rib eye. And that's what you usually order, right? Is it not okay?"

"It's fine. *It's fine.* It looks delicious. I just..." His mouth curved slightly. "I've never known you to cook meat."

"Oh, right." I smiled. "North showed me how to grill the steaks in a cast-iron pan on the stove and finish them in the oven. I was surprised how easy it is, actually."

Cash's face twisted up into a confused expression, but he was still smiling, which I decided had to be a good sign. "It's pretty rare for you to *eat* meat. I can count the times I've seen you do that on one hand."

I laughed. "Yeah, well, about that...a *lot* has changed in the last week. This is the least of it, I'd say. Carolyn Talbot led me completely and irrevocably astray. Apparently, I'm now this insatiable carnivore. I'm going to try the Mediterranean diet, I think, but this felt like a special occasion."

"It is?"

"Well, I hope it will be." I smiled at him. "Eat your dinner. Please. Can I get you anything?"

"I can't think of a thing." He cut a bite of his steak and delivered it to his mouth. "Mmm."

"Is it really okay?"

"Remarkable." He squinted at me. "Are you sure this isn't takeout from Hall's Chophouse?"

I laughed so hard I snorted a little bit. "No, and I'm pretty sure it doesn't taste *that* good."

"It's the best steak I've ever had." A smile crept up his face. "Is that actually bacon I see on these potatoes?"

"Yep. This is Liz's recipe for twice-baked potatoes. Sarabeth gave me the mushroom cream sauce recipe—it's Tucker's favorite. The salad and the sourdough bread I figured out on my own. And there's cheesecake for dessert, but I ordered that from Carnegie Deli."

"Wow. This is all amazing. Thank you."

Suddenly we were shy with each other. We ate quietly for a few minutes. Finally, he said, "I'm really glad you called."

"I'm so happy you came." I winced. "Cash, I'm so sorry about everything...and I'm so sorry, I was going to let you eat first, but now, I feel like I can't possibly eat another bite unless I get this out."

"Get what out?"

"I wasn't putting you first. I see that now. I mean... I saw it before, but I let myself get carried away. And we have to—always—put each other first. And I should've called you first when I was shot at. Immediately. Like...the second it happened. I don't know what came over me, but if you'll give me another chance, I promise I won't ever do it again. I'll do better...I'll—"

"Hadley..." He shook his head gently, a look I couldn't decipher in his eyes. "Please stop."

My stomach dropped. "What?" Oh no. It was too late. He was done with me. He was only here as a friend...or to be kind. And now I was embarrassing myself—

"I've realized some things too," he said.

My throat tightened. "What things?" I whispered. This was it. Here came goodbye. I had to stop him. I couldn't let him say it. I couldn't bear to hear it.

"I know now what the most important thing in my life is—"

I nodded quickly. "Your career. I know—"

"What?" His face screwed up like something tasted bad. "No. Not my job."

"Not...not your—?"

"Not my job." He shook his head. "The most important thing to me is you. *You* are the one thing in my life that is nonnegotiable."

"I am?" I could feel my lip quivering.

He nodded. "Hadley, I know you're on a mission to save the world—or at least as many people as you possibly can. And I, Hadley...*I* am on a mission to spend my life with you. I will find another job. One that can't possibly come between us."

"You will? Wh-what might that be?"

"I don't know...maybe I'll become a professional kite tester. They need someone to take high-end prototypes out in unpredictable coastal wind patterns. It's all very hush-hush—NASA adjacent, obviously—but I'd be off the grid most days. Just me, the wind, and a series of color-coded silk dragons."

"What?" I laughed. "You're insane."

That's when he got down on one knee.

He looked up at me, his soft brown eyes full of hope and radiating so much love.

Everything inside me fluttered dangerously. Happy tears rolled down my cheeks. *Please don't let me pass out right now.*

"Hadley Scott Drayton Legare Cooper, will you marry me?"

I nodded so fast I nearly gave myself whiplash. "Yes. Of course. Absolutely. But I have another idea on the job thing. Not that the kite testing thing doesn't sound fabulous—and honestly, whatever you want to do—"

He stood, pulled me into his arms, and kissed me silly.

When we finally came up for air, Cash glanced over my shoulder and laughed. "We have an audience."

I turned. Goose and Nala sat side by side on the pool deck, tails curled around their paws, watching us with what I could only describe as feline approval.

"How in the world...?" I looked from the cats to the house and back again. "I know I closed that door. Hey, you guys are indoor kitties."

"Didn't you tell me they escaped from a house just down the street and somehow ended up stuck in your lattice?"

"Well, yes, but—"

I stopped mid-sentence as a thought hit me like a wave. What if Momma had led them to me? She'd appeared that very morning, told me to help Bridget. And there were Goose and Nala, waiting for me when

I got home—two cats who would turn out to be the key piece of evidence linking Corey to Bonita's murder. Corey had brought them from West Ashley to the house he was sitting, just a few blocks away. They could have gone anywhere when they escaped. But they came to me. What if that wasn't a coincidence at all?

"Hadley? Everything all right?"

I blinked. "Yeah. Sorry. Just thinking."

I hadn't told Cash about Momma appearing to me. And this didn't seem like the moment to bring it up—*Oh, by the way, I saw my dead mother the other day, and I think she orchestrated events from beyond the grave, including guiding two cats across Sullivan's Island to help me solve a murder.* That was a conversation for another day. Maybe after the wedding. Maybe after we'd been married for years. Maybe...

Maybe never.

Some things a girl should maybe just keep to herself.

"Face it, Hadley." Cash grinned, oblivious to the rabbit hole I'd just tumbled down. "You've adopted a pair of Houdini cats. They probably have a whole secret life you don't know about."

Goose yawned elaborately, as if to say he'd neither confirm or deny such allegations.

I laughed and leaned back into Cash's arms. "I guess I'll add 'figure out how the cats keep escaping' to my to-do list."

"Right under 'plan wedding,' I hope. I'm thinking soon sounds good. How about you?"

"Soon is perfect. Maybe Poppy can help me plan it." I shook my head, still marveling at how much had changed. "I still can't believe I have a sister. I always wanted one. Two weeks ago, I had no cats. No sister. No fiancé. Now I have all three."

"I'm really happy about that fiancé thing, by the way. What a relief. I've been trying to propose for a month and my timing has been comically bad. I was starting to really worry." Cash pulled me closer. "I can't wait to meet your sister. The cats...I'm still trying to warm up to that whole development."

I gave him a look that said, *oh please, you know you love these kitties.* I hoped they'd grow on him anyway. "Momma always said everything happens for a reason." I turned in his arms to face the water. Moonlight shimmered across the ocean, and I thought of Momma on that beach at sunrise, glowing in her blue sundress. She'd given me three things that morning: an apology, a mission, and a promise that it was real. Help her, she'd said. And I had. I'd helped Bridget, yes—but in doing so, I'd found Poppy. I'd found a sister I never knew I had. I'd found a whole nother family, really, if I wanted them.

And I did. I wanted all of it.

The breeze picked up, warm and soft, carrying the scent of salt and jasmine. For just a moment, I could have sworn I felt Momma there with us—a whisper of presence, a flutter of peace. Watching. Approving. Maybe even taking a little credit.

I forgive you, Momma, I thought. *And I think Poppy does too. There's nothing to forgive, really. You did your best for both of us. And thank you. Thank you for nudging me in the right direction. And for the cats. Finally, you let me have pets.*

Goose stood, stretched, and sauntered over to wind between my ankles. Nala followed, bumping her head against Cash's leg in what I suspected was a gesture of grudging acceptance.

"I think you've been officially approved," I said.

"By the Houdini cats? I'm honored."

I smiled up at him. "Welcome to the family."

And there, on the pool deck, surrounded by tiki-torch light and escape-artist cats and the lingering presence of a mother who loved me enough to break the rules, I felt something I hadn't felt in a very long time.

I felt like I was exactly where I was supposed to be.

Want a bonus scene?

Find out what happens next at
susanmboyer.myflodesk.com/tttl-bonus

**Liz Talbot & Nate Andrews Return
October 27, 2026**
in
Hard Candy Christmas
A Talbot & Andrews Investigation #1

Preorder your copy at
susanmboyer.com/hard-candy-christmas

Acknowledgments

It takes a team to publish a book. I am ridiculously blessed with the following people, who I have assembled into what I like to call "my team." I am over-the-moon excited to work with my team, and deeply grateful to each member. Thank you, thank you, thank you...

...Kristen Weber, editor extraordinaire. I'm so happy we could work together again on this book.

...Trish Long, for your sharp eyes and careful copyediting and proofreading.

...The enormously talented Courtney Patterson and all the folks at Curated Audio for everything they do to create the audiobooks.

...The fabulous team at Dreamscape Media who makes the audiobooks widely available.

...Marina Kaye at Qamber Designs for the gorgeous original artwork used in my cover.

...Elizabeth Mackey for turning the artwork into a cover I adore.

...Susan Beckham Zurenda, the other half of the "Two Southern Susans."

...Ciera Washington, my retail assistant. Ciera handles a long list of things, including packing and shipping signed personalized books from the Worldwide Headquarters of Stella Maris Books, LLC. (Ciera is also one of the grand darlings.)

...Kate Huff, my Marketing Assistant, who ably handles whatever I throw her way.

...Veronica Adams, my fabulous Marketing Manager, who has made herself indispensable.

...MaryAnn Schaefer, my Director of Everything Else, who I would be hard-pressed to function without.

...Marc Duroe at New Wave Media Design, for excellent website design and maintenance.

Readers...as always, my heartfelt thanks go out to every reader who has connected with my novels. Because of you, I get to spend my days doing the job I love. I am endlessly grateful.

Booksellers and librarians...as ever, I deeply appreciate every bookseller and librarian who has recommended my books to a reader or hosted me for an event.

I also need to thank all the members of The Lowcountry Society, for your ongoing enthusiasm and support. And thank you to all the members of The Lowcountry Book Club for hanging out with me online and chatting about one of our favorite topics—books.

My heartfelt thanks to my family. I adore you all. Thank you beyond measure to my husband, Jim

Boyer, for your ongoing love and support. I could have looked the world over and not found a better man.

Last, but certainly not least, I am forever grateful to my Creator for giving me an overactive imagination and a love of words. I sincerely believe I'm doing what I was designed to do, and it is a joyful thing. If there is anything good in anything I have ever written, the credit is entirely God's.

If I have forgotten someone, please know it was unintentional and I am deeply grateful to everyone who has helped me along this journey.

About the Author

Susan M. Boyer is the award-winning, *USA Today* bestselling author of fourteen novels. She grew up in a small North Carolina town and has lived most of her life in South Carolina. She loves beaches, Southern food, and small towns where everyone knows everyone, and everyone has crazy relatives. You'll find all of the above in her novels. She and her husband call Greenville, South Carolina, home and spend as much time as possible on the Carolina coast.

If you'd like to be among the first to hear about new releases, events, and sales, sign up for Susan's newsletter on any page of her website by scrolling to the bottom or waiting for the pop-up.

susanmboyer.com

Seaside Southern Mysteries
BY SUSAN M. BOYER

Carolina Tales Series

Big Trouble on Sullivan's Island

Beginnings: The Sullivan's Island Supper Club (*prequel*)

The Sullivan's Island Supper Club

Trouble's Turn to Lose

The Liz Talbot Series

Lowcountry Boil (A Liz Talbot Mystery # 1)

Lowcountry Bombshell (A Liz Talbot Mystery # 2)

Lowcountry Boneyard (A Liz Talbot Mystery # 3)

Postcards From Stella Maris (Five Liz Talbot Short Stories)

Lowcountry Bordello (A Liz Talbot Mystery # 4)

Lowcountry Book Club (A Liz Talbot Mystery # 5)

Lowcountry Bonfire (A Liz Talbot Mystery # 6)

Lowcountry Bookshop (A Liz Talbot Mystery # 7)

Lowcountry Boomerang (A Liz Talbot Mystery # 8)

Lowcountry Boondoggle (A Liz Talbot Mystery # 9)

Lowcountry Boughs of Holly (A Liz Talbot Mystery # 10)

Lowcountry Getaway (A Liz Talbot Mystery # 11)

The Talbot & Andrews Investigation Series

Hard Candy Christmas (*coming October 27, 2026*)

www.ingramcontent.com/pod-product-compliance
Lightning Source LLC
LaVergne TN
LVHW090035080526
838202LV00044B/3327